The Malice Box

The Malice Box

MARTIN LANGFIELD

MICHAEL JOSEPH
an imprint of
PENGUIN BOOKS

MICHAEL JOSEPH

Published by the Penguin Group

Penguin Books Ltd, 80 Strand, London WC2R ORL, England

Penguin Group (USA) Inc., 375 Hudson Street, New York, New York 10014, USA

Penguin Group (Canada), 90 Eglinton Avenue East, Suite 700, Toronto, Ontario, Canada M4P 2Y3
(a division of Pearson Penguin Canada Inc.)

Penguin Ireland, 25 St Stephen's Green, Dublin 2, Ireland
(a division of Penguin Books Ltd)

Penguin Group (Australia), 250 Camberwell Road, Camberwell, Victoria 3124, Australia
(a division of Pearson Australia Group Pty Ltd)

Penguin Books India Pvt Ltd, 11 Community Centre, Panchsheel Park, New Delhi – 110 017, India

Penguin Group (NZ), 67 Apollo Drive, Mairangi Bay, Auckland 1310, New Zealand
(a division of Pearson New Zealand Ltd)

Penguin Books (South Africa) (Pty) Ltd, 24 Sturdee Avenue, Rosebank, Johannesburg 2196, South Africa

Penguin Books Ltd, Registered Offices: 80 Strand, London WC2R ORL, England

www.penguin.com

First published 2007

1

Copyright © Martin Langfield, 2007

The moral right of the author has been asserted

Set in 12/14.5 pt Monotype Garamond
Typeset by Rowland Phototypesetting Ltd, Bury St Edmunds, Suffolk
Printed in Great Britain by Clays Ltd, St Ives plc

A CIP catalogue record for this book is available from the British Library

Hbk ISBN: 978–0–718–14866–9
Trade pbk ISBN: 978–0–718–14867–3

To my wife, Amy, and my son, Christopher
To Andrea, Eddie and Tom
And to my parents, for the gift of loving words

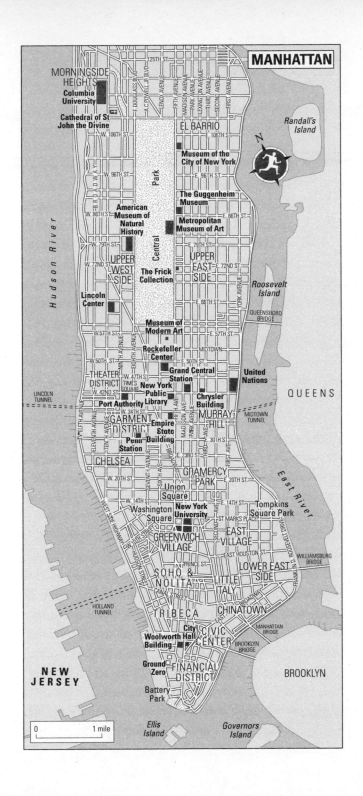

MANHATTAN

MORNINGSIDE
HEIGHTS
Columbia
University

Cathedral of St
John the Divine

EL BARRIO

Randall's
Island

Museum of the
City of New York

The Guggenheim
Museum

American
Museum of
Natural
History

Metropolitan
Museum of Art

UPPER
WEST
SIDE

UPPER
EAST
SIDE

The Frick
Collection

Roosevelt
Island

Lincoln
Center

QUEENSBORO
BRIDGE

Museum of
Modern Art

Rockefeller
Center

MIDTOWN

THEATER
DISTRICT

Grand Central
Station

United
Nations

QUEENS

New York
Public
Library

LINCOLN
TUNNEL

Port Authority

Chrysler
Building

MIDTOWN
TUNNEL

GARMENT
DISTRICT

MURRAY
HILL

Empire
State
Building

Penn
Station

CHELSEA

GRAMERCY
PARK

Union
Square

Washington
Square

New York
University

Tompkins
Square Park

GREENWICH
VILLAGE

EAST
VILLAGE

WILLIAMSBURG
BRIDGE

SOHO &
NOLITA

LOWER EAST
SIDE

LITTLE
ITALY

HOLLAND
TUNNEL

TRIBECA

CHINATOWN

MANHATTAN
BRIDGE

Woolworth
Building

City
Hall

CIVIC
CENTER

BROOKLYN
BRIDGE

Ground
Zero

FINANCIAL
DISTRICT

Battery
Park

BROOKLYN

NEW
JERSEY

Ellis
Island

Governors
Island

Hudson River

East River

FRANKLIN D. ROOSEVELT DRIVE

WEST SIDE HIGHWAY

Central Park

0   1 mile

Contents

Acknowledgements

I am greatly indebted to the following people: Michael Sissons and all at PFD; Mari Evans and Alex Clarke at Michael Joseph; Donna Poppy and Larry Rostant; David Schlesinger, Betty Wong, Paul Holmes, Tom Kim, Mark Egan, Stephen Naru, Chad Ruble, Soren Larson and Bernd Debusmann at Reuters, as well as my co-workers, over the years, in the San Salvador, Mexico City, Miami and New York bureaux; Nicki Kennedy, Sam Edenborough and Tessa Girvan at ILA; and George Lucas at Inkwell Management in New York.

I am grateful to several people who read part or all of the early drafts of this story, though any inaccuracies or infelicities in the final version are of course my fault, not theirs: Pilar Prassas, Allison Tivnon, Manuela Badawy, Rasha Elass, Jonathan Lyons, Patricia Arancibia and Bettie Jo Collins.

For their hospitality at different stages of the book's gestation, I am grateful to Daniel Soucy and staff at the Auberge Les Passants du Sans Soucy in Montreal, Randy St Louis and colleagues at Café Un Deux Trois in New York, and Gwen and Gary Fadenrccht in Mill City, Oregon.

For help in glimpsing some of the hidden nooks and crannies of New York, I am indebted to Glen Leiner, Suzanne Halpin, Maya Israel and Peter Dillon; Luz Montano and staff of the MTA and the New York Transit Museum; Janet Wells Greene and the General Society of Mechanics and Tradesmen of the City of New York; to Kevin Walsh, creator of the Forgotten New York website at http://www.forgotten-ny.com, and to Jim Naureckas's New York Songlines website at http://www.nysonglines.com.

Thanks also to Father Michael Relyea of St Mark's Church in-the-Bowery, Nathan Brockman of Trinity Church Archives and Colleen Iverson of NYC Marble Cemetery.

On matters of fact: the magic cube featured in the fourth trial was discovered by Walter Trump and Christian Boyer in November 2003, though I have imagined it already known to previous ages. Diana Carulli painted the labyrinth Robert walks at a key point in the story, the artwork he views at Grand Central is the creation of Ellen Driscoll, and the digital clock he sees at Union Square is the work of Kristin Jones and Andrew Ginzel. I have slightly altered the actual dates of Hurricane Georges, and imagined a section of Central Park to be open when it was not.

I owe a special thank you for encouragement and advice to Toni Reinhold, Clive McKeef, Stacy Sullivan, Jason (Jay) Ross and Nicole Revere. For musical accompaniment, thank you to Raquy and the Cavemen, Ken Layne and the Corvids, Tsar, Matt Welch, Don Collins and Alien (Chris, Libby and Jeff), as well as to Steve Deptula of Liberty Heights Tap Room.

George Short, Keith Stafford, Dave Nicholson, François Raitberger, Anneliese Emmans-Dean, Leslie Crawford, Juliette Aiyana, Donald Coleman, Vincent Sherliker, Ian and Fiona Gausden, Janie Gabbett, Robert Lethbridge, Alison Sinclair, Joe Cremona, Stephen Boldy, Andrew Paxman, my brother Graham Langfield, Kristin Roberts, Barbara Brennan and Catherine Karas, among many others, have helped me find and follow my own path.

Last, but not least, I am grateful beyond words to my wife, Amy, who sent me to Montreal to start writing and whose deep insight and love – together with a sharp editor's eye – allow me to make sense of it all.

Prologue
New York, September 2, 2004

An all-knowing eye – beautiful, pitiless, irresistible – stared into Robert's soul. He fought to control his breathing, to transform his fear.

I offer myself in their place. Take me. Let them go . . .

His heart was pounding. He was on the brink of success or failure. Millions of lives hung by a thread.

. . . I pray for my captor . . .

He could hear and see nothing, but he knew the Device was near by. He could feel its power rippling through him.

. . . as we forgive those who trespass against us . . .

He fought against panic.

. . . deliver us from evil . . .

Its raw energy was terrifying. The light of a thousand suns. His mind raced, deducing, estimating, remembering: downtown Manhattan, underground.

. . . thy will be done . . .

The air was dense, crackling with hostile energy, with words unsaid, like burning breath on his skin. His senses crept outwards, feeling menace, hurt to come, yet something else too: some desire not to harm him, an awareness that he provoked caution, even fear.

. . . fill my heart with compassion . . .

He felt the eye's searching gaze reach into the most hidden corners of his soul. The Device – the Malice Box, the Ma'rifat' – wanted to know him. It was a bomb about to blow, a barely contained chain reaction, feeding on the hearts of those around it. It asked questions: *Who are you? What are your most secret desires?*

He had chosen to be here, wanted it, sought it out with his actions. He fought to close his fear off, hold it to one side.

. . . turn fear into love . . .

Shapes and fragments of city scenes played before his eyes.

Curving arches, tunnels and squares and vertical monuments, fingers and spines pointing from the earth to the heavens, spirals and hexagons and numbers and stars.

. . . mind like a mirror . . .

Seven days earlier the hunt had begun, and with it the destruction of everything he'd thought of as his life.

He'd cracked one code after another, followed strange and wonderful trails through the city, traced lines of light and longing, lust and fear. A scavenger hunt, a geo-caching game. Decode the city. Penetrate the labyrinth. Read the secret story before the enemy do.

The clock always returns to zero. Here he was facing his end, and he was back where he'd started.

. . . merciful heart . . .

He peered deeper into the blackness as he lay on the ground, straining for a glimpse of the Device. He twisted his head. Then he saw it: an intricately carved gold and white drum, gleaming dully, its sides decorated in what looked like Arabic script, inlaid with precious metals. In the half-darkness, it defied focus, as though sitting in its own geometry. Its upper and lower rims appeared to rotate slowly in opposite directions. The Ma'rifat'. It was armed, on the verge of detonation.

A man's voice, hoarse and violent, jolted him like a bolt of electricity.

'Robert.'

When he tried to speak, his mouth was sticky, his throat clogged, and nothing came out.

It was time to fight. He was ready. He cast his mind far into the past.

. . . forgive him . . .

PART ONE
The Initiation

Cambridge, England, March 1981

Robert ran, his footfalls booming in the mist. The veneer of everything had been stripped away, and nothing was as it had seemed. Familiar sights were raw and strange. The great white limestone blocks of King's College Chapel, its spires lost in the fog, spoke of power and menace. The shop signs along King's Parade were written in a foreign tongue, its symbols threatening and new. His body seemed distant, not his own.

The terrifying image flashed again in his mind's eye. There was a door, flames licking beneath it, a baleful, unnatural light.

Blood pounded in his ears. He ran along Trinity Street in the darkness, his white carnival mask dancing between his shoulder blades like a cowboy hat, his star-strewn cape billowing behind him.

The clocks struck midnight.

The door was at the end of a dark corridor. He knew whose room it was. He knew what they were doing there. He did not understand what had happened. But if he did not reach them in time, he knew that they would die.

The evening had begun with a single red rose.

At eight thirty sharp, Robert Reckliss, freshman linguist, arrived at the college room of a young lady he did not know, following his instructions to the letter: face fully masked, attired as a warlock, sealed envelope and long-stemmed rose in hand.

He tapped on the door.

Katherine Rota, third-year philosophy student at King's College, who, in keeping with the game, had taped over her name on the painted list of residents at the foot of her staircase to maintain the mystery of her identity, called out in a sweet sing-song: 'It's open. Come in.'

5

Robert pushed the door open with his finger. A young woman dressed as a witch looked up from her desk and smiled.

'Now who, I wonder, are you, good sir?'

Amused blue eyes twinkled at him through a black half-mask. As witches go, she was punk Halloween. She wore black lipstick, black tights with holes torn in them, combat boots, a black dress that appeared to be from an Oxfam shop and several necklaces of black beads. A broom leaned against her desk. Her black hair was tied off to one side in a kind of jagged ponytail.

Robert applauded politely and, with a stiff bow, handed her the rose.

She performed a mock curtsy. 'Thank you, good warlock.'

Behind her, posters of the Clash and a Gustav Klimt painting decorated the wall. A large typewriter sat in the middle of her desk, in a small clearing amid undergraduate bric-a-brac. Classical piano played on her stereo.

'Truly you do not speak? Very well, then, please sit.' She pointed him to a broken-down armchair. 'Would my gentleman visitor care for coffee or tea?' She gestured to a small electric kettle on a low table by her desk. 'Or a cocktail? I could give you a straw to feed it in there somehow?'

He shook his head, raising his hand to decline politely. There was something intriguing about her accent, amid the educated London vowels. A hint of West Country? Even American, perhaps?

She moved to her sleeping area, which was in an alcove to the left. By the bed she had a screen to change behind. Robert found that very classy. She produced a tiny pointed black hat from behind the screen and, returning to the sitting room, tried it on in the mirror over a disused fireplace.

'I feel very witchy tonight.'

He did not reply. He was forbidden to. He nodded in what he hoped was a courtly fashion.

Her bookcases were crammed with textbooks on history, advanced mathematics and philosophy. Posters from student plays half covered another wall. He had butterflies in his stomach. She was very pretty. But would she go for him if she knew who he really was?

Tonight was a game invented by a certain Adam Hale-Devereaux.

A kind of ornate blind date for six people, to be consummated at a costume party later in the evening at the School of Pythagoras, a twelfth-century building in the grounds of St John's College. Adam was a charming dabbler in his final year. The son of a diplomat, he was a minor aristocrat and major drinker who was heading for an effortless first in the languages he had spoken fluently since he was a child.

Robert had met him at a linguists' sherry evening towards the end of his first term and been forthrightly rude to him, tagging him straight away as a feckless child of privilege.

'So you didn't actually have to *learn* your languages, you just picked them up as your father moved around the world,' he'd said to Adam. 'You're lucky.'

'I'm extraordinarily lucky.'

Robert's parents worked for a titled couple at a stately home in East Anglia, his father a gifted gardener and carpenter, his mother a cook and housekeeper, living in a tied cottage on the grounds. An only child, he was the first of his family to go to university.

'My father moved us around so often I used to fantasize about just being from one place,' Adam had continued. 'But no complaints, we were certainly privileged.'

'I really don't think you should be allowed to read something you find so easy. It doesn't seem fair.'

'But it's not about the ability to speak a language, is it? Isn't it more about what you say in it? Have you tried medieval French? *Le Roman de la Rose* is no picnic. *La Chanson de Roland* is an utter nosebleed. Rewarding, but . . .'

He'd said it with a disarming smile, before switching the subject to cricket. 'I know what you mean, though. No offence. How do you rate the Aussies this summer?'

And, on that common ground, they had enjoyed a civil conversation about the merits of Brearley and Botham and the future of the Ashes.

Then, at the beginning of March, an invitation had arrived in Robert's pigeonhole in the porters' lodge at Trinity Hall, hand-lettered on thick card, asking him to take part in 'a blind date, or preliminary activities towards the founding of a new Society dedicated to the exploration of unconventional wisdom', signed by Adam with the line 'would be honoured if you'd join us'.

Robert, still keen to keep his feet firmly on the ground and not fly off into the upper climes of undergraduate pretension, had accepted on what he termed anthropological grounds: he would study these strange creatures in their natural habitat and undoubtedly learn something, even if he disapproved. An additional deciding factor was that it was a way to meet women.

Under the rules of the game, participants were not supposed to know each other. Three gentlemen were to step out into the chill misty evening in full disguise, bearing a sealed envelope on which were written the college and room number of the unknown lady they were to call upon at eight thirty. This he had done. The ladies too had received instructions from the game's master.

'Adam's envelope says you are not allowed to speak this evening until ten o'clock,' Katherine said into the mirror. 'If you do so, I'm to send you away.'

He nodded.

She pinned her pointed hat in place at a coquettish angle, turned to receive Robert's approval, then poured herself a glass of red wine.

'That's a little difficult. Adam likes things difficult, doesn't he?'

Robert shrugged, inclining his head to indicate he didn't know.

'His note said I should expect someone surprising. Someone I wouldn't expect. I was thinking he might come himself, in disguise. That'd be typical.' She smiled. 'You're not Adam, are you?'

Robert sat motionless. She gazed intently at him. Adam and he were of similar height and build, though Adam was three years older than Robert. In the warlock outfit, each could easily have been the other. It seemed clear that she fancied Adam.

She giggled as the idea took hold in her mind. 'You're not, are you?'

Robert had the strangest thought: they both wanted it to be true. Robert felt outclassed by the older man. He wanted to acquire Adam's magnetism, his aristocratic ease and breadth of knowledge.

And he felt that Katherine would certainly respond if he could conjure up some of those qualities. Robert feared she would lose interest the more he revealed of himself.

After a moment he shook his head very slightly.

Katherine masked her disappointment, getting up and walking to the window. 'You know, I think I just don't care about finals. But the idea of leaving this place in three months – I can't bear it. How about you?'

He ran a finger down his mask, indicating a tear. After a moment he placed a hand lightly on his heart. She smiled at him.

In setting up the evening, Adam had chosen the couples and the personas based on what he knew of each of the participants. Katherine and Robert, for reasons not entirely clear to the latter, were witch–warlock; the others were damsel–knight, and tart–vicar. Before meeting up at the ball, each of them was to solve a riddle, contained in their envelope, that led to a certain location. Once there, the instructions said,

. . . you will find a second puzzle to be solved. Certain magic words are to be found, noted down and brought back with you. Then you are to fulfil a secret wish. To win the prize, you must return with the correct answers and solve a third riddle. Special honours will go to the most imaginative or scandalous adventures *en route*. Flirting is encouraged. Unwelcome groping is not. True identities will be revealed at 10 p.m.

'Let's get to the clues,' Katherine said.

Robert unsealed his envelope and removed two cards. On one was written: 'Clue: I am an echo of the Holy City.' On the back, it added: 'Suggestion: She has a secret wish involving this place. Once there, do the first thing she tells you to do. Remember you must not speak.'

The second card showed an array of dots and lines, and was marked: 'Save this for later.' He showed her the dotted card and the clue. Katherine took a letter-opener from the desk and slit her envelope open. 'Clue: Seen from the sky, I am an eye . . .' She thought about it and turned the card over.

'Mmm.' She did not share what it said on the back. Her envelope contained a second note, sealed with red wax, which she tucked into her dress. It was marked: 'Only to be opened at the location you seek.'

She drew an eye on a pad of paper and held it up to him. 'Mean anything to you?'

He shook his head.

'What is the Holy City? Jerusalem. Al-Quds. Christian, Muslim and Jew. There must be others, but . . .'

Katherine took down from a bookshelf an illustrated guide to Cambridge and riffled the pages back and forth. 'An eye. Seen from the sky. An echo of the Holy City . . .'

Robert signalled to her to hand him the notepad and jotted down: 'Irises and pupils are round. What about the Round Church?' Cambridge's Round Church, built in Norman times, was less than ten minutes' walk away.

She looked it up in the guidebook and gave a squeak of delight. 'Of course,' she said. 'You are clever! It says the Round Church is a copy of the Church of the Holy Sepulchre in Jerusalem. All the round churches in the world are. It was a Templar thing.'

She grabbed her broom. 'Let's go!'

New York, August 25, 2004

Late-summer heat stood in the streets, trapped by metal and glass. It was humid. A storm wanted to come.

Robert stopped without thinking at a shop window on Fifth Avenue. It was one of those stores that sold tacky New York souvenirs: the World Trade Center buildings in a snow globe, plastic Empire State Buildings with King Kong hanging from the top, Statue of Liberty lighters. Inexplicably, he was fascinated by them. He kept buying them. Little Chrysler Buildings. Tiny Flatirons. Katherine said it was a sickness.

He went into the store, feeling faintly guilty.

Katherine had her weakness for food porn: glossy colour cooking magazines, the Food Channel on cable, an unhealthy obsession with Mario Batali. But he had developed his own weaknesses: walking tours, coffee-table books on city architecture, crappy models of significant buildings.

A cheap silver-painted paperweight caught his eye. It crammed twenty-odd notable sights on to an oval base: the United Nations, Chrysler, Empire State, Brooklyn Bridge, Statue of Liberty. He decided to buy it when he saw it had a Rockefeller Center and Washington Square Park Arch he could perhaps chisel off. You couldn't find those on their own.

He made the purchase. He was sweating, and slightly dizzy. Dehydrated, maybe.

As he walked to Times Square and west along 42nd Street to the Port Authority bus station, his thoughts dwelled on Katherine, and on the gulf that had opened up between them. It had been eight months since the miscarriage. He didn't know how to fix it.

Katherine looked tired when he got home. His purchase amused her to a degree, until he took out the chisel.

'Now you're going to destroy it. Wow.'

'It's hard to find a miniature of anything to do with Rockefeller Center.'

She lacked sympathy. 'Feed your habit, if you must.'

'How was your day, Kat?'

She gave a dry laugh. 'I feel eighty years old.'

In his study was a map of Manhattan on a table. He had been putting his small souvenir buildings on it, as though building a scale model of the island in three dimensions. The Rockefeller Center building would fit perfectly.

Katherine observed him sadly from the doorway. 'Robert, no good will come of this. Truly.'

'Just . . . one . . . minute.'

She came over to see more closely what he was doing. The paperweight cracked, and part of the United Nations and the Brooklyn Bridge came flying off. The torch arm of the Statue of Liberty narrowly missed hitting Katherine in the eye. The Rockefeller Center's GE Building came off more or less intact.

'Stop!'

'OK. OK.'

Katherine eyed him with exasperation. 'So when are you going to open the mystery package?' she asked.

A parcel had arrived in the mail that morning, addressed only to 'Rickles'. Postmarked New York, no return address. She'd called him about it, knowing who it was from, concerned it might be important.

Only one person had ever called him 'Rickles'.

Robert's first thought had been to suggest she put it in a bucket of water outside the back door. Adam Hale's little gifts and games were like that. Instead she'd left it sitting on the desk in his home office, next to all the intractable crap that he kept in his 'too hard' file.

'It *might* be from someone else,' she offered.

But no.

The package was a cube of roughly three inches by three by three.

He pointed to the door. 'Would you go into the next room for a moment? One of us will need to be around to sue him if it explodes.'

She laughed absently and stepped away.

He held the package on the desk with one hand and started to slice the brown wrapping paper with a box cutter. His right hand, non-sensically, was trembling. Robert took a deep breath to calm himself. Adam's games could be self-serving and irritating, even downright upsetting. But this time it felt different – as though they might all have been merely dress rehearsals for the one that was about to begin.

He carefully finished slicing the paper and peeled it off to reveal a stout cardboard box, taped shut across the top. He punctured the seal of Scotch tape and let the blade run smoothly along the crack between the top flaps.

He opened the box.

Inside was an envelope and a mysterious object sheathed in bubble-wrap and tissue paper. He gently took the box cutter to the bubble-wrap. Still his hand shook.

He stopped and took a breath. Then he cut it free.

It was a round metallic box, platinum-gold in colour, about two and a half inches in diameter. It reminded him of a pillbox, or a small drum. Concentric rings ridged its top. It seemed remarkably lightweight.

The envelope contained a handwritten note, in careful capital letters, that said simply: 'PLEASE HELP ME.' On the back, in a more rushed hand, had been added: 'Out of time.' There was no signature, but Robert recognized Adam's handwriting. He closed his eyes.

One day you'll be called upon. He could hear Adam's words even now, more than two decades on. An acrid taste filled his mouth. He dropped the note in a drawer.

The pillbox had geometric motifs on its sides. There was no obvious way to open it. He turned it every which way, pressing and pulling and looking for cracks into which he could insert a fingernail. Nothing. The longer he held it, the more frustrated he got. After a while it even seemed heavier, and so he put it down and summoned Katherine.

'Typical Adam. Take a look at this, would you? It's a bastard,' he said. 'It's sealed tight.'

Katherine took it from him and gazed at it, holding it under his desk lamp and then close to her eyes. 'This is some kind of metal? It's almost like glass. Do you think Adam's starting another one of his games?'

She put it down on his desk. He smiled wryly at her.

'I hope not. I'm not sure our insurance would cover it.'

She surveyed him for a moment. 'You don't like being called Rickles, do you?'

The box sat on his desk like a toad. Now it looked more reddish gold.

'It always irritated me, yes.'

'Was there anything else with it?'

'No,' he lied.

She went upstairs.

Robert fought with the damned thing for half an hour longer, trying not to think. At one point the top rim slid a sixteenth of an inch counter-clockwise with a smooth click, as though he'd triggered a precision mechanism, then could not be coaxed further. He tried to reproduce the hand-and-finger positions that had made it happen, but failed. He gave up and went to join Katherine.

'When I was a girl, I had a special secret box that was very hard to open, a bit like that one,' she said, turning from the computer screen to look at him. 'A friend gave it to me on one of our summer holidays in France. It was made of wood, very tightly fitted, so you had to know an exact sequence of moves to open it. I wrote down all the hurtful, malicious things people said or did to me and kept the pieces of paper in it. It trapped the hurt inside.'

'I could use one of those at work.'

'I called it my Malice Box.'

Robert frowned. 'If I remember, *boîte à malice* means something more like "box of tricks", if that's what you were thinking of,' he said, walking to the bookcase and reaching for a French dictionary. 'Yes, look here, it's a mistranslation.'

She didn't look.

'I know. I was mixing up English and French. I was only thirteen, Robert.'

'It's wrong, but I do like the phrase. *Malice Box*. Very serendipitous. Very doomy. Adam would be thrilled, no doubt. Anyway, I'm going to smash it with a poker.'

'Don't.'

'Don't smash it?'

'Everything you're doing right now. Just don't. Just stop.'

'What?'

'Trying to diminish me. Being a pedant. Resenting Adam.'

He grunted.

'Let me have another look at it, anyway. It looks Moroccan, maybe? Egyptian? Whatever it is, don't smash it. It could be quite valuable. And it's beautiful.'

He handed the box over and left her to it.

The Malice Box, when Katherine eventually got it open, contained a snugly fitted leather pouch. Inside were two keys and a folded slip of paper, with an address on one side and a single word on the other: *vitriol*.

How appropriate, Robert thought.

The address was for an apartment in the West Village.

Katherine had become animated. 'How exciting. I'm glad he's doing his riddles again.'

'Show me how you opened it?'

'I'm not sure I can. I was trying different finger positions, and twisting and squeezing it in different places, and all the while I was staring at the top, and there's something about it. Look, you see? How it looks concave one second and convex the next? It's weird. Like looking into a staring eye. If I didn't know better I'd swear I hypnotized myself for a moment staring at it.'

'That's crap. You just lucked out, and now you can't do it again.'

He took it from her and retired to his study to work out what Adam might be playing at.

What information did he have?

Adam, who lived in Miami and had barely been in touch for several years, had mailed him a package from New York, or had had someone do it for him. He'd not put anything on the outside of the package, or indeed inside, to identify him as the sender, except to Robert and Katherine.

Adam was directly asking for help, in a way that was not typical of his previous puzzle challenges, which had involved mostly enjoyable requests for favours, introductions to women, solicitations of cash and an array of other dubious-to-actionable wheezes.

And he was running out of time.

Robert picked up the Malice Box and stared at it. He felt chilled to the core. Something wasn't at all right.

Cambridge, March 1981

The mist was thicker than ever, the air crisp. Katherine took Robert's arm as they walked north along King's Parade, past the Senate House and into Trinity Street. Almost no one was out in the

15

streets. They looked like dream creatures in the shop window of Heffers bookshop, lost between worlds. Katherine had brought a torch, which she played to and fro in front of them, to little effect.

They passed the Great Gate of Trinity, Adam's college, and the lawn outside it where Newton's Tree grew, then the front gate of St John's with its mythical creatures, called yales, supporting the founder's coat of arms: elephant tails, antelope bodies, goat heads, horns pointing backwards and forwards at once.

Just before they got to the Round Church, Robert caught another reflection out of the corner of his eye in a shop window, and for an instant he thought there was someone with them. He blinked and it was gone.

A low wall surrounded the Round Church, which Robert had walked by many times but never visited. A guttering light seemed to be on inside. Katherine squeezed closer to him as they entered the grounds.

'It's spooky like this. Are you a churchgoing man?'

He shook his head. The round-arched entrance was closed. He walked round to the left, on to the grass of the former graveyard, inspecting the stained-glass windows, which glowed faintly from within.

'There are only four others like this in the country, according to the book,' she said. 'Founded as a wayfarers' chapel in the twelfth century by a Fraternity of the Holy Sepulchre of which nothing else is known. Returning Crusaders, perhaps?' Let's see what the next clue says.'

Katherine took out the sealed note and cracked the wax, then walked over to him and handed him the torch. He read over her shoulder: '*You seek a magical bird. Name it and the reasons for its magic. Bring back the words it nests upon.*'

'I don't suppose he expects us to break in, does he?'

Robert shrugged and pointed to the carved pillars of the entrance porch. They inspected them. No bird. They left the graveyard and walked all the way around the church to the back, where later extensions had added boxier, more regular church architecture. The red-brick Victorian edifice housing the Cambridge Union debating society loomed behind them.

16

They stared up at a stained-glass window depicting the Cruci-fixion. In the light of Katherine's torch they scanned it for details. Robert made out a date, written backwards since they were viewing it from outside: 1942.

A man's voice spoke out of the mist. 'It was blown out in the war.'

Katherine screamed and grabbed his arm. Robert, forgetting his oath of silence, let rip in the direction of the voice. 'You silly fucker! You nearly gave us a heart attack!'

'Sorry to frighten you,' the voice said. A man in a tubular duffle coat and Wellington boots stepped forward, his face hidden in a deep hood.

'Who are you?'

'I'm just a watchman. I like to keep things tidy. People always littering in the grounds. You look pretty frightening yourselves in those get-ups. Are you going to a party?'

'Later,' Katherine said.

'It sounds like you need help? Solving a puzzle?'

He had the voice of a man in his fifties. Not local. A gentle voice.

'Well,' she said doubtfully. 'Know of any magic birds hereabouts?'

'Ah. Pelican-in-her-Piety.'

'Pardon?'

'You'll be wanting the Pelican-in-her-Piety.'

'What is that, exactly?'

'Stained-glass window. West-facing, so you'd see it on the way out. It's at the front. Bring your torch.'

The watchman strode off into the mist. Katherine hung back, raising her lips to Robert's ear.

'I had a secret wish about this place, but he's rather spoiled the mood,' she said with a smile.

Robert grunted at her.

'Don't say another word. At least I'm not sending you away. Come on, let's find him.'

They walked back round to the front of the church. The watch-man was standing stock-still, one arm raised, a furled umbrella in his hand giving him the impression of a deformed creature. He was pointing at a window above the porch.

'Follow my arm with your torch,' he said. 'Can you see it?'

An abstract, rounded form in white on a blood-red background shone into view. As he looked more closely, Robert made out the curve of a neck, and a wing. It looked as much like a dragon as a pelican.

'Oh, God,' said Katherine. 'It's eating its own heart.'

It was true. The creature's beak was slicing into its chest.

'To feed its young,' said the watchman. 'Pelican-in-her-Piety. Like Christ's sacrifice, among other things. See the nest and the chicks?'

Katherine played the light from her torch lower. There was a nest, and below it a chalice and a scroll of some kind. Below them was some lettering.

'Those are the magic words,' she said. 'Write them down. They're backwards, wait . . .'

'I can save you the bother,' the watchman said. '*Hic est enim sangus meus novi testamenti* in something or other *peccatos*. There's a missing word, illegible. How's your Latin?'

Katherine pulled a face. 'Quite rusty, actually.'

'Well, it should strictly be *sanguis*, not *sangus*, and the last phrase is garbled, but what it means is: *Here is my blood of the new testament* in something or other *of sins*. The missing word is "forgiveness", or "redemption". Got it?'

Robert took furious notes. He nodded.

'You don't say much when you're not swearing, do you? Take a look at the top of the window.'

Katherine shone the torch up. Robert made out a dome in red and white.

'Jerusalem,' said the watchman. 'The original Holy Sepulchre, built over Christ's tomb. Round.'

'You've been very kind,' said Katherine, in a tone that suggested he leave now. 'Thank you very much.'

'Pelican-in-her-Piety,' the watchman said in a ruminatory way. 'In heraldry it's called vulning. Vulning her breast. Self-sacrifice, you see. People used to believe the pelican fed its young that way. Nonsense of course. But you can see how it became a symbol for

Christ. For self-sacrifice. Are you Christians, would you say?' His eyes moved from Robert's star-strewn cape to Katherine's pointed hat and broom.

'Of a sort,' said Katherine. 'We must be off, then. Bye.'

The older man bowed slightly to them. 'Perhaps we'll meet again.'

She shivered and steered Robert away, pulling him over the road towards St John's. Robert looked back and saw the faint outline of the watchman, still looking up at the Pelican, slowly being erased by the fog.

New York, August 25, 2004

Adam Hale stood before the three white-haired men, fear in his heart. They wore exquisitely tailored suits in sober tones, discreet but very expensive cufflinks and signet rings, understated ties. They exuded an air of unhurried power.

'Adam Hale. Thank you for accepting our invitation,' said the tallest of the men.

'I had little choice, in the circumstances.'

'Quite so. Still, we are grateful.'

They were in the Empire State Building, in a 78th-floor office suite.

'Please sit, Mr Hale.'

'I prefer to stand.'

'As you wish.'

Only the tallest man spoke. The others sat on either side of him at the mahogany boardroom table, staring coldly at Adam.

'Our last meeting was just over a year ago.'

'That's right. August 14, 2003.'

'The Great Blackout.'

'Or whatever you want to call it. We all know what it was.'

'Since that day, we have been, shall we say, *bound* to each other in certain ways.'

The man barely moved his jaw as he spoke, his clipped vowels those of an old-money patriarch discussing real estate. Adam's fear ate at the limits of his willpower. They were very powerful, too powerful for Adam alone. And they were burrowing their way into his soul, inch by inch, day by day.

'We feel it is time to call upon you.'

'So soon?'

In the hidden depths of his heart, Adam repeated to himself the oath he had sworn more than twenty years earlier. To protect the innocent. To keep the secrets. He needed to slow them down, whatever it took.

'What is it, exactly, that you want? I want to understand you.'

The man to the right of the spokesman laughed. The other two crinkled their eyes in appreciation, as if he had uttered a well-turned witticism.

'We work, as you know, through others. We are patient. We have existed for a long time now, as has the group to which you belong. We have no address. Tomorrow, this suite will be empty. You cannot find us unless we wish you to.'

He took what Adam thought was a silver pen from his jacket pocket and twisted it, flicking up a gleaming metal blade. Then he stood up and, leaning forward, sliced four letters into the exquisite surface of the table: IWNW.

Adam flinched at the casual ease of the gesture.

'We are sometimes referred to as the Brotherhood of Iwnw,' he said, pronouncing it *yoonu*, the final vowel just a faint breath. 'We have had many names, in many countries.'

Adam snorted in derision. 'You just look like three thugs in Savile Row suits to me.'

The leader's eyes drilled into Adam's. For a moment he weighed the insult, then made a show of ignoring it. 'Iwnw is the name of a city, a sacred place. A place of power where our ancestors and those of the Perfect Light first, shall we say, *disagreed*. Myths in many lands reflect the battles between us since that time. They are all fragments.'

'You always lose in those stories, don't you?'

'It depends where you stop the story. It is never over. Neither of us can ever fully prevail. We will always be in the world. In fact, you need us. Your people also have many names, not all of them accurate. You might consider, you know, that you are actually on the wrong side in all of this.'

'You will fail. I stopped you before. Last year.'

'Indeed. But at considerable cost to you, Mr Hale, would you not agree? You are not strong enough to do so again. It is, in fact, quite pleasurable to be able to draw you towards our fold. Our kind – yours and mine – have always existed, have we not? A handful of people in the world at any given time, able to hear the higher harmonies, to see worlds beyond the physical? To serve higher masters?'

'It is a blessing.'

'It is also a curse, I think you will find. For you, personally.'

The leader of the Iwnw walked slowly towards Adam as he spoke.

'We are of the opinion that such knowledge – the ability to perceive and harness such forces – should be used to shape the world of ordinary men and women. It should be used for political purposes. To build a certain kind of society. We prefer to separate the wheat from the chaff, so to speak. We do not care much for America, or the world, under its present leadership. A polluted earth, heading for disaster. Endless squabbling. Power in the hands of the ignorant.'

He walked right up to Adam now, standing slightly behind him. Adam could feel the intensity of his gaze, but he refused to turn his head to meet it.

'What form would the Iwnw prefer the world to take?'

'Obedient. Submissive. At the service of benevolent, strong rulers. People like ourselves. People like you.'

'You can go to hell.'

Suddenly iron hands twisted Adam's body forward and slammed his head on to the table. His whole body exploded with pain. He heard words whispered into his ear: 'Our moment has come. You will do our bidding. You know what will happen if you do not.'

Adam struggled to free himself from the man's grip. His head was slammed into the table again, and his field of vision filled with bursting stars.

'Undo what you have done,' Adam spat at them.

'Your unborn child, and the mother. Help us, and they may yet live.'

'How can I? What you ask is unforgivable!'

'Oppose us, or attempt to trick us, and they will die. We require you to serve as our instrument.'

Adam closed his eyes. He saw darkness hurtling in towards him from all sides. He took shelter deep in the place where his most precious intentions lay hidden. He drew as much strength as he could there. Then he spoke: 'I will not sacrifice them. Spare them, and I will do your bidding.'

He felt the hands loosen their grip slightly. At least he had bought some time.

'Instruct me.'

The man smiled. 'Good. Well done. There is a man named Lawrence Hencott. We want you to pay him a visit. Tonight.'

Little Falls, New Jersey, August 25, 2004

Robert approached Katherine at bedtime, putting his hands on her shoulders and rubbing them as she sat reading. She was knotted tight. She gave a sound of enjoyment. He slid his fingers inside the neck of her blouse and worked the muscles harder. He whispered in her ear: 'How about I take you upstairs and pay a visit to your room and iron out these kinks more fully?'

It was his most direct invitation in several weeks.

Her posture and skin tone changed. She said nothing, then, after a while: 'Not tonight. Sorry. Not yet.'

He kept on working her shoulders for a minute, then stopped.

'I'm going to turn in,' he said.

'I'm going to read for a while. I'll look in on you.'

'Aren't you glad we heard from Adam, Kat?'

'You don't seem to be.'

'It feels different.'

'You seem almost . . . scared.'

'I'm not sure that's the word.'

'He's been like a brother to you. Or a faintly insane cousin.'

'I know.'

'What's eating you?'

'Nothing. I'm going to read for a while too.'

They had chosen the name Moss for the baby. He would have been born in late May, but they'd lost him at Christmas. He'd been their miraculous little Blackout baby, conceived the day the lights went out all across the north-eastern United States. August 14, 2003. He'd been their first, an utter surprise, given Katherine's age; and there would not be another. Adam's late brother had borne the name, and Adam had explained once that it was a variant of Moses, the little boy set adrift in a basket on the waters. It had seemed fitting to them.

Sometimes Robert would speak to Moss, great, long, whispered monologues that would make sense to no one. Tonight he just sat for a while in the room that would have been the boy's, alone with his thoughts.

When Robert got to bed and fell asleep, it seemed just a matter of seconds before the phone rang.

'Hello?'

He heard someone talking in the background, banging, breaking glass. Cursing.

'Hello? Who is this?'

He had no idea if he'd been asleep five minutes or five hours. Adam? Why would it be? He strained to hear the words. Then there was no need. Booming straight into the phone in pain-ridden shards, slurred and screaming, came a man's voice: 'You . . . fool! Going to . . . hurt you . . . bullet . . . you and everyone . . . in the ground . . . you . . . scavenger . . . die!'

Robert cut the line, and immediately started wishing he'd shouted back. His heart thumped. He looked around the room, as though the caller had been in the house. He was breathing fast, feeling attacked. His hands were shaking.

He hit *69 to call back, but got nothing. He got up to check the locks and look in on Katherine, who was fast asleep, then went back to bed and sat up in silence, trying to trace the voice in his memory.

His rational mind said odds were it hadn't even been intended for him: some sad-sack drunkard angry at the world, randomly dialling numbers and mouthing off. Despite his efforts to think, he drifted in and out of sleep. At one point he found himself staring straight ahead at patterns of light that dissipated before he could focus on them. He dozed.

The phone rang again, jerking him awake. Male voice.

'Robert Reckliss, wakey wakey! Are you ready to meet your maker?'

For a moment he was back in the room at Trinity, the night they'd almost died.

'Who . . .'

'No more sleep for you. Can you hear that thunder? You have an appointment with death.'

'Go to hell,' he shouted down the phone. But the line was already dead.

A bleary-eyed Katherine appeared in the doorway. 'What the hell is the matter with you? Who are you talking to in the middle of the night?'

'Some drunk.'

He abandoned any thought of sleep. It was nearly 5 a.m. on Thursday, August 26, the first day of his destruction.

New Jersey/New York, August 26, 2004

It rained on the way into work. The drumming of the rain on the car roof was hypnotic, a steady fine beat.

Katherine and he were in Little Falls, New Jersey, just outside New York through the Lincoln Tunnel. Driving in New Jersey was not for those of a nervous disposition, especially if the roads were slick. Despite three coffees, he was barely awake, and every couple of miles he lowered the window a crack to get some air, even though it sprayed rain into the car.

Each time he went under a bridge or overpass the bass drone of the rain would stop for a second, and start again almost before he'd noticed it was absent. Like those moments at parties when everyone falls silent at the same time: an angel passes, they say. Bridge, window. Bridge, window, punctuating the rain and the drone of the tyres.

There was other help too in staying awake: boy-racers and the infirm of mind hurtled by, snaking and weaving their way along the straight dark strip of Route 3.

From time to time in the distance the silhouette of Manhattan and its absent sentinels would appear on the horizon in shades of grey.

The crank calls and Adam's plea for help chased each other around in his mind. He tried to ignore them.

The commute was usually his time to work through permutations of and possible solutions to work problems – as if he were tackling a puzzle cube or those games where you move fifteen squares and an empty space around in a frame and try to get them into a certain order. He'd envisage staffing or resource problems as a series of coloured spaces or balls, or letters in an alphabet, and move them around until a meaningful combination came up that he could leaven with a little bribery, or flattery, or threats, to make it work for the operation as a whole. The inside of his head looked like a Mondrian painting.

He'd been in the news business for nearly twenty years, never really as a hard-charging correspondent in exotic climes like Adam; more of a safety-first company man, the kind who makes sure all the dull, necessary stuff gets done. More of a plumber than a poet, perhaps; more of a family man than a lover. You might say he was a responsible adult, always had been, ever since school days. He'd been raised never to let imagination get the better of him.

That's not to say he hadn't had his moments. He was sturdy. He was the unflappable man you need in the middle of a crisis. It was

Robert who had commanded the news troops in New York on September 11, when the towers came down. He'd held things together during market crashes, hurricanes, assassinations, currency collapses.

Unlike Adam, though, he'd never actually *caused* any of those things.

A cherry-red sports car rocketed past him on the right and cut in front, quivered for five seconds and shot off into a tiny gap in the traffic to his left.

The Republican National Convention was just days away. There was the usual fine-tuning and last-minute problem-solving to be grappled with. He liked that. He liked process. He liked things to run like a well-oiled machine.

GBN was on seven floors of the former RCA Victor Building at 51st and Lexington, through some grandfathered arrangement from the 1950s he'd never fully grasped. It was insanely Art Deco, gorgeous to walk into. Its designs had been seeping into his dreams in recent days: living lightning bolts, stylized radio waves, glorious patterns on the inside of his eyelids.

The previous night when he'd woken up, still half dreaming between the two crank calls, he'd seen a blue-white lightning bolt standing there right before him in the dark, as though frozen, and watched it slowly fade as he fully woke up.

On the great curve down to the Lincoln Tunnel mouth, in the purple E-Z Pass lane, he looked ahead and tried to gauge the levels of police activity. He couldn't describe exactly why, but it seemed higher than usual. Sooner or later someone would try to hit New York again. It was only a matter of time. That was why he had gone along with Katherine's desire to live outside Manhattan when they'd learned she was pregnant. They'd found a modest manse in Little Falls, a pleasant leafy town. Their house with too many rooms.

At the tunnel, a couple of trucks were being inspected. The number of cops was the same as usual, the regular black-and-yellow-striped radiation detectors were there, but there seemed to be an informed alertness about everyone's faces, a sense that there was more worrying and more surveillance going on than was immediately visible. With the Convention coming, it was hardly surprising.

It was not yet 7 a.m., and the Lincoln Tunnel's lighting towers, hollowed-out obelisks with spiral staircases running up through their core, were still on, illuminating the late-summer drizzle.

He thought of something sexual as he entered the tunnel mouth, and the next thing he knew he was at work.

You never see the one that gets you. The Blackout and the attacks of 9/11 (and Katherine and Moss, for that matter) weren't the only things that could come out of a clear blue sky. The tedious meetings he'd worried about on the drive in were blown away by a call he received as soon as he sat down at his desk.

'Robert?'

'John.'

John was his new boss. He was in Washington, DC, a city he inexplicably preferred to New York.

'Explain, if you can, this ghastly mess?'

Robert did not think it wise to ask *which* ghastly mess. He made a non-committal sound.

'This Hencott business. Ghastly. Mess.'

'Did something happen on Hencott that I don't know about?'

'Depends whether their lawyers have reached you yet.'

His heart sank. Lawyers were lawyers.

'They can fuck off.'

'Well, not entirely, it seems. Clearly you don't know. The CEO shot himself two hours ago.'

Hencott, Inc., was a medium-sized, privately held industrial firm with chemical and mining interests. One of GBN's business reporters, thanks to Robert, had managed to interview the CEO, an intense man of military background by the name of Lawrence Hencott, who in the ordinary run of things would have cut off his right arm rather than talk to the press.

Lawrence had a brother, Horace, who was an entirely different kind of character, a shiny-eyed architecture enthusiast and some-time academic Robert had met on a walking tour of downtown

27

Manhattan. Horace, an Anglophile, looked to be in his sixties but reminded Robert of a schoolboy. He wore a bowtie at all times. They hit it off, sharing an enthusiasm for New York history. Robert was the unschooled partner in their conversations.

Robert had met Lawrence at a party thrown by Horace to mark the publication of a slim volume he'd written on Egyptian Revival architecture. Several months later, having seen Horace a few more times, it occurred to Robert to ask whether his brother would talk to GBN. Not that he'd pursued Horace for that purpose, but why not ask, he figured. He could only say no.

Months had passed without a response. Then, on Wednesday, Lawrence had called to say he would do it, if Robert could send a reporter to him within two hours. In the interview Lawrence had said something market-moving about closing down several of their old, exhausted mines and some associated research and development facilities on the sites. The reporter wrote the story, the price of gold went up a tad on it: it was a nice little scoop for them over Bloomberg and Reuters and Dow Jones.

The company PR man then called, his day clearly ruined, to demand they kill the story. He was given a polite negative. He insisted. Eventually his call came up the chain to Robert.

'But it's wrong,' he sweated down the phone. 'Very embarrassing.'

'You mean he didn't say those things?'

'Your story doesn't reflect what he meant to say. He misspoke.'

'What he meant to say?' Christ. Of all the interviews to go wrong.

'I know. Robert, he made a mistake. Just said something wrong. You know he never talks to the press. He's not used to it. The mines aren't closing, nor are the R & D labs.'

'Then he should fix it. Don't ask us to. Your CEO doesn't know what he's talking about? Come on. We have the interview on tape. We quoted him directly, and in context. He wasn't drunk, the ground rules were clear, he was speaking on the record. What am I missing here?'

Horace would never forgive him. That said, he found it impossible to believe that Lawrence had ever been confused about anything in his life.

'He's been under a lot of stress recently. You know how tightly wound he is. Health problems. Between you and me, his marriage has fallen apart. He . . . got confused.'

Robert had no time for this. Poor man, if true, but . . . He sighed down the phone, censored his more lurid thoughts, tried to help. First the professional part.

'If this is true, you need to think about putting out a statement saying he made a mistake. In fact, I'll put you on to a reporter and you can say that right now, and we'll write about it right now. The market's open and you can't be withholding that information.'

The PR growled at the other end of the phone. Robert went on: 'I'm sorry for his pain, but if your CEO is out spouting nonsense in interviews, that's a fact Hencott needs to put in the public domain. But don't go accusing us of misreporting him.'

'I know, but —'

'I'll put you over to the reporter.'

They did a new story with Hencott's flak saying the CEO had misspoken. The gold price reacted again, dipping slightly; the reporter pulled it all together in a considered piece about what it all meant for Hencott; all sides got to comment.

Robert had tried to call Horace as soon as he could to try to explain what had happened. He hadn't been there, and his answering machine had been turned off, as usual.

'Oh, God. Oh . . .' His mind reeled as he tried to absorb the awful news.

'He's dead, in case I wasn't clear. He'd been up all night drinking in a hotel room off Times Square. Left a note that makes the company's lawyers very keen to sue us. Named you. Says he tried to speak to you last night to plead his case.'

The phone calls. Dear God. And poor Horace.

John ground on. Despite his sombre tone, he seemed pleased by the turn events had taken.

'Senior minds wonder whether *you* messed up, my friend.'

Robert's thoughts were playing catch-up. Would Lawrence have got his home number from Horace?

'Are you there, Robert?'

'He did call. He called me a fool and said it was time I died, if that's what you call pleading his case. While trashing his room, from what I could tell. I told him to go to hell. I thought he was some nutcase. This is bullshit. It's worse than bullshit.'

'No need to get overly emotional. We'll get the lawyers on it, of course. No one's saying you *caused* this.'

'Good.'

'There is perhaps a question of *judgement*, but . . . Do you remember saying anything else to him?'

'No.'

'Robert, between us, there are a few people who are going to use this as a weapon against you. I'm in your corner, but watch out. Times are harsh.'

'You want my badge and my gun?'

'Don't be ridiculous.'

'The man was drunk, for Christ's sake.'

Robert gave a preliminary statement to the GBN lawyers. He was jumpy throughout. What a ghastly mess indeed. He recognized that he was mildly in shock, tried to snap himself out of it. He attempted to call Horace again, got no answer. Katherine the same. He didn't know what to tell her and left no message. He got his friend Scott from the legal department involved, to watch his back and keep an eye on the others.

Then at noon John called him again.

'Take a break. Go home,' he said.

'What?'

'You're on paid leave for the rest of the week. It's been a terrible shock for everyone, but the company feels you, more than anyone else, should take a little rest.'

'I don't need a rest,' Robert spat down the phone. 'This is outrageous.'

'You may not need a rest, but the company needs you to need a rest. There will be a probe.'

He made it sound more like a gleeful colonoscopy than an impartial investigation.

'I am not leaving, John.'

'Yes, you are, Robert.'

And suddenly there were Gerry and Dave from the security department, standing outside Robert's office, looking embarrassed but monolithic.

'Do not do this.'

'Goodbye, Robert. Until Monday.'

He was speechless. John was giving him a perp walk. As the former NYPD boys with gammy knees escorted him out of the newsroom, some of his own people looked at him as though he had suddenly become a pariah.

He walked, in a daze, through the yellow chrome light of the lobby of 570 Lex and out into the street. The rain had stopped.

He made a right, down past the great hulk of the Waldorf-Astoria, right again on 49th Street towards Park Avenue, past the unmarked bronze elevator doors that led to the hotel's private railway siding beneath, one of the secrets of the city he'd always wanted to explore. He turned right again to head north on Park, lost in his anger and confusion, to the steps of St Bartholomew's Church.

There was something exotic and inappropriate about St Bart's that had always drawn Robert to it. Its great Byzantine profile squatted amid the stone and glass and steel blocks of Park Avenue like a grumpy turtle.

He walked into the narthex and paused by the bookshop under the gilded mosaics and Guastavino domes to let his eyes readjust. Each dome illustrated a scene from Genesis, set in a field of gold. He breathed deeply.

This was bullshit; there was no way Hencott could make anything stick against him. GBN would fight the case on principle. Scott would cover his back. Robert stepped outside and called him. He left a message saying he'd been sent home and asked Scott to keep him posted. They had internal procedures for such things.

To be fair, he wasn't really in a state of mind to work, though there was no excuse for frogmarching him out that way. When it was over, he'd make sure John regretted coming after him. This wasn't how GBN worked.

31

He went back inside, entered the darkened nave and walked along towards the altar until the sharp blues and reds of the rose window came into view to the right. He sat at a pew. He was not a churchgoer, but there were times, especially since they'd lost Moss, when all he craved was to sit silently by himself, and be still.

Suppose they sued him personally too? It would be a low trick. He'd been haemorrhaging money as it was, with the pregnancy and the bigger house.

Robert leaned forward and rested his head in his hands, his elbows on his knees. The fear was returning. All his life he'd worked for stability and safety, for predictability. There was a dark world, a world of fear and death and hatred, and he'd pushed it as far away as possible from him and his loved ones. But now . . . He was so tired. He felt darkness rising around him. Seductive. Irresistible. He slept for a moment.

A deep bass note sounded on the church organ, pervading the world between dream and waking. Not musical, not a melody, just the note, sustained. He lost himself in it entirely, not knowing where he was. When it stopped he came to in an altered silence, almost in a different world. Other notes sang out, higher, without structure. Then again the bass, so low as to be almost beyond his hearing, though he could feel it in the very vibration of his bones.

In the dream of the lightning bolt was a word too, a stream of words run together like a chant that he could never remember when he woke . . . Just its rhythm stayed in his mind . . . something like: Mary, Fat Mary, Fat Mary, Fat Mary . . .

His cell phone vibrated in his breast pocket. He'd missed a call while dozing, and there was a message.

Horace's tremulous voice, the dear man: 'Robert, Horace Hencott here. I just wanted you to know that we've had some very sad news about Lawrence, the worst, I'm afraid. I suppose you might already know, being in the news business. I've had some unpleasant dealings with the company people already, so I just wanted you to know that I don't want you to feel responsible in any way for what's happened. Please don't. Perhaps you could call me?'

Robert stared into the rose window.

Suddenly it was unbearable to be sitting still. He went outside and called Horace from the street.

His friend sounded terribly shaken. He spoke quietly, accepting Robert's condolences.

Then Horace asked a question that left Robert floored. 'Robert, I believe you know a gentleman named Adam Hale?'

How had Horace even heard of him? Robert gathered his thoughts. 'Er, yes, how –'

'How much do you know about Adam?'

'Quite a lot, and not very much. Why do you ask?'

'Because he went to see Lawrence at his office a few hours before he killed himself.'

Robert's mind whirled. 'What on earth?'

'Robert, I need to see you. Where are you?'

'Just outside St Bart's, on Park.'

'Go back inside. Wait for me. Please. It's very important.'

On the way back in, Robert asked about the organ. It was receiving its weekly tuning, he learned. He sat and listened, his mind racing. It seemed only minutes before Horace slid into the pew next to him.

'Thank you for waiting. We don't have much time. Please tell me all you know about Adam Hale.'

He seemed agitated, not in bereavement now but in worry. In anger.

Robert gathered his thoughts, then spoke in a subdued tone, though he could see no one else in the church. 'He was a friend at university. Sort of a mentor to me. Viewed me as a kind of social project, perhaps – a bumpkin from the Fens he wanted to help along. He was kind to me. A practical joker, enjoys setting up riddles and games for his acquaintances. He's involved me in a few over the years. They can be fun, though sometimes they can be a bit dark. Uncomfortable, for some people, but you usually end up happy you took part. He's a charming man, mischievous. A little troubled, in recent years. Not malicious.'

'Do you know of anything unusual about him? That may have happened to him?'

'A lot. Things tend to happen around Adam. And he's had some difficulties. Some tragedies. I should add that he and Katherine were married for a couple of years in the 1990s. Didn't work out.'

'Your Katherine?'

'The same.'

Robert heard Horace's voice quaver very slightly. 'What else?'

'Horace, I'm so sorry about Lawrence . . .'

'Yes, thank you. Go on, please.'

'Well, he went off after university to be a foreign correspondent, fell in love with an astonishingly smart and beautiful woman, naturally.'

'Yes.'

It dawned on him that Horace was trying to gauge what Robert *didn't* know about Adam.

He continued: 'Name of Isabela. Had a passionate affair in Central America during the civil wars there in Nicaragua and Santo Tomás. But she died. There were unusual circumstances. With Adam there usually are. Around that time I helped him out, got him a staff job with GBN for a while, which he hated, but he needed the cash. There was family money, but he and his father had some terrible feud that went on for years.'

'Thank you. What about these games you mentioned?'

'He'd send sets of postcards torn into two halves to people he wanted to see get together, send us off on mysterious jaunts, some-times matchmaking, sometimes throwing people into situations he knew they'd hate, setting up whodunnit train rides or risqué nightlife outings.'

'Have you seen him recently?'

'Not for a few years. That is, until . . .'

'Yes?'

'Until yesterday. I didn't see him, but I got a package from him in the mail. Rather mysterious. An ornate little puzzle box and a request for help. No details. And an address in the West Village.'

'Have you been to the address?'

'No, I –'

'If I might make a suggestion, Robert, I think you really must go.

34

But first there are a few things you need to know. Adam is in great danger. We all are. Tell me about the night of the fire.'

Robert's stomach twisted. 'The what?'

'The night you saved Adam's life in Cambridge. And Katherine's.'

Robert stared at Horace, speechless. He had buried the memory so deeply away he had almost made it someone else's story, an event in someone else's life.

'How did you even know about that?'

Horace hesitated, trying to gauge just how far he could push. He had to strike a most careful balance. Reveal too little, and Robert might not be convinced of the danger they all faced. Reveal too much, and he could be lost to them for ever, even driven to insanity. He had watched over them all for decades, from near and far, in Britain and America. Taught and mentored Adam in the Path, even after he broke away and tried to follow his own star. Advised Katherine from a distance as her powers waxed and waned over the years. Robert was the only one who did not know, because until now there had been no need to call upon him.

'I apologize for any deception, Robert. I have been taking a quiet interest in your well-being for many years, since I met Adam in England. Tell me about that evening. It will help you understand.'

Fear again twisted in Robert's gut. This was insane. Horace had been tricking him? What had Adam told the old man? He couldn't talk about that night. He had never been able to.

Horace's eyes were pools of kindness, but of an intensity Robert would never have suspected. He felt the old man looking all the way through him. He felt naked.

'Horace, there is a rational explanation for that night.'

'But you don't believe it.'

'I believe in reason. I don't believe in haunted houses, poltergeists, dowsing, the pricking of my thumbs or monsters under the bed.'

'Goodness, neither do I.'

'I believe in what I can verify for myself. What I have before my eyes. What I can see and touch. That night was just silly undergrad games. We were almost children, for Christ's sake.'

'You would agree that some invisible things are real? Gravity, perhaps? Most of the electromagnetic spectrum? Love? Fear?'

'Kat and I never speak of that night.'

'There was no need to. But now, Robert, it is time to wake up.'

'What?'

'You must awaken. Katherine and Adam need you.'

Robert found himself breathing deeply, his head buzzing, heart hammering. '*What are you talking about?*'

'We are all in your hands. We and many, many others. You are the only one who can help us.'

Deep down, stirring in his heart, Robert felt something mixed in with his fear: the knowledge that he had been waiting his entire life to hear the words Horace was speaking.

But this was insane. 'What do you mean, Horace?'

'Robert, something has happened. Something dreadful. I recognize it will be a surprise for you to hear such information coming from me, but please trust me.'

'No –'

'Please listen. You need to know this. Adam has put his life – more, his soul – at risk to prevent an act of great obscenity from taking place in this city. An event of great destructive power.'

'An attack? Is he working with the police? Do the FBI know about it? The CIA?'

'The regular authorities don't know about it. They can't. Their very knowing about it might cause it to happen.'

'I don't understand.'

'Robert, the world is far richer, far deeper, far more wondrous, and far more dangerous, than –'

'Than is dreamt of in my philosophy?'

'Yes.'

Robert stared off into the distance, trying to calm his mind. Images and sensations of 9/11 played through his mind. The reverberating hatred of the attacks. Disbelief turning to fear and horror. Courage and anger and dreadful loss. Could it be true? That it was

36

happening again? How? He rubbed his face with his hands. 'You're talking nonsense.'

'Many inexplicable things happened on August 14, 2003. The Blackout was more than you might imagine.'

'It was caused by power lines brushing against tree branches. Poor maintenance, then system errors. I read the report.'

'It was a psychic event. An *entanglement* event. Like the night of the fire. Lives were joined.'

'Crap. Who the hell are you, Horace? And what is this about an attack? Who will carry it out? Osama's boys?'

Horace stared deeply into his eyes. 'Adam will. He is being eaten away from the inside by . . . we could say, by a kind of devil. He is resisting. He is a brave soul. But he will lose, and he will activate the weapon. Unless you stop him. Unless you save him.'

A wave of anger hit Robert, surprising him with its intensity. Adam, always thinking he was exempt from the rules. Adam, always thinking he could go where angels feared to tread.

'How did this happen? Did he push his luck once too often?'

'No . . . and yes. There was a previous attempt to carry out this attack. On August 14, 2003. Adam stopped it, almost single-handedly. That is what caused the Blackout. A misfire of the Device. Now he is paying the price. He became infected, as it were. Jammed open to things he cannot control.'

'How long can he hold on?'

'I give him a week, at most. Probably less.'

'How many people are at risk?'

'Millions. Imagine a nuclear bomb of the soul.'

'What? What does that mean?'

'Go to that apartment in the West Village. All the answers are there. That is the way in.'

Robert lowered his face into his hands again, trying to make sense of everything. Was it an Adam game? Was the old man in on it? He raised his head and looked at Horace. 'Do you think Adam killed Lawrence?'

'One way or another, yes, I do.'

'This is not a game?'

'Most certainly not. Just promise me this.'

'What?'

'You will go to the address in the West Village. And, once there, you will suspend your disbelief.'

Robert sat in wonderment. He closed his eyes and cast his mind back to the day of the Blackout. The lights going off across the entire north-eastern USA as he lay in bed with Katherine. Times Square unlit in the late afternoon. The joy of her pregnancy, and then the unspeakable loss, just as they'd been expecting her to feel the first kicks. The quickening that never came.

He looked into Horace's eyes again. He reminded Robert of his late father, who had spent his entire life persuading Robert of the futility of superstition and the merits of the rational mind. Now Horace was telling him the exact opposite. The old man's gaze pierced his soul. Should he walk away right now? Send Horace and Adam and all their works to hell? He broke away from Horace's gaze and stared into the blues and reds of the rose window. Walk away? Or at least find out what on earth was going on?

He made up his mind.

'I'll go. I won't promise beyond that, but I'll go.'

Horace slumped slightly in his pew, closing his eyes. 'Good. Thank you. I have to leave now, Robert. One other thing: don't tell anyone about this, not even Katherine. I'll contact you as soon as I can, but please, in any case, we must meet after the funeral.'

Robert spoke as if in a trance. 'What are the arrangements?'

'It'll be a private family affair, I'm sure you understand. Monday morning. I'd be very glad to see you again afterwards, though I suspect we'll be in touch before that.'

Then he was gone.

Robert sat for a few moments in the church, staring into his past. Then he walked out on to the street and tried to call Katherine. No answer. He remembered she had an appointment with the shrink. In irritation, he didn't leave a message.

Then, instead of going home, he went to the West Village.

Cambridge, March 1981

The School of Pythagoras was in the north-western reaches of the vast metropolis of St John's. Entering the college through the gatehouse almost diagonally opposite the Round Church, they walked through the sixteenth-century First Court, the mist and the chill penetrating their costumes now, the college chapel to their right almost eaten up by the low white sky.

'I'm glad we survived that,' Katherine said. 'Actually I'm glad he survived it. I thought you were going to deck him.'

She took his arm again, and, as they passed through the passage by the Dining Hall to the next court, she stopped and put her arms round him, shivering and pressing her face into his chest.

'Warm me up,' she said. He felt his body respond with a flush of blood. She warmed herself against him for a few moments, then pulled away.

'OK, let's go. You're doing very well with your vow. Calling the watchman a silly fucker doesn't count.'

In the deserted Second Court they stood in the centre and turned about, taking it all in. 'Any time in the last 400 years it would have looked just like this,' she said. 'Spin me. Spin me round. It'll be fun. I don't weigh anything.'

Gripping her wrists tightly, he wheeled on his heels and began to spin her. She lifted her feet from the ground and let herself fly. It was like spinning a small child. He dipped and raised her, slowing and speeding up, as she shrieked with delight. Only when he almost lost hold of one of her wrists did he slowly bring her back to earth. Her toes touched the ground, and she skipped and twisted and slammed to a halt in his arms. She reached up to kiss him.

'Take that bloody mask off.'

He grappled with the drawstrings holding it in place. He had been too conscientious in making sure it wouldn't come off at an inopportune time. His efforts at laughter came out like a roar of frustration.

She hugged him and walked on.

'OK, tiger, later, it was just a thought. Moment's gone. Let's keep moving.'

In Third Court, smaller and a century younger, she sprinted on ahead towards the cloisters that lined the river bank, shouting 'Catch me!' and scattering a gaggle of scarved and greatcoated undergraduates. On the far side of the court, at the passageway leading to the interior of the Bridge of Sighs, she stopped and waited for him, clouds of white breath emanating from her mouth.

'This looks so romantic from the outside, but I think it's just freezing and draughty on the inside.'

They crossed halfway and looked out from within the bridge at the River Cam, spectral and empty. The few trees they could see traced gaunt filigrees against the boundless white.

'Let me feel your heart.'

She put her hand against his chest, then her ear directly over his heart. He felt it respond to her. Deep, slow, strong, steady. She looked up into his eyes through her half-visage mask. She placed his hand over her heart, just below the warm swell of her breast. He felt it hammer. They held each other's gaze. Time passed without their reckoning.

'You have a good heart, mystery man. I see why Adam chose you.'

A group of harried-looking students interrupted them, screeching about being late for the Arts Cinema. Robert was struggling still to understand the strange nasalized vowel distortions people affected when they came to study at Cambridge. 'Oh, no,' one of them had said, though 'Aynay' had come out of his mouth.

He reached into his pocket for the envelope and waved it at Katherine, pointing with it in the vague direction of north-west.

They emerged from the bridge into New Court, a riot of nineteenth-century Gothic with an extravagant cupola in the centre known as the Wedding Cake. Robert closed his eyes as they walked, feeling Katherine again nuzzled against him, and imagined the outcome he wanted of this evening. He held in his mind the image of her smiling up at him, naked, her black hair flowing freely on her white skin. He surprised himself to find he could not imagine her without her mask.

They walked in silence under the Wedding Cake and emerged into the twentieth century – the 1960s, to be exact – in a widely despised array of award-winning concrete and glass.

'Quick, run, don't look at the architecture,' Katherine shouted and took off again, running across the court and under the raised Cripps Building. 'I can't see it, I can't see it!'

Robert chased her.

'Oh!' she shouted as she ran. 'I understand why Adam is doing this. I get it!'

He caught up with her by the porters' lodge.

'He's bending our minds. He and I have been writing this play. *Newton's Papers*. It's about Sir Isaac Newton, obviously. Read his papers? Heard of them? They're at King's, Keynes bought a lot of them at auction before the war.'

Of course he knew Newton. Robert had been tempted to study physics when younger, before opting for modern languages, which he saw as just another kind of system. Calibration and predictability appealed deeply to him.

She gave a high-strung laugh. 'So these papers show Newton spent more of his time on alchemy and theology than on the things we know him for now, gravity, and optics, and calculus, and so on, and he didn't really distinguish: it was all about knowing God's creation, and clues were everywhere, in the proportions of Solomon's Temple, and in the path of comets and planets, and in curves and numbers, and the properties of metals, and the hunt for the Philosopher's Stone. Keynes said he wasn't the first of the Age of Reason, he was the last of the magicians.'

Robert looked at her quizzically and shrugged. Newton had created the modern world. It sounded like artsy crap to him.

'So that's what the game is,' she said, smiling. 'I think he's trying to create an experience like that. The world as the Ancients up till Newton saw it, everything mixed together in a big riddle. With drinking and fancy dress thrown in. Isn't he entirely mad?'

He nodded, unsure how else to react. It all sounded rather dubious.

They headed further along under the raised modern concrete buildings and emerged into the final court. At the far end of the ghostly lawn squatted the School of Pythagoras, two storeys of old stone town house with a dormer roof, completely refitted on the inside with modern amenities, where the bop – a fancy-dress birthday party thrown by friends of Adam – was clearly under way. David Bowie thrummed from the ground floor. They made their way in and quickly found Adam. He was standing on a chair waving to them, dressed as a cross between a sultan and a fakir, all in white except for an emerald-green turban and a blood-red waistcoat. A long fake beard hung from his chin. Two of their fellow conspirators, the tart and the vicar, had already joined him, and now he boomed across at them to join the small coterie, off to one side of the party away from the dance floor, which was jammed.

'Well done, well done! Did you find it? Did you bring the magic words?'

He was beside himself with glee, the twinkle of a lovable madman in his eyes. 'We await only the knight and damsel, who had to go a little further afield. Drink? Drink!'

Robert did not recognize the other two players, both of whom also wore masks. The vicar looked especially odd, with a hook-nosed black carnival mask above his dog collar. His partner had gone for the French maid look, topping it with a stunning black feathered half-mask.

Adam returned from the bar with a pint of IPA for Robert and a glass of white wine for Katherine.

'Great to see you, O magus! How was it? Fun?'

Robert nodded.

'You can talk to me, you clot, just not to her. Just make sure she can't hear you.'

'Katherine's great. Thank you so much for inviting me.'

'Nonsense. You're key to the whole enterprise.'

'How so?'

'All in good time, my friend. I have been watching you from afar. Yes, she is great, isn't she? I thought you'd hit it off. May have a proposition for you later. Proposal, I should say. Did she talk to you at all about the play we've been writing?'

'A little, yes. About Newton, right?'

'Yes. Let's talk about it later. Come back to my rooms with Kat after this.'

At that moment two more people joined them. One was a tall, somewhat buck-toothed man in the long white mantle of a knight of the crusades, a red cross on the front, worn over silvery pyjamas intended to represent armour. Robert noted a thick layer of woollen long johns under the silver. The other was a red-headed woman of generous build in a flowing skirt, laced bodice and veiled headdress. The crusader's face was white, tingeing to blue.

'Adam,' he shouted. 'You bastard!'

'That's a little harsh,' Adam countered. 'Have a drink. Warm up. Recount.'

'Who did you pay? How much did it cost you?'

The knight was quivering, whether with anger or cold Robert couldn't tell. His partner wasn't laughing either.

'All will be revealed in the fullness of the evening.'

Kathcrine put her hands up to the knight's face. 'You're freezing. Where did you go?'

Before he could reply, Adam again stood on his chair.

'Ladies and gentlemen, if I could have your attention. Lady tart and good reverend, please recount your evening. What tales of cracked riddles have you brought us? The rest of you, drink, warm up and enjoy.'

The lady spoke first. 'Well. This shifty-looking reprobate in a dog collar and a muppet mask showed up at my door at Newnham at eight o'clock and gave me a lovely rose. I've always had a thing for men of the cloth, though quite how you knew that, Adam, I would love to find out. Catholic schoolgirl and all that, so I let him in and made him a cup of coffee and he whipped out this clue. *I am the ends of the earth*, it said. We thought about that for a while. As instructed, I had my envelope here' – she showed a garter, to applause – 'which he couldn't keep his eyes off, but we tried to work it out with just the first clue. Land's End? John

43

o'Groats? John's? Finisterre? The reverend here thought we should raid the communion wine to limber up our minds a bit, so . . .'

The vicar took up the story. 'After some suitably chaste sippage the good lady was prevailed upon to open her envelope and therein was the phrase *just a short walk for Wojtyła*. Now, being a trained theologian and geographer, I was able to deduce the following: Wojtyła is a pope, hence lives in the Vatican, from where a short walk in any direction leads to Rome . . . but Rome and *ends of the earth* do not sit well together –'

'But,' his partner interrupted, 'Wojtyła is also a Pole, and then it gets more interesting. The North and South Pole are at the ends of the earth, and *just a short walk –*'

'Captain Oates,' the crusader knight piped up, somewhat happier now that he'd sunk a pint. '*I'm just going for a short walk, and I may be some time.* Walked out of the tent to die on one of the polar expeditions so that he'd not be a burden to his colleagues.'

'Precisely,' the vicar said. 'Which led us within seconds to conclude we should be heading for the Scott Polar Institute on Lensfield Road.'

'Bravo,' Adam said.

She resumed. 'We walked. I wasn't cycling anywhere in this get-up. Once we got there, we looked at the second riddle. *QAPVD*, it said. *Decode it and bring back the words.*'

'We looked everywhere except in front of our noses,' the vicar said. 'It's carved right on the front of the building. Eventually we spotted it. *Quaesivit arcana poli videt dei.*'

Katherine asked: 'Meaning what?'

'It's a tribute to Scott of the Antarctic,' the vicar said. '*He sought the secrets of the pole but found the hidden face of God.* Those are the magic words we were to bring back, I presume?'

Adam applauded, sparking the rest to join in.

'And what secret wish was fulfilled?'

The vicar and the lady looked at each other for a second. 'Neither of us dared,' he said. 'Honest.'

'I don't believe you for a moment,' Adam boomed. 'Moving right along, you will have found in one of your envelopes earlier this evening a card showing a design against a background of dots, looking perhaps like a key, or a constellation.'

The vicar fumbled in his pocket and produced theirs, holding it up to show to the group.

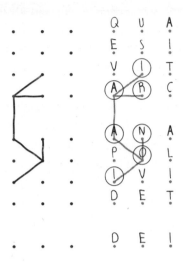

'Please jot down on the card the Latin phrase you discovered, one letter per dot, starting at the top. When you have done so, please call out which letters are touched by the design.'

The vicar did so. 'Let's see. I, A, R, A, N, O, I.'

Adam strode among them, thrilled at their diligence as they all made a note of the letters.

'In each of your adventures there is an absence,' he said. 'What is it in this case?'

The knight spoke up again. 'Scott never made it back. Oates sacrificed himself. There are lots.'

Katherine raised her hand. 'I don't know if it was his expedition or one of Shackleton's, but they said they had the feeling, when they were at the limits of their strength, that there was always one more person with them than could be counted. T. S. Eliot refers to it in *The Waste Land*.'

'Thank you,' Adam said, raising his glass. 'Yes. To absent heroes, and the spiritual succour they may bring. Now, witch, please recount.

Ladies and gentlemen, the warlock is under oath of silence until
10 p.m., still a few minutes hence.'

Katherine told their story in minute detail, including even her
secret wish to snog with a boy in a church graveyard. The watchman's cameo appearance was a big hit.

'*Hic est enim sangus meus novi testamenti* in something or other *peccatos*,'
Adam repeated. 'Let's cut it off after *testamenti*, since the last phrase
is mutilated. Speaking of which, what is the absence here?'

'The word "redemption", or "forgiveness",' Katherine said immediately.

'Thank you. Please write your phrase on your card and call out
the letters touched by your key.

Katherine did so. 'That would be M, N, I and V,' she said. They
all scribbled notes.

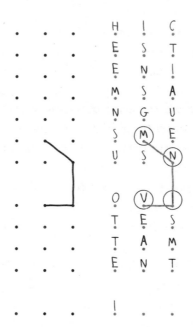

'Thank you. Now, knight and damsel, please recite.'

'First, you are truly a bastard,' the damsel said. 'My poor knight
nearly died of fright. You shouldn't play tricks like that.'

'I am intrigued,' Adam said. 'Please recount.'

'So this man in silver pyjamas and a Ned Kelly hat comes to my door. Lovely rose, and so on. The first clue was a biblical reference. Ezekiel 38:2. *Son of Man, set your face towards Gog, of the land of Magog.* Pretty clear directions. The Gog Magog hills just outside Cambridge, to the south-east. But they're big, easy to get lost up there.

'So we went pretty quickly for the second clue, which was as follows:

> *'I am the creature of this place*
> *I am its spirit, no magic wand*
> *Will bury me.*
> *A warrior might steal me away*
> *Wrote Gervase of Tilbury*
> *If he unseat my master*
> *On a moonlit night.*
> *I dwell within a ring.*
> *I am Arabian, and I am chalk.*
> *I am buried, yet I walk.*
> *Find me.*

'My *History of World Literature* got us as far as Gervase of Tilbury writing a book in the thirteenth century to amuse his emperor, part encyclopedia, part stories of marvels and local legends from around the world, but we couldn't get a copy of it, given the hour. We presumed there was some reference to the Gog Magog hills in there. We were looking at a local map and saying the clue out loud when we got it. Wandlebury. No magic *wand will bury* ... very cunning, Adam. Up in the Gog Magog hills there's an old Iron Age hill fort called Wandlebury. So off to the taxi rank we went and off we rode.'

'The driver was a complete card, asking what we were up to heading up there at this time of night in the fog, nudge nudge, and asks if we know about the legend of the knight up there. We don't, so he tells us. On any moonlit night, he says, if a warrior enters the ring of Wandlebury fort and calls out a certain phrase, a ghostly knight on a black horse will appear, and you'll have to fight him for his steed.'

'My partner claims to be a warrior of sorts, he's Officer Training Corps in the Army, and the driver tells us the phrase. *Knight to knight, come forth*, he says. *Don't say it unless you're serious.* Joker.'

'So we went up there and we're dropped off in the car park,' the knight went on. 'It's bloody desolate, it's freezing, we're looking for information boards or anything to solve the riddle and get out of there, and damsel here asks if I have a secret wish to freeze to death on a Fenland hill, because she certainly doesn't, and in any case who ever heard of a hill in the Fens, and I say, well I've always fancied a real swordfight with a real knight, Adam knows I fence, I've always wondered how good they were in the old days. So we walk into the ring and then we find this sign about the Godolphin Arabian. Has anyone heard of him?'

They shook their heads. Adam beamed.

'Inside the ring of Wandlebury fort there used to be a stately home, the Earl of Godolphin's seat, demolished in the 1950s, but the stables are still there, people live in them. In the stables is buried perhaps the greatest sire of racehorses that ever lived, the Godolphin Arabian. Died 1753. Legendary beast, apparently. Sired Regulus, Lath, Cade, all outstanding racehorses or studs. One of three stallions that virtually created English thoroughbred racehorses.'

He paused for a sip of beer and his partner took up the tale.

'So we have the Arabian and the mounted knight and his ghostly steed from your clue, and we've ticked off the ring too. We haven't got the chalk part, but we're feeling pretty pleased . . . but we keep on walking, away from the stables, into the centre of the ring. It's a big field. And in the middle this bloody fool shouts out the challenge.'

'*Knight to knight, come forth*, just like that. I belted it out, for a laugh.'

'And then . . .'

He licked his lips. Took a long draught of his pint. 'And then . . . there's this fucking black horse there. Staring at me. Nostrils smoking. Steam rising off it, like it's just finished galloping. Standing stock-still. Staring at me. I swear. Standing there in the fog. I have *never* been so scared in my life.'

'Who did you pay to do it, Adam?'

'Details, details. And so what is the answer?'

'The answer is *horse*, you twisted sod.'

Katherine spoke up, putting her hand on the damsel's knee. 'Did you see it?'

'I saw something. Hard to say what I saw. It could have been a horse. There was something there. I was bloody scared.'

'Horse from a field near by, must have escaped,' the vicar said. 'Either that or the two of you are winding us up.'

Robert jotted some lines down and handed them to Katherine. 'My good warlock says he thinks Adam paid two blokes from the village to put on a panto horse costume and stand up there till two silly buggers from the university showed up.'

'We ran down to the car park like fools. Taxi driver thought it was the funniest thing he'd seen in years.'

The knight insisted that the horse was there. 'That much I'm certain of. Who did you pay?'

'There was no knight?' Adam paused. 'I'll have to get my money back.'

'You sod!'

Most of them laughed. The damsel let out a high-pitched sound between amusement and hysteria. A smile slowly crept on to the knight's face too.

'Special points for intrepidity are awarded to our knight and damsel,' Adam said. 'Now, please write the challenge of Gog Magog on your card.'

Pencil-scratching ensued. *Knight to knight, come forth.*

'That gives T, C, M and O,' the knight called out.

'Just a minute,' the damsel interrupted. 'What was the chalk, then? I think we got the rest.'

'There is a great chalk figure cut into the hills up there, though it's overgrown,' Adam said. 'It shows a great horse or horses being ridden by a giant goddess with three breasts. Some people think it's ancient; others think the gentleman who uncovered it in the 1950s actually made it himself out of wishful thinking – there were old references to such figures, and he found it by bosing, which is

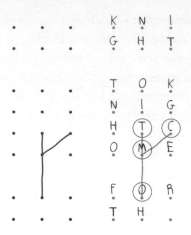

jamming a big stick into the ground to find disturbed earth and chalk. On the other hand –'

'Yes?'

'Well, it is right on the ley line that also goes through Wandle-bury fort, right by the Scott Polar Institute, and right through the Round Church, if you happen to believe in such things. There's also said to be a golden chariot buried in the ring. It is a place of power, they say.'

'It's a place of bloody freezing fog, I'll go that far,' said the knight.

Robert made a note to himself of the two new words he'd learned in the course of the evening. Vulning. Bosing.

'Ladies and gentlemen,' said Adam. 'It is almost ten o'clock. We are about God's work, forming a new Society. The penultimate challenge for this evening is to find its motto, hidden in the fifteen letters you have all just extracted with your keys. Find the three words that begin O . . . V . . . A.'

'Is it in English or Latin?'

'The latter. Each of your teams has someone who studied Latin at least to O-level.'

There was fevered scribbling and conferring.

'As you work, allow me to read you the constitution of the Society. *The as yet nameless Society is a social club dedicated to the setting and solving of puzzles, matchmaking, non-frivolous amusement and the pursuit of unconventional wisdom through playful exploration. Its methods draw on conventions such as the blind date, the scavenger hunt, spy fiction and the masked ball. Membership is by invitation only.'*

'You don't have a name yet?'

'We will guess the name. It will come from your adventures. A combination of what you discovered.'

'Shut up and let us think, then.'

Robert and Katherine huddled. From the Scott Institute: I A R A N O I. From the Round Church: M N I V. From the Wandlebury Ring: T C M O.

Robert drew them in a circle, Katherine in a square, each following their own crossword-puzzle technique.

Katherine whispered in his ear: 'Redemption . . . self-sacrifice . . . holy warrior . . . how much Latin did you do?'

Robert jotted in response: 'Warrior fights to win. Forgiveness conquers sin. No greater love than this . . .'

Suddenly he had it. He grabbed her by the shoulders and squeezed her. Scribbled furiously in capital letters. Showed her.

'Yes!' she shouted, raising her hand in the air. 'Bingo!'

Something of a crowd had gathered round to see what on earth they were up to.

Adam looked at his watch. Robert checked his own and saw it was ten o'clock. He shouted, in unison with Katherine: 'OMNIA VINCIT AMOR!'

'Ohhhhhhhhhh damn,' said the vicar, throwing his pen down in disgust.

'Love Conquers All,' Katherine hooted. 'Love Conquers All.'

She grabbed Robert's hands and squeezed them. 'You're my eternal hero! Love Conquers All.'

Adam was laughing so hard with delight that Robert thought he would levitate, clapping his hands and dancing a merry jig.

'Well done, Katherine Rota and Robert Reckliss,' he boomed. 'Ladies and gentlemen, unmask yourselves.'

Robert struggled again with the mask, managing with Katherine's help only to slide it down off his face so it dangled around his neck. She smiled.

'Hi, handsome.'

Her own she got off easily. She ran over and kissed Adam and held him in a long hug that Robert had been expecting for himself. Then she came and gave him one too. She was adorable. A blue-eyed imp.

The knight revealed himself as a third-year natural scientist from Downing. The damsel was a second-year medic at Emmanuel. Vicar and tart declared themselves to be a third-year geographer from Jesus and a most untartlike fourth-year linguist from Newnham, whom Robert recognized also as an actress from a show at the ADC theatre. There was applause, followed by more drinks.

Adam stood. 'Now the final challenge. What is the creature that combines all three of your explorations? What have you created in your exertions? After that creature we shall name our Society.'

The Newnham lady spoke. 'The ends of the earth, unknown territories where magical creatures dwell . . . horse-like, with healing powers born of suffering . . . redemptive but with a strong sexual charge . . . am I the only one getting this?'

The knight had had enough. 'Um . . . Pegasus?'

Robert couldn't help taking the piss. 'Rhinoceros?'

Five people shouted at the same time: 'Unicorn!'

Thus was the Cambridge University Unicorn Society founded. Adam claimed to have abolished it, a few months later, when he graduated. But some say it lives on, in a different form, with the same aims and methods.

New York, August 26, 2004

Robert stood outside the address Adam had sent him hidden in the Malice Box and tried the keys in the street door. The second one opened it. The apartment was a fifth-floor walk-up, which earned Adam no special thanks, in a 1930s white-painted brick building of 'railroad' apartments: one room wide, long and thin, running front-to-back through the building like a railcar or a submarine. The stairs to the top floor were narrow, tightly wound, bowed in the middle by the weight of walkers. The most recent paint job was starting to flake. Robert trod on a used condom as he walked up.

The other key opened the apartment.

He'd had no idea Adam kept a New York pied-à-terre, or love nest, or whatever he called it. The place was not set up in any great luxury, certainly not the kind of place one would take a mistress, Robert imagined.

But there was a computer, sitting atop a cheap black desk against the far wall as he entered. And computers took passwords.

The power was on. He dabbed the keyboard and got a prompt saying the screen was locked. Control alt delete. The username Adam was already there. He punched in the word on the slip of paper: *vitriol.* The Word document came up immediately.

Hello, Robert,

Long time no see, to coin a phrase. Very sorry it's been so long. I never write, I never call. Terribly sorry.

I won't bury the lead any further. I need to ask you to do some things, and they will seem rather strange. Some may be dangerous; others will take you to areas of life you might not ordinarily be familiar with. If you do them, you will help prevent a dreadful act from being visited upon us all. Something utterly hellish. You may also save my life.

It won't all be bad, and some of it will be right up your street, I should think, but some of it will be quite harrowing.

Why should you not bin this letter right now?

Because I pray you trust me. Because you and Katherine will be among the victims if you do nothing. Because you are one of the few people in the world who can stop it.

You'll need to begin this quite soon, and, once you begin, there'll be no stopping until it's over. Once again, I'm very sorry, but it's not just my wretched neck on the line. It's everyone's.

I've got in rather deep in something, to tell you the truth, and I don't know now how to get out. I may not be able to.

You'll need an internet-capable phone, the kind that takes pictures and transmits them from where you are and can handle instant messaging and Google searches and that kind of thing. One is provided, if you look in the cardboard box up to your right. I think it's called a Quad Plus, or something like that. It'll do GPS and maps too. I took good advice – it's a fantastic device.

You'll need a map of New York, Manhattan mainly, with the subways and bus routes showing, in case the technology fails you. Sometimes a pencil and ruler are a better bet.

Remember your Boy Scout days? Think of it as a scavenger hunt, with all the ugliness those two words contain if we take them separately and literally.

But most of all you'll need your good, stout heart, Robert, and guts, and your wits about you. There'll be clues and friends along the way, but enemies too, I'm afraid.

We must visit the secret chambers below the city, and the secret gardens and platforms above it, and the hidden places in between. We must also visit the secret places of the heart.

Let's call part of it a walking tour, and part of it a bit of self-help, and part of it a kind of meditation primer. We're going to need to get you up to speed pretty quickly, you see. Think of it as a crash course in certain matters spiritual, mental and carnal. If you can't pass it, you'll be of no use to anyone and an awful lot of people will die. Hot in here?

Cheers
Adam

Suspend disbelief, Horace had asked of him.

The letter was dated August 14. The first anniversary of the Blackout. He printed out a copy and closed the file.

There were no other recently opened files under 'Documents'. Clicking through the other programmes, he launched Explorer and Netscape browsers, found nothing in the bookmarks, then opened up America Online. There was just one screen name: AdamHD1111. He entered *vitriol* as the password. It worked.

AdamHD1111 had no mail, no old mail, no sent mail, no favourite places. But the Buddy List showed 0/1 – someone Adam chatted

54

with regularly, or wanted to remember. Whoever it was, they weren't online. Robert looked up the name. TerriC1111. And the user profile:

Name: Terri, 22/F
Location: Between Hades and earth. Eliot likes me 'throbbing between two lives'
Gender: Female
Marital Status: Open. To myself, to the divine
Hobbies and Interests: Vaticination. Seduction. Speaking the language of the birds, the green language
Favourite Gadgets: Myself; my eyes
Occupation: Seer, guide, lover
Personal Quote:

> Two snakes I spy, entwined in the act of love
> One I scotch, the female, and am myself made woman
> For seven years
> Till the same snakes I spy again, again lost in love's act
> The male I scotch, and am myself made male again
> So the seasons turn

Her AOL homepage had a picture of a headless but otherwise shapely female mannequin in a shop window, a snake on her black dress, a writhing mass of serpents behind her. In short, some deeply weird shit.

Robert looked inside the cardboard box Adam had indicated. Inside was a silver-and-grey device like a chunkier Treo or Palm Pilot, with a large screen. It nestled comfortably in his hand when he picked it up, despite its weight. There were also a few accessories: a charger, what looked like a foldable keyboard, an earpiece/microphone. He turned it on. It gave a beep and presented a startling array of icons. The GPS programme indicated the device had perhaps a dozen locations logged, all identified by three-figure numbers. He saw the battery was a little low and put it on to charge.

He imagined himself talking to Adam as he puttered about the apartment:

'This time I've crossed the line.'

'You've really done it, Adam.'

'This time I'm on the other side of the veil.'

'You've pulled it off.'

'I can't get back.'

'The Rope Trick.'

'I really did it.'

'The vanishing trick. Poof! Gone from the face of the earth.'

'You shouldn't follow. You mustn't.'

'I always feared you'd do it.'

'Always knew I could.'

'Adam Hale! Climbed the rope to the top . . .'

'I'm scared. I've met some people. Serious people. I don't think they'll let me come back.'

'It begins with a letter.'

'Hello, Robert.'

'Hello, Robert, it says. The world's about to end. Remember those dreams you've been having?'

Robert sat and tried to solve the puzzle. What was Adam up to? Visiting Lawrence Hencott? *Killing* him? It didn't make sense.

But then the computer gave the sound of a door creaking open, and TerriC1111 was on line. Robert wondered what the hell to do. It was ridiculous, but his heart was hammering again.

There was a trill. An instant-messaging window opened up on the screen. 'Hey, baby,' it said. From TerriC1111. She thought he was Adam. He hesitated. Should he pretend to be Adam or not? If he just said who he was, would she freak out and vanish?

'Hi,' he typed.

The cursor blinked for half a minute. A minute. His mouth was dry. Did Adam never say 'Hi'? Did they have a secret code? A lovers' code? *Unless I use the word 'rhubarb' assume I am captured?*

The sharp trill again.

'I've been trying to reach you, you crazy bastard . . . are you OK?'

Here he was, more than twenty years on, being mistaken for Adam again. And, despite himself, he liked it. He liked the idea of being someone else for a few minutes. It was a vacation from pain. It was exciting. It was relief.

'Yes. Tired.'

'Where did you go?'

Robert took a leap into the void. 'I was right here in New York.'

He could almost feel her thinking. The trill again.

'Did you get everything done you needed to do?'

'I hope so.'

'You're not sure? Were there any difficulties?'

'Hard to ever be sure, I guess. Then I went to see Hencott.'

'Who?'

Shit. Now how could he get out of this? She was his link to Adam. Or was it the other way round? He typed: 'The goldmines guy? Lawrence Hencott?'

'Oh, sorry. Yes. When did you see him?'

'Yesterday, I think. I haven't slept. I'm losing track of time.' It occurred to him that she was hurt. 'Sorry, I wanted to tell you where I was. But I had to see him first.'

'I think you might be forgiven, in the circumstances. Is it safe for us to meet? I soooo want to see you.'

'I really want to. But not quite yet.'

'How hard was it, my darling?'

'Lawrence is dead.'

She was quiet for a few seconds.

'You said he would die one way or another. What happened?'

'Killed himself. Shot himself. He made a call first.'

'Who to?'

'Robert Reckliss.'

'Is that good or bad?'

He paused, trying not to let the conversation spin out of control. 'He's trustworthy. Didn't I tell you that?'

'Yes. I can't believe you've done this. Were you scared?'

'Yes. I thought of you. A lot.'

Now he could almost feel her smile.

'I got something for you,' she wrote. 'Want to see?'

The blinking cursor. He felt like a teenager.

'I'd love to.' He added a smiley face.

'OK. What's the password, baby?'

Now she asks for a password? Fuck. 'The password to your heart?'

'The password to all of me, lover.'

He took another educated punt. 'Vitriol.'

'Interesting one. OK, baby. Sending.'

For a moment nothing happened. Then, in that vapidly cheery AOL male voice, the computer said: 'You've got mail.'

Terri trilled again. 'Hope you like it, sweetie.'

He clicked on the little yellow envelope. She'd sent a photograph, inserted in the body of the email, no other text. It began to reveal itself from the top, counting off in percentage points of completion: 8 per cent, 23 per cent . . .

The top of a woman's head began to appear, black hair . . . forehead . . . He realized it was a painting. Eyebrows spiralled into eyes like spinning galaxies in a heart-shaped face, very white, a long swan neck, a black form-hugging dress with ample décolletage, black gloves to above the elbow . . . an attractive, half-abstract head-and-shoulders rendering of a young woman in her twenties, with a little Goth about her . . .

'I shot it yesterday on the street in Chelsea. Doesn't it look like me?'

Did it?

'Beautiful. Very nice.'

The blinking cursor. His breathing. His mouth was still dry. He licked his lips. Now he felt embarrassed, creepy.

He was reaching for the keyboard when the asinine friendly AOL voice kicked in again. 'You've got mail.'

Another picture from Terri. He hesitated, his finger in the air over the mouse.

Another trill, another IM: a little red devil face from TerriC1111.

He opened it up and watched it slowly reveal itself on the screen. It was a photograph of a real woman this time, short black hair, slim with implausibly long legs, wearing a long black evening dress slit almost to the waist, one hand on her hip, the other parting the dress just enough to reveal a hint of black lace at the top of her stocking.

He felt a rush of blood away from his brain. Katherine and he had barely made love in eight months.

'Stop,' he wrote.

'No,' she replied. 'Just getting started. It's my latest photo shoot. Tell me a story.'

'Wait. Please.'

'You don't like?' Pouty face.

He hesitated. 'I like. Very much.'

'You're not Adam.'

He couldn't afford to lose her. But he didn't know how to sustain the fiction. Fearful of losing the connection to her, he cracked. 'No,' he typed.

The blinking cursor. A minute passed.

'I'm . . . intrigued.'

'I'm trying to find him. To help him. I'm a friend.'

Silence. Another pause.

'Why?'

'I believe he may be in danger.'

'From whom?'

'I don't know. I was asked to come here. To trust. Are you and he together? I assume you are? An item?'

'Lovers? Ohhhh, yes.' Winky face.

'Do you know where he is?'

'Adam is elusive at the best of times . . .'

How not to frighten her off?

'I'm sorry for pretending to be Adam. I didn't know quite what to do when you appeared here.'

'Yes, you're a bad boy . . . Did you like it?'

'Seeing your pictures? Yes, they are lovely.'

'Pretending to be Adam. I think you liked that.'

'OK. Maybe.'

'I take it you are Robert Reckliss? The man he calls Rickles? I hear you share everything.'

What the hell?

'How did you know who I am?'

'He said there were three options: it would be him, it would be you, or he'd be dead and it would be his killer. You have no idea what he just did. What he just risked. He said if it wasn't him, I'd have to guess whether the person imitating him was the killer or you.'

'How do you know which of us it is?'

'He said if he were dead, the killer would imitate him perfectly, but that I'd feel he was evil.'

'And I didn't imitate him perfectly?'

'The real Adam would have been more direct in his lust by now. Especially after just surviving what he went to do.'

'What did he go to do?'

'One thing at a time. He talks about you a lot, Robert. Says you saved his life.'

'I did. A long time ago.'

'He saved mine. In a way. So now we have a triangle to close. I save yours?'

'How did he save your life?'

'He protects me from a bad place. Makes life seem joyful and happy even when it's not. Do you know how he does that?'

Robert smiled, almost laughed. It was Adam's maddening gift. He suddenly felt as though Adam were in the room. He could make you laugh even while you were knee-deep in manure. Usually the mess you were in was of his making, of course.

'I don't. But I know exactly what you mean.'

'He makes things turn for the better, even if it feels like a train wreck.'

She knew him, that much was clear.

'Does this mean Adam is safe?'

'No. I'm not sure what it means. I think it means he's not dead yet.'

'What's going on? Please tell me.'

'I need to think first.'

'You said Adam knew Lawrence was going to die?'

'One way or another, he said. I didn't understand.'

'What can I do to help?'

'Slow down. I need to think.'

They were both silent for a moment.

'Where are you, Terri?'

'Adam calls me his Red Hooker.'

'Red Hook. Brooklyn.'

'Got it in one.'

'Tell me something more about you? And him?'

'We've been lovers for about a year. Since the Blackout. As for me, here's my usual line, I have it saved: *I'm a retired bike messenger. I'm in identity management. I seek God. I make videos. I'm an empath. I switch. I blog. I'm a geo-cacher. I like sex in public places. I'm an ex-suicide girl, but I won't tell you which one, I'm a tour guide. I'm a healer. I scare people.*'

'Er . . . I don't even know what some of those things are. How old are you?'

'I'm twenty-two. Don't fret. You are so serious. And about you: he says you are entangled for life. He says it's shared history.'

Images Robert had forbidden himself to recall for two decades suddenly came hurtling back at him. He saw himself kicking over the table in Katherine's college room and knocking its terrifying contents to the floor. He felt again the raw fear and confusion of that night. He saw Katherine making love to Adam, and to him. He saw fire ripping through Adam's room at Trinity, and the face of death in the smoke – the single, unblinking, beautiful eye – staring into his soul.

He fixed his eyes on the wall, remembering, his hands motionless on the keyboard. He lost track of time.

She typed: 'Now I'm losing patience.'

His heart started as he came back to the conversation. 'It's hard to explain. Shared history's a good way of putting it. We shared a woman once.'

'Just one?'

'Just one. As far as I know. Look, Adam asked me to help him. Do you know what kind of trouble he's got himself into?'

'Do you?'

He didn't know how much to reveal of what Horace had told him. He opted for caution. 'No. Something about some people he's fallen in with, who won't let him get away from them. Something about an act of great obscenity. He says I can help.'

Terri was silent again.

'Terri?'

'I'm making up my mind about you. Wait.'

Suddenly he felt a sharp sensation of being watched. The hairs stood up on the back of his neck. But it was as though he were being seen ... known ... *from the inside.* The sensation deepened, becoming more acutely physical. He breathed in sharply. He was being ... *strummed. Teased. Explored.*

'Jesus! What the hell is that?'

The sensations faded as quickly as they had come. Then Terri was back. 'OK. You check out. So be it.'

'Woah! What did you just do?'

His head buzzed. It was as though he'd been kissed, such was the unexpected intimacy. Had that really been her? Or had it been just his imagination, a reaction to the intensity of his flashback? Who the hell were these people?

'I just tried to get a read on whether you're up to this. You have a lot of fear, Robert Reckliss. But we can work on that. Now pay attention.'

She sent him another email. It was a letter. To Terri, from Adam.

My darling Terri,

Soon I will be going to the dark place I told you about. You know I must go, that I would rather stay with you, that more rides on my going than simply our own lives, and that therefore I have no choice. I must undo the potential harm I have created.

Here's what you may say:

A plot is afoot. A device of extraordinary power is hidden somewhere in Manhattan. It goes by many names, including Gnosis, Ma'rifat', the Soul Engine. The Ma'rifat' is a window into the place where our potential darkness resides, where we are called to turn our fear into light, or else perish. It is at once a place in the mind and a state of matter. The science that made it is astonishing and very ancient.

It can be disarmed only by beings of great psycho-spiritual power. Such

62

a being is rare indeed, but there are two in Manhattan at this very moment. One we may call a Unicorn, a creature of pure light. The other is a Minotaur, a lost one. The Minotaur serves evil masters. It is within me, corroding me. It has no interest in disarming the Device. On the contrary, it wants to drive me to detonate it, as do the people I am now going to see. I am resisting. The Unicorn is within a sleeping man, one unaware of his power. If I die, my killer or the sleeping man will come to you, I don't know which. You must help him awaken. You must take him as far along the Path as you can, so that he can become powerful enough to stop what is going to happen.

The Device is armed. To deactivate it will require seven minor keys and a master key. The seven minor keys are hidden in Manhattan, in a geometric array, and must be recovered.

The master key has been sent away for safe keeping.

Perhaps, please God, I will succeed in this endeavour.

I am doing this for us. Please forgive me if I fail.

'This was written just before he vanished?'

'Yes. He went to see these people he refers to yesterday. I've heard nothing since. Until you.'

'What else did he say about this damned Device?'

'The Ma'rifat'. That's what he called it most of the time.'

'Arabic?'

'Yes.'

'Meaning what?'

'Meaning, among other things, knowledge of the divine. Knowing as you know a person, not as you know a fact. And he kept saying the last thing we can do is call the cops. None of us can. They'd need to send in a priest or a chaplain, and you can bet your ass they wouldn't. Can you imagine? Cops defending New York? Army, even? If a SWAT team got within fifty yards of it, knowing what it could do, they would set it off. It would read their fear. Like I just read you.'

It didn't make sense to him. Then it did.

'Only psychopaths aren't afraid,' he said. 'Ordinary people are scared, soldiers and cops are scared, but they learn how to put it aside. The fear is still there.'

'Adam said the Device would find it out. Amplify it. Feed off it to detonate.'

'And?'

'Think Hiroshima, if the authorities find it. If the Minotaur's masters set it off, think something far worse. A kind of soul bomb. Think of what people do when their souls are poisoned, turning on each other. Think Auschwitz in America. Think damnation.'

Robert thought of his friend facing down such evil. The dilettante finally facing his destiny. Choosing to fight, not to cut and run. He felt irrationally proud of Adam.

'I think he sent me the thing he called the master key. I've been calling it the Malice Box.'

'You have it safe?'

'Define safe. It's in my pocket.'

'Jesus Christ.'

'What is the Minotaur?'

'A parasitical thought-form, an unappeased soul. Suffering. It was once good. It has become evil.'

'And the Unicorn?'

'Work it out.'

'Tell me.'

'It's in you, Robert. It *is* you.'

He closed his eyes. By all that was holy . . . He swore to himself. Fear and panic surged again.

'No. I don't believe it.'

'Believe. Look into your heart.'

She had seen something he had been trying to hide even from himself: the unspoken knowledge, forced deep away into the depths of his mind, that one day this would happen. And, in the midst of dread, a sense of *pride* that it should be him.

His mind spiralled back to his parents, both now long dead: hard-working, honest people who'd insisted the old ways were nonsense, that backward superstition was a family curse, to be finally laid to rest in their son. They had brought him up to disbelieve, alone on the great estate, cut off from distant aunts and uncles and half-heard stories of dark events thirty years earlier, during the war. There were no family get-togethers among his people.

Only once, when he reached eighteen, had a relative contacted him. He'd received a single, unsigned letter in his first weeks at university.

You are of my kin. There are things it is your right to know. Neither side of your family will tell you, so I will, God preserve me. This is the marrow of the knowledge. You will understand each line when you have need of it. Preserve them.

The rest of the letter had consisted of seven sentences on a single page. He had dismissed it as bunkum and burned the letter at the end of his first term. But he had never forgotten what it said:

> *To live well, know death*
> *In love, give to receive; seed is not sensation*
> *Seek freedom's far bourns*
> *Walk the path of the Other*
> *Be your own weather, through intention*
> *As above, so below; as within, so without*
> *Die to live*

They were both silent for a moment. Then Terri came back. 'OK, I'm going to help you, I've decided. Brace yourself, because things are going to speed up from now on. The clock has started ticking.'

'Since when?'

'Since you began to believe.'

Another email landed. It was a photograph of a small monument of some kind, surrounded by railings.

She asked, 'Do you know what that is?'

'No. A gravestone?'

'Yes. It reads as follows:

'Erected to the Memory
Of an Amiable Child
St Claire Pollock
Died 15 July, 1797
In the Fifth Year of His Age

'It's up by Riverside Church. A child. Caged off in perpetuity from everything that goes on around it. Hold that image in your mind. You'll need it later. Trust me. It's going to look like a game, but it's not. Is there a Quad Plus there? You know what that is?'

'Yes, he left one.'

'That's going to be our main means of contact from now on. He set it up as a way we could help him. Call home if you need to. You may be late. Don't tell your wife what's going on. It won't help. It might make things worse.'

'How so?'

'Listen. You are going to need to go somewhere, solve some riddles, post some pictures to a website. It's the first bookmark. The email and URL to use are already loaded into the Quad. Do a test now. Hurry. We can help him, but there isn't much time.'

'Stop. Hold on.'

'Adam is in great danger, Robert. Trust me now. Go to GPS Waypoint 025. Meet me there. Go.'

'What? Why?'

'When you find the waypoint you are going to have to solve a riddle. When you solve the riddle, you will find a cache. In the cache will be one of the keys to the Ma'rifat'. These are also stages of the Path. Each stage will be meaningful, in a way you will need to show you understand. I will help you as best I can.'

'How did you get these GPS locations?'

'Adam captured them on Blackout Day. There were hundreds in a PDA that belonged to the creator of the Device. Most were dummy waypoints, but the good ones have all been loaded on to the Quad. I just don't know which are which. I received a text message to tell you to go to Waypoint 025 just a few minutes ago.'

'Who from?'

66

'That's the thing. I don't know. Adam just told me to trust anything I received from the Watchman. So we're both flying blind here. Now go.'

Then the computer made the sound of a slamming door, and she vanished.

He sat staring at the screen, utterly bewildered.

He had to make a decision. Meet her? Believe her? Believe Horace and Adam? His mind spun. Dismiss them all and go home? Disbelieve?

While his thoughts raced, he cut and pasted their IM exchanges into an email and sent them to himself, from Adam. Ditto Adam's letter and the pictures she'd sent him.

Decide.

He needed more information, which meant meeting her.

Adam had asked him for help, and he would not walk away.

He made up his mind.

He grabbed the Quad and checked its settings. He did a test of the camera, snapping a photograph of a 'New York Skyline' paperweight on Adam's desk and posting it to the webpage at the first bookmark. Username AdamHD1111 and a password were already loaded, he noted. He called up the webpage and confirmed it had gone through. He called up Waypoint 025. The street map on the Quad GPS screen showed a marker between Broadway and Church, near Fulton. He racked his memory, trying to recall what was there.

He called Katherine. It went to her voicemail. 'Hi, darling. I'm having a really screwed-up day. I may be late home. I'm fine, but I'm going to try to find out more about that thing Adam sent us.' He wondered what else to say. 'Call me when you can. I need to tell you about a couple of things.'

Katherine, Adam and Robert went to Adam's rooms in Nevile's Court at Trinity, above the elegant north cloister where Newton had tried to measure the speed of sound in the seventeenth century by stamping his foot and timing the echo. They walked up one flight of stairs and entered a long dark corridor. Katherine led them, turning left towards Adam's set of rooms at the far end.

Something about the hand-painted names, white on black, at the foot of the staircase intrigued Robert. 'Are you the only under-graduate on this staircase, Adam?'

Everyone else seemed to be at least a Ph.D., if not an actual Fellow.

'Yes it's dreadful, isn't it? You'll hate the reason. Not very egalitarian I'm afraid.'

'I was just curious.'

Adam opened the door and ushered them inside. 'It was my grandfather's doing. He is quite esteemed hereabouts. Had a good war. Something to do with the SOE, intelligence and so on. Created a couple of scholarships, quite generous ones. The only condition was that any direct descendants who could get here on merit should be allowed to occupy his old rooms, if they wished.'

'Nice.'

'I did wish, naturally. It's actually quite handy that they can't take it away from me; otherwise they would have done so by now. I am not entirely in the good books of the Master. More of that anon.'

The sitting room was huge, high-ceilinged, book-lined. The furnishings were old and expensive. It did not look like an under-graduate's room at all.

'You come from such a different world,' Robert said.

'Don't get judgemental on me now.'

'I'm not. Just observing. Was your father here too?'

A cloud crossed Adam's face. 'Dad? No. He was a little too thick.'

'Adam and his father are estranged,' Katherine said. 'Adam is a little bit disinherited. It's very dashing.'

'Quite. Care for a drink? Red wine? Pimm's? G and T?'

They had both said he'd been chosen and that he was key to some enterprise. What on earth had they meant?

Adam fussed with bottles and glasses as Katherine prowled the room. Robert plunked himself down in a beanbag.

Father. Estranged. Disinherited. He had to ask her about her accent. It was very sexy.

'Katherine, there's something about your *r*'s . . .'

Adam and Katherine burst out laughing. He felt his face burning.

'That didn't come out right.'

'You're too sweet,' Katherine said. 'It's OK, Robert. My mother was American, if that's what you're asking about. My grandmother was from California. She spent a lot of time over here during the war. I was brought up here. My dad's a Brit, Anglo-Argentine to be exact. Wanted an English rose for a daughter, and that's what he got.'

She settled on the sofa and drew up her knees, cuddling herself dreamily. Robert leaned towards her. 'So how long have you been writing this play? When do you plan to put it on?'

Katherine's eyes flickered towards Adam.

'Most of last term and all of this,' she said. 'I wanted to write something to do with the history of science for my thesis, and I got into the Keynes papers thinking I'd find some correspondence that might help. Typical me. Once I started I couldn't stop.'

'This is Keynes the economist? John Maynard Keynes?'

'The same. He bought all these papers of Newton's at auction in 1936, so they wouldn't fall back into private hands. Left them to King's when he died.'

'And you've done a lot of theatre?'

'My first two years I practically lived at the ADC. This year I want to write. Adam and I have a pact.'

Adam handed her a glass of red wine, a smile playing on his lips. 'What's that?'

'We won't sleep together, so we can write together.'

'Kat, really,' said Adam, reaching out to Robert with a gin and tonic. 'Behave.'

Adam discarded his false beard and turban and settled into a large armchair, surveying the two of them like a proud paterfamilias.

Katherine stretched. 'That's why I said I'd do the blind date tonight, to help Adam foist me off. You don't mind, do you?'

'Foist away, frankly.'

'Then I thought he'd show up in disguise and ravish me and pretend he was someone else.'

'Sorry to disappoint.'

'You didn't, Robert. You've been the perfect gentleman. Just what a girl would wish for. Will you walk me home tonight?'

He couldn't help checking Adam's reaction. Studiously neutral.

'I'd be delighted to.'

'With regard to the play, I wanted to ask you a favour,' Adam said. 'We want to put it on on the lawn outside the front of Trinity.'

'Where Newton's Tree is?'

'Yes, but not just because of that. In Newton's day it was a walled garden, and his laboratory was inside it. His rooms were between the Great Gate and the chapel, on the first floor, so he could just walk out on to his veranda, down some stairs and into the garden. The laboratory was at the chapel end of the garden.'

'Would they let you?'

'Well, that's where you come in. They wouldn't let *me*, you see. There was some unpleasantness and misunderstanding last year about my borrowing some college punts – quite a few, actually – for a re-enactment of the Battle of Waterloo on the river . . .'

'That was a land battle, wasn't it?'

'Literal-mindedness will be the death of you, young Robert.'

'So . . .'

'So it occurred to me that you might like to be the producer of the play. Front for me with the Trinity authorities, certainly, but also help us put it on. Do the organizing.'

'You don't mind pretending to be Adam, do you?'

He held Katherine's gaze. Was he being insulted? Played with? He didn't think so. He decided to risk it. See where it took him.

'Not at all, in the right circumstances. But why me?'

'I'm sure you'd be good at it, first of all. You exude trustworthiness and matter-of-factness and solidity. Is that how your friends back home think of you? I'm sure it is.'

It was barely six months since Robert had left home, straight from the local grammar school, to take up his place at Trinity Hall. All that was solid and real in his life was there.

'My friends back home would probably find this entire evening too pretentious for words, but I've found it enchanting so far. Yes, I'm good at organizing things. I'm thrilled to be asked. Thank you.'

'Adam's been watching you, you see.' Katherine walked over behind Adam's armchair and put her hands on his shoulders. 'He said he'd found a diamond in the rough and he'd like to think of some way to give you a leg-up.'

Robert's pride flared. 'A leg-up into what?'

'Into this place,' Adam said. 'Into not being afraid to dream. Into not letting the chip on your shoulder or the mud on your boots hold you back from enjoying three years of unfettered wonder, whatever your friends back home think of it.'

'I'm getting the hang of it. I don't quite have your languid ease, I'm sure, but –'

'You'll do an excellent job, I have no doubt. Keep our feet on the ground. Make it happen. Think of me as a talent scout.'

'Is this where I get asked to join MI6?'

Adam laughed. 'Nothing so sinister. Though if you're interested . . .'

Robert turned to Katherine. 'So you knew it was me all along?'

'Oh, no, don't think that.' She seemed genuinely concerned. 'I had no idea who Adam would send. He just promised it would be someone I might fancy. Seems a little bit kinky, I suppose. But I liked the idea. I could just as easily have thrown you out, though.'

'I'd talked to Katherine about you and the play. But tonight was completely separate, I swear. What do you say, Robert? Will you do it?'

'What do I need to do, to start with? Is there a copy of the play I can read?'

'I suggest you go right to the top and contact the Master. Nothing like a spot of fresher chutzpah. As for the play –'

'The first two acts are pretty much done,' Katherine said. 'We're both a bit stuck on the third. The climax. There's a fire, you see.'

'A fire?'

'The laboratory catches fire. Caught fire. In the winter of 1677/8. While Newton, rather uncharacteristically, was on a visit to the chapel. He didn't hold much with what the Church had become.'

'Bit hard to stage.'

'Something was lost in the fire. Irreplaceable work. A candle fell on to some of his papers and a book was burned. Whatever was in it, he would never undertake the work again. Some people say it was mainly what we'd now call chemistry. Some people say it was less conventional than that.'

Adam smiled. 'He had a remarkable mind, Newton, everyone knows that. Some people even recognize now that he dabbled in alchemy, though they dismiss it as so much nonsense.'

'As they should,' said Robert.

'You might not think that if you'd seen what I've seen. Keynes didn't get all the papers at that auction, you know. A German group bought some. My grandfather recovered them from the Nazis, during the war. One in particular, he brought back here to Trinity. He was its keeper, so to speak. As I am now.'

'What does it say?'

'I'm afraid I can't tell you, old man. Not as yet, at least. One thing at a time. Katherine wants to know too. I can't tell her either.'

'Or won't,' said Katherine.

'It's a single document. It's partly charred around the edges, looks like it was in a fire. I'm not sure I fully understand what it says, but I'm slowly learning.'

'Is it here?' Robert looked again around the room.

'It's in a safe place. Anyway. Kat and I have known each other since last year. We met at a fancy-dress party, funnily enough.'

'Let me guess. She was a witch and you were a warlock?'

Katherine laughed. 'You catch on quickly.'

'An innocent little inside joke with Kat,' Adam beamed. 'Please forgive. So . . . when she told me about all this material she'd found, I put it to her that it wasn't a thesis at all, that it was something she was much more uniquely equipped to create, given her background, that it needed something much more attuned to the subject matter. Since –'

'*Since theatre involves enchantment and suspension of disbelief,* you said. *Whereas academic theses largely do not.* And you had such good ideas.'

'So we started writing together. I have a kind of mentor myself, who sparked the idea in my mind. What if, he asked –'

'What if Newton took the fire as a sign from God, in whom he undoubtedly fervently believed in his own heretical way, that he had taken his research down a forbidden path – it was in 1677, remember, before the *Principia* – and as a result changed course, and as a result of *that* –'

'Created the world we now live in. What would the world be like now if he had continued down that lost path? What would the word "Newtonian" mean to us in that world, and how different would it be to what it means to us now?'

'And,' Katherine said, 'what was in the burned papers? What discoveries did the lost book contain?'

Robert shifted uncomfortably. It was all a little too esoteric for his taste. He tried to get them back on track. 'On a practical note, what about the tree? And would you want to put up scaffolding for seats? Or just put chairs out on the lawn? What about damage to the grass?'

'Well, what do you think?'

'The tree's right in the middle of the lawn. You can't ignore it. Perhaps incorporate it somehow. Have him sit under it. Or cover it up and put a red light inside and make it a furnace for his lab. Scaffolding for seats would be expensive, and you'd have insurance to worry about. Depends how many people you expect to come and see it.'

Katherine waved her empty wine glass in the air. 'We thought the audience could be on two sides, south and east, roughly where the garden walls used to be. Tree in the middle. Like the Garden of Eden.'

'The Tree of Knowledge, I take it.'

Adam took a bottle over to Katherine and replenished her glass, glancing sideways at Robert. 'Or the Tree of Life. Anyway, these are all good ideas. And I'm sure they could put down boards or something to protect the grass. Perhaps 200 people a night? I already feel like we're in good hands.'

Katherine sipped her wine, peeping over the top of her glass at Robert. 'I was going to do some writing tonight. Would you like to help me?'

This time Robert saw she'd annoyed Adam, who turned away from them and studied a bookcase.

'I'm not sure writing's my forte but –'

'Katherine has some unusual writing techniques,' Adam said, his voice as light as ever. 'I'm sure you'll enjoy them.'

Katherine reached into her bag and produced a scrunched-up packet of cigarettes. 'God, I've been trying not to all night, but do you mind if I do?'

Robert suddenly wished he smoked. He looked around for matches, but Adam beat him to it, leaning towards her with a lit match he seemed to have produced from nowhere. Katherine pulled his hand towards her and held it steady. She kept holding it for several seconds after her cigarette was lit, smiling saucily at Adam till the match was almost burned down. He lowered his head and blew it out, holding her gaze throughout. For a moment it seemed to Robert that he wasn't in the room at all.

He coughed.

'So . . . what are you both thinking of doing next year?'

The words were out of his mouth before he could stop them. He could have kicked himself. Asking people in their final year about the future was almost guaranteed to kill a conversation, or an evening, stone dead. He'd been doing so well, and then out popped the boy from the Fens.

Katherine looked for a moment as though she would cry. Adam, instinctively diplomatic, saw his discomfort and moved immediately to dispel it. 'Glad you asked, Robert, actually. I was just talking this week to a couple of contacts I have on Fleet Street. I was thinking of trying my hand as a foreign correspondent. Small country, nowhere grand. Somewhere in Africa, perhaps, or Latin America.'

'Wow.'

'Just freelance, you understand.'

'This time next year he'll be toppling governments,' Katherine said, brightening.

'And Kat will be lighting up the London stage, or living on beans in a theatre collective in Bermondsey.'

'Not mutually exclusive,' she said, smiling. 'What else am I going to do with a first in maths and a third in philosophy?'

'You switched?'

'Yes, after my first year. They're the same thing, really, I thought. Maths I was good at, philosophy I haven't been. I switched for love, and I was disappointed. Plus I did all the acting.'

'Disappointed? How so?'

'I'll tell you another time. It was *scandalous*. I'll write about it one day. *Katherine Grows Up*, it'll be called.' Her high-strung laugh returned.

'What about the Unicorn Society? Now that we exist?' asked Robert.

Adam gave a bark of satisfied laughter. 'It was rather fun this evening, wasn't it? I really was very pleased.'

Katherine sucked deep on her cigarette, then blew a long wraith of smoke into the air. 'Adam said we needed someone on my team to earth me. Stop me flaming out. I'm too flighty, he says.'

'"Volatile" was my word, I think.'

Robert kept talking to Adam. 'You want to do another event?'

'I'd like to fine-tune a little. I'm not sure how to extract what everyone might have learned. I'm not even sure myself what it might be. I know what it looks like. I know what I think's in it, I know what I think the elements are. It was an experiment. I'm trying to learn how to create *experiences* for people. We all need to digest it a little.'

'Some light is so intense it can be experienced only as darkness,' Katherine said. 'Some presences are so intense they can be experienced only as absence. And vice versa. I can see what you're reaching for.'

'Actually I think *Newton's Papers* could be the Society's next project. Our knight's a military man, scientist, he'd be damn good at lighting and all of that; his damsel is an excellent seamstress, if you noticed her outfit, all home-made. Our vicar's a born stage manager. Dear old tart's a damn good actress. Kat directs, you produce, I meddle: it's perfect.'

'We'd better get writing, then,' Katherine said. 'I'm going to work on the lost material. Adam, thank you, darling. Good night. Robert, would you escort me?'

Robert scrambled to his feet as Adam and Katherine clinched in a vigorous hug. Then, as they reached the door, a question popped into his head. 'Just out of curiosity, why was I not supposed to talk till ten o'clock tonight?'

Adam smiled. 'I have observed in social settings, my friend, that when nervous or trying to impress, your words-per-minute rate approximately quadruples. This is a natural response to stress, and the same phenomenon as its opposite, clamming up or becoming tongue-tied.'

'When exactly have you been observing me?'

'Robert, my spies are everywhere. Since I imagined we all had an interest in your making a favourable impression on young Kat, I thought we could shut you up tonight, thus obliging you to practise silent flirting and charm her off her feet without speaking – which you certainly seem to have done.'

Katherine slipped her arm through Robert's and faced Adam. 'It also allowed me, Mr Hale-Devereaux, to think for a while that it was you under that costume, not Robert.'

Adam beamed at them. 'Good night, dear friends.'

Katherine didn't move. 'How much did you have to pay to get that black horse to stand there up at Wandlebury fort? Was there supposed to be a knight too?'

'Ah, now that's one of the evening's surprises. You see, I didn't pay anyone to do anything. I've no idea whatsoever what that horse was doing there.'

New York, August 26, 2004

The Watchman blinked several times and opened his eyes wide, sitting perfectly still as he reaccustomed himself to his surroundings. He had been in a deep state of meditation. Now, as he returned to the quotidian world, he found that his worries were slightly eased. He was even a little excited. The game was on. Help had been enlisted. The risks were immense, and there were things he could not see. But the first steps in the battle had been taken.

His eyes rested on the corkboard by his desk, where the photographs of two men and a woman were pinned amid scribbled notes, geometric diagrams and postcards showing landmarks of New York.

Three remarkable talents, chained together by fate, linked through the years in an unending dance . . .

There would be trials. It was the only way. Trials, deception and pain.

The clock was ticking. One week, at most.

He could feel the intensity of Adam Hale's mighty will. He was fighting.

The Watchman closed his eyes, directing his attention inward. He prayed.

First would come the Trial by Earth. It might end right there. There was no option but to take the risk.

Then Water, Fire, Air. Four trials, four days, four caches. Four keys to the Device. Four chances for Robert to die. Four deaths he must face.

Then the mystery would deepen.

Passing the four trials – if he did – would give him mastery of the four basic elements. Combining them in balance would create a fifth, a gateway, invisible in itself, even more rarefied than air. Ether, or quintessence. And if he could survive opening the gateway, he would be led to two more, both invisible unless he learned how to see. The sixth was Mind, or light. The seventh was Spirit, or love, which imbued and cradled all the rest. It was the Path. It was the only way. And he would help where he could, but primarily he would watch. For he was their Watchman.

He closed his eyes again and deepened his prayer.

The Watchman had mentored many men and women, and he knew there were as many variations to the Path as there were individuals.

Three days earlier, as Adam prepared to make his visit to the Iwnw, the Watchman had met him in Central Park, at the octagonal brick Chess and Checkers House, and discussed the events they knew were now coming. They had sat at one of the outdoor chess tables, shifting pieces around as they conferred. And then the Watchman had sent Adam away, and, sitting alone, he had mapped out the trials of Robert Reckliss.

It would be a race against time: bringing Robert along the Path fast enough to keep pace with Adam's decline, without destroying him by going too fast. The Watchman would need to balance Adam's will to resist against the capacity of Robert to evolve. One falling, one rising.

Robert would have to endure the Path of Seth. There was no other option. He would have to be torn apart and built up again, in seven days, no more. Adam would not be able to last any longer than that against the Brotherhood. Even the Watchman had not undergone such a path. He would not have been able to survive it.

The trials would have to be multidimensional, involving place, pattern, action and experience in a carefully woven whole. In taking each one, Robert would have to be brought to know, and tap into, specific physical and psychic energies, one after another, each building on the previous one.

The trials would also have to be mapped to the impending detonation of the Ma'rifat' – Robert would have to recover the keys and neutralize the grid they were arranged on, as he progressed along the Path.

The Watchman held the grid in his mind's eye. It was a known shape to him, a particular key used to harness the energies of the physical and spiritual worlds. The maker of the Ma'rifat', working with the same forces, had chosen it to amplify the power of his

Device, linking two focal points in downtown and uptown Manhattan. Robert would trace it on the city as he advanced through the trials.

Robert would have to be carefully drawn in. He had been raised to be more than sceptical, to be actively hostile to the tenets of the Path. So the Watchman had framed it initially as one of Adam's games, to put him on familiar terrain. The Watchman had told Adam to send the major key, the core, to Robert before going to see the Brotherhood of Iwnw. He needed to rid himself of it anyway. That had allowed Katherine to help shape his initial experience.

The Path of Seth was named after an ancient Egyptian myth, in which Osiris, a benevolent and civilizing king, was murdered by his brother, Seth. Seth dismembered his victim and dispersed his body parts far and wide. Osiris's wife, Isis, who was also his sister, re-assembled his remains and conceived a child by him, whom she hid among the marshes until he came of age. Then the child, Horus, attacked Seth to avenge his father. In an epic battle, each wounded the other, but neither was able to prevail. Eventually a tribunal of gods ruled against Seth, who was cast into the darkness as the evil god of the desert, chaos and storms.

The myth itself, like similar ones in cultures around the world, partly reflected the millennial battles between the initiates of the Watchman's Path and the Brotherhood of Iwnw. In China the Watchman's predecessors were known as Fan Kuang Tzu, or the Sons of Reflected Light. In ancient Mexico they were the followers of the civilizing priest Quetzalcóatl, the Bird-Serpent, and the Iwnw were echoed in his enemy Tezcatlipoca, or Smoking Mirror.

Each stage had a dilemma, and this one's was simple: kill or be killed. The Path of Seth would begin with death.

They would have to expose Robert first to the most powerful, rawest, least organized energies latent within him: those to do with tribal responses, fighting and killing, survival and territory. These were the earth powers.

To pass the trial, he would have to immerse himself in actions and experiences surrounding death, access those survival energies within himself and find a way to escape their shadow side.

Some aspiring walkers of the Path never got beyond this stage, and their lives came to consist purely of fighting. For such people, unable to free themselves from the shadow of survival energies, life became simply a brutal struggle for dominion.

Robert would face attack from the Iwnw. He would have to fight for his life, with a real risk that he might lose. And he would have to see into the heart of these energies, see what lay at the heart of hatred, of contempt, and acquire their strength while seeing beyond their shadow.

He would recover a key, which would have a circular form.

The Watchman prayed for him.

Cambridge, March 1981

At the door to her room, Katherine looked up at Robert and sighed. 'Will you come in?'

'God, yes.'

The first kiss was electricity and blood, wine and cigarettes. She made small vulnerable sounds, trembled, grabbed him hard. Banging into furniture and grappling with buttons, they cut a trail of destruction to the bed.

She pulled up her black witch's dress. Then they were face to face and joined, and she was whispering and babbling sounds he didn't recognize, and their breathing was scented honey and deep violet-orange, and sex consumed them.

He dozed on her bed for a while, still semi-clothed. When he awoke, she was freshly showered, moving about her sitting room in a man's dressing gown. She came to the bed and stood over him. He untied her dressing gown and started to kiss her body. She pulled back, smiling.

'Time to do some writing,' she said. 'A little magic, a little writing, a little more sex. Yes? Help me?'

Following her instructions, he moved a table to the middle of the sitting room and arranged chairs so they could sit on each side of it.

'A few candles, perhaps?' She lit them and placed them around the room.

He watched her, fascinated. 'You like your atmosphere. Very conducive. Are you really a witch?'

'Adam thinks so.'

'He's very attracted to you.'

'Yes, he is. But he wants the play even more than he wants me. Which is why we don't sleep together. Just bottle it up. Still, I have my little tricks. Witchy tricks.'

'Do they involve surrogates? Such as myself?'

'You're not a surrogate. You're Robert Reckliss.'

'Why does he think you're a witch, as opposed to just finding you bewitching?'

'Ever heard of magick? With a k? Sex magick?'

'Makes me think of Tommy Cooper.'

Down on the floor by her desk, her kettle came to the boil and clicked off.

'Mm . . . not really. It's a taboo. I love taboos. They're so sexy.'

'So what is it?'

'It's not real. I just play with it. It's just a way of releasing the unconscious. But the unconscious is very powerful. Far more than we realize.'

'You mean chants and incantations and things like that?'

'Sometimes.'

'What were those words you were saying while we were making love?'

'Just a way of making it more powerful. More intense.'

'Words can do that for you?'

'If you believe them, yes, of course they can.'

'So it is real.'

'Define real. We all make our own real. Tea?'

Katherine got up and poured hot water from the kettle into two mugs on the low table by her desk. She brought them over to the table. 'You'll like this. Magic tea.'

'What's in it? Eye of newt?'

'Yes. And a few other goodies.'

He eyed it with caution. It was green. 'How legal is it?'

'Trust me. You'll love it.'

He took a sip. It was bitter, but not unpleasant.

'What was the scandal you talked about over at Adam's?'

'I had an affair with my Director of Studies. Most of my first year. Switched to philosophy so I could be more fully his dream creature, his creation, since that's what he taught, and that's what he wanted.'

'What's wrong with that, in the bigger scheme of things?'

'You'd have to ask his wife. I broke it off the same day he left her, poor man. That's the danger with dream creatures. They can turn on you.'

He sipped some more tea.

'Do they have many girls like me in the Fens?'

'Oh, we have lots of witchcraft. It can be pretty weird. My family has ... practitioners. Cousins, aunts. But I've never met them. I wasn't allowed to. I was brought up to disbelieve. And I do choose not to believe in it.'

'Why not?'

'Because if I did believe in it, the world would be a terrifying place.'

'But Robert,' she said, 'it is.'

'How so?'

'I lost my mother when I was twelve. Adam's brother died in his teens.'

'Really? I mean – I didn't know. I'm so sorry.'

'Later. There's nothing to say. Let's try to get some material for the third act.'

'How?'

'We'll ask the Weej.'

'The what?'

'The Ouija board, silly. Let's see what it says. It's worked before. I don't see why it shouldn't work now.'

He sat absolutely still, staring at her. This was nonsense.

Katherine brought a round board out from behind the screen and put it on top of the table. Letters of the alphabet were arrayed around the rim, black on a crimson background. She sat down opposite him, a water glass in her hand. 'Do it with me.'

He didn't move.

She giggled. 'There's nothing to be afraid of. It's not real. It's just our unconscious. It's just a way of tapping into it. Have some more tea and do it with me.'

Reluctantly, he joined hands with her as she intoned an incantation.

'Be Adam,' she said. 'You think it's complete nonsense too. You do it to keep me happy.'

'You want me very much to be Adam, don't you?'

'If you're very good, maybe we'll do some real sex magick later. I love saying that. Sex magick. You'll love it. I'll make love to both of you.'

He had some more tea and placed his fingertips on the overturned glass, touching hers.

'Wait, something's missing,' she said. 'I know what.' She went over to the bed and picked up the mask and cape he had discarded during sex. 'Put these back on. It'll help with the atmospherics.'

He laughed, though inwardly he felt fear.

Katherine held them out to him. 'Please, Robert?'

For a moment he hesitated. But hell, it was only a game. 'Your wish is my command.'

When he had put them on and settled back in his chair, his fingertips once again brushing hers on the glass, she took a deep breath. 'We can begin. We seek an answer. May we pose our question?'

Nothing happened. He closed his eyes. This wasn't real.

'We seek an answer. May we pose our question? We mean no harm.'

Still nothing.

'My disbelief is spoiling it,' he said. 'Sorry.'

Then the glass moved. Katherine began to breathe deeply, her eyes closed. The air went cold. Their fingertips were barely touching, resting gently on the glass. He forced himself to stay calm, to observe.

The letters came one by one: Y . . . E . . . S.

'Let time and place elide. We are in the winter of 1677. We are in a wooden shed, a laboratory, just south of the chapel of Trinity College. There is a fire. Can you see the fire?'

The glass moved again. He could not see how she was moving it. But the answers were what she wanted. She was creating her own dream creature, he told himself: a spirit that quarried words and feelings from places she was afraid to visit herself.

Y . . . E . . . S.

'The fire is now, the place is here, join me and Adam . . . I mean, join me and Robert at that place so we can see the papers that are burned.'

N . . . O.

Now, suddenly, his head swam violently. He closed his eyes.

'I cannot see the papers. Can you show me the papers? Please show me the papers.'

F . . . O . . . R . . . B . . .

He felt himself hurtling through space. He opened his eyes. He was sitting completely still in his chair. Katherine was breathing evenly, more heavily. Sweat beaded coldly on his forehead. The glass started up again.

I . . . D . . . D . . . E . . . N.

He closed his eyes. The hurtling stopped, and he was inside someone else's mind, six years ago. Grief and guilt hit him in a tidal wave. He was lost in thoughts of a brother he didn't have. Adam's brother. He could not remove his fingertips from the glass. He was in the big old house in Buenos Aires, aching for Moss to come home, knowing he never would. Moss Hale-Devereaux. Dead at fourteen. There were doctors, priests, unbearable pain. Parents bitter and distant. Irremediable guilt. He wrenched his mind away.

'I'm Adam,' he said, hearing himself speak, feeling his mouth move. He heard Katherine's typewriter pecking at the paper. He couldn't open his eyes. 'What's happening to me?'

He felt a gravity in the darkness, a dense mass drawing him to its source. Then he was lying on his back, Katherine above him, her face close to his, insubstantial like mist. In Adam's room. In Adam's bed. She was making love to him, and he was Adam.

'Time and place elide,' Katherine said, her voice far away. 'What do the papers say? What is the content of the burning book? Show me.'

The glass lurched crazily under their fingertips. He heard the typewriter clacking again. He opened his eyes and met hers, and she gazed right through him in lust and fear. The glass shot to an F, then an L. . .

'Remember this,' she shouted. 'Remember this!'

A . . . M . . . M . . . A . . . U . . . N . . . I . . . C . . . A . . . C . . . L . . . A . . . V . . . I . . . S . . . M . . . U . . . N . . . D . . . I.

Unbearable, skull-splitting light burst from behind his eyes. It was the light he had been brought up to fear, to deny existence to, if he ever felt it glimmer in his mind. Now it was bursting forth for the first time inside his head, exhilarating and terrifying in equal measures. The light was washing away the borders between Robert and Adam, Robert and Katherine, till all three danced together, folded into each other. He felt his body ignite with intense white flame that leaped from his fingers to Katherine's to Adam's. It was too strong. It was forbidden. He couldn't stand it.

He screamed at the top of his lungs. Enough. He kicked over the table and knocked the board and glass to the floor. He couldn't see Katherine. He twisted the mask roughly to one side, its cords tangling around his throat. He broke one and forced the mask backwards over his shoulder. The typewriter fell silent. He leaped across the room and ripped the paper from it. He read:

```
'MADAM I'M ADAM
MADAM I'M ADAM
MADAM I'M ADAM
FLAMMA UNICA CLAVIS MUNDI
FLAMMA UNICA CLAVIS MUNDI
FLAMMA UNICA CLAVIS MUNDI.
```

'The key to the world is a single flame,' he translated.

His blood ran cold. Were they words from the forbidden document? He would swear neither of them had gone anywhere near the typewriter. But where was Katherine now? He felt an unearthly connection still to her, to Adam.

Then Robert wheeled as white-hot pain seared his face. In his mind's eye he saw flames flaring into life, bookcases dry as tinder starting to smoke ... Adam's room ... Katherine making love to Adam, Katherine making love to him, oblivious of the flames ... unnatural light, yellow, terrifying ...

Head swimming, knees buckling, he lurched to the bed, shouting for Katherine. Then hands were on him, angelic, soothing. He blacked out.

When he came to, she was gone.

He struggled to his feet, cataloguing his sensations. Light-headedness. Strange clarity of thought. Fear. The fire. Oh, God, the fire.

Robert ran. Down the corridor, down the stairs, out into the mist-shrouded court, out on to King's Parade, past the Senate House. The image was so real he could feel the mounting heat. Flames licking beneath the door. Unnatural light. He had to save them.

He hammered into Trinity Street, past Caius, as the clocks struck midnight, cape flowing, mask twisted backwards on his back.

Reaching the Great Gate of Trinity, he beat on the window of the porters' lodge and shouted until they let him in.

'There's a fire! In Nevile's Court!'

'Now just a moment, sir, let's calm down a moment, shall we?'

'I tell you there's a fire. Help me!'

'And how would we know this, sir? Are we a member of the college?'

He pushed past them, sprinting into the Great Court. He heard them in pursuit. 'Oi! Come 'ere!'

He cut a straight line across the court, ignoring the footpaths, running on the forbidden grass. Then he was through the passage and into Nevile's Court. He jumped down a flight of stone stairs and ran along the northern arcade, his footfalls cracking and boom-ing like Newton's stamping, echoing feet 300 years before. He

86

pounded up the stairs to the first floor, ran left along the dark corridor, saw a fire extinguisher and wrested it free from the wall.

The flames were shadow-dancing under the door.

It wasn't locked. He charged in, saw the fire leap up at him, saw Adam and Katherine motionless on the bed in the next room, still locked in an embrace, saw the face of death in the black clouds of smoke churning in the room. It was a single eye, a bottomless black core staring out of a rippling iris of yellow and blue, long red filaments flaring off it like lightning.

'Begone!' he yelled, the word welling up from somewhere deep in his panicked soul.

He dragged Katherine free. She was still breathing.

Two porters appeared behind him. He handed her off to them. A fire alarm began to sound. One porter began to bang on the other doors in the corridor. Robert went back in. He fired the extinguisher at the base of the flames as he went, clearing a path. In the bedroom he saw fire feeding on loose notes and script pages at the side of the bed. He dragged Adam out through the sitting room and into the corridor. He was semiconscious, babbling.

'Moss?'

'It's Robert.'

He heard sirens in the distance. People were emerging from their rooms. One helped him semi-carry Adam down the stairs and out into the cold fresh air. A porter was wrapping Katherine in a blue blanket as she sat on the grass. She saw him. She shouted: 'Robert. Something happened to you!'

'I started the fire.'

'Are you OK?'

'I kicked the table over. It started the fire.'

'You kicked the table over. You were shouting about a fire. You frightened me. You went very strange. I thought you were going to hurt yourself.'

'I blacked out.'

'I helped you to the bed. You passed out. Then I came to see Adam.'

'I was Adam.'

87

'You were saying all kinds of things. Mumbling to yourself.' Her face screwed up, and she started to cry. 'You frightened me!' She began to shake.

'She's in shock,' the porter said. 'Best to leave her alone for a while.'

Firemen and ambulance men were appearing. Robert knelt down to give Katherine a hug, but she sat like a statue, tears pouring down her cheeks.

'Katherine, did you put something in the tea?'

She swung her arm and hit him, and hit him again.

'Don't be silly. It was just a game. It was chamomile.'

The porter pushed him away.

'You're upsetting her, sir. Leave her alone now.'

They met several days later, in Katherine's rooms. She had just been released from hospital. They drank coffee, no one wanting to be the first to speak. Eventually Adam broached the subject. 'Robert, you saved our lives.'

'It was nothing.'

'Not to us. We both owe you an eternal debt.'

Dreadful images leaped into his mind. They wouldn't stop.

'I can't talk about it. I'm sorry.'

Katherine put a hand on his arm. 'Adam thinks you had an awakening. A spontaneous opening up of psychic powers. He'd seen them in you, seen your potential.'

'Please don't talk this way. It's nonsense. If you say you didn't put anything in my tea, I believe you. I'd had a lot to drink, remember. I think, in the end, I was just jealous. After I freaked out at the Ouija board, I was just jealous of Adam, that you'd gone to sleep with him. So I went to hammer on the door, or throw stones at the window, or fight, or something childish.'

'Robert, I don't think that's it,' said Adam.

'Let him think what he wants,' Katherine scolded Adam gently. 'I think, though, that perhaps we all should not see each other for a while.'

'We're bound up with each other for ever,' said Adam. 'Entangled. But a hiatus seems a sensible idea. Some of us have finals coming up, after all. And I'm afraid we'll have to put *Newton's Papers* on hold. It's too dangerous a play to write now. Perhaps ever.'

Robert snorted. 'What nonsense.'

He felt raw fear pulsing just below the surface of his rational, daylight-shedding, system-building mind. He willed it away, deep into the darkness. There were dreadful things at the edge of consciousness, chaotic, evil things, and it was wrong to pursue them. Harmful to himself and others. His parents had been right to keep him away from them. Now he did what he had been brought up to do. He set his mind in a cold, clinical cast that denied such things any existence, and he crushed the life out of them.

'Believe what you must,' Adam said with a kindly smile. 'You may turn away from it now. But a time may come when your powers will be needed, a time of great danger, and you'll be called. Just promise me you'll not turn away when the call does come.'

Robert met his gaze without speaking, then looked away into Katherine's eyes. She was so beautiful. 'I can't promise anything like that,' he replied.

Katherine leaned forward and rested her hand on his knee. 'You were very brave, Robert,' she said. 'You're my fearless knight.'

Robert raised her fingers to his mouth and kissed them, then stood up and shook Adam's hand.

'I should go,' Robert said. 'I'm sorry.'

PART TWO
The Trials

⊙

I

Trial by Earth

New York, August 26, 2004

Robert left the apartment and walked down the stairs, the Quad in his hand, the earpiece in his ear. The air was thick and humid, and within a minute he was sweating as he paced on Greenwich Street, waiting for the device to pick up the GPS signals from the satellites overhead. It was 3.30 p.m.

The Quad gave an incoming-call chirp, and he hit answer. There was a crackle of static but no voice. He said, 'Terri?'

Nothing.

He said, 'I'm leaving the line open. OK?'

Maybe some breathing? He couldn't tell.

He needed to meet her. Understand what was going on.

The Quad screen showed a small stick man standing on a tiny globe with four blinking satellites overhead. 'Wait . . . Tracking . . .' it said unhurriedly, and faint dotted lines snaked up from the hand of the homunculus to each of the satellites, growing more solid as connection was established with each one.

'How long does this take?' he said into the open air.

He heard a crackle of static but no response.

After four minutes the Quad gave a beep. The screen said: 'Ready to navigate. Accuracy: 70 feet.'

He selected Go to Waypoint 025. An arrow came up on the screen, and he started walking. It seemed to get a good reading on him and pointed south-east, flashing up: '1.6 miles, speed 2.5 m.p.h.'

He jogged along in the shade of the trees on the west side of Greenwich Street, crossed the road and made a left on to Christopher Street, heading for the 1 and the 9 subway station downtown.

Then, without warning, just after he crossed Hudson, a young woman's voice was in his head, and the street beneath his feet was full of stars and diamonds.

'Hello, Robert. Can you hear me?'

'Yes.'

'Good. I'm going to help you. I'll be watching your back.'

'How?'

'This is where it gets hard to explain. Assume I can see where you are, that I can detect what's around you.'

'How? Can you read the location of the Quad? Through GPS?'

'Something like that. It'll do as a metaphor. I'm . . . alive to what's around you.'

'If someone's going to follow me, are they going to try to stop me solving this riddle or finding this cache? Are they looking for it too?'

'I don't know. They may end up helping you to understand it. They may try to hurt you. It's an unusual situation. Now go quickly. I'll contact you when you get out of the subway.'

He walked east, sweating hard now, snatches of neon and impressions of building details seeming to fly at him from the walls and sidewalk. Video. Tattoo. Two spirals in the brick to his left, something compelling and hypnotic about them. In the shop windows as he passed there were action dolls of Freud, Christ. Sex clothing for girls and boys, a Cuban restaurant . . . crossing Bleecker, there were flowers on the corner, a locksmith half hidden underground in a basement store, an old church with a sign exhorting passers-by to love one another, New York Fetish, Boots and Saddles gay bar. Then Village Cigars, with its strange triangular plaque in the sidewalk, the smallest piece of real estate in Manhattan. He walked down the steps into the subway.

A train arrived almost immediately. As it clattered and rattled along the five stops to Rector Street, they passed through the closed Cortlandt Street Station directly under Ground Zero, built to replace the one destroyed when the 9/11 attacks had sent debris smashing through its ceiling on to the tracks below.

At Rector he turned right off the train and jogged to the exit, out through the curved iron bar gates and up the stairs. He emerged on Greenwich Street, where the waterfront at the edge of Manhattan used to be, outside a topless bar called the Pussycat Lounge. He crossed the street and walked east up Rector to Trinity Place, where the huge mass of the retaining wall below Trinity Church stood. The wall breathed, expanding and contracting by almost an inch with the heat and cold, like a great chest. He'd met Horace for the first time on a walking tour around this very area. Above, the Trinity spire – once the tallest structure in the city – jostled in the deep blue sky with latter-day rivals along Wall Street, Numbers 1 and 40, a fluted off-white Deco tower and a steepling green pyramid.

Robert passed under an overhead walkway linking Trinity church-yard to a building next to the American Stock Exchange, the latter a riot of Neo-Egyptian frontage and 1930s-style carved represen-tations of modernity and progress: a ship, a factory, a steam engine, what appeared to be oil wells, giant earth-movers. It reminded him of the declamatory style of Rockefeller Center. Progress! Industry! Wisdom!

Set into the massive wall of Trinity were several gates. He took the one in the middle called the Cherub Gate.

He walked up some steps, through arches at the top and into the graveyard. Robert held up the Quad, waiting for it to reacquire the satellite signal in the open space.

As he headed east towards Broadway along the path through the graveyard, the Quad came to life again. Terri.

'Don't go on. Branch off to your left. Do you see a big monu-ment? There's a headstone, a grave. Leeson, James Leeson . . . Crack the code. Use the website. Show you were here and you cracked it. Hurry. You're being watched.'

'Code?'

'You'll see.

'Are you OK?'

'Just do it. Please.'

As he walked, the white-and-gold entrance to the Bank of New York at 1 Wall Street came into view again. The GPS signal returned weakly, pointing him north as it should have, and faded again.

Robert saw the Gothic brown stone monument, 'sacred to the memory of those great and good men who died while imprisoned in this city for their devotion to the cause of American independence', looming over the north-east end of the graveyard.

He surveyed the stones around it. The gravestone in question was easily found. 'Here lies deposited the body of James Leeson who departed this life on the 28th day of September 1794 aged 38 years,' it read. Along its upper rim, above a winged hour-glass and other mysterious symbols, was a series of markings that reminded Robert vaguely of codes he'd seen in Sherlock Holmes stories. In this case they were not little stick men but dots placed within partial or complete squares.

He squatted in front of the headstone and gazed at the code. Shut out the world. He'd seen something like this before when he was a kid, in a spy story or a puzzle book, or one of those boy-soldier manuals that sometimes came with toys, or Action Man, or Clarks Commandos' shoes. He remembered those shoes had had animal tracks imprinted on the bottom, so wherever he went playing around the grounds of the estate he was himself and also a bear, a deer, a badger. He cast his mind back to that time, to a special copse he had known, where he used to go to puzzle through things that confused him as a child. There was a smooth stone in the middle of the copse that he would sit on, and lose himself in the birdsong that echoed there, sometimes for what seemed like hours at a time. He remembered now the language of the birds, the endless sea of voices and harmonies, twittering and whistling and singing in a torrent of sound that had seemed to him to be the very voice of the world. He'd never left the copse without an answer to what troubled him. He let his mind roam free in the same way now, lost in the memory of the harmonies he no longer heard.

He was hungry, he noticed. He thought of a diner on Route 3 that he sometimes would go to on the way home, the Tick Tock Diner – neon and gleaming metal cladding. There was another diner called the Tick Tock on 8th Avenue, neon and chrome, at the street level of the hotel New Yorker. Tick Tock. He'd sometimes imagined walking into the Tick Tock in New Jersey and emerging from the Tick Tock on 8th Avenue. Maybe all Deco diners were connected. Maybe they were all just one diner. Tick Tock. Tic-tac. Tic-tac-toe. Noughts and crosses, as the Brits called it back home.

Then he had it. Tic-tac-toe.

He wrote down the letters of the alphabet in a noughts and crosses grid with A in the top left, B in the top middle, C in the top right, and so on. He saw three grids side by side, the first containing the letters A to I, the second J to R, the third S to Z . . . so on the first grid, E was represented by a closed box, B by a box open at the top, H by a box open at the bottom. How were the grids distinguished from one another? Some boxes on the gravestone bore one dot, some two, some none.

He stared at the grids. If a single dot signified the first grid, and two the second, none the third, then he got: Q . . . E . . . L . . . E . . . L . . . B . . . E . . . Q . . . D . . . E . . . A . . . S . . . H.

It made no sense. Something was off. Wait. Wait. What happened if he treated I and J as the same letter, and U and V, as gravestone lettering often did?

R . . . E . . . M . . . E . . . M . . . B . . . E . . . R.

The lower word was: D . . . E . . . A . . . T . . . H.

A chill ran down his spine, mingling with the thrill of cracking the code. 'Fuck,' he said out loud, partly to banish the fear.

*

Robert used the Quad to post it to the website with the pictures.

'Well done, Robert. Remember that, you'll need to. Now go north, till you get the GPS signal again. Follow it. Here's a rhyme. A clue. I just got it by text message. Remember it.'

'Who is sending you this stuff, Terri? How do they know when to send it?'

'I told you, it comes from someone called the Watchman. Adam told me to trust him. You'll need it to find the first cache. I received it as soon as you posted the decoded gravestone message, so it was a response. A reward, perhaps.'

'This wasn't the first cache?'

'No. It's near by, I think. Take it down, quickly.'

He got his pencil and notebook out.

> *'Our zero's a place for heroes*
> *Ground of being, way of seeing*
> *Don't have a conniption, seek something Egyptian*
> *Kind of a digit, to find the widget*
> *Our secret cache is where the ashes*
> *And bones of Éire*
> *Aren't laid to rest. By the star, you'll go far*
> *To prove your worth, pass the Trial by Earth'*

He heard heavy breathing. Then she spoke again: 'Got it? Go.'

He walked north along Broadway, stepping on five-pointed stars in the sidewalk honouring an eclectic mix of sports stars, war heroes and foreign dignitaries who had received ticker-tape parades on Broadway in the 1950s.

Hopping and scooting between pedestrians, he passed on his right a large red cube sculpture poised implausibly on a point; and to the west the buildings fell away to reveal the vast absence of Ground Zero. Behind the site loomed the twin solid masses of the World Financial Center, their glass panels ablaze with orange light.

He jogged across Cortlandt Street, looking down to the giant Century 21 Department Store, past the New York Stocking Exchange lingerie shop, crossing Dey and then Fulton. There, right in front of St Paul's Chapel, the signal came back on the Quad, with an accuracy reading of 43 feet. It pointed west. He headed down the hill towards Ground Zero.

Robert crossed Church Street and leaned his forehead against the metal fencing overlooking the huge pit. There was a cross made of two girders from the site. Holy ground, land laden with hate, yet not heavy with it, not overwhelmingly charged with evil; there was something else, not in the tribal Christian sense of the Cross but still . . . there was something that felt like the opposite of fear, that felt like the Pentecostal winds that had swept Manhattan on the first anniversary of 9/11, a scouring wind that carried *forgiveness*. Could that be possible? He looked into his heart, deep into his memories of that day. No, it was not possible. He couldn't.

'What the hell, Terri? Am I in the right place?' he said into the air. Nothing back.

Now the Quad pointed him back towards the chapel. He'd gone too far west. He entered the churchyard through the gate facing Ground Zero and watched it count down: 184 feet, 181, pointing him east, 44 seconds to go, 43, 2.3 m.p.h., 150 feet, 147 feet, counting him down as he walked along the graveyard path parallel to Fulton, 96 feet . . . 2.5 m.p.h. . . . The words 'Arriving Destination' flashed up on the screen at around 69 feet, and still it counted lower. Then, at 37 feet, the signal blinked out.

Cursing, he got his notebook out and read Terri's clue. Looking directly ahead of him due east was, most certainly, something Egyptian, and a kind of digit.

A big old pink-grey stone obelisk.

He tramped off the path across the grass to it and surveyed the thing.

Very faintly, on the west face, he saw what looked like a mixture of digits and letters. On the east side, he could barely make out the name of Thomas Addis . . . something, over lines and lines of faded script.

Standing back from the red and creamy white flowers around the base of the obelisk, he noticed, at the edge of the flowerbed, at foot height, a five-pointed metal star in a metal ring, the letters 'US' in the middle, that he had seen before at the graves of Revolutionary War veterans. *By the star, you'll go far*, the riddle had said.

Terri came back. 'There's a cache. Get it . . . the secret is in the ground.'

'Just a minute. Sinking my fingers into the soil of someone's grave is not doing it for me. When do we meet, Terri? You have to meet me.'

'There's no corpse underneath. Trust me. Get the cache.'

'Explain to me what's happening here. I'm going to meet you, and you're going to tell me what's going on.'

'Robert, you don't have the initiative here. You need me to help protect Adam. To help stop this awful act from being carried out. If you think it's all just a stupid game, hang up right now.'

He stared out over the gravestones towards the great empty pit where the towers had stood. He'd been asked to help stop something even worse happening, in a city he'd adopted as his own. He'd been asked to help his friend. As crazy as it all sounded, good people said they needed him. And, deep down, he was recovering a part of himself that had been cut off, almost exterminated. If he lost Terri now, he might never discover what it was. And if it was all a twisted game of some kind, he wanted to find Adam to beat seven bells out of him.

'I'm not hanging up.'

'I didn't think you would. If I cut the connection, you'll never find me again. Robert, I swear I want to help you. But you have to do it by my rules. It's the only way.'

He barked: 'How?'

'You'll see. And I'll meet you. But first do what I say.'

He knelt before the obelisk and feigned paying his respects in front of it, or possibly catching his breath and buckling his shoe, and, as he did so, sank his fingers into the earth to either side of the small metal star. Nothing. He dug further, sinking his left hand into the earth. Still nothing. And then, deep down in the flowerbed, his fingertips touched something smooth and hard and plastic.

He fished it out and hid it up his sleeve as smoothly as he could. Then he made his way back along the footpath.

He went into the chapel, his earth-covered hand hidden under his jacket, and found a pew. For some reason he felt safer inside. He sat at the Broadway end, facing the altar, and took up a discreet praying position in order to look at what was in the cache. He unplugged the container, which was a clear plastic cigar tube, and felt a hard metal item fall into his hand.

He looked around. No one was paying attention to him. His eyes fell on the altar: the gleaming golden rays representing the glory of the divine presence was above it, the name of God in Hebrew at its centre. Right to left, Y . . . H . . . V . . . H. Yahveh. The greatest puzzle of all.

The altar, he'd heard from Horace, had been designed by the same man who'd gone on to lay out the core streets of Washington, DC: Pierre L'Enfant. Some people thought he'd tried to make the city into a giant sundial, or something similar.

He looked down again. In the palm of his hand he held a spent bullet cartridge.

'I have it,' he whispered to Terri.

'Praise heaven. Keep it safe.'

'Now what?'

'Get out. Need your thoughts. Find a place to write. Then report what you've done. Post a picture of what you found and what you think about it. Then you'll need to carry out an action.'

'What kind of action? We're going to meet, remember? Terri?'

No answer.

Robert walked out of the churchyard on to Broadway. He looked about him and crossed the street to John, heading for the closest bar he knew, a place called Les Halles.

It was a classic dark-wood mirrored bar with a kaleidoscopic array of bottles and mirrors behind the bartender, and an elaborate display of hard-boiled eggs in a wire holder on the bar in front of him, like a model of the solar system. There was almost no one there. Looking into the restaurant away from the street, he thought the light was almost amber. Yellow-gold lighting fixtures stood out against a dark brown, almost black wooden background. Something stirred in his memory. He couldn't place it at first. He realized he had been in Les Halles before. Drinks with colleagues after an awards ceremony of some kind, Katherine dressed to the nines, and they'd gone off to the bathrooms at the back, up the stairs, pursued by a waiter saying no, no, ladies only, and she'd lifted her dress, and they'd thought about making love right there in the bathroom but chickened out. They had been the first awards after 9/11, and after drinks they'd walked out and gone down to Ground Zero and wept.

Robert went to the bathroom to wash the dirt from his hands. Then he ordered a beer, trying to gather his thoughts.

After a while, the Quad buzzed. 'Terri?'

'Yes. Just listen. Don't speak. This is where we begin. We are at the foot of Jacob's Ladder. We build the ladder by climbing it, from darkness to light, from fear to love. Each rung is a trial. Hold that in your mind. Then write what you're thinking. Post it.'

'This is not sane or helpful.'

'Do it. Please.'

'Meet me.'

'After you do it.' Then she was gone.

He rubbed his face with his hands. Should he walk away? He had to meet her. 'Fuck it,' he said under his breath.

He took the bullet casing off to the bathroom and photographed it with the Quad, not wanting to do so in a public place.

Then, back at the bar, he tried to look at himself in the mirror panels. Not rational. Oddly emotional, panicked, feelings all over the place, nothing purely digested. But he realized: part of him wanted to be doing this.

He unfolded the portable keyboard contraption he'd found at Adam's pied-à-terre. He wrote and posted some lines to the website at Bookmark 1.

Proof of Good Faith

I am writing this in accordance with your instructions. I can demonstrate that I've done the following things:

– I went to the first location you gave me. The coordinates correspond to a churchyard overlooking Ground Zero in Lower Manhattan.

– I recovered the cached item. I am posting a photograph of it, as

requested. A spent bullet casing, hidden in a clear plastic cigar tube. I don't know what it means. Should I guess? I have brought it with me.
– Terri, I wish to help you. Are you all right? You sounded as though you were in pain. Who else is looking at this blog? Who set up this website?

He put up the picture of the bullet casing. He stayed online. Within two minutes she had replied, in the comments section.

Robert, please realize what you will be doing. You will receive a series of clues, or provocations, or challenges, and in each case you will have to look within yourself to find your response. It is a scavenger hunt of the soul. It is the only way for you to help. For each inner state there is an outer state. Link the site of the cache to its contents. Write your impressions. Show that you are evolving. It is the only way. I am fine. This is hard. Adam set up the website to help the Watchman, right before he vanished. Write more.

He wrote more. Drank more beer first. He was starving. He ordered a sandwich, dug into himself and wrote again. He put up photos of the grave-marker obelisk and the view of Ground Zero that she'd wanted him to see. He even put up a shot of the view from his bar stool.

What the first cache said to me
Terri
I don't know how you want me to do this. Connect the cached items and the site, you say. The inner world and the outer.
   So: I am getting lots of death, naturally. You sent me to two graveyards, venerated places, one to crack a code about death, one to dig in the grounds of one of the oldest buildings in Manhattan, you sent me back to the beginnings of this city among flowers and stones and grass to gaze upon the great gaping hole at Ground Zero . . . the church that was somehow spared when the spars and beams of the Twin Towers came hurtling down towards the ground. You had me gaze upon the place that fills me with anger at the primitive emotions it arouses in me, and you had me root around like someone not entirely sane or presentable among

the gravestones till I found your cache and, in it, a bullet casing. So, yes, death. Death and survival, and the willingness to lash out and hurt in order to survive. Primal things. Are you going to send me all across the city sinking my fingers into graves? Is this enough? Help me. I don't understand.

George Washington had his own pew at St Paul's; you can still see it. He prayed there after being sworn in down the street at Federal Hall as the nation's first President. Birth of a nation, from war. Now another war. Destruction, survival. Is this where you want me to go?

I had a friend who was downtown when the towers fell, in fact I sent her there. She said those clouds of dust you see on the videos of that morning were full of flying fragments of metal. I drank with her at this bar. It was an act designed to provoke a tribal response. We are all reasonable, civilized people, until someone touches our tribal core. Then we change, or maybe we remember. We will kill and more for our tribe. We are all potential torturers. Some things are impossible to forgive.

Terri, what more do you want of me?

Again she replied:

Robert, you have made a good beginning. Dig deeper along the same lines. Learn to look within, and you'll learn to see without. This is our first step on an arduous road. You are being prayed for. Start to pay closer attention to your surroundings. If something draws your attention, pay heed to it. Photograph it. Post it.

He had to get moving again. He got up and left the bar.

He tried to call Terri back on the Quad, impatiently jabbing the buttons, but the number was masked. He couldn't get her.

Directly outside Les Halles was a beautiful brown terracotta building, housing both a Christian Science reading room and a Manhattan Muffin store. It was 11 John Street, and in the ornamentation was a kind of half-formed version of that medical symbol he'd seen sometimes, snakes climbing a staff, except they were kind of twisted little lizards snaking up a column. He had never noticed it before. In the same ornamentation were several fierce, bearded

106

heads with vegetation springing forth from their faces. He found them unsettling.

He walked back to Broadway. At the Stocking Exchange across the street, in black-and-gold accents, under the shop window displays of semi-risqué lingerie, strode a line – into the store, naturally – of single gold barefoot female legs. He took a picture, then retraced his steps and snapped the terracotta birds and the foliage heads.

He headed further south, again passing the giant red cube on its miraculous angle at Liberty. This time he noticed a round hole that pierced it through. He looked at it more closely. It was an illusion of a cube. The sides were of different lengths. A true cube wouldn't look like one, presumably.

Terri was silent.

He walked two more blocks south. Trinity Church was again on his right. He came to the scalloped corner of 1 Wall Street that he'd seen from the graveyard earlier, the Bank of New York Building: glorious Art Deco, white stone and blazing gold, like a cathedral made of draped fabric. As he stood at the main entrance on Wall Street, the sun caught the red-and-gold lobby interior – the fabled Red Room, closed to the public since 9/11 – and made it glow like a brazier. He stood transfixed. Crimson, white, gold.

This was where the wooden wall had once stood at the northernmost end of New York to keep out invaders. The *northernmost* end, barely a mile from the southern tip. On the Broadway side of the Bank of New York Building, the bronzed windows reflected the spire of Trinity against a deep blue sky, and again the crimson flame of the interior leaped out.

'Robert.'

'Terri? Where have you been?'

'Hell.'

'What's –'

'Head west. Find an angel. Quickly.'

'What?'

'I can't explain. Not now. Do you remember what I've been saying?'

'Terri, I won't be forgetting any of this for a long time.'

'Go west.'

'I am. I'm crossing Broadway, heading along Rector, along the south side of Trinity Church.'

On the railings outside the church he found what she'd told him to look for: a plaque marking the original site, across the street, of Columbia University, when it was still King's College. It held two oval seals. On the left a sunburst, like the one above the altar at St Paul's Chapel, shone at the top of the seal, the name of God in Hebrew nestled within it.

'Yod, heh, vav, heh.'

'Terri?'

'Unutterable name . . . Unknowable . . . Robert, find the Man of Light.'

On the right of the plaque, in what he took to be the Trinity Church seal, was the most remarkable image. He said out loud: 'Swirly Man.'

'Yes,' said Terri.

One foot in the sea, the other on land, the sun ringing his face: in the centre of the seal stood a figure like a man composed of spinning wheels, or whorls; or it could have been a man wearing a garment of spirals that ascended up his body from groin to head. A line of vortices ran up the centre of his body, while others were off to either side of his spine.

'Mighty angel, wrapped in cloud . . . Robert, when you look into yourself, as far and as deeply as you dare, and then further, hold the image of this figure in your mind. This is what you will see. It is what you truly look like, your body of light. You are protected . . . we are . . . believe me. Now go west. Further west.'

He photographed the figure of light with the Quad and walked on, along Rector, under the arcades where a Berlitz Language School was, back towards the subway stop, ending up again right opposite the Pussycat Lounge.

'Robert: go home now.'

'WHAT? No, no, no, no. I'm going to meet you, right now.'

'I think the danger is past. You've done enough for today. We've done enough. Trust . . .'

Her voice trailed off and the connection died. He stood at the subway entrance, fumbling for something to do, wanting at that exact moment, more than anything else, to hit someone very hard. Anyone.

Was she safe? Had she exhausted herself? She hadn't sounded at all sure the danger had passed.

The Quad buzzed. It was a text message, saying simply: 'Take the 1 train north. Meet in the last car.'

He replied: 'Terri?'

'If you want to see Terri again, take the 1 train.'

'Who are you?'

No reply.

Robert stood at the mouth of the subway, feeling it pull him in and down. What would happen if he didn't take the train?

He had no choice. He strode down the steps.

A cramped ticket area led through low turnstiles down on to the platform. The *R* of Rector Street was picked out in pleasing purple, blue and green mosaic tile. He hadn't noticed it before. Everything seemed brighter, sharper.

He walked to the far end of the platform, where the last car would be. He heard distant shrieking and clattering as the train came towards Rector from South Ferry, the first and last stop on the 1 line. The last car was empty.

Robert got on and waited, sitting as far towards the rear as possible.

As soon as the train began to move, the sliding door connecting the car to the rest of the train slammed open. A figure dressed entirely in black, face masked by a balaclava, ran towards Robert so quickly that he barely had time to stand before it was on him. Instinctively Robert lowered a shoulder and leaned into his assailant, trying to hold his ground. With a crunch of bone against bone, he felt himself lifted into the air and slammed against the metal door at the end of the train.

As soon as he hit the floor, Robert felt a knife at his throat, a hand gripping the top of his head. He gasped with pain and fear as the cold metal pressed into his flesh, his ribs and spine screaming.

An acrid smell filled his nostrils. Desperation. His assailant might be more afraid than he was. But of what?

'Give it to me.'

He tried to get a reading on the voice. It was hoarse, dangerous. He knew it. Did he? Brisk, confident, but distorted somehow.

'You want my wallet?'

'The cache.'

'That's fine. Take the cash.'

'What you found in the cache. Give it to me. Where is it?'

'I'll have to reach into my jacket pocket.'

'Which?'

'Inside left.'

It was a lie, but Robert figured his assailant would find it hard to reach into the pocket without moving his knife hand.

Fingers reached into the pocket, found nothing. Robert's head exploded with pain as it was slammed against the metal door.

'Where is it?'

The assailant wanted Robert's link to Adam. No way. Robert chose his moment. A detached calm came over him, and he pushed up violently with his legs, hitting bone. He wouldn't give it up.

Powerful hands twisted him round. He took punches on the mouth and nose. He went down on one knee, scrambling for footing.

He began to feel dizzy, and the quality of the light around him began to change. A tenuous yellow light, richer and darker with each second, seeped into the air around his attacker. Robert's face started to go numb, a fist gripped his mind with cold, and he was back in the dream . . . geometric shapes . . . lightning bolts . . . searing pain stabbed behind his eyes. It was evil. He wanted to vomit.

Words came into his head. Terri's voice: 'Hide with the child and the Man of Light. Hide with them.'

The picture of the caged-off monument to the child that Terri had sent him sprang into his mind's eye. He took refuge there. And with Moss. And with the swirling angel figure.

Outside, the pain doubled.

Hands went through his other pockets, found the bullet casing and took it.

Robert felt himself hauled to his feet. Then he was suddenly watching the scene from above, from far away. He thought of Katherine, tried to gauge whether he was going to die. He thought he was. He saw the world shatter like pond ice.

Then, just as suddenly, it stopped. His mind was released. His knees gave way. The man was walking back towards the rest of the train, stashing the bullet casing in a pocket on the sleeve of his jacket.

'No!'

Robert, with a sheer act of will, launched himself at the man as he slid open the metal door that led to the next carriage. He forced them both out into the narrow metal and chain-link cage between the cars. The metal platforms shimmied and bucked beneath their feet. Rushing air tore at his skin.

He looked into his assailant's eyes, and it was like looking into a malignant sun. He was staring again into the face of death from the night of the fire. The face spat hatred, arcing and warping into a single black hole, drawing him in and down. They grabbed each other by the throat, slamming off the doors and metal harnesses that hung between the cars. They roared through the closed subway station at Cortlandt Street, directly under the Ground Zero site, thrown from side to side, their feet slipping on the metal plates. The tracks rushed beneath their feet.

Closing his eyes to block the bilious yellow light, Robert twisted out of the stranglehold and took one of his assailant's wrists with him, turning it until it was between the attacker's shoulder blades. He jammed a hand into the zippered arm pocket and grabbed back the bullet. Then he slammed his assailant's head against metal and forced it over the chains towards the speeding tunnel wall.

'Who are you?' he shouted. 'Who are you?'

No reply.

He forced his assailant's head and torso further out into the tunnel.

'Who are you?'

To his amazement, tears of anger filled his eyes. He wanted to kill this creature. He loosened his grip for a moment, disconcerted.

An elbow slammed into his belly, knocking all the breath out of his body. His assailant twisted away from him and tried to open the door back into the rear car as they pulled into Chambers Street.

Doubled over with pain, Robert felt his entire body fill with weight, as though he were being pumped full of lead. It pooled into his legs, rooting him to the earth. Time distended, like poured molasses. Yet, to his astonishment, he was able to stand, feeling the heaviness pour through his body, displacing the pain, filling his lungs and chest with a strength he had never felt before.

He slung his weight forward in one mighty step and his torso twisted round like a slingshot, propelling his fist into the back of his assailant as he stepped through the open doorway into the last car. The man flew forward, lifted clean off his feet, as though hit by a shotgun blast. He flew past the metal poles along the midline of the car, hitting one halfway along and rolling and tumbling to the far end, where he slammed into the metal door at the back of the train.

Robert stared at his fist in disbelief. And he recognized something else too: excitement, and pride. He felt molten metal pouring through his veins and muscles, though already now it was beginning to seep back down into the ground, towards the centre of the earth. His attacker picked himself up and fled into Chambers Street Station as the train doors opened.

Strength now flowing from him, his head spinning, Robert stepped from between the cars on to the platform and made straight for a trash can. He threw up into it. Then he staggered to a wall, squatted against it on his haunches and held his head in his hands. For a moment or two he blacked out.

Little Falls, August 26, 2004

Katherine stared into the mirror, shaking.

She'd seen the fight. She'd seen her husband attacked, seen him survive. The images had come to her unbidden, sensations of anger and pain hitting her like a hurricane as Robert fought for his life. In the depths of the mirror, for just an instant, she'd seen through Robert's eyes, and stared with him into the seductive, hating eye.

It really was happening, at last. The long chain of events begun more than twenty years ago – perhaps twenty lifetimes ago – was winding into its final, choreographed, elegant form. All the events of the Blackout Day were finally coming to fruition.

What she needed now was the instruction to go ahead with her final assignment.

So many years of waiting for orders, of setting up and carrying out missions, of living in a world of deception and half-truths and betrayal. All of it for nothing, except the tainting of her soul.

And now the only secret mission she had ever really wanted. She awaited the word from the Watchman to go undercover one last time.

She loved Robert. Was she still *in* love with him, as the cliché ran? Did it even matter after so many years together? Deceiving him was painful. She was ashamed, even when it was for his own good. She was too good at it. Always had been.

She walked out into the back garden and lit a cigarette, her first. There were days when she could barely abide herself, but today she felt she could finally get there. Finally find a form of redemption.

There were costs for having lived for so long in the secret world – a world she'd seemed born to, that she'd been so good at inhabiting.

Today she'd amused herself for an hour with Grief Counsellor Sarah, making all the right noises about knowing the stages of grief, recognizing where she was in the process, embracing her pain. She was still in a period of magical thinking, she had been told, when it was quite natural to try to bargain with God, associate bad things she'd thought or done with the terrible loss she'd suffered, as though she had somehow caused it. It was natural to cling to the belief that somehow her little boy wasn't really gone. Everyone knew it was nonsense, of course. A natural, childish, false response to loss. This is what Sarah had said.

Except Katherine had learned more terrible things than most people. How to deceive, blackmail and extort. How to betray. How to use people up and throw them away like litter.

And she had known for many years that magical thinking was more than just a stage of grief.

The counselling sessions were a crock. She'd been going to them for three months to keep Robert happy, with and without him, biding her time. It had been a way of protecting him. She had always sworn she would shield him for as long as possible, until the moment arrived to call upon his gift. Deception was not always a bad thing.

The phone rang.

She listened carefully to the Watchman and hung up.

She stared for a moment into space. The race was afoot, the Watchman had said. Robert had made contact with Terri, embarked on the quest and found the first cache. He'd had to fight to keep the key. Everything was balanced on a knife-edge. If she had any doubts, now was the time to confess them.

Katherine had no doubts. It would be terribly dangerous if she were discovered. But now at least she had the clarity of final marching orders. She had broken one code, and now she had to break another, for the greater good.

There was equipment to locate, a role to prepare.

And, above and beyond her formal mission, she would complete her own secret task. She didn't know how, but she would make things right.

At last, the quickening had come.

She wrote a note to Robert, explaining her absence in a way that would help him take his next step. Then she left the house.

New York, August 26, 2004

Dabbing his bleeding mouth on a handkerchief with a shaking hand and feeling thankful that no one was paying much attention, Robert took the subway from Chambers Street to the parking garage where he'd left his car in the morning – it seemed several days ago – and drove slowly across town towards the Lincoln Tunnel.

It was 6 p.m.

His mouth and throat were sour with vomit. He wanted very much to be with Katherine.

He kept the Quad firmly turned off in his pocket. He focused on the robotic tasks of driving a vehicle in close traffic. Everything else he shut out.

This worked well until a Ryder truck cut in front of him, forcing him to brake hard and setting off a barrage of horn-blowing from the car behind. His heart started to hammer, he wanted to urinate, he wanted to weep, he wanted to punch someone in the head and keep punching till their skull cracked. What. The. Fuck. He slammed the steering wheel with the heel of his hand. Again. Again.

He breathed out long and hard. Collected himself. Edged into the tunnel lane. Crept forward. Calmed down. Miraculously, he made it across to New Jersey without killing anyone.

Robert stopped off along Route 3 at the Tick Tock Diner, all gleaming chrome and burgundy panelling, for coffee and a sandwich and to try to get cleaned up. The décor around the entrance was patterned like the cracking ice of his dream. He looked like he'd splintered into a dozen versions of himself.

Metabolized alcohol and adrenalin sloshed around in his bloodstream and fought with the coffee and the digestive rush of blood to his stomach as he downed a BLT. He got the Quad out to call Katherine, but closed his eyes first for a moment to think about what he'd say. He didn't know what to tell her. He called anyway and got voicemail again. He told her he was on his way, not to worry.

Then he crashed: dozed off, right there in the booth, till the waitress nudged him awake so he could pay up. As soon as he sat down in the car, he realized he was no longer fit to drive. He fell asleep again.

When he came through the door he expected Katherine to be aghast at his swollen lip and nose. His mind was running at a hundred miles an hour, shooting off at different tangents. What could he tell her? What had to remain secret?

But she wasn't there. All he found was a note.

Darling Robert

I need some time to clear my head. I love you, but I know I'm not being the wife you want or need. I feel hopeless, sexless, lifeless. I've gone for a drive. I'll be back late. Don't worry about me, I just need some time.

Kat

He took a deep breath.

She had done this before, heading off on her own to see a movie or eat dinner or occasionally see a friend. Mostly she said she was alone, and he believed her. She always came back.

He felt bone tired. He didn't know how to help her return to him.

Should he worry? He dismissed the idea. She wasn't going to hurt herself, he was sure. But his fear was that one day she just wouldn't come back at all.

Drained and aching, he cleaned his face up in the bathroom, then poured himself a drink and sat in his study. One thing at a time.

He tried to pull it all together, retracing his steps and interpreting everything that had stuck in his mind since he'd left Adam's apartment.

Stars beneath his feet: a magical path. A yellow-brick road?

Masks and costumes: disguise and deception. Not all is as it seems.

Spiral designs: ascent and descent.

A breathing wall: things that seem dead coming to life.

Code-breaking: find the deeper reality.

'Remember death.' As if he could do otherwise at Ground Zero, a place of death and hatred, courage and sacrifice.

A grave, a bullet casing, the attack. More death. His desire to survive, to kill. His shame in being ready to kill. His pride in surviving. He had literally seen red. He could still feel the echo in his body of the power he had been able to tap into while fighting for his life.

Trying to still his mind, he plunged into automatic behaviour, which for Robert was research. He started googling, printing out results, making piles of related-sounding findings. He needed to understand. He called Horace. No reply.

He went to the website she'd told him to post to and checked if there were any other responses or comments. There were none.

He took a look at how the website worked. It was a free weblogging service. Very simple to use. He posted the pictures Terri had sent him, and some more of the photographs he'd taken with the Quad during the day. Maybe they had someone else doing the same thing with a different URL to compete with him. Blog versus blog. A blog-off. The prize? Adam. Or Adam's life? Everyone's life?

It occurred to him that Terri might not know his email address. He signed on as Adam on AOL and continued his research.

Then there was a trill, and Terri was online. He messaged her immediately. 'Are you OK, Terri?'

'Adam?'

'No, sorry. Robert here.'

'I didn't expect you to pretend to be him again this evening. You must really enjoy it.'

'There are limits.'

'Do you know your limits, Robert?'

'I nearly got killed after you vanished.'

'I know. I'm sorry, I couldn't help you. You fought. You survived. You still have the first key. I felt it.'

'That's what it is?'

'Yes. And you still have the core on you, the major key, don't you? You did well to survive. Protect them now.'

'I will.'

'What did you see? If you had to blurt out one thing. Say it.'

His mind flashed back to the moment he'd released his assailant, blinded with tears of rage. He'd wanted to kill the man. Hurt him. He'd made him a nothing, a creature beyond the pale, meriting no human consideration.

'Something happened to me. My rage stopped, when I saw myself about to grind his face into the tunnel wall. I let him go. Just for a few seconds. Then I was as strong as an ox. Made of steel. I punched the guy into the middle of next week.'

'But what did you see?'

'Hate. Fear.'

'And?'

'That's all. I had to stop.'

'You did well.'

'I let him go.'

'You had to.'

'I would have killed him.' Robert sighed. 'This blog ... Can Adam see it?'

'He's on the run, but I hope so.'

'It's not him sending you the GPS waypoints? The little clue ditty wasn't from him?'

'I don't know who they're from, I told you. All I know is this: Adam doesn't know where the caches are. They were placed by the maker of the Ma'rifat'.'

'What for?'

'I don't know.'

'Explain those trances – or whatever it was you were doing when you were giving me directions. You sounded as though you were in pain?'

'I'm not guiding you out of full knowledge, Robert. I'm picking up fragments of meaning from your surroundings and passing them on to you. We are *both* trying to solve the puzzle, you see? I get spatial perceptions – go right, stop here, turn left – and I get images of what is there that is relevant – buried stuff, or a shape, or an emotion, an echo of past activity at the site, or a sense of geometry, of the figure you are making as you go. Sometimes it's like a set of coordinates, but in time and emotion as well as space. Sometimes it's shapes, or rhymes . . . and I *can't remember what I say.* I need a record, I need the blog . . . so I can try to work it all out. You need to ground me and relate what I see to the material world, here and now.'

'That's astonishing.'

'You have greater abilities than I do. In potential. I work with some strong women who've taught me how to use it, but you outstrip us all. You've always known it. There's always been part of you that understood what we call the green language, or the language of the birds.'

'You don't understand. I was brought up to kill it off in myself.'

'And you nearly did. I've felt the fear around it. I'm going to help you bring it back. I need to, for the sake of us all. You're a real Unicorn. You've no idea what a privilege it is to help you.'

Robert rubbed his eyes with the heels of his hand, fumbling for the right response. 'Thank you. What's so special about a Unicorn, exactly?'

Her response seemed to take several minutes. When it came, he felt his chest fill with a gratitude he had no idea how to share.

'A Unicorn is the most powerful kind of healer. It is a being who can take the full array of human energies – and I mean the full array, starting with the energies of killing – and channel them all into building a body of light so intense that no evil can penetrate it, or withstand its touch.'

'Body of light? Like the Swirly Man?'

'That's what it looks like. Adam said it's so intense that even unawakened people can see it. It shines around you. Makes you look seven feet tall. They show up in myths as giants, as luminous teachers, as angels . . .'

The first line from the letter he had burned over twenty years ago lit up in Robert's mind: *To live well, know death.*

He had wanted to kill that man. It had been necessary to want to kill him. And now he had to convert that power.

'I think I understand. What happens if a potential Unicorn cannot channel these energies, cannot convert them?'

'They die.'

They were both silent for a while. Robert looked within himself. He would find the strength. He had to.

'May I ask you a favour, Robert?'

'What?'

'Could you stop pretending to be Adam? He might try to contact me. He can't do that if you're using his profile . . . I do know your email address.'

'Oh . . .'

'Please? You need to rest. Gather your strength.'

'I want to see you tomorrow.'

'Be at the site of the first cache. Tomorrow at 2 p.m.'

'Will you be there?'

'You'll see me. Now go. I'm going to send you something to listen to tomorrow. It's part of the puzzle. Till tomorrow. We'll meet. I'll explain. You'll like it. Trust me. Please.'

And she was gone.

He took the bullet casing and the Malice Box to the hidden safe he and Katherine used for their valuables. Then, back at his desk, he continued to look things up, his mind haring in a dozen directions at once.

The image of the Man of Light burned in his brain. Robert found him in the Book of Revelation 10:1–4:

Then I saw another mighty angel coming down from heaven, wrapped in a cloud, with a rainbow over his head, and his face was like the sun, and his legs like pillars of fire. He had a little scroll open in his hand. And he set his right foot on the sea, and his left foot on the land, and called out with a loud voice, like a lion roaring; when he called out, the seven thunders sounded. And when the seven thunders had sounded, I was about to write, but I heard a voice from heaven saying, 'Seal up what the seven thunders have said, and do not write it down.'

Seven thunders. Each a sealed secret. Had he just heard the first thunder, in the subway under Ground Zero?

He shook his head, fatigue in every bone. He worked on.

The obelisk at St Paul's commemorated Irish patriot and former New York State Attorney-General Thomas Addis Emmet, brother of executed Irish patriot Robert Emmet, but it covered no grave. Thomas Addis Emmet's vault was across town, at St Mark's in-the-Bowery. Carved into the obelisk was its own location, latitude and longitude, in minutes, degrees and seconds.

None of it made sense. He rubbed his eyes in frustration. Terri's email landed. It contained nothing but an audio file and the admonition not to listen to it until she told him to. He loaded it on to the Quad. Terri had asked him to dig deeper. He gathered his thoughts, wrote again and posted to the website.

Ground Zero, Lower Manhattan

If I look within myself at this place, I return to a memory so painful it still causes me to twist my head away as though ducking a blow. It is the image of a street covered in thick black dust, under thunderclouds, and at the end of the street the still-standing remains of a section of the World Trade Center towers, twisted and blackened and looking like the very mouth of hell, those Gothic arches backlit in the afternoon gloom from the arc lights of the searchers, the damp dust like cinders under my feet and the sheer hatred of the attack reverberating weeks after the towers fell. It caught me by surprise even though I knew it was there, as Katherine and I walked in the rain and held each other, in downtown Manhattan to spend some money to support the local vendors, the only time I could bring myself to go.

There was beauty still: the arches persisted, they were not all thrown down. Something defiant remained in their shattered suggestion of a cathedral entrance, of praying hands, of a portal that said: through these arches lies a womb, beyond this defilement there is rebirth, even here there will be love.

But the overriding pulse in that place was of such anger and hatred that I could not look at it for more than a second or two, I had to walk away, east, towards the South Street Seaport. It will never leave me.

We have been locked in a labyrinth since that day. How do we react, how does anyone react, to an act of such wickedness and still remain ourselves? You cannot be good unless you survive. But there is a monster within us who out of sheer fear says: do anything, hurt anyone, I don't care: to anyone beyond the bounds of my tribe, anything may be done.

Today I thought I would die. I was so scared that for a moment I wanted anything, anything at all to happen to prevent it. Then suddenly I wasn't afraid. We were right underneath Ground Zero. I stared into the face of death, and I fought for my life. I saw something in myself I had not seen before, and I came out on the other side. It was the ability, the desire, to kill.

It was dangerous, inchoate, raw energy that poured through me. Blood energy. I know now, with complete confidence, that I can draw on it again, whenever I need it.

Many years ago, someone within my family wrote to me with seven lines of wisdom. The first line was this: 'To live well, know death.' I think I understand: these were the first energies I had to tap into on the quest I have embarked upon. Raw, powerful, potentially murderous. If I can't yoke them, I won't have the strength to survive. But how to harness them?

At Ground Zero the towers fell and St Paul's was left intact, not a window broken. A friend of mine, a masseuse, volunteered there for weeks, working on cops and firemen and construction workers, offering real physical compassion as others put together the chapel's ministry of meals and water, a place to sleep, a place to find some solace for the heart. Yet this was all for 'our' people, for those like us who had suffered, those with whom we identified. For 'identity' comes from *idem*, 'the same'. It is easy to pray for our friends. How many of us can truly pray for our enemies, for those who actively seek our death?

Robert had just finished posting when there was an IM trill from AOL. He figured Terri wanted to respond. But it was from AdamHD1111.

'So you've met the delicious Terri.'

'Adam?'

'She probably means to fuck your brains out tomorrow. Problem with that?'

Then he was gone.

Robert stared at the computer screen, willing him to come back, and praying he wouldn't. Eventually he could bear it no longer and went to bed.

New York, August 26, 2004

Adam took a deep breath and slowly exhaled, alone and racked with pain. He walked away from his computer and curled up in a ball on the bed, praying from his most secret inner place. He had taken a hell of a risk in attacking Robert. Either might have killed the other.

Compelled by the Iwnw to carry out the attack, and feigning complete obedience to them to buy time, Adam had prayed the experience would launch Robert on to the Path. It had worked, he felt, though only just. But Robert had passed the Trial by Earth. Drawn on his raw will to survive. Faced down death and fought for his life. And he'd seen its shadow side, known the tribal savage, the executioner, the torturer within. And he'd turned away from it. From pure earth towards water, which washed away the dross.

The pain was growing. Adam steeled his will again to force away the Iwnw's creature that was eating into his soul, into his very DNA, the Minotaur lodged within him. He recited his mantra of defiance: . . . *death shall have no dominion . . . death shall have no dominion . . .*

Only one in a thousand survived the road that Robert was taking, he knew. Adam would stay with him until the end. He couldn't go on much longer. A few days more. Just long enough.

A Martyr's Love Song: The Making of the Ma'rifat'

I am the maker of the Ma'rifat'.

I am not a hateful man. I love God with every pore, with every atom and breath of my body. I am in love with God. I wish only for everyone to see what I see in God. Please do not think of me as a primitive, tooth-gnashing kind of man. I am educated to a high level. I am almost what you might call a rocket scientist. I studied in the finest halls of Cairo and London, before coming to live in America. I worked at what I like to call the Ring of Gold — its official name is the RHIC, or Relativistic Heavy Ion Collider at Brookhaven, on Long Island. We smashed things there, to see what would happen. Not large things, though a secret part of me has always wanted to smash large things, like all boys, to see what happens. But we smashed together atoms of gold, at very high speeds. At speeds so close to the speed of light that time and space started to warp. My father taught physics and chemistry in Egypt and Iraq, and this would have been his dream. We created such powerful energies in the collider that particles appeared that have not appeared in nature since the first few nanoseconds after Creation. It is a marvel. It is almost like prayer: it gets us that close to the energies of God.

My mother is American, and I am an American.

You may call me Al-Khidr. I take the name of the great instructor and guide in hidden knowledge of God, the one who instructed Musa himself — Moses, as you call him — because I will teach you the greatest lesson of your nation's history, and the lesson will be in destruction and rebirth, in wiping clean, in making holy once again that which is defiled.

My true name is unimportant. I shrugged it off long ago. I lived among you, studied in your schools, ate in your homes, slept with your women. I held security clearances. You would not find me a prig or a bore. I know your literature and music. Do you know mine? I know your laws and institutions, your holy books and prayers. Do you know mine? I know your fears and nightmares. Do you know mine? My name is Al-Khidr, the ancient guide, and I am bringing you your lesson, which is the same lesson we must all learn.

I am not filled with hate. I am filled with love. I have come to love freedom, but I love God more. I have come to love America, but I love the earth more.

It seems to me that America must experience submission to the will of God. America must be shattered in order to emerge more whole and humble. America must learn that true freedom is found in submission, not in being the biggest, loudest, dumbest, horniest kid on the block. This is why I chose to destroy New York. But do not say I did it out of hate.

∞

2

Trial by Water

Little Falls, August 27, 2004

Katherine returned home sometime after midnight and came to Robert's room. She lay with him in the dark, saying nothing, inches and light-years away. It had been seven years now since she'd walked away from her career, six since they had met again and fallen in love.

Neither liked to argue, but it was rare that they would make up like this. She just lay next to him, and they drifted off to sleep, fingertips barely touching, each showing the other that they hated the deadening frost between them, even while acknowledging that it was there.

Robert dreamed they made love.

He dreamed that they awoke to find themselves making love, and that their relief and delight was so great they burst out laughing.

Then in the dream he opened his eyes and realized it was Terri he held in his arms. He willed her to become Katherine again. She wouldn't. As Terri smiled up at him, he dreamed Katherine stood over them, watching.

'I can't blame you,' she said. 'Everybody wants Terri.'

Then he caught a glimpse of himself in the bedroom mirror. He was Adam.

He awoke with a start. Katherine was gone. His body aching, he stared into the darkness till dawn broke.

August 14, 2003: Blackout Day

For months Adam had tracked his quarry, using the skills of the Path, sometimes working alone, sometimes directed and aided by the Watchman. Now he stood at the intersection of Tesla and

Robinson Streets in Shoreham, Long Island, and surveyed the abandoned buildings. A brick tower rose above the main one, a disused laboratory, and he knew as soon as he saw it that his target was inside.

He pressed his fingers against the talisman Terri had given him, then pulled it out of his shirt and kissed it. He was totally calm, totally alive, more alert than he had ever been in his life.

It was five minutes to four.

He checked the position of the security guard. He was over by the far entrance. Searching in his mind's eye, Adam saw his enemy's movements that day, his arrival at the site, his entry through a disguised hole in the fence.

Adam felt Katherine's power with him too. To her, he owed the final tip-off: that today would be the day of the attack.

Adam found the entrance and moved towards the laboratory's ground-floor windows. He saw a device like a shallow drum, glowing softly with gold light, on a simple wooden table, and a stocky man in his late forties, his eyes closed in deep meditation, sitting on a chair before it. The man held a smaller version of the drum, of the same translucent red-gold metal, between his fingers. The rim of the drum seemed to rotate in contrary directions at once, and geometric forms traced into its sides glowed white and gold. At the limits of his perception, so tenuous that he wasn't sure if it was there or not, he could make out a faint cloud above the Device. As it swirled in and out of visibility, he thought for a moment it was an eye.

Adam prayed. *Let me stop this act of defilement from taking place, even if it costs me my life.*

The man suddenly stood up and took a step towards the Device, eyes still closed. Adam saw that he was weeping. A wave of great loss, of deep hurt and anger, rippled off him. Adam moved to the door and walked in. He moved towards his target in plain sight as the man opened his eyes and calmly put down the core.

When Adam was almost upon him, the man raised a hand and planted it firmly palm-first into Adam's chest.

In the split second before it hit him, Adam clearly saw the

tenuous eye above the Device twist and melt into his opponent's body. Then a shock-wave tore through Adam that sent him flying twenty feet across the room. Stunned, he scrambled to get back on his feet. He looked up to see the man again walking calmly towards the Device.

Adam stilled his mind. He called out, firmly: 'Stop.'

'No. No, no. Why stop?'

His quarry placed the core into the top of the Device, which doubled its speed and began to emit a deep bass throb. The air around it began to vibrate, to warp. Then he removed it, wrapping it in a cloth. The Ma'rifat' slowed again.

'It is complete. It is armed. You cannot stop it. I will take it into Manhattan now, where the fuel is richest. The greed. The fear. The hypocrisy. Then I will insert the key again. And it will feed.'

Adam stepped closer. The Device flared and spat light.

'It is responding to me,' Adam said. 'I have no hate in my heart.'

'Step back,' the man said.

Adam took another step forward and spoke again. 'And I have no fear.'

'Step back!'

Adam launched himself forward, trying to wrest the core from the man's right hand. They fell to the ground and fought. The core rolled loose, and they both lunged after it. Adam grabbed it and tried to rise but felt his wrist twisted savagely backwards. He dropped the core into the hands of his enemy, who leaped forward and slammed it back into the top of the Device.

The Ma'rifat' began to spin again, glowing deep blue and red from within. A sound like slow thunder rippled through the twisting air.

Adam shoulder-charged him, and both men fell, grabbing at each other's throats. They hurled themselves over and over on the ground, trying to gain enough leverage to stand. They smashed into the table and cracked one of the legs, and before either could react they saw the Ma'rifat' slide off the falling surface and drop towards the concrete floor.

'I have no forgiveness,' the man said as it fell, and then the Device hit the ground and detonated.

Time and space twisted as Adam watched, aghast. A seething, swirling eye of lightning formed around the damaged Ma'rifat', flaring yellow and electric-blue as it shot towards the two men, dousing them in fire. Adam made his mind a perfect mirror. He saw his enemy's body atomize in a flash. Then he knew nothing.

Generating its own warped geometry, searching for fuel, for an energy it could engage with, sliding down the ladder from finer to denser, from spirit to ether to matter, the Ma'rifat' fed on the echoes of its creator's pain, his hatred and anger, and flared out into the world. Specks of space and time randomly distorted around the Device. Snatches of time and place became conjoined, and from the void at the heart of the Ma'rifat' a great surge of energy flowed, arcing in the air.

But then it lost its grip on the souls it could feel all around, the great agglomeration of spirits it detected . . . Weakened by Adam's calm, his stillness, its power spiralled down to become a raw electromagnetic pulse, hugely powerful but disorganized, its spiritual force diluted to a fraction of its potential. The pulse see-sawed back and forth along power lines, tripping safety systems, blowing out fail-safes, spreading like ink in water. With a surge of physical energy like an invisible thunderbolt, the Ma'rifat' blew out all the lights across the north-eastern United States.

Little Falls, August 27, 2004

Robert lied to Katherine over breakfast, telling her a spurious story about trying to break up a fight in the street between a taxi driver and a customer and getting punched in the face for his pains.

'No good deed goes unpunished,' Katherine said. 'You'll heal.'

It was a role she hated playing, but already she was performing the Watchman's wishes, settling into her secret assignment. With the genuine difficulties she and Robert had had since the miscarriage, it was not proving hard. She despised her own skill.

Robert told her of the death of Lawrence Hencott, saying nothing about Adam's supposed involvement. As for Robert's ignominious removal from the offices of GBN, she had little sympathy.

'John's a dick. He's scared of you, that's why he's doing it. Sees you as a rival. He can't think any other way. Scott will look after you.'

She announced she was going out again. 'If you find out any more about what's going on with Adam and that weird box, let me know. I'll be at yoga.'

'I'm going into Manhattan again. I need to see Scott to sign some documents.'

She stopped by the door. 'When I worked at the Foreign Office . . .'

She still couldn't say what she'd really done, even after all these years. They'd trained her to the bone and beyond.

'. . . we were taught to listen to our instincts very closely. First impressions. Intuition. The hairs on the back of our necks. It could save our lives.'

'You did well to get out when you did. I'm eternally grateful.'

'Something about you right now feels wrong. Just so you know.'

'Something about us feels wrong.'

'No, I mean something new. Something very recent.'

'Such as?'

'You're afraid. I've never seen you afraid before.'

'Of what?'

'I don't know. I don't think you do either.'

She considered him for a moment. 'You're a rock, Robert. Don't stop being a rock.'

'I am Gibraltar.'

'Don't get into any more fights. We're out of peroxide.'

Alone in the house, Robert thought of Terri. There was no chance of anything happening with her. He wouldn't allow it. But he recognized that he wanted it. It was one of the things he was afraid of. He was ready for something to happen.

He cast his mind back to the weekend he and Katherine had fallen in love.

Miami, September 1998

They all convened on a Friday afternoon in the lobby of the Biltmore Hotel.

Robert, who had been covering the march of Hurricane Georges across the Caribbean for several days, was exhausted and irritable. Scores of people had been killed in flooding in the Dominican Republic, thousands driven from their homes across the Caribbean. The Keys were going to get hit, and maybe Miami itself. He'd evacuated the downtown GBN news bureau and set up a temporary operation deeper inland at the hotel. Now he'd come down to the lobby to politely withdraw from Adam's upcoming mystery weekend.

Adam, who was mostly living between Havana and Miami Beach, had invited a small group of people a fortnight earlier to meet at the Biltmore at this hour, using his customary riddles, torn postcards and invisible writing. Robert wanted him to call it off.

'Georges is very big, and very powerful,' he'd told Adam by phone. 'If it comes this way over sea, it'll hit Miami like a bomb. A big one.'

'I know. Delightful, isn't it? Adds such an element of doom to the mood.'

'Promise me you won't have people out in the streets chasing bloody clues.'

'They'll all be lashed to masts on Miami Beach, Robert.'

'You're joking?'

'Relax, I promise I won't kill anyone.'

'I'm going to have to pull out.'

'I understand. At least come down and say hello.'

'I have a job to do.'

'Delegate. Just for an hour. The lobby, five o'clock. Please come. People want to meet you. I have a surprise.'

Now they stood among the ornate octagonal birdcages in the cavernous lobby hall, awaiting Adam's entrance. The finches and nightingales swooped and twittered with agitation at the approaching hurricane.

A man Robert didn't know, beautifully blazered, twinkled at him.

Robert tried from the depths of his fatigue to twinkle back but didn't have it in him. The man introduced himself as a William, American. He was with a Penny, British, whom he'd met on a boat trip to Cuba organized by Adam the previous year. There was Carmen, a tall black Cuban-American lady, electrifyingly dressed in all white and yellow, and a watchful man of sallow complexion called Vladimir. William appraised Carmen with a moneyed leer. Suddenly Robert perceived a woman approaching him at high speed from his left.

'Miaow,' she said. 'You must be the one Adam warned me about.'

'Katherine,' he said, smiling. So she was Adam's surprise. 'My God. How long has it been?'

She had a nautical effect going on, white shorts and a matelot top and tanned legs. She kissed his cheek.

'Too long. You look tired. Busy?'

He hadn't seen her in nearly ten years, since London. Her ill-fated marriage to Adam. The performance of *Newton's Papers*.

'Adam told me to expect a surprise but . . .'

Katherine looked slimmer than he remembered her. Worry lines around her eyes crinkled when she smiled, but, despite her tan and vigour, she seemed not fully at ease. Haunted, he thought.

'How long have you been here?'

'Posted here as bureau chief from London. About eighteen months.'

'Any family with you?'

'Jacqueline didn't come. We called it a day.'

'Oh, sorry. Kids?'

'Never happened. You?'

'I left the Foreign Office. Free as a bird. Oh, look, here he is.'

Adam, the self-elected shaman to his friends, appeared from the direction of the elevators, wearing a white jacket, jeans and sunglasses, looking like a gigolo. He kissed everyone kissable.

The group sought out the bar downstairs. They all liked themselves, especially when people were looking. And in their different ways they all loved Adam way too much. Feeling like the token local dullard and yearning to get back to work, Robert began whispering asides to Katherine as they settled around a table.

'I suspect we're the only ones with real jobs.'

She smiled and squeezed his arm and sat down next to him. 'Vladimir looks like he was grown in a laboratory.'

All the participants had received through the mail a riddle and half a postcard in a manila envelope. In Robert's case, his half of the postcard showed a curve of tanned flesh and a line of fabric that was probably, though not certainly, a breast in a bikini top. The riddle was as follows:

Complete the picture to a nicety, find the creature known for piety. Share a table, if you're able, with a hottie (not for totty). The name and day are Mercury, Icks ecksive at eye.

The Pelican Restaurant. A Wednesday, Mercredi, Miércoles, the day named for Mercury. Icks ecksive was IX XIV, 9/14. Eye was I, one o'clock. Reservation in the name of Frederick Mercury.

A similarly personalized riddle had been received by Penny, which led her to the same Miami Beach restaurant, at the same time and the same table. The lunch date had allowed the two of them to join together their torn postcards, which, when combined, indeed gave a complete bikini top as well as the jumbled name of the Biltmore Hotel, today's date and a time.

Adam framed it as a summoning of heroes from the four corners of the earth, or at least a parlour game in which those were the roles, in order to solve a great mystery.

Ensconced at the head of the table, he spoke: 'I have asked you all to come here today because . . .'

Little Falls, August 27, 2004

Robert, his notes in one hand and a souvenir paperweight in the form of an obelisk from Buenos Aires in the other, pored over his horizontal map of Manhattan, squatting at the table's edge to squint along streets and sight lines. He placed the paperweight, a gift from Katherine's father, downtown at Fulton Street and Broadway, muttering to himself: 'First waypoint. First cache. Obelisk.'

He took a box of map pins from his desk.

'Before that, Adam's pied-à-terre.' He stuck a yellow pin at Greenwich Street and Charles.

'First waypoint again. St Paul's Chapel.' He stuck a red pin next to the obelisk at Fulton.

'Join the dots . . .' He tied a length of string between the two pins, then squatted again and looked south-east along its length with one eye closed. He moved around and did the same looking north-west.

If something draws your attention, pay heed to it. Photograph it. Post it. But nothing leaped out at him.

He took his notebook and drew a diagonal line, imagining the full page as Manhattan.

What else? The bullet casing.

He'd been in a few fights in his time. Never sought them. But he was solidly built, and people didn't usually mess with him. He'd taken a couple of bullies apart to protect smaller kids in his schooldays. Getting banged in the face didn't bother him too much. But this had been different. The knife. And then the face that wasn't there. That sickly yellow light where a face should have been and, pulsing at its core, the hypnotic staring eye. He knew it was death, stalking him through time, from the burning bedroom in Cambridge to the New York subway. The fire in Adam's room had been rekindled, and he couldn't put it out. Why did it want him? How could he fight it?

He focused his mind on the bullet. An ad caught his eye on the back cover of a magazine on the stack by his desk. A red dot within a red circle. A Target ad. He tore the logo from the page and pinned it through the centre on to the map by the obelisk. A bullet and a target.

Robert whispered to himself: 'Is Adam the target? Am I? Who's shooting?'

He picked up the Malice Box. The master key, they'd called it. 'Let's have another look at you too, you evil bloody box.'

He went out into the backyard, seeking some sunlight. The box resisted his initial twists and squeezes.

'So help me, Hale, I will break your neck when I find you.'

He tried pressing lightly on the various geometric patterns traced in its sides. Nothing. It gleamed a translucent reddish bronze in his hand. The concentric raised rings on its top seemed to flip from convex to concave and back . . . then they seemed to turn in a slow spiral. He stared into it. Lost himself. It was like a tiny black hole. He shook his head clear. Grabbed the Quad from his breast pocket and photographed it in the palm of his hand.

Then he put it, together with the bullet casing, in the safe upstairs and got ready to head into Manhattan.

August 14, 2003: Blackout Day

Adam awoke to find himself in darkness, facing the eye. He could not feel his body. The eye was irresistibly beautiful.

'You have thwarted us,' it said. 'Or at least you have thwarted our proxy, our creature. But there is a price. Now we have entered your being. We have become entwined, through him, in your very DNA. And we have entered your seed.'

Adam became aware of the burned-out, smashed Ma'rifat' somewhere on the floor near his feet. But the encounter was taking place elsewhere, in some deep corner of his consciousness.

An image entered his mind, unbidden: tendrils of light spiralling from one double helix to another, from himself to Terri, Terri to Katherine, Katherine to Robert, all linked as though they were one. He felt a foreign presence within himself, one he must contain, a contaminant of hatred and loss.

He saw another image, of Terri. He saw her body as though in a living X-ray. He saw a fertilized egg.

'She's pregnant?'

'She was. She may yet become so again. But we are entangled now. The man you killed. This woman. You with us. We have halted this pregnancy before it begins. We have made it into something else and frozen it in time. Until you do our bidding.'

'What are you?'

'We are Iwnw.'

'What is that?'

'We have fought your kind for many years, though we are the same as you in many ways. We dwell equally in your world and the next. We reach you through the maker of the Ma'rifat'.'

'He's dead.'

'He lives in you now. He is entangled with you. He is what we call a Minotaur, trapped between worlds, consumed with loss and fear. A powerful creature, become weak. He will be our gateway into you. We will not be denied. Do as we wish, at the time of our choosing, and we will reverse what we have done. Deny us, and cell division will proceed, in a form of eternal life.'

'Eternal life?' Adam spat. 'How?'

'There is a form of physical immortality available to everyone. It is caused by an enzyme called telomerase, which stops cells from dying when they are exhausted. It allows them to divide for ever. And there are some conditions in which the foetus doesn't grow, but the placenta does, in an abnormal manner, in a way propitiated by this enzyme. It can spread rapidly to the rest of the body. Do you know what it is?'

'Tell me.'

'It is called cancer. We have altered the cell structure to ensure this is what will happen if we unfreeze it. And we will ensure it is of the most virulent kind, if you do not attend us when we call on you.'

Miami, September 1998

'. . . I need your help. There has been a killing. An unusual one. Your remarkable powers are required.'

Adam's guests exchanged amused looks.

'The looming hurricane has forced a change of plans . . . but for the killer, as well as for us. We are all confined here in this magnificent lodging for the next twenty-four to thirty-six hours. No one may leave. We are locked in together. *But so is the person we each seek.* Among us.'

He took some green folders from a briefcase at his feet and passed them around the table. 'Here, among other materials, you will find a photograph of the person you seek.'

Robert opened his folder and laughed. He looked around the table and saw everyone had the same photograph.

It was a chalk outline, the kind police drew around a dead body in *noir* thrillers, white outline on a black surface. Sans body.

'This was someone we all love very much. The victim fought to the very end. It was a brutal struggle. The hunt for the killer will take place inside this splendid hotel. Outside, there is nothing. Just the gathering storm. I'd planned certain outings for this event that will have to be cancelled. But we can do it all here perfectly well.' He paused and gave a rueful smile. 'If we survive . . . Now, please read through the rest of your materials and begin. Oh, and one last thing. The identity of your target is contained in a sealed envelope.

Each of you has one. Under no circumstances may you open the envelope until you are ready to confront him . . . or her.'

Robert's cell phone buzzed. It was his deputy. 'The mayor's about to speak again, Boss.'

'On my way.'

He picked up his folder and mimed regrets to Adam. For Katherine, he jotted down his room number on a business card and slid it into her folder.

Robert returned to the lobby. The birds were shrieking and banging into the bars of their cages now. Before going back up to the makeshift bureau, he stepped out on to the front steps of the hotel and looked up at the sky. It was livid green and purple. It was starting to boil.

Katherine came to Robert's room shortly before midnight, as the edge of Georges flayed the hotel with sumptuous rain. He was on the phone with his news editor, wrapping up coverage plans for the coming twenty-four hours. He waved to her to sit. She riffled through her folder until he was ready.

'You look exhausted.'

'I have six hours off now. I'll pick it up from Mike again in the morning.'

'Is it coming here?'

'They usually head straight for Miami and veer off at the last minute. This one hasn't veered yet.' He rubbed his eyes. 'If it comes, we'll know about it. This thing's the size of Texas. Enough energy to light Manhattan for a decade. If I tell you to get into the bathtub and cover your head, do it.'

'Will it protect me?'

'No, but it'll give me a good laugh. It's full of water at the moment. In case we get hit.'

She smiled.

Robert got up and perused the contents of the mini-bar. 'Want anything?'

'Jack Daniel's, straight. Thanks.'

He cracked open a small bottle of wine for himself. 'So . . . what's Adam got you all doing?'

'Chasing clues. It's been fun. We all just compared notes over dinner. Everyone's all over the place.'

'Teams of two?'

'No, everyone's on their own but collaborating.'

'I'm sorry I can't take part. I think.'

'There are clues every few floors, starting in the basement. Want to hear one?'

'Not now. My brain is shot.'

'Want me to leave?'

'Not in the least. Tell me about you. All about you. It was rumoured you became a spook.'

'Foreign Office.'

'Based where?'

'Everywhere. Paris, some of the time. London. Short stints elsewhere.'

Beneath her calm, she was as tense as a wire.

'And you quit.'

'There are things I can't talk about.'

'I understand. But you quit.'

'I did a lot of work in non-proliferation. Of sorts.' She snorted to herself, an expression of disgust on her face. Then she looked out of the window for a long time.

'Why did you come?'

'I didn't plan to. It was a last-minute decision. I was thinking that Adam and I had seen quite enough of each other for this lifetime.'

'Did you get his letter from Havana?'

Adam had written to several friends earlier in the year, after the Pope's visit to Cuba, announcing among other things the death of his mother, his coming into a small inheritance and his retirement as a foreign correspondent. He would now dedicate himself, he wrote, purely to what he termed the Rope Trick: the pursuit of wisdom and a good laugh, though not necessarily in that order.

'I thought he'd gone batty.'

'Me too. Nice to see him happy, though.'

'So this is part of the Rope Trick?'

'He said it was a way of sharing the Rope Trick with friends. Experimental, he said.'

'So why did you come?'

'It was a free air-ticket. Change of scene. Adam said you'd be here. And I wanted to tell him I finally understood.'

'Understood what?'

'Losing someone. Having them torn away. Losing them to violence. Like he lost Isabela.'

'What happened?'

She got up and walked to the window. She was rigid. 'I couldn't go on, that's all.'

'Your work?'

'I ended up caring. You can never care. Not about people. Just about the cause. And sometimes you forget you're not actually even serving a cause, you're just serving a country.'

'Was there something specific? A particular incident? You said you lost someone.'

'Christ, did I ever.'

'What happened?'

'Clumsy. To lose someone. To fumble a life. Oops. Butterfingers.'

'You blame yourself.'

She was fighting back tears. 'Can we talk about something else? Tell me about Jacqueline. Or your job.'

New York, August 27, 2004

Robert stood on Broadway outside St Paul's Chapel at 2 p.m., looking at the obelisk through the railings. The Quad showed four satellites engaged, accuracy of 29 feet, ready to navigate.

It rang.

'Robert. Waypoint 064.'

'And good afternoon to you.'

'Hi. You can take the subway to Canal Street.'

The Quad showed the new waypoint as a location in SoHo, just over a mile north and slightly west. As he walked, he was treading on stars in the sidewalk again.

Robert crossed Broadway near the giant clock at Vesey and walked north, heading in the direction of City Hall. On the corner of Barclay a green octagonal information booth offered free maps of New York. He took one, unable to resist.

The signal faded. Trying to reconnect, he walked into City Hall Park and found himself staring at polished granite slabs laid into the sidewalk showing scenes from the area as it used to look. The granite was so smooth he could see his reflection, as though he were staring through the ground directly into the past.

An image of the burning room flashed again into his mind. The past had never felt closer. He walked back to Broadway. The GPS signal returned as he reached the R and the W subway station, the gated grounds of City Hall itself to his right, closed to the public for security reasons.

The Quad now said 0.9 miles.

Something about the station entrance railings leaped out at him. A form like a fish was welded into the design. Green metal. He took a picture of it.

'I'm going to tell you a story as you go,' Terri said. 'I hope you like it.'

'I'll let you know.'

'Did you see the reading of *Salomé* by Oscar Wilde that Al Pacino did last year at the Barrymore? Marisa Tomei was in it?'

'Missed it, sorry.'

'She did a Dance of the Seven Veils, very Middle Eastern. Made her butt shimmer and vibrate. The night I saw it she ripped her top off, flashed her breasts. It was very erotic. She didn't do that every night.'

'Wish I'd seen it.'

'The Dance of the Seven Veils isn't in the Bible, though the scene where John the Baptist loses his head is, of course . . . not everyone realizes.'

'Hadn't thought of that, but, yes, think you're right.'

144

'There was no Dance of the Seven Veils as we now think of it until Wilde wrote that play in the nineteenth century . . . in French, no less . . . but this story is where it comes from. It's on a clay tablet. Very, very old. The story of Ishtar.'

'The film version didn't do too well.'

'Shut up and listen. It's the MP3 file I sent you last night. Start it as you go down the steps. It's about what's happening to you. When you get to Canal, take the left-hand exit and cross Broadway to the west.'

Then she was gone.

Robert found the icon on the Quad screen and clicked it as he descended past the green ironwork.

The station was a utilitarian brown-and-yellow riveted oblong box, dotted with grubby dark blue mosaics of City Hall on the far side of the rails.

Her voice was closer, more intimate, in the recording. She'd used a good microphone.

'Hi, Robert. You'll like this. Ishtar, goddess of love, daughter of the moon, has chosen a lover. She has taken Tammuz, the shepherd, to be her husband, and now he has become the god of fertility. Life on earth flourishes. But Ishtar has a sister, who rules the land of the dead, and she captures and imprisons Tammuz.'

The R train came. He got on and found a seat.

'Ishtar goes to her sister's realm, the land of no return, the house of shadows, the place of darkness, to free him. There is no way back from this road, no exit from this house, where clay and dust are the only sustenance. The dead resemble birds, in this telling. Ishtar demands entry. Her sister, Ereshkigal, perhaps in joy, perhaps in fear, orders her to be admitted.'

Robert closed his eyes and let his mind drift into the story. Entering the land of the dead . . . to reclaim a lost soul . . . that is what they were doing. Rescuing Adam . . .

'The gatekeeper welcomes Ishtar to the land of the dead and opens wide the first gate. She is wearing no dress, only items of personal adornment and modesty. He takes the crown from her head. She asks: "Why do you take my crown?" And the gatekeeper replies: "Enter, my lady. Such are the decrees of my queen."

'At the second gate, he makes her take off her earrings.

'At the third gate, he makes her take off her necklace.

'At the fourth gate, he makes her take off the ornaments of her breast, made of precious metals.

'At the fifth gate, he makes her take off her girdle, inlaid with charms of birthstones.

'At the sixth gate, he makes her take off her bracelets and anklets.

'At the seventh gate, he makes her take off her final undergarment.'

Robert smiled, holding the erotic image at a distance. Terri was stripping for him? She'd narrated it deadpan, but with just a hint of mischief at the edge of her voice. Was he going to let himself be seduced today? He'd never been a philanderer. He just wasn't that kind of guy. He'd resist. He had to. That's what the trial had to be.

'Thus Ishtar is naked when she meets face to face with the queen of the dead. Ishtar immediately attacks her sister. The seven judges of hell turn the eyes of death upon Ishtar. Ereshkigal unleashes upon her a host of diseases, like a pack of hounds. Ishtar dies, and her corpse is hung upon a stake. The earth lies barren. Fertility dies. Man and woman sleep alone. The bull does not mount the cow, and trees and plants do not quicken.'

Wow, Robert thought. Erotic charge dispelled, no problem.

'But Ishtar has left word that if she does not return from the land of the dead after three days, she must be rescued. The messenger of the gods, seeing sterility all around, speaks with the sun and moon, and pleads with the god of wisdom, to restore fertility. The god of wisdom forms a being of radiant light to rescue Ishtar. The being's name is Asushu-namir, which means "face of light". The gates of the underworld open to Asushu-namir, who is taken to an audience with the queen of the dead.'

A Unicorn, Robert thought. Like the Man of Swirling Light. What he must become.

'Such is the radiance of this extraordinary being that when Asushu-namir asks the queen of the underworld for the water of life, she curses and spits but finally cannot refuse, and orders Ishtar to be sprinkled with the life-giving water and removed from her sight. Ishtar is restored to life.

'At the first gate, her undergarment is returned to her.

'At the second gate, she puts on again her anklets and bracelets.

'At the third gate, she puts on again her girdle, studded with birthstones.

'At the fourth gate, she puts on again the ornaments of her breast.

'At the fifth gate, she puts on again her necklace.

'At the sixth gate, she puts on again her earrings.

'At the seventh gate, she puts on again her crown.

'Tammuz her lover appears by her side, restored to her. Vegetation enlivens the earth. Fertility returns, and the earth lives.'

The story ended as the train pulled into Canal Street Station. The ride was barely two minutes. He got off, its images still echoing in his mind.

The exit was in the middle of the platform, by a sign saying WAITING AREA in Chinese and English. Robert took the left-hand stairs and crossed Broadway to the north-west corner of the intersection, as instructed. Opposite him rose the off-white National City Bank of New York, built in Egyptian Revival style in 1927, now housing a shoe store. The GPS signal returned with an accuracy of 40 feet, and he headed west. The Quad directed him to make a right turn as soon as he could. The waypoint was just under half a mile away.

He passed shopfronts selling knock-off bags and belts, perfume and clothing, a backrub place, a music equipment and electronics store with huge speakers in the street, a closed hardware store, an industrial plastics store covered in yellow graffiti, and arrived at the corner of Mercer Street.

He made a right. The smell of urine hit him immediately on the heavily spray-painted, run-down first block. Then, as he approached the corner of Grand Street, the Cast-Iron District began and elegant former SoHo warehouses came into view, housing galleries and up-market clothing stores, residential lofts and trendy restaurants.

The Quad buzzed and Terri returned. 'Once you're on Mercer just keep going straight till you recover the signal, and listen. There'll be a stop or two along the way —'

'That story?'

'Did you like it? It contains today's agenda, a little bit at least.'

'The being of light? That's me?'

'It's all you, Robert, in a sense. We are stripping down your identity, piece by piece. Then, if all goes well, you clothe yourself again. But in a new form. In light. Imagine me taking off my crown now. Can you? And stop when you get to Eve's Delight.'

It was just north of Grand, a glass shopfront leading to a virtually empty foyer, with the wares discreetly set further back from the street. It was half past two. It was a sex shop, one of the classier ones, run by women. Not his usual kind of haunt, though Kat and he had playfully explored a couple in their earlier days.

Robert stopped and looked up before going in. To the south, the Gothic tower of the Woolworth Building was perfectly framed against the deep blue sky. To the north, framed equally perfectly, he saw the metal spire of the Chrysler Building. Its seven parabolic arcs shimmered in the sunlight.

'Go in, Robert. There's something waiting for you here.'

'This isn't the waypoint. Is there a cache here?'

'No, the cache comes later. This is just a present, to help with today's activities. Ask at the counter.'

He went in, feeling slightly awkward. A friendly woman with multicoloured hair and a nose stud greeted him.

'I understand there's something here for me to pick up? My name's Robert.'

She gave him a relaxed, welcoming smile. 'Hi, Robert. How are you today? Let me check.'

She looked under the counter. 'It's your lucky day. Your wife left this for you.'

She produced an orange-and-black plastic bag with his name clipped to it on a card. 'She did?'

'Would you like me to go through it? She asked me just to explain a couple of things.'

'Er . . . sure.'

She took on a happy, matter-of-fact, unalluring voice as she removed the items from the bag.

'You may want to stretch the cock ring a couple of times before you use it the first time, and lubricate it a little . . . it goes on before you're fully erect. There's a diagram included.'

'Wow.'

'If you're not fully familiar with them, the main thing of course is to take it off if you feel pain or discomfort, and don't leave it on for too long after sex . . . there's some lubricant here . . . the blindfold is self-explanatory . . . oooh, I love pin-wheels. They won't pierce the skin, but they can be very intense, you might want to start slowly with that . . . I think that's it?'

Robert stood in a speechless daze, feeling completely awkward. He couldn't use these things with Terri. He didn't even know how. Yet she had read him well: part of him was enjoying being teased.

'Is everything OK, sir?'

'My wife's been . . . busy.'

She smiled. 'Will there be anything else? No rush, if you'd like to look around.'

'No, that's . . . how much is all that?'

'It's taken care of, sir.'

He emerged on to the sidewalk. 'I've just taken off my earrings, Robert. Let's walk.'

'That was . . .'

'Yes?'

'I mean, I'm not unfamiliar . . .'

'No.'

'But I hadn't ever . . .'

'Relax, Robert. You and I have some talking to do. If you need some help with it, I can promise you it's all a necessary part of the Path.'

He passed Pearl River on his right, the giant Chinese goods store that went all the way through to Broadway, like some of the graffiti-sprayed vacant lots. He crossed Broome.

'Count the lotus flowers, Robert.'

'Huh?'

'Learn to look and you'll see.'

He stopped outside a children's store called Enchanted Forest and looked around him. 'Don't see anything.'

'Learn to look and you'll see.'

On the other side of the street there was a design in the black iron columns of an old warehouse. He crossed to look more closely. It was a flower like a lotus, repeated on several of the columns, a flower of black iron. He counted. 'There are eleven, Terri.'

'Look at it another way.'

'Another way? How?'

'You'll see. Learn to say yes. Use your eyes.'

'I am.'

'Use them better.'

What was she getting at? Eyes. I's, to say yes. Aye, aye. II.

'I have it. Roman numerals, I and I.'

'So what's the answer?'

'Two.'

'Good. Remember that. It fits the sequence. Part of the next password. What did Ishtar take off next?'

'After the earrings? Her necklace, I think.'

He passed a big warehouse of Indian goods, then a hip clothing store.

'There goes mine.'

He was at the corner of Mercer and Spring.

'It was all brothels along here in the nineteenth century,' Terri said. 'Keep moving. What did she take off at the fourth gate?'

He could sense water flowing underground. Streams and grass and greenery long gone.

A sign drew his attention, and he photographed it with the Quad: DANGER. HOLLOW SIDEWALK. Indeed. He no longer trusted anything, even the ground under his feet.

'Umm . . . breast ornaments.'

'There goes my bra . . . You read *Neuromancer*, Robert?'

'William Gibson, right? No.'

'Scene where the hero Case is plugged via computer into the sensations of the street samurai chick so he can follow where she goes and see what she sees . . . they call it simstim?'

'Didn't read it.'

'She runs a finger around her nipple to give him a taste of how it works . . . I love that scene. It's so hot.'

Robert wanted to say he was married. The words wouldn't come. She knew anyway. And just in one sense, just for a few hours, he realized he didn't want to be. He was starting to no longer recognize himself.

He passed an antiques and bric-a-brac store, then a lingerie store with mannequins in provocative poses in the window. He looked away, trying to cool himself down. He came to the corner of Prince Street, outside Fanelli's Bar. The GPS signal kicked back in, accuracy 62 feet, and 'Arriving Destination' flashed up on the Quad screen.

'I'm at the waypoint,' he said. It was nearly three o'clock.

'Well done. This was a brothel too. And a speakeasy. It has a hidden room downstairs. Secret entrance via a closet in the bar. Now, you'll need a clue.'

'I'm ready.'

'First, what was the fifth thing she took off?'

'Her girdle of precious stones. Didn't know they had them back then.'

'Think studded belt, maybe belly-chain, garter-belt, that kind of thing. There goes mine.'

'What's at the end of this, Terri?'

'I am, Robert. And you are. Ready for your clue?'

'Yes.'

'When I saw where the waypoint was, I couldn't resist. I've had some time to prepare this one. I did it myself. It's better than the one the Watchman sent me.

> *'In a curtained room, in a secret bower*
> *Seek the sacred rose, find the holy flower*
> *She's on display, and ready to play*
> *And none can resist her, once they have kissed her*
> *To rescue moon's daughter*
> *Pass the Trial by Water.'*

Robert scribbled it down.

'I'm your dream creature, Robert. Come find me. There go my anklets and bracelets.'

He started to walk back towards Eve's Delight, confused. It was too far from the waypoint, though. What did she mean? The secret room at Fanelli's?

He'd barely begun walking when he stopped again. *On display.*

'You're getting warm.'

The window of the lingerie store.

Curtained room . . .

He stared at the mannequin on the left. Long black hair, wearing just black panties and thigh-highs, black opera gloves . . .

'You're getting very warm.'

'You're inside.'

'Hot . . . come in and ask for your wife. But take a good long look at the mannequin in the window, the one who's standing up on the left. That's what I'm wearing.'

'Terri —'

'Please. Do it now.'

He walked into the store. The décor was silver-grey and pink. A woman in her twenties in a form-fitting pink uniform came to greet him, her breasts pushed up into a welcoming décolletage. Two other women, dressed identically, fussed with the displays in the background. He was the only man in the store.

'I'm looking for my wife? My name is . . .'

'Robert? Hi, how are you? I'm Gemma. She's expecting you.'

She led him past racks of lace finery to a mirrored space at the back of the store. She gestured to a circular sofa in deep red-orange. There were several changing rooms against the back wall, each with a silver-grey curtain.

'Please have a seat for a moment, I'll tell her you're here.'

She put her head behind the second curtain from the left and spoke in a low voice. Robert heard giggling.

Gemma looked over to him and beckoned. 'She has something she wants to show you,' she whispered.

Robert went over to the curtain. Gemma gave his arm a squeeze and walked away. He peeped behind the curtain.

And there was Terri.

'Hi.'

'Hi.'

She was wearing a short silver-grey silk gown. Short black hair. Silvered wrap-around sunglasses. Petite. Smiling at him.

She let the gown fall to the ground. She wore just a black thong, black stockings, black opera gloves. Just like the mannequin.

Blood raced from his brain.

'We meet at last, Robert. Give me your left hand.'

He put it through the curtain.

She took it and made it into a loose fist, separating out just the index finger. She raised the finger to her lips and blew softly on it. She gave a crooked smile.

'Robert . . . don't say anything . . .'

She parted her lips and, with the tip of her tongue, teased the very end of his finger. She stopped, looked at him, smiled to herself, licked very softly again. He tried to pull his hand away.

'This is forbidden, isn't it?' she said. 'That's why it's so . . . delicious. Don't speak.'

He stopped trying.

She opened her mouth and placed the tip of his finger just inside. She breathed heat but did not close her lips. Removed his finger. Licked along its length with the tip of her tongue, barely touching.

'You . . . and I . . . have some serious . . . talking to do.'

She made a circle of her lips and closed it around the first joint of his finger. Electricity tore around his body. He leaned into the curtain between them. She placed her left hand on his chest through the curtain.

'Pleased to see me?'

She began to suck his finger rhythmically, slowly, slightly deeper each time.

'Stop,' he said.

She slowed, halted, kept her lips squeezed together on the tip and slowly pulled his finger away, letting a string of saliva form. She stretched it till it broke.

'I can't resist this,' Robert whispered. 'I'll fail.'

'Silly . . . you're not supposed to resist it. Now help me buy a corset.'

She pushed his chest through the curtain.

'Step back, I'm coming out.'

He went back to the sofa, trying to hide his erection. He felt light-headed, his ears ringing. Terri emerged from behind the curtain in her silk robe and called to Gemma. 'We'd like to try a corset or two. Can you suggest anything?'

She moved in a way that suggested both vulnerability and iron self-possession at once. Gemma brought a flimsy black number and a solider pink creation with black drawstrings. Terri held them both against herself for Robert, over her gown.

'Which do you like better, darling?'

'The pink.'

'Would you lace me up in a moment, Gemma?'

Terri walked back into the changing room with the corset and drew the curtain.

'She'll look so good in that,' Gemma said to him. 'She has such a beautiful neck and shoulders.'

Robert smiled and nodded.

'She said it's your anniversary? Congratulations! How many?'

He coughed.

'First?'

Terri came out from behind the curtain. Gemma moved behind her and placed one hand on Terri's back as she pulled the laces taut.

'Tighter,' Terri said. 'It feels so sexy to have it tight.'

'You look great,' Robert said.

'Buy it for me? I'll keep it on.'

She took his arm as they left the store. She wore a sharp executive black jacket and knee-length skirt over the corset and stockings.

'We're not going far. Stay close.'

They headed back to Fanelli's at the corner and crossed Prince Street. Almost immediately, under a great iron clock, Terri steered them through an unmarked black door in a nameless red-brick building.

A lobby like a hipster library greeted them. Books lined a full wall to their right. A few people sat at low tables, pecking at laptops or chatting among themselves. A whitewashed blank wall ahead dazzled Robert. Terri led them past the reception desk, where the young lady smiled and waved at her, directly to the elevators.

New York, August 27, 2004

When Horace assumed the role of the Watchman, sinking deep into a meditative state, a detached coldness came upon him. As loyal as he was to his charges, he could no longer be their friend. As the Watchman he had to be ready to take unsentimental decisions, even be prepared to sacrifice one of them if necessary. He hoped it would never come to that. He held the details of the plan in his mind and examined every detail. It must not fail. It would not, he fervently prayed, though at every stage there were great risks.

He watched the players in motion, each pursuing their fragments of the puzzle, each acting on the instructions given to them on a need-to-know basis.

Time was running out, but they were all on schedule.

The seven minor keys were arranged along Manhattan in a special array. The maker of the Device had extended them like an antenna, the Watchman now understood, in order to increase the power of his original intended attack.

It had been Adam who had captured the maker's PDA on Blackout Day, but the Watchman had not trusted Adam with the information it contained. From the very day of the Blackout, it had been clear that souls had been conjoined. Entanglements created. The seed of Adam's corrosion had been in him since that day. The Watchman had instead entrusted the PDA to Katherine, in deepest secrecy. Urged her to decode the files, thresh the good data from the noise. It had taken a year, but she had cracked them. Mysteries remained. But she had been able to extract the good waypoints, without realizing their full significance.

As soon as she'd accessed them, barely a few days earlier, the PDA had lit up and fired off a signal. The maker of the Ma'rifat' had clearly booby-trapped the PDA to send it if the waypoints were decoded.

Kat had told the Watchman immediately. And the Watchman had concluded a second Device had now been armed. The clock had started ticking.

The Watchman had seen what the waypoints traced. He saw the full picture. He was able to maintain control of the game and to dole out the parts as required. To Adam. To Katherine. To Terri, in part behind Adam's back. To Robert. Each would have to experience loss and pain in order to play their part. Without a delicate balance, all would be lost.

Once Kat had cracked the codes of the PDA, a summons had quickly reached Adam to attend a meeting with the Iwnw. For a year Adam had been resisting them, and they had not pushed too hard, mysteriously waiting for the moment that now clearly had come. He could no longer refuse. It was then, as soon as the invitation arrived, that Horace had decided what form Robert's trials would have to take.

The second trial would be sex. Robert would be led to a situation in which he would be subject to the powerful, disruptive forces that dwelled in sexual desire. These were the energies of water – second only in raw power to those of earth. To pass the trial, he would have to tap into those forces and fold them fully into his progress along the Path, neither squandering them nor weakening them. Like many people, he was cut off from their full force.

The Watchman saw the necessary changes in Robert's relationship with Katherine that would be brought about, and in Terri's relationship with Adam.

All must suffer, he said to himself. Alas, all must suffer.

Robert would be forced to choose between being true to himself and being true to a sacred vow. They would tear him down by beginning to destroy his marriage.

He would recover a second key, in the form of one circle splitting from another. And he would begin to reassemble a body, his own new body of light.

Adam had asked to meet Robert at a couple of points along the Path. The Watchman had been unsure, not intending to share the specific waypoints with Adam, wary of fully trusting him once everything had begun. Adam had claimed it would help them both: as Robert grew stronger, that strength would help to slow Adam's own corrosion. And it would help Robert focus his powers by confronting Adam at key points. He'd suggested the first and third trials, maybe the fifth. The Watchman had refused, saying only he would monitor Robert's progress. If Robert needed to confront Adam, he would send Adam the coordinates in due time.

The Watchman reviewed the remaining five trials, one by one. As Robert climbed the ladder of the different stages of the Path, each energy he tapped into would become less raw and more organized; finer and more capable of intentional direction. And each one would become more lethal. Without the combined powers of earth and water, he would be killed by the higher energies themselves, if not by the Brotherhood of Iwnw, before he could go any further.

May heaven help us, the Watchman said to himself.

Miami, September 1998

Adam smiled in delight as Robert joined them at dinner on Saturday evening. He boomed: 'What news?'

'Georges is giving the Keys a real pounding.'

'Do you think he's related to the pianist in the lobby?'

'Good one.'

'Does your presence mean we're safe?'

'Taking a break. But I'm afraid I have to miss your grand finale.

157

We're not out of the woods yet. Looks like it'll veer towards the West Coast and the Panhandle. But it could still switch again and come straight back at us.'

Everyone else was already finishing their main course. Katherine had kept a seat vacant for him next to her. He grimaced an apology.

'And so,' Adam said, without rancour, 'we must solve the mystery without the services of our good friend Robert. Let us apply ourselves.'

❖

Later that night, Katherine stretched on the bed in Robert's room.

She recounted the whole experience Adam had put together for them, more in amusement than in puzzlement. He'd locked them in hotel rooms, sent them hunting for clues in ice buckets, had them cracking rudimentary codes. At one point, in one of several rooms rented for the event, he'd pulled a conjuring trick on them, asking them to place all their money, passports, driving licences and photographs of loved ones into a metal bin, and then appearing to set fire to its contents. 'He almost got himself lynched right there,' Katherine said.

At the climax, in a breathtaking vaulted suite on the thirteenth floor that had once housed a Prohibition-era casino, Adam had told them the murderer was in the room among them. Then he'd said the victim was too. He'd asked each of them to open a sealed envelope containing the true identity of both the killer and the victim.

Katherine's envelope had contained a photograph of Katherine. They found they all had photographs of themselves. And, just as they realized this and puzzled protests were starting, Adam had set off some kind of high-intensity flash, like a magnesium flare, and vanished. All that remained was a note inviting them all to stay through Sunday night at his expense, together with a passage translated from a twelfth-century masterpiece of Persian literature, *The Conference of the Birds*, which he recommended to them. Their experiences had been intended to dramatize and reveal the fabled mystical work in a fresh light, he added.

'I think he lost a couple of friends, but to be honest I really enjoyed it,' Katherine said. 'It was all about the language of the birds, I guess.'

'I've no idea what that means.'

'That's OK. Let's not talk any more about Adam.'

Now she spoke from the depth of her memories, her eyes still on the invisible, secret world she had left behind, the one of which she could never fully speak.

She told him about the man she had lost.

'He was as brave as a lion, in his own way. Went in to spy for us. To betray his country for the greater good of the world. He was one of the people who actually think that way.'

Robert assumed it had involved nuclear secrets of some kind.

'He was already being squeezed by his own intelligence people, by the local Mukhabarat. He didn't care for them. They put pressure on him through his family. It was tawdry and stupid – he said they weren't even asking him sensible questions. So he came to us. And I made myself the greater good of the world. That's what I was to him. For him there was no world without me, and its future happiness was whatever made me happy.'

'You were his . . . controller? You ran him?'

'He ran himself. But, yes, in the organigram of who was to blame, I was the one. I didn't discover him. Finders don't usually get to be keepers. He was actually a walk-in. *I wish to betray my country, sooner rather than later, and I am also in a great hurry to fall in love.* But he was mine to exploit, and I was good at it.'

'You shouldn't despise yourself.'

'I wonder, if it hadn't been me, whether anyone would have done. For him, I mean.'

'To the extent that they were male with bad breath and a hairy back, I doubt it.'

'Any woman, then.'

'Were there that many of you? In your line of work?'

'Enough.'

'But he was given to you.'

'Yes.'

'And there are strictures, I assume, about falling in love with those one is controlling. Running.'

'Yes. *Verboten*. Whereas vice versa may prove useful.'

'Was it your head for maths he loved?'

'The fact that I could discuss the science at a professional level was helpful. You know how well trained we were. And it was platonic.'

'Willingly so?'

'No, of course not. He wanted to consummate, and I didn't let him.'

'But you didn't crush his hopes.'

'Not once I saw which way it was going. That it would serve as a tool. And then one day . . .'

'Yes?'

'He said something. It won't sound shattering or epic or anything. It was silly, really.'

'What?'

'He said he was always afraid. Every day, all night, all the time. Except when he saw me, and we talked about mathematics. He said it stilled his mind.'

Robert looked at her quizzically.

'And something broke for me. I realized I couldn't treat him like that. That doing so made me part of the problem. Definitively, resolutely, not the greater good of the world. Quite the contrary.'

'And you told your superiors and were pulled off the case and never saw him again.'

'No.'

'I imagine they call that being unprofessional?'

'They have lots of words, if they find out about it.'

'But they didn't.'

'They didn't. And I sent him in because if I didn't, we wouldn't be saving the world. There was no way not to send him. He could love me only if that's what we were doing. And somewhere along the line I started to believe.'

'Can I ask where this was?'

'Does it matter? His name was Tariq. He was giving such a lot. Everything. I felt I had to give him something in return. Something of value to him, something commensurate.' She sighed. 'I gave him something I shouldn't have.'

'What?'

She frowned. 'We'd talked a lot about the great Arabic thinkers. The philosophers, the scientists, the alchemists. He was intensely proud of his lineage, as he called it.'

'Yes.'

'You remember the Newton document that Adam was the guardian of?'

'I do.'

'It quoted several of the great Muslim scholars. On the nature and manufacture of the great secret. On the ways to combine glass and metals. I gave him a copy.'

'Did Adam know?'

'No. I trusted Tariq. And the formula wasn't complete. But it's haunted me ever since.'

'What did he do with it?'

'He called it just a beautiful artefact, and a reminder of lost knowledge. Then he gave it back to me. Trust for trust. For several years we had good material. The best. No one else had it. Not the Americans. No one. Grandma would have been proud of me.'

'And then?'

'And then he wanted to come out.'

'Not so keen on saving the world after all?'

'You've no idea of the strain he was under. I was told to keep him in-country.'

'He wouldn't be much use once he'd been let out, I imagine.'

'He was priceless. We owed him. But we pushed harder. Eventually it was agreed he could come out, but only if we squeezed every last drop of intelligence we could from him first. So we did. And we said we'd arrange something for his family. His father. Get him out of the hands of the Mukhabarat.'

'Around when is this, now?'

'1997, late summer. So I arranged his extraction.'

'Just you?'

'A team of us. I was in charge.'

He sat still, waiting for her to go on.

'We were all set. Van, secret compartment, funny passports. He'd confirmed he was coming. Yellow chalk mark the previous day, pre-set location. It was a grey morning. Overcast.'

'Cold?'

'Yes. And . . . he never came. He just . . . wasn't there.'

'You waited.'

'Till it was dangerous. Beyond dangerous. We all agreed to push it. But we couldn't stay for ever.'

'He was arrested?'

'Never knew. Probably, after a fashion. They would have hurt him. For days. Then I assume he died. I never heard. It makes it harder to grieve, in some ways, but in other ways I'd rather not know. There's always the slim hope that he survived.'

'I'm so sorry.'

'And so I got myself out of the service.'

'I'm glad.'

'There was one other thing.'

'Your gift?'

'It died. I hadn't truly realized I had it, until it went away.'

He tried to react kindly, without abandoning his scepticism. 'Kat, I always had the idea it was empathy, or being highly aware of body language, or something similar. Intuition, or tapping the unconscious. You remember how you used to talk, at university.'

'That's what I said, I know. But it was much more than that. When I was a girl, I thought everyone could do what I did. But no one else heard what I heard. It was like music, like wonderful harmonies. It was as if everything resonated, and I could attune myself to people and things, and *learn* from them. I'd talk to people, or even just touch them, and *words* would form in my mind.'

'You heard voices?'

She sighed. 'No, not voices. Or maybe inner voices. But the words that came would be exactly what people most needed to hear, or wanted to say. I'd find my lips forming the words even before we'd spoken. Words like *lonely*, or *vulnerable*, or . . .' She stopped and smiled.

'Randy?'

'Quite often, Mr Reckliss.'

'And you lost it all?'

'I lost some of it, the night of the fire.'

'Let's not talk about that.'

She looked at him in amusement. 'You're still terrified of that night. After all these years.'

'It's dead. It's in the past. Go on.'

'Then when I lost Tariq, it turned off completely.'

'Just like that?'

'Like creeping cotton wool. Over several days.'

'Has it ever come back?'

'I'm not sure I want it back. It was very useful, when I was doing that work. Now I associate it with loss. With betrayal. I've gone as far as I ever want to go down the danger road. I'm finished with it. The older I get, the more I realize I need solidity. A man who'll always be there. A rock. Someone like you.'

Robert kissed her.

'Stay with me.'

'I think I will.'

New York, August 27, 2004

Robert and Terri rode up to the sixth floor.

The hotel-room doors were of heavy solid grey metal, like brushed steel. A little green magnetic sticker on their door said *Yes, please.*

In the room, they stood facing each other. Terri filled the room with her presence. She was sexual gravity.

'Robert. Time to talk. You think I'm going to have sex with you now?'

163

'I was hoping you would want to. And I was hoping you wouldn't want to.'

'Understandable. You are married, after all.'

'I haven't been touched in six months. I could melt for a woman's flesh on mine. But . . .'

'I know.'

'Who are you?'

'I am your needs. From the Robert who is still a gauche horny fifteen-year-old, all the way through to the Robert who is a gauche, horny 42-year-old. All the Roberts are OK. All the Roberts who want to fuck me are good. There's no need to feel bad about any of them. And all the Roberts who feel guilty about wanting to fuck me are OK too. You're a good man.'

She held her head with such self-possession. Yet she looked entirely vulnerable. He marvelled at her.

'Robert, these next few hours are a sealed-off time and place. It's all about us. It's sacred, and it's necessary, and no one will ever know. I need you to do some things for me, and to me . . . And you need me to do some things for you, and to you. It will make you feel good. It will make us both well. It will strip you of your fear and fill it with well-being. It will give you something you've never had, something everyone needs, that everyone should have.'

'What is that?'

She kept her tone light, almost playful. 'Everyone is unique. No one responds in the same way, no one has the same psycho-sexual needs. But we all need the same outcome. It's just a question of finding the right path for each person to get there.'

'What is that place?'

'It can't be talked about. It can only be experienced. You're afraid of the God in the sex. You're afraid of what you'll experience if you fully lose control, or fully take control. It scares you to be fully in the moment. Sex is like a spell or a charm, but you've never let it take you to the end of the line. You always pop back out and start observing yourself. If you fear the God in anything, it's because you fear the God in yourself. You've locked something away so deeply behind a veil of fear that you can't let it out any more, and it's killing you. And we need to free it. Otherwise you're no use to anyone. And certainly no use to me.'

He should leave, he knew. But he also knew he wasn't going to.

'Sex is sex,' he said. 'It's wonderful, but at the end of the day it's just a physical spasm.'

He remembered the night of the fire. Sex with Katherine. His first time, though he hadn't told her. And ever since that night, the association of sex with destruction, with harming others, with starting the fire ... ever since then, the disconnection from his own body as he let it pursue its own rhythms, the delightful but empty physical release ...

'It's never too late to learn something new, Robert.'

'Terri. Look me in the eyes.'

'You've worked out my secret?'

He saw himself reflected, distorted, in the silvered curves of her sunglasses. He hadn't before, but now he did.

'You're blind.'

'I am. And yet I see.'

'How? What happened?'

'I got hurt on the day of the Blackout. A lot of things went down that day.'

'Tell me.'

'I will. But we have something more pressing to take care of first.'

She slowly unbuttoned her jacket, lingering over each button, and let it drop from her fingertip to the floor. The corset emphasized the grace of her neck, the full curve of her breasts.

'Terri, you're amazing.'

'You have no idea. I love this hotel. Feel the sheets. To be honest, the thread-count alone is going to make me come at least once.' She unzipped her skirt and let it fall, then stepped daintily out of it. 'Make love to me, Robert.'

A heartbeat rocked his body so hard he thought he'd fall. He was dizzy, his ears ringing, heat and heavy blood flushing through his body. Her sexual magnetism gripped him, pulling him towards her smiling lips, her mesmerizing perfume. The sight and smell of her body ignited purples and violets in his eyes, birdsong in his memory, aching lust in every fibre of his being.

He stepped forward and lifted her clear off the ground, pushing her up against the wall as she wrapped her legs tightly around his waist. She moaned, arms around his neck, one hand pulling his hair, the stiff ribs of the corset pressing against his chest as he kissed her mouth, her face, her neck.

He wheeled around and took two steps towards the bed before flinging them both down on it, landing with his elbows either side of her, then kneeling up to unbuckle his belt. He undid his shirt, then stopped for a moment, breathing hard, as she held up an open palm to him.

'Take everything off,' she said. 'I'll be here.'

She slipped off her thong and leaned back, one hand behind her head and the other flitting over her body, over the stockings and black lace, to her neck, to her thighs. When he was naked, he leaped straight back on to her, beside himself, not knowing himself, thrusting deeply, thrilling to her cry of surprise and pleasure, lost in his own body and its sheer pounding weight as she pulled him into her.

He was lost to himself, lost to the world, pushing and pushing. Time ceased to pass. Only when he had felt her peak twice, and was preparing to let go, did he notice her hands snaking up his back, from his tailbone to his shoulder blades and the base of his skull. He heard her intoning words softly, none he understood, as she breathed deeply under him, drawing him in, pulling him down.

She cooed into his ear: 'Slow down now, lover. Stop for a moment. Time to show you something new.'

She held him tight inside her, running her hands down again to the base of his spine, whispering calming words. He breathed deeply, staring down at her taut cheekbones, smiling lips, pale transparent skin.

'Most people don't understand,' she said, 'that orgasm is a full-body experience, and a full-mind experience, a full-soul experience, that has very little to do with ejaculation in the man. I won't let you ejaculate. If I do, you'll disperse all the energy we've been building up, and are going to build up in the next few hours. But I'll show you something better.'

He felt a shuddering heat ignite at the base of his spine, licking like flame along his back and out to the tips of his fingers and toes. She was holding her hands just over his tailbone, then weaving her fingers up and down above his back. His whole body began to rock as his mind filled with torrents of violet light. A deep growl began in the depths of his chest. And then he was consumed in a roaring, lung-emptying, body-racking howl of pleasure that lasted till he no longer knew who or where he was.

When he recovered consciousness, he was still inside her, as erect as ever.

'Good boy,' she whispered. 'Good boy.'

They made love for hours.

Every square millimetre, every tendon and joint and curve. Recounting and honouring and full attention given, full and loving care given and received. Naming and knowing each corner, each pore, each lash, each taste, each limb. Interconnecting of all. Knowing of all. Endless and without time. The tracing of the body of the lover is the tracing of the pattern of the city, and the honouring of each part of the body is the rebuilding of the mystical body, the building and remembering of the body of light.

Eventually they rested, her head nestled on his chest. He reached to the bedside table for a bottle of water from the ice bucket. Her silver shades and necklace lay next to it, along with his wedding ring. Her eyes were a wild, piercing green. He watched her in the mirror.

'You can't see me.'

'I can feel you. That's all I need.'

'You have great imagination.'

'No, I have great perversity. It's far more fun.'

'I've never felt so alive.'

'We're not done yet, baby.'

'I've no idea what time it is.'

'That's a good thing, Robert. Recover your power . . . with some sex in the shower.'

'In a moment. Not quite yet.'

'They have great showers here. They have jets of water that fire all the way along your spine. Or if you turn round . . . they just seem to hit all your erogenous zones at once.'

He kissed her head. 'So I think I've worked out the location of cache number two.'

'Tell me.'

'It's you. Your body.'

'Bravo.'

'The cached object is on your person.'

'It is. Or it was.'

'Your necklace? The one that was nestling so happily between your breasts until I took it off?'

'The same.'

'If you know where the caches are and what's in them, why do you need me to go and empty them?'

'I don't know where the rest are. But since this trial involved meeting you myself, I had to know where the waypoint was. And the Watchman sent me the original clue early enough for me to work out where the cache was. It was hidden on the roof of this hotel, actually. I knew this would work better if I could wear the key myself. So I took it and strung it on a chain.'

'Who writes the clues? The ditties?'

'I don't know. But, as for the rest of the keys, you need to collect them all. It's because of what you become each time you find one.'

'What do I become?'

'More powerful. More beautiful.'

'How so?'

'More able to help Adam. To help all of us.'

'Can I do it? Can anyone do it?'

'You've made a good start. Don't go thinking it's all going to be like this, though. You need to build sexual energy on top of the fighting energy, the killing force, from yesterday. Then tomorrow is a different challenge. You won't survive tomorrow without today.'

He was silent for a moment. His body was glowing with relaxed heat, with the memory of her touch. Yet death was stalking them, somehow.

'I understand now the second line of a letter I received. When I was eighteen. *Give to receive*. That's just good advice on dealing with others, I guess, but good love advice too. Good sex advice. Then *seed is not sensation*. That's what you showed me. I thought that was just a thing yogis did.'

'There's a core wisdom behind lots of practices and beliefs that might seem different,' Terri said. 'You are on the Path of that wisdom.'

He reached over and picked up the necklace. The pendant was made of a light metal and was a reddish gold, like the Malice Box.

'I recognize this shape,' he said. 'What's it called, this fish shape?'

'Vesica piscis.'

'Is this the object? I need to take it.'

'Take it. Guard it. Keep it safe.'

'What kind of keys are these, Terri?'

'To hell. If they are misused.'

'To hell. So how does this all work? Who's behind this impending attack? Horace said it was some kind of soul bomb, not just a truck of ammonium nitrate. Tell me.'

'All I know is this. Adam was terrified about going to see the people he went to see on Wednesday. They are the ultimate bad guys in this. They need people to work through. They wait and wait, and then, when they see a chance, they attach themselves to someone in psycho-spiritual distress and slowly twist them to their ends. This Device, this Ma'rifat', is built using very rare materials, impossible to find, and using very old knowledge, the kind of knowledge you find on the Path. It resonates to people's souls. Amplifies what it finds there. There's a reason that the true Path is not widely advertised. It's too dangerous. It was built by someone whose pain and suffering attracted the Iwnw, and now it serves their purpose.'

'What is their purpose?'

'Well, the last time they got any traction in the world was in

Bosnia. And they were able to influence some key Nazis in World War Two. People around Heinrich Himmler. They ride that kind of wave. Adam's grandfather fought them, back then.'

'The SS? The Nazis?'

'These people. Adam called them the Brotherhood of Iwnw.'

He stared at the ceiling. 'I was nearly killed yesterday for the bullet casing. Was that them?'

'I told you, you were protected.'

'It damn well didn't feel like it.'

'If you hadn't been, you would have been killed.'

'I take it someone's going to want to kill me for this one too?'

'It's already harder to kill you. You're already stronger. Let's hope not.'

'Are you in danger too?'

'I can look after myself. But there is danger for all of us. And somehow, it even involves your wife. I don't know how.'

He spoke sharply. 'Why Katherine?'

'Something to do with the Blackout. That's all I understand. Everything's to do with the Blackout.'

'That's the day our baby was conceived.'

'I know. Something changed that day, for all of us. Adam and I have only been truly together since that day. Since . . . I can't tell you some of this.'

'I want to know everything.'

'I'd had very deep intuition all my life, it was normal to me. But after that day my abilities increased – tenfold, more. It was as though I'd been kicked, slam. As though I'd expanded within myself, somehow, as though my inner body, the one I imagined being made of light, suddenly amped up and blew through my skin. It blew my eyes to hell, I don't know how to describe it . . . Suddenly I couldn't see, but I could start fires in people's minds. Suddenly I could feel whatever it was that people were yearning for in their lives, what buttons to press. It wasn't all good, believe me. At all. I could make things happen, I could just *know* things about people, I could do things I'd only dreamed about . . . read people to their core . . . read their needs . . .'

'How well can you read me? Stupid question?'

'I can read you as though you were made of glass, my dear.'

'Can you turn it off?'

'I have to. I have to shield myself from it. The acuity of perception is too great. I'd die. At first it made me live way too much for other people. But I've found my centre now. When it's worth while, I can turn it full on. You, Robert. You're worth while. That's why I can be your dream creature. I can see what you need. And I can give it to you.'

'What do I need next?'

'Actually let's talk about what I need next.'

'And what's that?'

She handed him the cock ring. 'Take a wild guess. This will help.'

They made love again, ate, showered, made love, each exploration melding into the next. They were drunk on each other, on pleasure. Terri seemed to live one perpetual orgasm. She gave him two more all-consuming, full-body climaxes that left him gasping, shattered, yet bursting with raw energy.

As she floated between peaks at one point, nearing another, she handed him the nerve wheel. It was a rounded metal device with dull spikes that looked like spurs for a horse.

'Very, very gently . . . very . . . run this over my skin,' she said. 'I can only take it when I'm this turned on.'

She sighed and closed her eyes as he did so. She trembled at the sensations, cooing and moaning, 'Softly . . . softly . . .'

She reached a slow and intense peak, shaking against him, then took the wheel from his hand. After a few moments of deep breathing, she took his hand.

'The path you are on is called the Path of Seth. It is based on the idea of dismembering the subject – that's you – and building him up again. In a moment we're going to do a kind of ritual around that. Something to help you on your way.'

It was getting dark outside. He barely recognized himself.

'Tell me more about Terri. Where are you from?'

'New York. Brooklyn. The rough part.'

'So what is identity management? You're a computer whiz?'

'Oh, Robert. Now you sound like an old man. Please.'

'What?'

'*Computer whiz?* I have lots of names, lots of identities. This one is all for you. And yes, I know computers. I put myself through college.'

'Is Terri your real name?'

'No.'

'Do you have anything as mundane as a job?'

'No. With gifts like mine, money comes to you.'

'Do you really make videos?'

'Maybe. Nothing you've ever heard of, if I do.'

'And you seek God.'

'If I had to choose a religion, I'd say I'm a Sufi. But all labels are meaningless: the question is what's in your heart. I am what I do. If I said I was a Buddhist, would it make a difference? A Wiccan? What's in my heart?'

'What about the vesica piscis?'

'Get it. Look at it.'

He took it from the bedside table.

'Second rung of the ladder. It's the shape you get when two cells divide. It's creation. A circle with a point in the centre, then another circle, each with its edge going through the centre of the other. It makes a fish shape. It makes a pointed oval shape. Church entrances are shaped like it. And vulvas. Not a coincidence.'

'I want this to last for ever.'

'It will.'

'But in this world, I'll have to go home at some point.'

'Everything in its time. We're not done.'

'We're not?'

'Lie back.'

She handed him the blindfold.

'What kind of ritual is this?'

'Trust me.'

She sat up and locked her eyes on his. Mesmerizing emerald

depths drew him in, drew him up. She leaned down to kiss him. He closed his eyes and lost himself in the kiss. He felt her slip the blindfold over his eyes.

She whispered some words, nothing he could understand. Musical, resonant words. Then he felt the nerve wheel moving slowly across his skin, marking where his arms joined his torso, then his legs, then along his sternum to his chin. It was intense, but neither painful nor sexual. She drew it along each side of his neck, then put it to one side.

The light in the room changed. The quality of the black grew lighter. She pulled off the blindfold and was kissing his still lowered eyelids. One. The other. Then both together. Then his forehead. He cracked his eyelids open and saw golden-yellow light flooding the room.

Terri was smiling at him. There were two of her. He saw an identical twin of her splitting from her body and moving to the right. A twin of light. They both glowed golden-yellow. Then they both leaned forward and kissed him on each side of his neck. Kissed down along his chest. Two tongues traced interlocking patterns down his breastbone, along his stomach.

They both looked up at him and spoke in unison. 'We're just getting started.'

'How the hell do you do that?' he hissed. 'Jesus God.'

They kissed all the lines Terri had drawn with the wheel, as though symbolically stitching him back together. This time he trembled with pleasure.

'When you build up enough power, enough energy of the right kind,' they said, still speaking in unison, 'you can project a body of light outside yourself. Like this.'

They kissed him everywhere, sharing, alternating. Then one lay down against him and slowly began to fade, seeming to melt into his flesh, while the other solidified slowly back into Terri's pale skin.

'Rest now,' she said. 'I've made a gift of my energy to you. May it strengthen you.'

*

173

He slept for a while, a smile deep in his body. The whole world was singing in his skin, and skin was all he and the whole world were made of.

Several scented candles in small glass pots burned all around the room in the half-light. She got dressed.

'I'm going to leave you to pull yourself together now,' she whispered in his ear. 'This was wonderful. You were wonderful. The clock is stopped for tonight. There is no time for us right now. But tomorrow it will run even faster. Be ready.'

'Terri –'

'Be quiet.'

Robert dozed again, this time for almost two hours, before eventually getting up and running a bath.

He had been lying in the water for a few minutes, Terri's necklace wrapped around his fingers as he gazed at the design, one vesica piscis within another, when he heard the door open.

'Terri?'

No reply.

He sat up, ready to climb out of the water.

He shouted: 'Hello?'

A figure appeared in the bathroom doorway, holding up a bedsheet between them. He vaguely saw what he thought was a woman's silhouette behind the sheet before it flew at him, covering his face and chest. A hand came behind it, forcing his head under the water, forcing the wet sheet over his nose and mouth.

Robert fought to remain calm, jamming his hands up where it seemed his attacker's head would be, trying to hold his breath. He missed, flailing against wet cloth. A gloved fist punched him in the solar plexus, and he shouted involuntarily, inhaling water. The linen tightened around his face. Now panic kicked in. He thought he heard a woman's voice as the blood roared in his ears, and he lashed and kicked upwards. He felt a hand grabbing for the necklace in his closed fist. Glass shattered as he kicked candles over.

Darkness started to rim his vision. He was at the bottom of a deep, dark well, the stones wet and slippery to the touch, clawing

174

with his fingers to pull himself up . . . He felt the water heating up as he struggled. It began to scald him. Through the sheet over his face, he suddenly saw his own arms and hands, flailing upwards, outlined in a grey-blue viscous light. The light was hot, fluid but dense, dripping from his fingers. Burning hot. With his eyes closed he could see it even more clearly. He reached upwards and grabbed the arms of his attacker. She screamed. He felt the crackle of shrivelling flesh as his hands burned into her skin.

Then the figure was gone, the bedsheet suddenly limp and knotted around him. The heat had gone out of his body as suddenly as it had come. He heaved his torso over the edge of the bath, coughing up water, gasping for breath. Steam rose from the bathtub. The necklace was still wrapped around his fingers. The door slammed.

Robert pulled himself out of the bath and rolled on to the bathroom floor. It's real, he said to himself, over and over. It's real. Dear God, it's all real. Part of him had still not quite believed that the spiritual threats Horace and Adam and Terri had spoken of were about real physical violence in the real world. He'd told himself the fight on the subway could have been a mugger, the whole thing could somehow still have been a macabre game that was spinning out of control.

Now he knew for certain: there were people who were trying to kill him, and he had the power and strength to fight back.

Little Falls, August 27, 2004

When Robert got home, no one was there. A note in the kitchen said Katherine had gone to visit her friend Claire in the West Village. She'd be back late again.

He felt relief. He couldn't lie to Katherine. It wasn't in his nature. Yet he dreaded confessing to her what he had done. It seemed to him he still smelled of Terri, smelled of sex.

It was after ten at night. He had the necklace safely in his grasp. But he didn't have his wedding ring. When he'd gone to pick it up from the bedside table, it hadn't been there. He'd uprooted everything. Nowhere to be found. He'd tried to reach Terri on the Quad. Number blocked.

He changed clothes, put his things in the washing machine, ran it. Showered. Called Katherine to say he was going to bed soon. Left her a message again. Called Claire's landline and learned Katherine was fine and had just left.

He sat alone and stared into his returning fear.

When attacked, he'd had no qualms about fighting back. He'd protected the keys. He felt good about that. And he was becoming more powerful. He felt more alive. But at what cost? He'd done a thing he'd sworn never to do, broken a vow he'd sworn never to break. There would be consequences, and he wouldn't avoid them. Yet it had felt so necessary, so right, to make love to Terri. He might not even have survived without the power she had given him. But it was going to happen again. Would he be as strong next time? He felt his stomach knot. It was real. He had no choice but to go on.

He looked for a message from Terri. She had sent him another audio file. Nothing else. It was called 'Two Knights'. It was password-protected. He tried various variations of vesica piscis. Then he remembered the black iron flowers. Two was part of the sequence, she'd said. Part of the password.

It opened to Vesica2. It was a haunting piece of operatic music for two male voices. He listened again and again. They were singing in German. Eventually he identified it through internet searches. It was from *The Magic Flute*. He found several translations, some freer than others. The part she had sent him was incomplete. It said, more or less:

> *Whoever walks this path of pain will become purified*
> *Through fire, water, air and earth.*
> *If he can overcome the fear of death*
> *Then he takes flight for heaven . . .*

He fired up the Quad and posted a short note.

What the second cache said to me
Today was the Trial by Water. Find God in the sea of sex. I have never felt
so fully known, so fully electrified, so fully comfortable with another
human being. Having her utterly in my power. Being utterly in her power.
   But my sexual desire cannot be for Terri. It has to be for Katherine. I
have to fold it back towards her.

A response came within a few minutes, but not from TerriC1111.

You have done well, Robert. You have passed the second trial.

The Watchman

A Martyr's Love Song: The Making of the Ma'rifat'

I do not address you with the splendour and flourishes of my native tongue, for I am well versed in American ways and know that you will find too much 'God is greatest' and 'praise be to Allah' discomfiting.

I was killed by my own creation on August 14, 2003.

Can you believe a man can be killed by his sins? For this is how I died, sparking the great discharge of energy that plunged the north-eastern United States into darkness on that day.

I failed in my mission, for the detonation was unintended. I came under attack at the key moment of arming the Device, and I was not sufficiently pure in my heart, mind and soul to respond safely. Although the effect was great, the power released was only a fraction of its potential.

Know simply this: there is another Ma'rifat'. There were two Devices. When the second is detonated, it will slice away that which is impurest in the impurest of cities in the impurest of nations: it will destroy Manhattan, the clitoris of the great whore, because in Manhattan it will find the richest fuel for its detonation, because Manhattan is so riddled with greed, and lust, and envy, and pride that the chain reaction, once begun, will erupt like 10,000 suns. An apocalypse of souls.

You may think what I have to say is gibberish. Let us explore that term. For what is 'gibberish' to you, what sounds like the jabbering of a madman, may simply show your prejudice and ignorance. Do you know where this word comes from? And 'alchemy', 'algebra', 'algorithm'. 'Alcohol'?

Let us look at some of these words.

For, while some will say 'gibberish' merely imitates the sound of nonsensical talk, others will tell you of Jabir ibn Hayyan, known to you in the West as Geber, the greatest Muslim alchemist of all, also a geometer, a mathematician, all knowledge being one to the wise; for his language and concepts were so subtle, and his encoding of the great secrets so effective, that none but the finest minds could pierce the 'gibberish' of his writings to discover the gold beneath.

Or perhaps we should take 'algebra' — once also used in English to mean bone-setting, did you know that? — which derives from al-jabr, *Arabic for bringing broken parts back together, used by the ninth-century mathematician Abu Ja'far Muhammad ibn Musa Al-Khwarizmi of Baghdad as the title of his* Kitab Al-Jabr w'al-Muqabala, *or* Rules of Reintegration and Reduction, *his great treatise on equations.*

Or 'algorithm', which simply mangles the name of the same man, Al-Khwarizmi, who also gave you our Arabic numerals.

Or 'alchemy' itself, from Al-Kimiya, from Khem, an ancient name for Egypt, the black land, land of the black earth. There is more. Let us not speak of 'alcohol', for example! But I do not wish to tire you.

Looking backwards in time, the Muslim stands between the modern world and the ancient wisdoms of Egypt and Greece; we are the door through which your world passed; we are the filter of that knowledge, and the saviours of it. Without us, there would have been no you.

△

3

Trial by Fire

Little Falls, August 28, 2004

Robert awoke early, feeling like a stranger in his own house. His body was singing. His whole being was singing. But he could not imagine being anywhere else. Katherine. The memory of Moss. Their life together.

Surely he smelled still of Terri. He could taste her, smell her, feel her on his body. He felt complete. Fully alive. He had never felt so physically jubilant, never felt his body resonate so fully with joy. In his skull. In his mind. In the tips of his fingers. In his heart, for God's sake. From the sex. From fighting and surviving the second attack.

He looked in on the room that would have been Moss's. Suddenly tears burst from his eyes, and he stood crying silently for the loss of his baby boy, shoulders shaking.

He left without waking Katherine, leaving her a note. He couldn't face her. Told her he'd been summoned urgently by Horace. Another lie, though he felt oddly, coldly detached from it.

New York, August 28, 2004

In Manhattan, Robert left the Port Authority bus station and fired up the Quad on 8th Avenue. A text message was waiting for him from Terri giving the new waypoint: X62. It was a couple of miles south-east, at a corner of what looked like Tompkins Square Park. The message had said eleven o'clock, and it was barely ten. He decided to walk east along 42nd Street to the F train at Bryant Park and take the subway to Delancey.

It was a humid, brilliantly sunny day. A fever was building in the city. The Republicans were coming. There had been armed National Guards in camouflage uniform around the Lincoln Tunnel. The Fujifilm blimp was overhead but now painted with NYPD markings. Whenever he looked up, it was there, an unblinking eye in the sky. Groups of police cars sped by, making sudden rushes from one part of Manhattan to another. A motorcade of five black vehicles, windows tinted, forced its way through an intersection in the oncoming traffic lane, lights flashing. Already there were police everywhere. Even the skyline was weaponized. He talked to a couple of cops at Times Square.

'Ready for the Republicans?'

'Ready for anything.'

'Protesters?'

'Anything. You're in the safest place in the world right now. See all those rooftops? There're sharpshooters on most all of them.'

Many New Yorkers were away on vacation. Few Republicans and protesters had arrived yet. But something momentous was coming, for good or evil. Regular rules were eroding; space was opening up for extraordinary things to happen.

He was burning to see Terri. He jogged up the subway stairs at Delancey and pulled out the Quad. As soon as he had a fix on the waypoint – just over half a mile north – he ran along Essex Street.

There was a giant clock face on the side of an apartment building's water tower as he approached Houston. All the numbers were screwed up: 12, 4, 9, 6 ... He shook his head and looked again. They were still screwed up.

As he came to the south-west corner of Tompkins Square Park, 'Arriving Destination' flashed up on the Quad screen. He looked about. No sign of her. Five minutes to eleven. He examined the immediate area, looking for anything meaningful.

Where was she? What was she doing to him?

He walked into the park. Five or six guys, down at heel, were congregated around the stone chess tables. One was speaking Spanish. No one was playing. He sat in one of the green slatted chairs at a chessboard and waited.

Every inch of his body was smiling at him. Every second of

pleasure was recorded in the memory of his skin. The slightest friction of his shirt against his chest conjured her hair and fingertips brushing over him, her breath on him, her eyes on him, her heat, her sugar-wet, her salt-wet, her honey-wet.

He checked the Quad: 'Ready to navigate, accuracy 75 feet.'

Someone settled into the seat behind him, their back to him.

'Don't turn round, Robert,' a man's voice said. 'It's time for us to talk.'

'Adam?'

'Just don't turn round.'

'What the hell?'

'This is a place of great holiness and great loss, you know? Terrible sadness. Lots of homeless people, lots of desperation, lots of lost faith, lost hope. Then there's some joy too. Dancing and singing. If you know where to look.'

'Where's Terri?'

'We'll get to her in a few minutes, don't fret.'

'Are you safe?'

'No, old friend, I'm not. Not at all safe.'

'What's going on?'

'You're saving me, I think. I hope you are. Are you?'

No words came. Robert made to twist round in his seat. Adam's voice was sharp: 'Don't. For Christ's sake, don't.'

'I don't know what's going on, Adam.'

'Just make like you're enjoying the sun, or something. Talk softly. In a moment you'll go for a walk. For now, relax a little and listen.'

Robert clenched his jaw.

'You asked if I'm in danger. Yes, I am. So are you, so are we all. You need to come further into the game if you are to come out on the other side. There is no way out but in.'

'I –'

'Please. This scavenger hunt we are all involved in has, I'm afraid, an evil core to it. I'm being compelled to take part, I have no choice in the matter. I'm in it, there's no getting around the fact.'

'In over your head?'

He heard a sardonic laugh. 'In so far over my head I can't even see the sunlight any more. Just the occasional glimmer. When I do see it, it's so beautiful it would break your heart.'

'You can run.'

'No. There's no hiding from it.'

'I want to help you.'

'Thank you. You've always been an extraordinary man, Robert, in part by being so ordinary. You're kind, you're direct, you're honest – all with the possible exception of yesterday, admittedly, a necessary interlude – and an amazing thing about you is that you can't see your own power. You don't know what you are. The night of the fire, when you saved my life and Katherine's, our lives were . . . entangled. Whether we like it or not. Are you familiar with the concept?'

'Tell me.'

'Imagine identical twin sisters. They both have an amazing trick. They both only ever wear black or white, but they never wear the same colour at the same time. And they never make up their minds which they are wearing until someone looks at one of them. As soon as a gaze falls upon one of them, her clothes take on a specific colour. Say white.'

'I like your metaphor. What are their names?'

'They're both called Phoebe. But here's the thing. They have to add up to zero. They have to add up to grey. As soon as Phoebe One's clothes turn white, Phoebe Two's clothes turn black, instantaneously. No matter how far apart they are in time and space. Information can't travel faster than the speed of light, yet somehow it happens, when there's no way for it to happen. Entanglement is what the scientists call it.'

'That's impossible. I've heard of this, now that you describe it. It's what Einstein called "spooky action at a distance". He didn't believe in it, didn't like it, didn't want it. I'm with Einstein, I have to say. God doesn't play dice, as he said. It's simply a flaw in our understanding.'

'Well, it's been done in the laboratory with photons. The first time was in Paris, nearly thirty years ago. Not with colour but with something they call spin. It's been repeated many times since. It exists as a physical phenomenon. But I'm not talking about physical phenomena or black and white dresses in our case. I'm talking about souls, Robert. Yours. Mine. Katherine's. Terri's.'

'Terri's?'

'We are all entangled. You, me and Kat since the night of the fire back in '81. Terri with me, and hence with the rest of us, since the Blackout. There's a level of reality for living beings where we are like those girls, like those photons – where something that affects one of us, affects all of us. Now, answer your Quad when it rings.'

Robert closed his eyes. He tried to keep a lid on his fear. He didn't understand. He let the Quad ring and ring. Eventually he answered.

'Robert?'

It was Adam. He twisted round in his seat. No one was there. He darted his eyes around the park. Couldn't see him.

'Adam. Where did you go?'

'Walk. Get up and walk east. I assume you have a riddle?'

'Wait. No riddles. Not yet.'

'Robert . . .'

'Lawrence Hencott. You went to see him right before he killed himself.'

'Ah.'

'How on earth did you even know him?'

'Please let's not talk about this now.'

'We talk about this right now or I walk away.'

'You can't.'

'Watch me.'

There was a pause. Did he have any leverage? Or had he just lost Adam? And maybe Terri?

After what seemed an age, Adam answered. 'I had to see him. I was . . . compelled to.'

'Why did he kill himself?'

Adam gave a cry of pain. 'I am . . . shielding us from . . . Iwnw . . . scavengers . . . I can't do it . . . if we talk about this now.'

'Why did he kill himself?'

'Please . . .'

'Tell me.'

'To . . . protect . . . you.'

The line went dead.

Robert tried to recall Lawrence's words in the phone call. *Hurt you . . . bullet . . . scavenger . . . die.*

Had it been not a threat but a warning?

The Quad buzzed again. 'Robert.'

'What do you mean, to protect me?'

'Find the cache first, and I'll tell you. Please.'

'Don't you know where the cache is?'

'No – not this one, not any of them. They won't tell me. Don't trust me.'

'Who?'

'Find the cache, Robert. Didn't they send you a clue?'

'No, not yet.'

'Check your Quad again.'

'Who's sending it?'

'The Watchman.'

'Who is the Watchman?'

'You'll find out very soon, I'm sure.'

Then the Quad buzzed, and Robert had a new text message:

> *A living tree's the place to be*
> *Steer your helm towards an elm*
> *I'm not barmy, I'm just a swami*
> *The first of three, a trinity*
> *How fire entangles, in love triangles*
> *Yet to atone, you walk alone*
> *To survive your desire*
> *Pass the Trial by Fire*

At the end it gave two more waypoints.

Beautiful curved railings in black forged-iron lined the park's paths. Robert followed the path that took him most directly eastwards, scanning his surroundings for a sight of Adam. He came almost immediately to a tree with garlands around its trunk and flowers strewn among its roots. It was an American Elm. *Ulmus Americana.* He found a plaque on the chicken-wire fence near by. It told him that, on October 9, 1966, A. C. Bhakhtivedanta Swami Prabhupada and his followers sat beneath the tree and held the first outdoor chanting session outside of India of *Hare Krishna, Hare Krishna, Krishna Krishna, Hare Hare . . .* The Beat poet Allen Ginsberg was there. The event was recognized as the founding of the Hare Krishna religion in the United States.

'Robert.'

'Yes.'

'You have it?'

'Yes.'

'Concentrate. Find the cache. Read me the clue.'

Robert read it to him.

'Did you become a Krishna and not tell anyone?'

'No. That's not the point. Just go with the notion of the joy. If it helps, Jimi Hendrix played in this park. It's also named after the guy who abolished slavery in the state of New York. Look away from the specific.'

Robert wheeled around the tree, looking for a hint of something buried. He looked over it for crannies and cracks . . . Nothing. Back to the plaque. To the fence. He ran his fingers around the bases of the fenceposts. Nothing. Then something drew his attention higher up in the tree, a hollow well above head-height.

He called over a beaten-up-looking man sitting on a nearby bench and offered him five dollars for a leg-up. They settled on ten. With the man's back against the tree and his hands making a stirrup, Robert was able to climb up and dig his fingers into the cavity. He felt a fishing line and pulled on it. It was attached to another clear plastic tube.

'I have it.'

'Discretion, Robert. Please.'

He dropped to the ground and looked about. No one seemed to be paying attention. Upon inspection, the tube contained an irregular four-sided piece of metal, perhaps an inch long. It seemed to be made of the same alloy as the Malice Box.

'I need to put something on the website.'

'Not yet. This is a three-parter, I suspect. Now walk north. There's something you need to see.'

Robert slipped the metal shape into a zipped pocket on his trousers. A pattern was forming in his mind, just beyond his ability to recognize it. He followed the park's curving paths towards the northern end, where a one-storey building of men's and women's lavatories stood, with a gate in between them to a garden behind. He passed a curious structure that on closer inspection turned out to be a fountain, a mythical water carrier atop it on a pyramidal stone roof with the word TEMPERANCE carved into it.

'Keep moving, Robert.'

He passed a ship's flagpole and came to the comfort station. Through the gate he could see a pink marble stela, maybe nine feet tall.

'Go take a look, Robert. This is death by fire.'

It was a monument, with bas-relief renderings of two children's faces.

In memory of those who lost their lives in the disaster to the steamer General Slocum, *June XV, MCMIV*

> *They were earth's purest, children young and fair*

'More than a thousand died, mostly women and children,' Adam said. 'Look at that little boy's face.'

'Are you trying to fuck with my head?'

'Not in the least, Robert, not at all. But I'm saying Moss's death will be as nothing if you don't come further into the hunt.'

'Further in? What do you mean further in? I already said I want to help you.'

'The *General Slocum* caught fire as it headed up the East River. It was a day trip for the children of Little Germany. You'll notice there isn't one of those in New York any more. Not after this. The captain beached on North Brother Island in the East River to try to save the passengers. That's where Typhoid Mary was interned and died, if you didn't know. The *Slocum* disaster was the greatest loss of life for any fire in New York City. Biggest disaster before 9/11.'

'And?'

'9/11 was, what, about three times bigger?'

'More or less. Different category.'

'What we are dealing with here – what you'd be helping to stop – would be perhaps ten thousand times bigger. We can stop it, but only if we continue the game for now.'

'What on earth are you talking about?'

'Death by fire. You need to give me the keys you have so far.'

'That's not going to happen.'

'You need to think. I understand that. You should expect another waypoint soon.'

'I already have it. Number 101.'

'Start walking, I'll be back to you.'

Robert walked through the asphalt basketball courts where kids shouted and hollered, and got a Quad signal at the corner of East 10th, accurate to 37 feet. It showed Waypoint 101 was about two thirds of a mile to the west, near Washington Square Park.

Robert racked his brains as he walked along East 10th. *Record anything that leaps out at you. It'll be important.*

He passed a red-brick Gothic Revival church, St Nicholas of Myra. Something struck him about it. He stopped and stared till he saw what it was. There were strange sculpted heads on the walls, their faces . . . peeling away? Cut up? Maybe made of leaves? They were like the ones he'd seen on John Street. They made him shudder.

Across the street he noticed a curios and antiques store, a dressmaker's mannequin outside on the street, old military and anatomical items in the window. There was another one on First Avenue, across the street from the Coyote Ugly Bar, selling old typewriters, musical instruments, lamps, models of military missiles, a beautiful black girdle. Compared to SoHo, the neighbourhood had a grungier, student-rich feel. He passed a store called Vinyl Market selling techno twelve-inch records.

The GPS signal kept cutting out mid block and returning at the corners. 'Need clear view of sky' flashed up on the screen.

As he reached Second Avenue, a church came into view, angled in defiance of the Manhattan grid, its pediment and steeple above a colonnaded porch echoing those of St Paul's Chapel downtown.

Adam called again. 'Robert, where are you?'

'Can't you tell where I am, like Terri?'

'I'm not psychic the way she is. I can't do what she does.'

'Aren't you watching me? I'm just opposite St Mark's in-the-Bowery. I'm crossing the street to go into the graveyard now.'

'A rich man's corpse was stolen from there and held for ransom at the end of the nineteenth century, did you know? His widow had to bargain to free his body.'

'I didn't know that.'

'We're about ransoming the dead too, my friend. The future dead. Our man Tompkins, the freer of slaves, is buried there. Also your man Thomas Addis Emmet lies in a vault there. The one who's absent from his obelisk at St Paul's.'

'You know about that, huh?'

'I read everything you posted. It's part of the game.'

'I'm going to start needing better answers than that.'

'Calm down. You'll have them.'

Emmet's vault was a stone slab in the paved churchyard. The image of an empty chamber beneath an obelisk teased at his mind. He noticed a large cracked bell in one corner of the churchyard, heavy iron bolts holding it in its frame. The bolts meant something to him too. Indefinable images rushed at him. He placed his hands on the bell, closing his eyes, hearing again the chanting in his dream.

Fat Mary Fat Mary Fat Mary . . .

He couldn't. He willed the images away, and with them the fear.

The Quad pointed him directly along Stuyvesant Street, diagonally across the Manhattan grid. Less than half a mile to go. He crossed Third Avenue in front of Cooper Union, past the Budapest-inspired Astor Place subway entrance, one of a handful of reproductions of the original elegant subway entrance designs. As he neared Lafayette Street, a great lamp glowed red to the north atop the Con Ed Building.

He passed alongside a Barnes & Noble bookstore to the corner of Broadway, along what used to be called Obelisk Lane. Now the spire of Grace Church came into view as he looked north. Then, as he crossed Broadway, the Woolworth Building swept into view to the south. The two Gothic towers connected, drawing lines like the threads on the map board in his study. Great sweeping geometries flashed in his mind.

The signal returned again at Broadway. A tenth of a mile to go.

He walked south past cheap low-rise stores and right on to Waverly Place, following the arrow, 460 feet to go. It pointed left on Mercer, then right on Washington Place . . . 177 feet . . . directly ahead to the corner of Greene Street. 'Arriving Destination' flashed up, 79 feet, pointing directly at a building on the corner of Washington Place and Greene. At around 30 feet the arrow began to go round and round, slowly spinning within its own range of error.

He looked about him for any further clues. Then the Quad rang.

'Are you there yet?'

'Standing right at the waypoint.'

'Where is it?'

'Washington Place and Greene.'

'Oh . . . I see. Yes. Of course.'

'What am I looking for?'

'You're going to need a bit of time to absorb that place. Read the plaque on the building at Washington Place and Greene, north-west corner.'

'What is it?'

'More death by fire, my friend. This is what you'd be helping to prevent if you do what I say.'

He read the plaque: 'On this site 146 workers lost their lives in the Triangle Shirtwaist Company fire on March 25, 1911 . . .'

'Oh, God.'

He knew the story, but hadn't recognized the location. The awful sound of women screaming, falling through the air, some hand in hand, like the poor people who jumped from the Twin Towers, smashing into the sidewalk on Greene Street. Young women trapped behind locked and blocked doors on the top floors as the flames tore through the factory, driving them to the windows. An inferno at their backs. Leaping to their deaths. He could feel it. He could see it. The pain was unbearable. The street resonated with violence. It was not his imagination. For a moment, he was actually there, psychically connected to the pain and fear of the women. He felt energy flare around him and subside. Then it was gone, as suddenly as it had come. He was like a broken radio, picking up snatches of signals from the air.

Adam was talking to him. 'Robert, what's the most precious thing in your life?'

'My marriage. The memory of Moss. The idea of him, rather.'

'Once again. You need to give me the keys you have collected so far. There'll be a ring or cylinder of some kind, a pair of interlocked circles, and the one you get today.'

'Can't do that, Adam.'

'If you don't, I'll make sure Katherine learns everything about you and Terri. Everything. We both know her. She'll leave you.'

'She wouldn't believe you.'

'When did you guys last . . . never mind. There are pictures. Video. Terri didn't know, if it makes you feel any better.'

'What? What has happened to you, you sick fuck?'

'The only way out is deeper in. You need to give me the keys.'

'No way.'

'You need to think about this very carefully.'

'Blackmail. You. I can't believe it.'

'Focus. You have to think of what's best for Katherine. Now go get the next cache. What's the clue?'

It was almost the same as before:

> *A hangman's tree's the place to be*
> *Turn your helm to another elm*
> *The second of three, a trinity*
> *How fire entangles, in love triangles*
> *Yet to atone, you walk alone*
> *To survive your desire*
> *Pass the Trial by Fire*

A cold detachment came over Robert, the one that possessed him whenever he felt himself under attack. Had they really been videotaped? Did it matter?

He was beginning to see a pattern. He felt himself gaining advantage. He would overcome this. He would not be treated like a plaything. He needed to play for time.

'The keys. I'll think about it.'

'Good. What's the clue?'

He read it to him.

'As you go, look out for old Garibaldi.'

As he walked into the park, Robert passed a dramatic statue of the Italian military genius, caught in the act of unsheathing his sword. What was salient? Garibaldi in exile had shared a house on Staten Island with a man called Meucci who'd supposedly invented the telephone before Alexander Graham Bell. A glass vessel was found under the base of his statue when it was moved in 1970, a glass time capsule containing newspaper clippings from the 1880s about his death and the erection of the statue. Something precious, delicate, hidden . . .

He walked towards the circular fountain in the centre of the park, looking about him and taking in the square. Henry James territory along its north side. New York University east, south and all around. A hulking red-brick NYU building reminded him of a nuclear reactor. Legend said one of the elms in the north-west corner of the park had been used for public hangings. He looked for the tree. The West Village lay ahead of him, where the quest had started at Adam's secret apartment two days before.

Turn your helm to another elm . . .

He found it. Even bedecked in leaves, it was a sinister, clawing, twisted creature. A tree of death.

The park had been a military parade ground, a potter's field, a place of public execution, whether from this elm or others. And before that a marsh, fed by Minetta Brook, the stream that still flowed under Lower Manhattan. In Native American lore, the Minetta, or Manetta, was a serpent.

He inspected the Hangman's Elm. Only a tiny green plaque on

its trunk identified it. He stepped over the low railings on to the grass to look more closely. Explored around the base. Found a green drawing pin driven into the earth. The cache was deep among the roots near by, below the ground in soft soil.

The tube contained two items identical to the first, oddly angled geometric forms that seemed to fit together in a form he couldn't fathom. He stashed them safely in his pocket. He walked over to the park's chess tables in the south-west corner and declined several offers to play a game.

'Tables for chess and checkers only. No loitering' a sign said. 'Two-hour limit per table. Free for public use. No gambling or fees.' He sat and loitered, waiting for the next call. He knew what he had to do. It was time to take control. He was afraid of the pain it would bring, but he had to do it.

His mind turned again to the strange faces on St Nicholas Church and at John Street. Flayed faces? Harvest gods? Disguises of some kind?

After a few minutes, the Quad rang: 'You have it?'

'I have them, to be exact. Same as the first one. I have three pieces now.'

'One more to go, then, I would guess. What's the next waypoint?'

Robert looked at the Quad. It was 036.

'I'll tell you when I'm there.'

He walked to the north-west corner of the park again, by the Hangman's Elm, and circled till he got a new signal. The Quad said just over half a mile, pointing west. He took Waverly Place. Crossing Sixth Avenue, he saw the turret of the strangely beautiful red-brick Jefferson Square Market Building swing into view to the north. A pyramidion atop a square clock face, atop a cylindrical tower, atop an octagonal base. He remembered an Art Deco prison had stood on the site of its garden, demolished now, that had featured a revolving altar for use by prisoners of different beliefs. It was the only prison he'd ever wanted to see the inside of.

The Watchman gauged Robert's progress, weighing the risks and the knife-edge balance of the plan. Half-formed images came to the

Watchman's mind. Adam pushing Robert, Robert resisting. Robert wrestling with dilemmas, with fear. Adam fighting the Iwnw, ceding ground, pretending to do the devil's bidding, concealing, dissembling. Straining towards the light. Deep inside Katherine, as she prepared to go deeper undercover, lay a hidden dark core. No one could see what resided there.

The Watchman saw the maker of the Ma'rifat', suspended between lives, latched into Adam's DNA, unable to forgive, unable to forget. Unable to die. Saw Terri's cancer, suspended in time. Then he looked again. He saw with impotent horror that it had now become unfrozen.

Soon, when he came out of his trance, Horace would return to the preparations for burying his brother. Pain awaited him there.

The Watchman prayed for himself, and for them all.

New York, August 28, 2004

As he walked, Robert soon found himself knee-deep in triangular motifs.

He reached the three-sided nineteenth-century Northern Dispensary, a street-naming anomaly: Waverly Place on two of its sides and both Christopher Street and Grove Street on the third side. Edgar Allan Poe had been a customer in the days when they handed out laudanum.

He came to Christopher Park, created as a triangular open space at the request of residents after a fire ripped through the area in 1835.

Next to the park was a bar with a triangular gouge out of its corner at street level, the shape etched into the sidewalk. Two strange carved artisans held up the lintel above the missing shape, seemingly crushed by its weight. In another of the carvings a naked woman rode a sea monster.

He realized he had come to the irregular star formation of streets where he'd taken the Christopher Street subway two days earlier.

He crossed the street to the triangular plaque in the street outside Village Cigars, commemorating the refusal of a former owner of the site to sell 500 square inches of his property to the city authorities.

Following the Quad's arrow, he retraced his steps of Thursday along Christopher, past the tattoo parlours, gay bars, fetish clothing stores. He came again to the stars in the pavement where Terri had first reached him on the Quad.

God, he wanted Terri. His body stirred at the thought of her.

He realized where he was going to end up, as the GPS unit counted down the feet to the intersection of Charles and Greenwich Street. He arrived outside a white-painted, higgledy-piggledy two-storey wooden house, its lines so out of true it looked like a Stealth plane design. Across the street was the building where Adam had his pied-à-terre. He stood and waited for the Quad to buzz again.

> *The third of three, a trinity*
> *You need to dowse a crooked house*
> *Our cache's host, an iron post*
> *How fire entangles, in love triangles*
> *Yet to atone, you walk alone*
> *To survive your desire*
> *Pass the Trial by Fire*

Robert kneeled by the iron railing of the gate that led into the wooden house's front yard. At its base, clinging magnetically to the railing and painted the same black, was the last part of the puzzle. He quickly pocketed it and stood up.

Then Adam called. 'Robert? Where are you?'

'I can't look at this house without getting dizzy. It distorts the space around it.'

'Dutch farmhouse from the early eighteenth century. Brought here on a truck in 1968 from the Upper East Side to save it from demolition. The lady who wrote *Goodnight Moon* lived in it before it was moved. Observe the garden.'

The house sat on a triangular plot of land. He gazed through the railings. Atop a feeding pole, he saw a tiny white bird house with crazy roof angles and canted angles: a perfect miniature and echo of the house itself.

'It's a bit like the key to the Ma'rifat' that I sent you,' Adam said. 'The small one is a perfect miniature of the big one. Now, there's something in my old apartment you need to see.'

'What's going to be up there this time? Is it you?'

'No.'

'Terri?'

'No. Sorry.'

'Anyone I know?'

'No one's in this time at the House of Spells. Go up.'

'As it happens, I really need to pee. I thought you'd never ask.'

Robert took out his keys and let himself in. He started up the stairs.

'Five flights. Thank you.'

'Enjoy.'

He opened the door. The apartment had been stripped bare. The blinds were lowered, and the only light came from a single electric-blue lava lamp on the floor where Adam's desk had been.

'You're going for a certain seventies minimalism, I see. Nice.'

'What music would you recommend to go with it?'

'Kraftwerk, maybe. Was this your love-nest with Terri? Others too?'

'I take the fifth. Do you have the complete key now?'

Robert held the four pieces of the puzzle in his hand.

'They go together somehow. Can't see how. What did you want me to see up here?'

'Wait. I'll be back in touch.' He rang off.

Robert went into the small kitchen at the rear of the apartment and raised the blind. All four pieces of the key were identically shaped, all magnetically charged. He twisted them against each other. And twisted. And twisted.

Adam called back a few minutes later. 'Are you done?'

'Almost.'

'Loser. It's supposed to be a fricking pyramid.'

'I knew that. I could see that.'

'Robert, give me the keys. You have to.'

'No.'

'You know, Katherine wasn't just seeing her friend in the West Village yesterday. She met me too.'

'What?'

'Listen. Please. I'm going to send you a photograph. We were in Washington Square Park. Look closely at it. We've been in touch for a while, but I asked her to keep it secret. She tried to help me last year. And she did. Now she wants to know what's going on. How much she could tell you. This isn't a threat. It's a reminder of what's at stake.'

The file landed. He opened it up on the Quad screen.

The photo showed Katherine, in the dress she'd been wearing the previous day, sitting on a park bench. Around her head was a cloud of darkness. And in it, Robert saw again the face of death. It was the single, beautiful, seductive eye, flaring with yellow and-blue light, the dead black core at its centre. Was this the face of Iwnw? Were they going to come after Kat? How much could he believe of what Adam was saying?

Robert shouted into the phone: 'Adam . . .'

'If you won't give me the keys . . .'

The connection went dead.

Robert stared out of the kitchen window, fighting his fear. Then he noticed a faint hissing sound coming from the oven. A glimmer of flame, like a spark, blinked into existence on one of the top burners. The spark grew and stretched into a tiny string of fire that twisted upwards from the burner, arching slowly into space. It was followed by a second, a snake of flame turning in slow motion in the air before his eyes.

A web of burning strands of light formed before him as he watched, frozen, spellbound; and slowly it formed into a shimmering human figure, standing before him in a filigree of flame. For a moment the figure held, then melted in upon itself and re-formed as a shifting, rippling face of fire.

'Robert.'

It was a voice he knew but couldn't place. 'Who . . . who are you?'

'I watch over you.'

The voice was a sonorous whisper, threaded with the hiss of the gas and a note of deep power, a distant thunder.

'What's happening?'

'The kitchen is exploding. It's already begun. This is all happening in a fraction of a second. But don't worry. I'm warning you in time.'

'How is this possible?'

'You are starting to learn to see.'

'This whole place is going to blow?'

'It already is. You'd never survive, normally.'

The strands of fire melted again and re-formed in a shifting human figure, as tall as Robert, that rippled like a reflection on water.

'How can this be happening?'

'Time exists differently for all of us. It is part of a cage we build for ourselves. You are opening the door of the cage. You are walking out of yourself. Out of your small, sleeping, ego-bound self.'

'I'm just trying to survive.'

The tendrils of flame started to fatten, swelling to obliterate the figure's body and face and coiling into thick ropes of fire.

Still he heard the voice. 'I hope there's more to it than that. You are being attacked by the ones who call themselves Iwnw. They are feeding on the psychic energy of Adam to do this. I am just able to intervene, to insert myself into their attack, long enough to give you a chance to survive. You'll need to use the window, by the way. You'll never make it if you take the door.'

'What is your name?'

'I am the Watchman. You know me as Horace. Robert, run!'

Robert reached over the kitchen sink and tried to pull the window up. It wouldn't budge. The flames thickened. He took a saucepan and smashed the glass, clearing out the frame as much as possible and then levering himself up on to the sink, poking his head through the window, then his shoulders. He twisted sideways, one hand on his eyes, one on his groin to shield himself from broken glass, and kicked with his feet against the wall of the sink.

He flew horizontally out of the window as the ropes of flame coalesced into a single ball of fire and exploded in a booming, roaring shock-wave.

He fell on to the roof of the neighbouring apartment one floor below, rolling and tumbling as debris fell all around him. Then he lay on his back, hyperventilating with shock, saying over and over: 'Dear God. Dear God.'

Bleeding from a cut on his thigh, his arms and legs shaking, Robert made his way down to the street on the fire escape, hearing sirens approach. He felt a voice in his head, an intuition that seemed like an order: *Get away. The authorities can't help. Get away.* He felt defiance in his heart. He was getting stronger. They had failed to kill him again. He was growing on the Path.

He limped north from the *Goodnight Moon* house along Greenwich Street, until he found a stoop to sit on for a moment to examine his wound. It was superficial, by the look of it, though a dull throbbing was settling into his leg. He'd been lucky. Or was there any such thing as luck?

He looked back at the apartment building. There was no fire now, and it looked like the explosion had, somehow, directed all its force outwards from the top floor, causing no damage below. Neighbours were pointing up at the blown-out windows of Adam's place, and a police car was arriving on the scene.

His hands were still shaking.

The slow-motion explosion was already like a dream in his mind. Had he seen Horace speaking to him in the midst of the flames? Had he been hallucinating? What was real and what were tricks of his imagination?

He couldn't go on much longer. Yet he had to.

He thought of Adam's threat of blackmail. Robert made up his mind. He would call Adam's bluff, take back the initiative. Tell Kat about Terri before Adam could. However much it hurt.

He turned his mind to practicalities. How to get home. How to warn Katherine.

Years ago she'd insisted they establish emergency codes in case either of them was ever in danger. With her past, prudence and habit died hard. He made the call.

'Katherine?'

'Robert? What's up? Are you OK?'

'Hi, my darling. I'm fine. Just to let you know I never got that migraine I thought was coming on this morning. I may have to work late with Derek, but I'll leave as soon as I can. And, hey, I got tickets for the *Lion King* at last. Very happy about that. Guess which night?'

'Which? Tonight?'

'Yes.'

'I'd better get ready, then.'

She hung up. His hands left damp imprints on the phone casing. The humidity had risen as the day wore on. He was drenched in sweat now. His eyes stung with salt and the throb in his leg was deepening.

He flagged down a cab and offered a generous fare to New Jersey. Just as they were nearing the Lincoln Tunnel, Katherine called back. 'You're going to have to take back those tickets, sorry. I just remembered we have Orlando coming to dinner.'

'Oh, shit. You're right. I'll do that. See you soon.'

Migraine and *Lion King* meant that she should go to a safe place outside the house that only he and she knew about. The fact that she'd called meant she was there.

Knowing she was safe, he went to their house first and cleaned up, changing his clothes and disinfecting his cuts. Their current safe location was their friend Kerry's house, a few miles from their own, and it was almost three thirty when he got there, after following a circuitous route. They both had keys. Katherine would look in on her cats whenever Kerry travelled for work, which was frequently. This week she was in Chicago. As he slid the key into the lock, he remembered the sound of his father coming home to the cottage in the evenings after working late on the grounds, the sense of security that it gave as he heard the door latch being lifted, the hope that he would come to Robert's room and talk about his day for a while. Yet, as he entered Kerry's house, he felt as though he were bringing something alien with him, something dangerous and unwelcome. Katherine was sitting in the front room in loose-fitting trousers and a light jacket. Her boots were on, and he knew she'd have a pistol concealed close by. She gave a barely audible 'Hi' to his whispered greeting. He walked over and kissed her head.

'It's all going to be fine,' he said. 'I'm sorry if I frightened you.'

'Crazy day. You showered?'

'Yeah.'

She looked straight into him. He felt a flutter on his flesh and behind his eyes. Was she trying to read him? He'd never had such a sensation before.

'Did you hear about the bomb-plot arrests?'

'No?'

'NYPD arrested two guys, an American and a Pakistani, for planning to blow up Herald Square subway station. Said they had all the intent but no actual explosives.'

'Did they really know what they were doing?'

'Sounds like it. No suggestion of links to organized groups, though. Is this anything to do with that?'

'No.'

'What's the threat?'

Katherine's training could make her very no-nonsense. They were well matched, that way.

'We have been deceiving each other, somewhat.'

'What's the threat?'

'What did Adam tell you yesterday?'

'Let's be clear about something. He came to me last year —'

'Asked you to keep it secret. I know. What did he want help with?'

'He wouldn't say. Back then all he'd say was that he was going to be going up against someone very powerful, and he wanted to know if any of my gifts had returned. I told him no, but he asked me to try anyway.'

'When was that exactly?'

'The morning of the Blackout. August 14. And he swore me to

secrecy. To protect you. He said he wouldn't involve you unless he absolutely had to.'

'And yesterday?'

'He said somehow the person he had to fight a year ago has come back. He said somehow we are vulnerable, because since the night of the fire at Cambridge we are all . . . entangled, he said. What do you have that's newer than that?'

He showed her the picture. She stared at the screen, wordlessly.

'Adam sent me it not a couple of hours ago. He's been drawing me into this same thing, you know that. But there's something very . . . dark going on with him. I don't believe he can control it. I don't know if he can win.'

'What do you mean?'

'I mean suppose he needs me not to stop this terrible act of obscenity but to cause it? Suppose it's all a trick? He threatens you, but he says it's to protect you. He threatens me . . .'

She looked him in the eyes. 'How?'

He couldn't meet her gaze. 'Just bullshit stuff. I'm not afraid of him.'

'You're afraid of something.'

'Less so than I was. I don't know how to explain.'

'This thing in the picture. Have you seen it before?'

'It's death. Foregathering. Don't ask me how I know.'

'You saw it the night of the fire. In Adam's room. I know.'

His head swam with secrets, with things he had seen and denied his whole life, things he'd considered forbidden, things he could scarcely credit he'd seen in the last three days. What could he tell her? What should he say?

'You've seen it too, Kat?'

'I have. In dreams. And I felt it in Adam's room that night in Cambridge, though I didn't know what it was at the time.'

'What is it?'

'It's malevolent. It lives in a potential world, not quite in existence but constantly seeking to exist. It feeds on pain, confusion, fear. It's connected to free will somehow. When someone chooses to do ill, or even has the opportunity to do so, it draws near. When people stumble into psychic areas they're not equipped to deal with, it sees an opportunity. It brings death, yes.'

'How is it related to these people called Iwnw?'

'I'm not sure what more I can say. Each of us has a role in this, Robert, and it has to be played out. Some things are only valuable to you if you discover them for yourself. I think, from what Adam said, that the Iwnw live in this world and the next. They have people in every generation who act for them, a kind of priesthood, if you like, and then they are also this . . . eye.'

'I'm starting to understand some of this. But I need help. There are people who fight them, yes? Horace? Has he been watching over us all this time?'

'You remember that night at the Round Church? That's the only time you met him while he was mentoring Adam in England.'

'Oh, my God.'

Hour by hour, his life was being remade. Nothing was as it had seemed. He saw protective forces everywhere around him, throughout his life, trying to shield him from his own nature. His parents. Adam and Kat. Horace.

'I have to be who I am now,' he said, not realizing he was speaking out loud.

Kat said nothing.

'I've been so blind.'

She smiled. 'No. You weren't ready until now. One thing you need to realize is that Adam says he is shielding us. Protecting us. I believe him.'

'I don't know if I do, Kat. I believe he wants to, but –'

His cell phone rang. It was Horace. He kissed Katherine and walked into the kitchen to talk.

'Robert, my friend. Are you OK?'

'You saved my life.'

'Only just. I was just able to tip the balance in your favour. I hadn't realized Adam was so powerfully in the grip of the others. They used him to get to you.'

'He's still resisting, though, isn't he? I felt he was fighting.'

'Yes, but he is losing faster than I thought. Robert, you must pay attention to everything, to every internal voice, every seeming coincidence, every sensation you receive from people.'

Anger flared in Robert's heart. 'I'm going as fast as I can! I've been attacked three times! People are trying to kill me, for Christ's sake.'

'You're not alone in that regard. I'm between bases too, we might say. Home is not the most recommendable location for me at the moment. If I go home, I'll be killed.'

'What?'

'It is time to grow up, Robert. For all of us.'

'I'm sorry, I –'

'Hush. I can't stay on for long. They'll find me, and Adam will kill me.'

'Adam?'

'Just like he killed Lawrence. Or forced him to die. I will die too, if I must. To protect you.'

'Horace?'

'Understand, Robert: understand what is at stake here. Truly.'

'Who are *they*, Horace?'

'The Iwnw are scavengers of the soul. In this world and the next. Parasites. They are using the Minotaur as a kind of gateway into Adam. Quickly, tell me everything else that happened today.'

Robert recounted everything.

'You must go on. You must stay in it with Adam. You must.'

'But you said he's going to kill you?'

'He is battling. He is not yet lost. But his willpower is not inexhaustible. When he tires, he is not in command of his actions.'

'Can he be saved?'

'Yes, Robert. You can save him. And everyone. But only if you risk losing.'

'Losing what?'

'Losing everything.'

His mind hared in twenty directions. He let it. He was learning to trust.

'Horace, have I completed the third trial? Have I passed?'

'Let me gather my thoughts for a moment.'

Horace fell silent. Robert recognized something in himself more strongly than before, something he knew from his regular life, that already seemed years in the past: he was committed now. He wanted to see it through, regardless of the cost. The alternative was too awful to bear thinking about.

'The third trial focuses on freedom,' Horace said. 'It places you in a situation where your autonomy and independence, your ability to stand on your own two feet and decide your own fate, are placed under unbearable pressure. These are the powers of fire, the energies that drive ambition, self-respect, the pursuit of achievement, the force of pride. This trial has brought you deeper into the nature of the race to stop the Ma'rifat' exploding. To pass the trial, you have to discover what lies at the outer limits of freedom and pay a terrible price: entering the shadow of this power, you have to choose between submitting to blackmail or losing your wife.'

'I have made that choice. I am going to tell her.'

'Many aspirants to knowledge of the Path fall at this stage, in one of two ways: they either fail to tap the fire powers to create a healthy ego and sense of independence, or they fail to transcend self-infatuation. Tell me, as you reject this blackmail and establish this freedom of action, what do you see at the outer limits of freedom?'

It was the same question asked by the letter, in a different way: *Seek freedom's far bourns.* 'Absolute freedom means absolute loneliness, absolute isolation. It will cost me Kat, but I've had no choice but to take these actions if I'm to survive.'

'Good. You will have recovered a key in four parts, forming a triangle or pyramid, and you will have discovered another part of your shattered body of light. If you had failed at this stage, you would have perished. I would not have been able to help you if you had not developed the strength to survive. You have passed the trial.'

Tears suddenly filled Robert's eyes. He was exhausted, frightened and bewildered. But he was alive, and fighting, and learning what he needed to fight better. He was proud.

'Robert, are you there?'

He composed himself, clearing his throat and scanning his mind for questions. 'One thing. I saw something that disturbed me on a church in the East Village. A head, a face, that looked . . . flayed? Leafy? It's hard to describe.'

'The Green Man,' Horace said immediately. 'Good. What you saw is a foliate mask. A lot of nonsense is spoken about him, but at heart there is something you need. It stands for life. Remember it. One other thing. Does the term "Water Tunnel Number One" mean anything to you?'

'The big new one they are building? That's going to take thirty years?'

'No, that's Number Three. Coming along quite nicely now, actually, with the new drills. But no, I mean Number One. Follow its path. You may find it illuminating. Now I have to go. It's dangerous to talk longer.'

'What are you going to do?'

'What I must do. I'm going to help you fight.'

Then he was gone.

Robert went back into the living room to his wife. He took a deep breath.

'How's Horace?'

'Katherine. I've been unfaithful to you. I had sex with Terri yesterday.'

A Martyr's Love Song: The Making of the Ma'rifat'

My father was not just a scientist; he was a dreamer and a man of deep spiritual concerns. He was a teacher, a physicist, a chemist and, beyond that, a mystic, an explorer of God's mysteries. There are no longer words in English for what he studied, though in Chaucer's time — yes, I am a learned Arab, remember? — he would have been called an alkamystere.

Take chemistry, take alchemy, take mystery, and combine them. That is the lost science. Alcumystrie, *it was later called. I sat at his feet. I learned. I have applied it.*

I had prayed that 9/11 would be enough. That America would learn. That the great wave of compassion and selflessness that it provoked would last and spread into the world. But it did not. And I concluded, amid tears, that something far bigger was needed.

I love New York. Even more was required of New York. Not only to show compassion and enormous heart in the face of attack but even more, for the sake of the world: to die. This great heart had to be stopped; it had to make the ultimate sacrifice, the ultimate leap into the divine.

When the Device was accidentally triggered, I died to the physical world. But now I dwell in a place of no time and no space, where light dwells. For particles of light, there is no time, and all places are the same place. Now I am a Man of Light, and I observe the workings of the world I left as one thing. I am a newborn child. I am a dying man. I am working at the RHIC. I am burying my grandfather. I am knowing a woman for the first time. I am holding my mother in my arms. I am building the Device. I am doing and being all these things.

From here I can see everything. I can see all of us. I see the afternoon of August 14, 2003 in every single detail. I circle above the north-eastern United States like an eagle and watch the spreading fingers of the Blackout. I see the electricity surging madly back and forth along the power lines. I see the darkness metastasize. I see the world cracking like ice. I swoop down and enter bodies and feel their most intimate sensations. I see each of us connected to the others along the hairline cracks and fault lines exposed by the detonation.

I see myself die.

I see Robert and Katherine making love. I see Terri hyperventilating, lost in sensation, lost to herself. I see her lose her sight.

I see Adam. I see him fighting. I see him in a burning room. Always I see him in a burning room. Always the same fire.

I see space and time bend.

I see deep into my soul. I see the flaw. I see, too late, the wrong turn I should have rectified.

I see myself fail.

There is a sculpture in the water off Battery Park. It shows sailors reaching desperately down to try to rescue a drowning man who is completely covered when the tide is high. So are we all subsumed into the sea of God when our individual fears are drowned in a greater love . . . when all the fear is gone, the love at the core of each of us can flow through. This is how I see the world of men from my new dwelling in light. Tiny packets of love, pinched off from one another and from the world itself by fear. All the borders in the world are made of fear. We need them so we may grow to maturity, but then we must learn to take them down again, to transcend them. What power can achieve this?

At Brookhaven, in the collider programme where I worked, we wound back the clock of time so far that we were able to create matter in a form that has not been seen in the universe since ten microseconds after the Big Bang. It is called a quark-gluon plasma, but you can think of it as simply this: a liquid universe. The ocean from which we all came. The machine we used to collide gold with gold is so powerful that, before we were allowed to go ahead and use it, studies had to be made to show that fears we would destroy the earth were unfounded. One of the concerns was that we might destroy the entire known universe. This is not a joke. The report examining these issues, and concluding it was safe for us to go ahead, is publicly available. You can read it for yourself online.

Many years ago, as I excelled in my studies in London, the men of the Mukhabarat sought me out. One does not turn down an invitation from the intelligence services. They wished to ensure I would be willing to serve, come the day, as an asset for them when I began work in other countries. All these years later, I do not even know if they were from the Mukhabarat of my own country or another.

I did not go to work for them willingly. I gave them as little as possible. Their questions were stupid, their understanding minimal. I was a particle physicist, I had no desire to work on bomb programmes or to inform on my colleagues. But eventually, in the 1990s, they asked me to infiltrate a bomb programme in a foreign country. They arrested my father to focus my mind.

I went along, but I decided secretly to strike back at them. I went to the British Embassy and offered to spy for them.

Now I am a man in love, and I burn with the pains of that love. It is a thirst that never can be slaked. I am a drop of rain, and my Beloved is the boundless sea. To join my Beloved I must dissolve myself back into the great ocean from which I came. I must seek annihilation in the joy of my love.

I knew my Beloved by a different name, but she told me her real name was Katherine.

□

4

Trial by Air

Little Falls, August 29, 2004

Katherine sat smoking. They'd talked into the early hours.

There was frost between them, distance and pain. The hurt he had caused her stood in the room. She had cried, and Robert's face burned where she had slapped him.

'You were my anchor. If all else failed, there would be you.'

'I've let you down. And myself.'

'Please. Let's just focus on me for the moment, shall we? Yes, you've let *me* down. You've hurt *me*.'

'I'm sorry.'

'I know you are. It doesn't help in the least. It changes nothing.'

She took a drag on her cigarette and angrily stubbed it out. 'I shouldn't smoke. Look at me. I'm a wreck.'

Robert saw himself from the outside. He was there in the room with her, absorbing the tide of her pain, taking her blows as she lashed out. She needed him, and he wanted her to expend her anger on him. Yet a part of him remained distant and watchful, coldly gauging how well the ploy to free himself was working.

She toyed with her lighter, flicking it on and off. 'When I decided to stay with you, I was coming out of a nightmare. Almost a decade, undercover most of the time. It was killing me, and I quit.'

'To my benefit.'

'I was lucky. I thought all the men like you were married already.'

'You made up your mind pretty quickly. And you were done with danger and dangerous men.'

'I was.'

'And you wanted someone dependable and reliable, but not over fifty, and not your actual father.'

'And you were safe. You made me feel important and safe.'

'Even with a hurricane looming. Our whirlwind romance.'

'And do you remember what I said to you? That night in Miami?'

215

'You said you would go to the ends of the earth to avoid betrayal. To avoid experiencing it ever again. And to avoid soliciting it ever again.'

'And now what have you done?'

Robert said nothing.

She stared out of the window. Her hurt seeped into him. He let it flow. She was right, but there was more to it. She too had her portion of blame. He bit his tongue. Losing his temper would be losing control, and this was about the opposite.

'Robert, after 9/11 something happened to me. I wanted to think it was noble, but looking back now I think it was just about revenge. It wasn't something I could tell you about, at the time. I shouldn't now, actually. But I'm going to.'

'You went back to work?'

'You knew?'

'I guessed. You disguised it very well. But something changed about you. You became harder, underneath everything.'

'You didn't say anything.'

'What could I say? I thought perhaps the spooks never really let you go. Part of me was afraid of what would happen if I asked you about it.'

She laughed. 'Whether I'd have to kill you? That old joke?'

'Whether you'd have to leave me. I assume you went back to the Brits?'

'Actually no. I went to the Americans. It was the American side of me that 9/11 really hurt. I had a few contacts. I got into counter-terrorism.'

He appraised her. 'On the analysis side?'

'And operations. I did some tough-girl training. Got back up to speed. That yoga retreat I did? Wasn't yoga.'

'Were you rusty?'

'I was the best shot in my class when I joined Six back in '86. I was so good I got specialist training. I was still good. Very good.'

'You're telling me this for a reason?'

She turned cold with anger. 'I'm sorry, Robert. Was I boring you?'

'No, I –'

'You selfish, self-seeking bastard. I can't bear to look at you.' She stared out into the night.

'I'm sorry, Kat.'

'I need to tell this story. So you can understand what I mean about betrayal.' Pain filled her voice. 'So you can understand what you've done.'

Unexpectedly, tears welled in his eyes. He'd hurt her far more badly than he'd imagined. An image flashed into his mind of a tiny, misshapen fool. Himself, his ego. Shrivelled, lost in self-gratification.

'I'm sorry,' he said again, more thickly. She saw his impending emotional release, saw where it would lead. She denied him it. There would be no crying in each other's arms, no reconciliation.

'Let me tell this. You can't understand me unless you know this.'

'Go on.'

'Something about one of the suspects we looked at in 2002 rang a bell with me. It wasn't nice work. We were looking at potential spies in the scientific community. There was a particle physicist, an Arab-American, working out at Brookhaven on Long Island, showing suspicious behaviour. He'd only been in the country two or three years.'

'Were you using your gift at all? I thought it died after you came out of the service.'

'After I lost Tariq?'

'Yes.'

'Guess what. I found him again. At Brookhaven. Working on the particle accelerator, and also showing a lot of interest in metallic-glass research.'

'You found him? He wasn't killed after all?'

'I didn't know whether to laugh or cry. He'd survived. But to have been released, then to have come to America – they must have forced him to spy on us. There was no other way.'

'What did you do?'

'I'm ashamed of what I did.'

'I thought you'd loved him. And you were his reason for living. For betraying. For everything.'

'I know. I used that. I sought him out. Accidental meeting. Amazement. Tears. Protestations of innocence, of miraculous escape. I didn't believe him for a moment. But it got me close to him. Got me to what he was doing.'

'You started seeing him?'

'Yes.'

'Did you sleep with him?'

She paused. 'No.'

'Did you make him think you would?'

'Yes.'

'And then?'

'America went into Iraq. A few weeks later, I led him to a secluded spot and handed him over.'

'To whom?'

'Interrogators.'

'Jesus.'

'I told myself it was the job. A necessary job. It was. Then when the Abu Ghraib things started to come out . . . The bestial things they were doing. I heard about them before they broke publicly. I was sick. It made me sick.'

'You hid it well.'

'You helped a lot. Though you didn't realize. I quit again. I've had happier years with you than I thought possible, Robert. And then there was the Blackout.'

'Our miracle came along. Moss. You a mother at forty-three.'

'And then I lost him.'

'We lost him.'

'And I was cold to you. Lifeless. Since then.'

It was what he'd wanted to say. Yes, she'd been cold. Yes, it was humiliating. To be turfed out into a separate room. To be so suddenly estranged that they killed desire in each other. And yes, in a dark corner of his heart he had wanted revenge.

'It wasn't your fault, Kat.'

'I always felt he was a twin.'

'That's what you said.'

'From the very start, when the doctors said there was only one,

I thought they were mistaken. Something had to have gone wrong.'

Katherine had slid from elation to numbness after the miscarriage. Despite all evidence to the contrary, she'd held on to the idea that somehow Moss wasn't entirely gone. It was a common traumatic response. She'd held on to her dream creature.

'I know it's impossible. But you thought I was going mad.'

'I didn't know what to think. I just saw myself losing you. I've ached to be touched. By you. And then just to be touched. When it happened, it was like life returning.'

She looked into his eyes. 'Was she good?'

'What does that even mean?'

'She wasn't a bore, at least. Some people are, you know. In bed.'

'Would it make any sense to say in some ways it's not even about you?'

She slapped his face, without warning, her face white with rage. 'Not about me? You couldn't even find your wedding ring to put it back on, and it's not about me?'

'I'm sorry. Kat, I –'

'I always thought I'd be able to deal with it if you ran around. Had an affair. I'd just leave. It's harder than that. But . . .'

She sighed, fought back tears. Made up her mind.

'I have safe places arranged that you don't know about. I have to. I'm going to one now.'

'Please don't.'

'This is what it costs, Robert.'

'Kat, please. Don't do this. I want to protect you. To do that I have to help Adam get out. Horace is adamant. I have to go deeper in to help him.'

'You don't trust Adam, though.'

'I don't trust whatever he's becoming. What he will become if I don't help.'

'Are you going to tell me that this fling with Adam's woman is part of helping him?'

'No. I'm not saying that.'

'It might be.'

'I'm not saying that. Not hiding behind that.'

'Maybe part of the cost of saving Adam is my trust in you. Maybe that's one of the sacrifices that's required. Because it's gone, believe me.'

'I'm not making excuses.' But it was hopeless. The anger surged in him. 'But you know what? I might want to fuck Terri again.'

'So it *was* that good, was it?'

'You bet.'

'You bastard. Don't try to stop me. You know you won't find me till I'm ready. Now get out of my way.'

Hours later Robert sat in his study, rubbing his eyes till stars shone, exhausted and alone. After Katherine had left Kerry's place, he'd returned home to their empty house. Now he was poring over his three-dimensional map of Manhattan. Yellow pins marked the Hare Krishna tree, the site of the Triangle factory fire, Adam's apartment. Coloured threads ran between them and the red pin at St Paul's, an orange pin at Mercer, just below Prince. He'd traced a shape that suggested a triangle, but wasn't one; that suggested a letter *G*, but wasn't one.

He felt the cost of the decision in his very flesh. He'd made himself immune to blackmail. Told Katherine about Terri before Adam could. Asserted his power to stand alone. Completed the trial. And now, in his utter freedom, that's what he was: utterly alone.

He knew he could be cold. Detachment had been a professional virtue. But this was something else: he had deliberately chosen to hurt Katherine. Set her pain against his need and found his need greater. And what if she never came back? He still found his need greater.

Forgive me, he whispered to himself.

His head spun. Part of him felt relieved to have told her. Even to have told her he'd like to make love with Terri again. It was the truth. But he'd taken the confession and twisted it on its head: he'd used it as a weapon, to hurt her. To gain revenge for the pain she'd caused him since the miscarriage. It was unforgivable.

Yet he was now free of the threat of blackmail. It was part of completing the Trial by Fire. He'd assumed responsibility for his actions, and he was paying the price. He could take it.

The way out was on the other side of the darkness gathering around him, around all of them. The way out was the Path of Seth.

He returned to his map of Manhattan, extrapolating lines on the map, seeing them shoot off into New Jersey and Queens and along Manhattan in his mind, seeking meaning.

Look at Water Tunnel Number One, Horace had said.

Tunnel Number One was an iron snake under the city, bringing fresh water, bringing life. Too vital to turn off for repair, too old to shut down safely, sustained by the very flow of water it carried, the tunnel coursed through the Bronx, under the length of Manhattan and away into Brooklyn, bearing water from an array of reservoirs to the north and west. Ninety years old. Slaking a one-billion-gallon-a-day thirst.

He looked at its route. Gravity bore the water south into Manhattan, through a chain of city parks. Central Park, Bryant Park by the New York Public Library, an intersection just by Madison

Square Park, down into Union Square Park . . . Sinking the tunnel-digging shafts on public land had presumably made sense, to avoid hassles with eminent domain.

He looked at the other water tunnels. Number Two never entered Manhattan, feeding Queens and Brooklyn and connecting to Staten Island. Number Three, a behemoth that had been under construction for decades, was designed to allow the other two to be turned off and properly inspected for the first time.

Without Tunnel Number One, Manhattan would die. Was that what Horace was talking about?

So far the waypoints of each trial had been located further north than the previous day's. If that continued, then the route of the tunnel would connect with his map at . . . Union Square. Would it then follow the tunnel's course back towards its origin? He stretched a thread over his map from St Paul's Chapel, past the waypoint on Mercer where he'd met Terri, through the site of the Triangle fire and towards the top of Manhattan. It led up into Central Park, first passing near the tunnel's shafts at Union Square Park, Madison Square Park, Bryant Park . . .

A shape formed in his mind and then vanished as soon as he thought he could see it. Maddeningly, he knew it was something that could give him an edge over the evil that was corroding Adam from the inside out. But it could not be looked at directly.

He stared at the map until he could think of nothing else. But after the initial flash, the pattern eluded him. He was left with just the conviction that he'd found part of the puzzle.

Doubts continued to rack his brain. To what extent was Adam telling the complete truth? Why had he asked to see Katherine?

He needed more information still.

He needed to find Kat, and win her back to him. He needed to find out more about Adam's and Terri's lives. And, being honest, he wanted Terri again. Perhaps he needed to fuck it out of his system. Or be with her again and find it less mind-blowing. Find fault with her. Something. He couldn't reach Adam. He had to meet Terri. All roads led to her. He looked at the map again. With a shout of rage and frustration, he swept his arm across it, sending the miniature buildings and pins flying across the room. He stared into the blackness.

The way out was the way in. He had his freedom, and now he had to make it right. He was growing in strength. Understanding was coming to him in flashes, fading immediately, but he felt tantalizingly close to breaking through.

He rubbed his temples. He closed his eyes for a moment, and slept.

Hours later he awoke with a start, fully clothed, stiff and cold, twisted in the chair in his study. The Quad was buzzing. It was a text message from Terri. Washington Square Park. 11.30 a.m.

He looked at his watch. It was after nine. He staggered to the shower.

Robert stood under the arch in Washington Square Park, facing uptown, waiting for Terri's call. If he was right, he knew where she was going to send him.

It buzzed.

'Hi.'

'Hi. Waypoint 057.'

'Union Square.'

'Very good. Impressive. South-west corner. You're getting quicker. But pay attention as you go. The point is the journey.'

'Where the hell were you yesterday?'

'Get moving, lover. It's a whole new day today. Check out Number 2, as you go.'

'Water tunnel?'

'What? No. Number 2, Fifth Avenue. What's with the water tunnel?'

'Ignore me. I'm tired.'

He started moving north on Fifth. Across the street was the NYU mews at Number ½, an Elizabethan-looking statue at the far end. To its left, the great Deco heap of 1 Fifth Avenue. Its bronze-plated doors reminded him of the Waldorf-Astoria and its hidden railway siding.

He took a closer look at Number 2, a nondescript apartment building. To the right of the main entrance, inside the lobby but visible through glass, rose a seven-foot-tall plastic tube, yellowish and clear, its lower half enclosed in a marble base. Water bubbled up into it.

'A brook winds its erratic way beneath this site,' he read on the plaque affixed to the wall outside. 'The Indians called it Manette, or Devil's Water. To the Dutch settlers it was Bestevaer's Killetje, or Grandfather's Little Creek. For the past two centuries familiar to this neighborhood as MINETTA BROOK.'

Devil's water, bubbling up. The snake under Manhattan.

The Quad pointed him away from Fifth, a block over to the east, taking him to University Place. There he headed north. The seven glistening parabolas of the Chrysler Building swung into view again along the avenue as he reached East 9th Street.

He walked on. As he emerged on to 14th Street, at the bottom of Union Square Park, the roof structures of Zeckendorf Towers appeared, three pyramidal forms that seemed to float on the horizon as he moved, momentarily aligning like the Giza Pyramids in Egypt. He walked towards them, seeing a fourth pyramid emerge from behind the other three. From trial three to trial four.

Off in the distance, he could hear drums in the still air, chanting and whistles and shouts. The temperature had to be in the nineties. He was already dripping sweat.

'Arriving destination' the Quad showed. Then it buzzed. 'Welcome to Dead Man's Curve,' Terri said. 'Right where you're standing.'

'Hell of a name.'

'Hell of a game. It's where the cable cars coming up Broadway used to crash or send people flying as they tried to negotiate the bend. There was no way to decelerate. Sound familiar?'

'I am that streetcar. Where are you?'

'Cross to the park and look down. There's a pattern in the sidewalk, a kind of wheel of time, in a horseshoe shape, wrapping around the south end of the park. Walk the wheel and you'll find me. Can you hear the march coming?'

The protest march against the Republican Convention was routed to end and disperse at Union Square after passing Madison Square Garden, the venue for the meeting. Hundreds of thousands of people were on their way. He looked about the square. There were some cops, but there were many hundreds more at a discreet distance, he was sure.

He crossed 14th Street and looked down at his feet. There were more inlaid plaques, like those near City Hall, but in metal instead of stone.

Pay attention to everything, Horace had said.

He walked the half-wheel along its western side first, looking for Terri and inspecting the rendering of Union Square Park at different times in history. It was a place of labour protests, free speech, activism, vigils. After 9/11 he'd been here and sat amid the glow of hundreds of candles at a makeshift altar, soaking up the dreadful loss, trying to believe in a force of love so mighty – like the heat and light of the candles at dusk, endlessly multiplied – that it could actually fight and defeat such violence, that it was possible to break the cycle of killing and revenge. There had been such urgent graffiti crying *Love*, *Love* and *Fight War with Peace* . . . and in his heart he had not been able to believe. He'd felt a black flint of cynicism lodged there, and he bore it still. Love was not enough. Sometimes you had to fight.

'Robert.'

'Terri.'

'Walk to the eastern tip of the wheel.'

'Coming for you.'

He retraced his steps and followed the other arm of the horseshoe back in time: 1859 . . . 1857 . . . 1855.

He didn't immediately see Terri.

His eyes were drawn to the corner of one of the larger historic plaques set into the pavement. It was a compass, showing north. But not just any compass design. It was a compass rose. It was made of four hearts conjoined.

Robert, Katherine, Adam, Terri.

Images flickered rapidly in his mind. The four of them, dancing through time, connected by strands of fire . . . and a shadow among them, hiding something he could not see. Was it the Minotaur, latched on to Adam? The image vanished.

Then came a long-stemmed rose, on a misty night many years ago in Cambridge, as he knocked at the door of a Miss Kathcrine Rota at the start of a blind date.

Then, destroying the rose, came the swirling, pulsing eye of death, staring at them all. A voice came into his head, unheard but understood, and he spoke the words as he received them, like a radio. *Turn the flint into a jewel.*

It made no rational sense, but he understood. Passing the trials would give him that strength. The power to turn the black flint into diamond. To convert fear into love, and make it enough.

'Boo.'

Hands covered his eyes softly as the word registered in his mind. He turned around and pulled her against him, kissing her long and hard. Waves of lust broke over him. The world fell silent, and there were just her lips, her touch, her taste, her heat against his body.

Then she stopped kissing him back and pulled away.

'What's wrong?'

Terri looked up at him quizzically. 'That was Friday. This is today. Different trial, Mr Reckliss.'

He was still flushed with desire, with the heat of her.

'Katherine has left me. I told her what happened.'

'You took a very courageous step.'

'I don't know what I did.'

'You did what you had to.'

Now he stepped back from her, his hands on her shoulders, taking her in, absorbing her. She stood motionless, unseeing yet seeing, supremely confident in her stance, perfectly poised. His sudden access of lust was fading. Something was wrong with her.

'A different trial now. I understand. No more sex.'

'Not with me.'

'It was —'

'Be quiet.'

Her lips quivered. And, to his amazement, a tear ran down her cheek.

'What's wrong?'

'None of your business. Listen. The marchers will be here soon.'

He sighed with impatience. 'I need to find Adam again, Terri.'

'It's not safe. Not for any of us.'

'He needs me.'

'Sometimes he acts like he doesn't need anyone.'

He saw the flash of pain again cross her face. 'He hurt you?'

She hesitated. 'I'm afraid I'll lose him.'

'Afraid he'll die?'

'Worse. Lose his love.'

'Because of what you and I did?'

'No.'

'Do you regret it now?'

'No.'

'What, then?'

'I don't know if you're ready for this. I shouldn't give it to you.'

'Terri, what's wrong?'

'I'm losing control. I never lose control unless I choose to, but I'm losing it now.'

'I don't understand.'

'We're at a crossroads. We all are. We're all interlinked, and we're all being changed. When you told Katherine about what we did, you did it for a reason beyond simple honesty and devotion, right?'

'I did it so that Adam couldn't blackmail me with it.'

'You did what you had to do to protect yourself. Now I have to do the same.'

She seemed to be talking to the air, to someone he couldn't see. Convincing herself, he thought.

The voices boomed louder as the great swaying, swarming snake of people burst into Union Square, banners waving, drums pounding, chants resounding.

'Take this.' She thrust a slip of paper into his pocket. 'It's your clue. Now listen: I'm in danger. I have to look after myself now.

Your wife is with Adam. He still loves her. She went from you to him. Which means he may not protect me any more.'

He grabbed her wrist as she twisted away from him. 'Terri! Stop!'

But she turned his wrist over with astonishing ease, throwing him off balance, and vanished into the oncoming crowd of humanity before he could recover.

Robert was stunned. Katherine had gone to Adam? A bark of rage and pain issued from deep in his belly. Katherine and Adam? The hypocrite! How dare she! She paid him back like this? He fought to control his breathing.

'No! No!'

He heard himself shouting into thin air. Passers-by avoided his gaze. Agonizing pain coursed through his chest, surging into his skull.

'No! Damn it!'

He felt all the power of killing, of sex, of pride, that he had gained on the Path pouring into a black place of rage. He saw himself punching Adam in the head, remonstrating with Katherine, even as Kat threw in his face the utterly irrational, hypocritical nature of his anger.

But it was dangerous for her. Adam was teetering on the edge of evil, of giving himself over entirely to the Iwnw, if he hadn't already. Had she no idea? Was she joining them too, to work against him?

Suddenly he felt a shadow brush against his soul. Something had passed through him, tried to infiltrate him. The eye. Jesus Christ, suddenly he saw the eye of death staring into his eyes, and it was the Iwnw. Trying to feed on him.

His eyes fell on a huge digital clock on the side of a building facing the south-eastern end of the park. It had fifteen flashing numbers and was part of an art installation that Robert had never fully tried to fathom. The central three numbers usually moved so fast that you couldn't tell one from another, with the outer ones moving progressively more slowly towards the ends.

But now all the numbers were speeding up and starting to race so fast they were just a blur. The clock was going haywire.

An image jumped into Robert's mind, a symbol carved into the

James Leeson gravestone he had decoded: a winged hour-glass, dancing before his eyes.

Time flies.

The Iwnw were talking to him, feeding on his jealousy, showing him something. Toying with him even.

The numbers on the digital clock all suddenly stopped at once, on the digit 7. Then, in lockstep, they started to count down: 6 . . . 5 . . . 4 . . . 3 . . . 2 . . . 1 . . . 0.

At zero, the clock burst into flames. People screamed and pointed as black smoke began to lick from the number display. A smell of short-circuited wiring drifted towards him.

You can't stop us.

The words appeared unbidden in his mind.

Instinctively he dived into the deepest, most secret part of himself and drew strength there, then filled himself with fighting, hostile light to force the parasite out of his consciousness. He felt it leave, flying back to the virtual darkness it came from.

He staggered into the park, heading northwards, and found a place to sit for a moment. Sweat was streaming from his body.

March organizers called for calm over megaphones. 'The bang you may have heard was just a malfunction of the clock, people,' one boomed. 'Let's keep it calm, let's keep it cool, there's nothing to be concerned about.'

He looked up and saw police milling about the foot of the building where the clock was housed, outside the Virgin Megastore.

He turned his mind back within. The Path. It was the only direction away from the Iwnw. He had to get stronger. He took out the scrunched-up piece of paper Terri had thrust into his pocket.

Amazing turns await the lover
Whose heart is turned towards another
Seek a snake that spirals in
For now it's time to shed your skin
Find wisdom's gate, it's not too late
To conquer despair
Pass the Trial by Air

Chants filled the park. *Bush lies, who dies?* Still they came, wave upon wave of people, puppets and banners and drums, their course through the city flanked by NYPD in blue and National Guard in green camouflage.

He tried to block the demonstration out and concentrate. There were just too many people. How the hell was he going to find anything with the square jammed with protesters?

He tried to walk towards the north end of the park but found himself carried back south by the sea of people.

A snake that spirals in . . . shed your skin . . .

'Hell is other people,' he said out loud, as he tried to steer himself towards the edge of the crowd.

He edged round the fringe of the demonstration as it massed into Union Square, and eventually almost reached the Barnes & Noble bookstore on the park's northern lip. Directly in front of him was an open area popular with skateboarders, when the Farmers' Market stalls weren't set up on it. Hundreds of people were milling all over. Under their feet he saw twisting, painted shapes in green, interrupted by sneaker after sneaker, boot after boot. He couldn't see the pattern, but something about it drew his attention. He stepped closer, eyes on his feet, watching the squiggly painted patterns circle. *Amazing turns . . . a snake that spirals in . . .*

He found the edge of one of the patterns, pushing protesters gently aside as he moved, staring intently at the ground and not at their faces. He wheeled to the right and then to the left, back upon himself, towards the park and back again.

Amazing . . . a maze . . . He realized he was walking a labyrinth, a painted spiralling snake in green and yellow and red. Again he turned and turned about, almost reaching the centre and then being twisted left and right back nearly to the rim in a teasing dance. It was in a way erotic, teasing, but also childish and innocent. He felt suddenly joyful.

At the centre, he stopped and looked south. A buzz of excitement rippled along his spine. He had followed the snake to its end, where the painted spiral split into a fork, like a snake's tongue.

Ahead of him was a grey stone pavilion at the park's northern end, like the comfort station at Tompkins Square Park, a children's playground on each side and, in its centre, an arched gate.

Find wisdom's gate . . .

He stepped forward into the crowd, making his way as best he could in the direction of the pavilion, allowing himself to be swept in the good-humoured sea of people towards his goal. But suddenly panic ripped through the crowd. He heard shrieks and shouts, incoherent voices mingling and rising like an ocean surge. Looking towards its source, he saw a tall, white-haired man staring right at him, a smile on his lips. Then the wave came, a current of jostling, running people that knocked his feet from under him and carried him ten feet to his right and down to the ground.

He knew with instinctive certainty that the Iwnw had got into someone's head in the crowd.

Fearful, conflicting shouts went up. 'They shot a cop! They shot a cop!'

'Don't panic! Stay calm!'

'The pigs are coming! Everyone get out of here!'

'It was a firework, people! Stay rational! Stay peaceful!'

'Fight the pigs!'

'There are children here, for God's sake!'

Feet kicked him, trod on him. He felt terror. He was going to be crushed. He tried to haul himself up but couldn't. He rolled up into a ball, shielding his head, scrambling for footing. Then bodies fell on him, shrieking. The air shot out through his teeth. He was being squeezed to death. He strained to twist out from under the bodies. Children cried and women pleaded in panic as the wave of fear swirled through the people.

With a supreme effort he freed himself, crawling and twisting, kicking and pushing others aside, and took juddering rapid breaths as adrenalin ripped through his body. The Iwnw were trying to kill him. He found shelter behind a concrete flower tub and gasped and spat in pain.

Then he saw a little boy fall under the feet of the crowd directly in front of him, screaming. He was maybe nine or ten. Without thinking Robert leaped forward, back into the crowd, and forced himself between a sea of shoes to reach the boy, trying to protect him.

He managed to get up on one knee. Holding the boy around the chest, he stood. He forced himself to take a deep, slow breath. Two. Then instinctively he spoke, whether to the boy or the crowd he didn't know. 'Don't be afraid.'

Once again he gave himself up to the ebb and flow of the mass as he held on to the boy, slowly feeling the power rise within himself to become the pole around which all the people turned. He didn't know how it was happening, but instinctively he drew from the same strength that had expelled the Iwnw from his consciousness a few minutes before, and poured it out into the crowd with insistent, gentle firmness.

He saw to his right a mother screaming for her son. He felt the boy in his arm try to free himself.

'Is that your mother?'

'Yes.'

'Go.'

He put the child down and freed him into the open space. Then suddenly he was watching himself from above. The crowd swirled about him in a spiral, like the turning masses around the Kabaa at Mecca, like a roaring hurricane around its eye.

Three heads in the crowd caught his attention, shoving through the crowd in different directions, moving away from him now. He knew who they were. He had made them retreat. Pouring the strength of earth, water, fire and air into the crowd, he stilled the people, calming them, allowing his feet to be lifted from the ground as the flow dictated. Then finally he rooted his feet in place.

'Don't be afraid,' he said again.

He felt the panic dissipating.

Voices went up. 'It was a firework.'

'Everyone stay calm.'

'It was the pigs!' Boos went up at that one.

'Peace, everybody. Peace.'

When the whirling stopped, Robert found he was standing right at the centre of the labyrinth.

He stepped forward and the crowd parted, no one paying him

particular heed, letting him through as though they were a single thinking creature. No one had noticed what he'd done, except the men he was sure were the Iwnw. But he knew he'd averted a stampede. They would have inflicted whatever collateral damage it took to kill him. For a moment, he exulted in his new-found strength, and in the instinctive use he had made of it. He had risked his life to save the boy, finding the power to save perhaps dozens more. *Walk the path of the Other.*

He still needed the key.

Ahead of him was the comfort station. *Wisdom's gate.*

A metal grille stood open at the top of a flight of steps, letting him into the covered central section of the pavilion. To the left he saw gardening and maintenance equipment; to the right were the rest rooms. He looked about for any obvious niches or ledges. Nothing.

Dulled glass bricks were set into the floor of the pavilion, suggesting there was a chamber below, though he could see neither steps down to it nor up to the balustraded top floor of the structure. He checked out the rest rooms, getting nothing but a lungful of disinfectant. Protesters were swirling calmly now around the pavilion, but for the moment none entered. He was alone, at the still point of the turning world.

He looked down at his feet again. There was a ring of green paint around one of the glass cubes set into the floor. Looking around, he saw no other graffiti. He knelt and inspected it more closely.

It was a primitively drawn snake, its tail in its mouth, painted around the central cube in one of the arrays of light-bricks. It seemed to echo the design of the labyrinth painted on to the pavement outside.

Seek a snake that spirals in . . .

He put a finger on the cube. It was loose in its setting. He took out his penknife and worked it free, and underneath saw a sealed plastic bag. He scooped it into his pocket, quickly replaced the light-brick and walked out of the pavilion, back into the great wash of people. He had the fourth key.

*

He let himself drift in the streets of the city, exhausted, heading vaguely north and west, trying to avoid the protesters.

Eventually, in a doorway, he slit open the plastic bag and carefully removed its contents. There were five squares of what felt like pewter, stamped with numerals, each about one inch by one inch.

25	16	80	104	90
115	98	4	1	97
42	111	85	2	75
66	72	27	102	48
67	18	119	106	5

91	77	71	6	70
52	64	117	69	13
30	118	21	123	23
26	39	92	44	114
116	17	14	73	95

47	61	45	76	86
107	43	38	33	94
89	68		58	37
32	93	88	83	19
40	50	61	65	79

31	53	112	109	10
12	82	34	87	100
103	3	105	8	96
113	57	9	62	74
56	120	55	49	35

121	105	7	20	59
29	28	122	125	11
51	15	41	124	84
78	54	99	24	60
36	110	46	22	101

Stacked together, they made a cube. He saw that the thin edges of each square also had numbers stamped on them, so that the cube was itself made up of 125 smaller cubes, each marked with one number.

He was too tired to puzzle it out now. He put the squares away and walked on, observing the city and its people.

After each of the previous trials, immediately after being attacked, he had felt drained of all strength, barely able to think or speak. It had been a more intense feeling of exhaustion each time. Now he felt it hit him again, even harder than before. He felt like a zombie as he walked.

There was a fever over Manhattan. It was a humid, electric fever, a fear-fever, a super-conducting, barrier-breaking fever, one of sirens and shouts and disrupted rhythms. There were sudden rushes of vehicles, there were police motorcycles snaking up and down the island's spine, lights glaring, and there were special traffic lanes marked in orange cones, speeding black vehicles on special missions, roadblocks where usually access was free.

The fever was eroding distances, giving people permission to challenge one another, to berate, to confront, to seduce.

The airship floated overhead, seeing all. For a moment he saw it as the eye of death, the stare of the Iwnw.

There were strangers in town. People were removed from their usual paths, and new ones appeared before and around them. Excitement and fear salted the air. There was humour, and there was anger. People who would not usually speak, spoke. There was fear of attack, and there was fear of what the fear of attack was doing to people.

There was danger, and the city was alive.

He came to 34th Street and 8th Avenue, where police manned checkpoints in the sweltering heat to control access to Madison Square Garden, site of the Republican Convention. There were TV mobile trucks everywhere, antennae deployed, cables helixing along the shaft like the spiral stairs up the core of the lighting towers at the Lincoln Tunnel. He saw that CNN had taken over the Tick Tock Diner on the corner for the duration of the Convention, adding its own electric-red to the green-and-blue neon and chrome of the Tick Tock itself and the faded Deco glory of the New Yorker Hotel it was part of. The two Tick Tocks, in New Jersey and Manhattan, were superimposed in his mind: two separate but identical gateways to an imaginary, timeless Perfect Diner.

A young woman with a nose stud and black ponytail, wearing a pink 'Buck Fush' button on her black unbuttoned shirt, talked up a planned demonstration and the glories of real-time text-message-coordinated protest to a reporter on the other end of her cell phone. With a smile of wry amusement he realized after a moment that she was talking to one of his own reporters.

To his surprise he realized he didn't wish he were in the thick of the coverage. Deep down, since he'd been frogmarched out of the newsroom, he'd felt relief. He'd been bored rigid, half asleep, dying a slow death while he built up layer upon layer of aversion to acknowledging it. In a way, the same had been slowly happening to his relationship with Katherine. The miscarriage had been killing them.

Now he barely recognized his former self. And he knew he wanted Katherine back. This close to the great round drum of Madison Square Garden – not a garden, not square, not on Madison – it felt like all 37,000 cops in the city were within a hundred yards of him. Hot, angry New Yorkers and tourists bitched and moaned about not being able to pass. Cops politely redirected them along long blocks to the east and west, around the security perimeter. Sirens blaring, a rapid-response team tore past them a block away in a convoy of at least six vehicles, five of them minibuses, traffic cops waving them through a red light.

He had walked himself to a standstill. He decided to go home.

New York, August 29, 2004

Sitting on Adam's bed, deep into the undercover role the Watchman had asked her to perform, Katherine prayed for Robert.

She had received no warning that the Path would entail losing her husband this way. The Watchman had said nothing about it. He'd simply given her the mission to get as close as possible to Adam, claiming to have left Robert.

She'd built up a scenario in her mind, based on the real difficulties they'd had since the miscarriage, understanding that she and Robert would have to be apart while he walked the early stages of the Path. She'd begun to exaggerate their estrangement in her mind, even while trying to help Robert understand what he was undergoing.

The Watchman had said she'd know when to begin her run to Adam without his telling her.

And then Robert's confession had hit her like a thunderbolt. After that, there had been no need to play-act. She'd been given everything she needed to be convincing. It was at once a shrewd move by the Watchman and a form of punishment – so she took it, in her anger and pain – for her part in causing everything that was now happening.

She tried to still her mind, looking back on the past year and the events leading up to the impending attack.

Two days before the Blackout, she'd received a frightening email from Tariq. It was the first and only contact she'd had with him since handing him over to the interrogators. He was free, he said, and wanted her to meet him in Las Vegas, at the Luxor Hotel, at 6 p.m. on August 14. He had some very important information to give her. The message had resonated with anger and fear.

She had gone to the Watchman and told him.

The Watchman had contacted Adam, who for months had been tracking the potential attack. He took it as a tip that the detonation would take place on August 14. It seemed to show Tariq wanted her out of town that day.

And so she'd helped Adam prepare to face him, and then Adam had gone and fought Tariq, and killed him. He'd brought the Watchman a PDA that he took from Tariq, and the Watchman had handed it on to her. It had been of a kind she'd never seen before. Seals within shields within seals.

For a year she'd worked on cracking its codes.

She'd found a ghost programme of hundreds of three-digit numbers.

One string of numbers seemed to denote longitude and latitude. But when she'd looked them up on a globe, they'd proven to be mostly in the middle of the Pacific Ocean, hundreds of miles from anywhere.

Eventually, she'd seen patterns in the three-digit numbers. She found a programme that linked the digits to the longitude and latitude numbers. They were waypoints for a GPS unit.

She knew something of Tariq's mind. She knew how playful he could be with words, with numbers. She found a file of ridiculous-sounding doggerel of the kind she and he used to improvise for fun when she was wooing him. Then she saw that each one was related to a waypoint.

She got the feeling – sickening and heartbreaking at once – that Tariq had been thinking of her as he'd put together the intricately structured codes.

Still she worked.

The sequence of the waypoints puzzled her. The presence of an X in certain numbers ate at her imagination. In groups of four, the numbers added to 252. But there was something else she wasn't seeing.

Her last breakthrough, the one that had started the clock ticking, had taken place just over a week earlier.

She'd realized the Pacific Ocean longitude and latitude points were mirrors of points on the other side of the globe.

She'd linked all that data on the PDA and run a programme to strip out all the codes and encryption. It showed that, when the calculations were done, all the waypoints were actually in New York. In a very specific pattern along Manhattan.

And as soon as the programme had displayed all the linked data correctly, the PDA had lit up and issued its distress signal. For several seconds it gave off a burst of energy on an array of wireless wavelengths, then started to erase the data she had uncovered.

She didn't know what the signal had contained – whether it had transmitted the decoded information, or broadcast her location, or somehow primed the Ma'rifat' to explode. It might have simply warned an unknown partner of Tariq that the seals had been breached on the PDA, or something else entirely. Fortunately she had copied the decrypted data on to her own computer. And she couldn't shake the feeling that Tariq, in one way or another, had wanted her to have it. So that she'd know what he'd done? So that she'd see how badly she'd hurt him, to drive him to build such a device?

She'd told the Watchman immediately, and he'd moved quickly to consult Adam and put together a plan of action. Robert would be made to walk the Path of Seth. It was the only way. She hadn't fully realized what it would entail, just how destructive it would be.

She was hurting Robert by walking out on him, she knew. She'd always intended to deceive him at this stage of the plan, and that would have been bad enough, but necessary. Now, after he'd slept with Terri, she felt that the hurt she'd inflicted was justified and deserved. For the first time in her life, she cursed and prayed for a man at the same time. *Robert, you bastard. Get through this so I can kill you myself.* She half meant it.

Katherine's first proper meeting with the Watchman had taken place more than twenty years earlier, after the night of the fire at Cambridge, when he'd helped explain to her what had happened to them. He'd spoken of his mentoring of Adam, of the need to protect Robert. Their Ouija board session, he'd explained, had gone so badly wrong because of Robert's presence, because of his unacknowledged psychic power. Her previous sessions had been harmless, well attuned to her own abilities; but Robert had served as a hidden magnifying lens, unbeknown to either of them. Their innocent thoughts and slips of the tongue – wishing he was Adam, confusing the two men's names – and the emotional intensity of the evening had acquired huge resonance, attracting forces that ordinarily would have been kept at bay. At the level of reality where psycho-spiritual entanglement took place, where time and place were fictions, they had been linked for ever: Robert, Katherine and Adam. Robert's jealousy and insecurity had twisted through a loophole in the world, starting the fire in Adam's room. And, briefly, when the fire had threatened to kill Adam and Katherine, a manifestation of Iwnw had been attracted: the eye of death. Robert, somehow, had dispelled it.

She hadn't fully understood then. She'd remained in sporadic touch with the Watchman through the years of her secret work, though on Tariq she had not consulted him. Too secret, she'd told herself. Now she wished she had.

She knew there were parts of the plan that she didn't fully understand. Losing Robert was killing her, and hurting him was killing her. But she would do what the Watchman asked. And, for now, that was to win Adam's confidence, so she could stay close enough to surreptitiously give him strength to resist the Iwnw. The gamble was: could she hide her secret purpose from the Iwnw, and could she herself resist the Iwnw's influence when she was in such close proximity to it?

Little Falls, August 29, 2004

Once home, Robert posted a photo of the cube to the website Terri and Adam had given him.

The middle digit of the middle square was missing, he noticed now. If he assembled them as a cube, that meant the innermost central cube would be blank.

He let his mind range over the numbers blearily, looking for any obvious relationships between them. They seemed random, at least to his tired mind. Then he put it in the safe upstairs with the other keys.

He wrote some notes, trying to summarize his feelings, yearning for the Quad to buzz. There was nothing. He called Katherine's cell phone. It was turned off. Anger made him silent. Even if she had answered, he didn't know what he would have said to her. He left no message.

He let his mind fill with static and draped himself in front of the TV, watching coverage of the Convention preparations and the demonstration. He saw Commissioner Kelly had announced about 200 arrests. There had been no major incidents at the big march, though a dragon float of some kind had been set briefly alight, sparking a small mêlée. Later in the evening smaller groups had tried to block the entrances of two midtown hotels where Republican delegates were staying.

A news item said someone was distributing a fake New York subway map, with non-existent stations and routes, to mess with the Republican visitors' heads.

He saw images of police corralling protesters and journalists together in orange netting, saw the day's placards and slogans and papier-mâché heads and street theatre.

He watched middle-America Republicans breezily going to Broadway shows amid all the ruckus, their attitudes ranging from insouciant to contemptuous as they blew off the protests. He saw priceless cameos, his favourite being a middle-aged woman from New York indignantly shouting *'Get the FUCK out of this city! Get the FUCK out of this city!'* at an anti-protest protester who was berating the marchers for aiding America's enemies.

He fell asleep, chuckling, with her words echoing in his ears.

Hours later he awoke, feeling refreshed. He'd missed a text message on the Quad that said simply: 'Post your thoughts, urgently – Horace.'

He gathered his notes, stilled his mind and wrote:

What the fourth cache said to me

Sometimes the devil's water brings life.

I am being torn apart, yet I am growing more alive.

I am beginning to hear and see things I would never have believed were possible.

Since these events began, I have lost my job and been humiliatingly expelled from among my people. Tomorrow I will reckon with them.

I have been attacked and beaten, and left vomiting in the subway.

I have been almost drowned.

I have been almost blown apart in a gas explosion.

I have had the breath crushed out of my lungs.

I have willingly broken my marriage vows and lost the ring that symbolizes them. I have insulted my wife.

I have experienced a new autonomy, a new self-respect, then hurt my most beloved one in order to retain it. I have indulged my anger and desire for revenge, and I have dressed it up as honesty.

Yet, in facing death, in the play of lust in my flesh, I have found strength I never knew I had. I have turned basic urges – kill it, fuck it – into spiritual weapons, those of earth and water.

In rejecting blackmail, in asserting my utter freedom, I have added the power of fire to those weapons.

241

In diving into the crowd to rescue that boy, when self-preservation would have had me stay sheltering and cowering where I was, I have, I believe, added the power of air. It is what I used, without knowing how, to calm the crowd.

I am growing stronger as I advance along the Path, though all this strength is only lent to me, is not my own, is not for my vanity or advancement.

It is for Adam, to help him to resist the corrosion of the parasites within him.

It is for Katherine, to help her on the lonely road I have driven her to. If her being with Adam will help him survive these ordeals, then so be it. But I will have her back.

It is for Terri, to help her overcome the hidden new fear I see in her.

It is for Horace, to guide and instruct me as he may need.

Other people are not hell. They are salvation.

There is a shape in my mind that defies words, just as the peregrinations I have been on across Manhattan – the shape I have drawn on the city, the experiences at each waypoint – are drawing a shape in my soul.

I am seeing connections where none were apparent, lines and images of new harmonies.

The capacity to speak the language of the birds is awakening within me.

All this, to defeat those who have caused these ordeals to come to us.

I pray for my enemy, since praying for my friends is no virtue.

I forgive myself, for everything I have done has been necessary. I ask the forgiveness of others.

I am ready. I am alive. I will fight.

After posting his words, he sat staring into the night, all the lights out, waiting to hear whether he had passed the fourth trial.

Eventually Horace called him: 'I have read your post. You are advancing,' he said. 'But we are running out of time.'

'Have I done what was required?'

'Let me tell you about the fourth trial, and about what comes after.'

The fourth trial, he said, had brought Robert to the main cross-roads, or transition point, of the Path. At Union Square, aptly named for this stage, the physically based powers accumulated so far met the higher psycho-spiritual powers not yet discovered. The motors of transition from one to the other were the air powers, or the forces of compassion.

To pass the trial, Robert needed to have shown he was beginning to live for others beyond himself, placing his own ego and even his own chances of survival in abeyance. The trial required recovering a key in square or cubic form and finding the heart of his body of light. Without the powers of air, Robert would not survive what was to come.

'So did I pass?'

'The setting fire to the large digital clock was not a promising sign,' Horace scolded. 'There are shadow sides to all these powers, and your jealousy and anger ignited them. They also let the Iwnw get dangerously close to you.'

'I know. I'm sorry. I learned.'

'Be sure you did.'

He was struck by a sudden pang of fear. 'Did I fail?'

'From what you have written, and from the fact that you risked your life to save that boy and stop the stampede, which was aimed solely at killing you, saving countless more lives, I judge that you have acquired the power of air. Yes, you have completed the fourth trial.'

'Thank you.'

'Don't get cocky. We are just beginning.'

Horace talked for a few minutes about the nature of the Path. It was about speeding up and intensifying natural processes, he said, and living them many times in a single lifetime. It was necessary for a spiritual warrior to experience the erosion of ego. All human beings underwent this, in the trials of love, of parenthood, of serving causes larger than themselves. The difference was in the level of intensity, the degree of disciplined focus and the number of cycles of refinement undergone.

It was in part too what lay at the secret heart of alchemy: the hundreds of evaporations and distillations, meltings and coagulations, of substances in the laboratory flasks mirrored the same process in the alchemist, in the seeker of wisdom – but the substance was himself.

Robert asked him what he should expect next.

'The remaining three trials can be attempted only by an aspirant who has folded together, in creative balance, the elements of earth, water, fire and air. When the point of equilibrium is struck, a fifth element, or quintessence, is formed – then you will be exposed to the powers of ether.'

It was here that most people fell from the Path, Horace said, for the ether represented the level of reality at which all things were connected – the level at which higher harmonies began to be fully audible, and where clairaudience, clairvoyance and clairsentience began to occur. Many simply chose not to believe it – it contradicted too strongly the world they had grown up believing in. It was the level where the language of the birds began to truly sing.

Robert would be required to tap the energies of the ether, both by expressing in complete truth his thoughts and feelings, and in subjugating his own will – his own ego – to a will greater than his own, the will of the Path itself.

Robert would pass the test if he demonstrated an understanding of how he could now affect reality itself by using his will, yoked to that of the Path – of how he could warp and alter aspects of the world around him.

His dilemma would be simple: to trust, or not, the Path.

Robert would recover a five-sided key, divided into three parts. And he would reassemble another limb of his broken mystical body.

Robert was quiet for a while, absorbing Horace's words. Then he asked: 'What am I becoming?'

Horace laughed. 'None of this will make you a Buddha, or bring you to the level of a great teacher such as the Christ, or Muhammad. You are undergoing but one cycle in an endless ascent to such levels. But it might just be enough to stop the detonation of the Ma'rifat'.'

Then Robert heard a sound in the darkened house, a muffled crack. He felt his senses light up like a Christmas tree, nerves suddenly straining, muscles tense.

'Horace, someone's in the house. I have to go.'

He hung up and sat absolutely still in the darkness. No sound but his own racing heartbeat. He breathed deeply, trying to slow it down. After a moment, it settled to a firm, insistent hammering.

He stood up slowly, trying to make no sound. Very slowly he stepped forward, heading for the stairs. He reached out with his senses in all directions, seeking any hint of who or what was in the house.

A door creaked faintly on its hinge, upstairs. He imagined he heard breathing. Then all was quiet again.

Katherine had kept a gun in the house, but she had taken it. He kept a baseball bat, though, near the front door. He crept over to it and picked it up. Its heft in his hands reassured him. Gripping his hands tightly around the handle, Robert stood at the foot of the stairs, ears pricked.

No sound. His heart hammered solidly in his chest.

He began to inch his way upstairs, placing his feet softly, avoiding the seventh step that always creaked, making his way cautiously to the top. As his eyes reached the level of the first floor, he caught a glimmer of red light, as from a torch beam covered by fingers.

Someone was in his bedroom, the one that had been theirs until Kat had taken a different room at the low point of their estrangement. Anger welled in him at the violation of their home. Reaching the top of the stairs, he gripped the bat handle more firmly, ready to swing as soon as he had an angle on the burglar. He walked towards the bedroom. It was not Iwnw, he felt. None of their corrosive energy was in the house. It was more like –

Suddenly a black-clad figure rushed out of the darkness, like the darkness itself uncoiling into his face, crunching into his chin, snapping his head backwards. He reeled and fell, lashing up with the baseball bat as he went down. He made glancing contact with flesh, heard a grunt of pain. Then a kick slammed into his groin, and his whole body exploded in agony.

The figure tore past him and ran down the stairs in the dark-ness, not missing a step. Then it turned and headed to the back of the house. Robert heaved himself to his feet and half fell down the stairs in pursuit. He saw the back door close as he rounded the corner, and then the figure was gone into the night. He ran to the door, but knew it was futile. From their backyard there were at least three different directions to take to escape.

He stepped out and stood in the middle of the yard, ears straining for any clue. Nothing. He ran down to the street at the front of the house, looking for vehicle lights. Again, nothing.

He ran frantically back into the house, up to the bedroom, to the safe. The door was hanging open.

He looked inside, desperately clawing among the documents kept there. All the keys to the Ma'rifat' were gone.

A Martyr's Love Song: The Making of the Ma'rifat'

Three things led me to my death.

The first was the Mukhabarat.

Every month I received a videotape showing that my father was unharmed.

They sought demeaning things. To begin with, that I should pass on scientific information that I knew they had no chance of putting to good use, or to any use at all. Then, later, that I should try to build a network of spies in my community, seek to embroil and blackmail my colleagues with women, with alcohol, with drugs, with money.

I gave them the minimum I could to protect my father. Worthless scientific information they could have found in the academic journals. Titbits they could not possibly derive benefit from.

To honour my father and cleanse my soul, I returned to the study of the honourable traditions he and my grandfather had passed down to me, to the science of the Black Land, where 'black' is correctly understood to mean 'wise', to the alcumystrie that is neglected by the modern ways.

My Beloved, Katherine, gave me a precious gift around this time. It was a summary of lost knowledge, some of it written by the sages of my people, assembled by no less a personage than Sir Isaac Newton himself. To the layman, it would have meant nothing. It contained lists of chemical substances and laboratory procedures, times of day and night for prayer and reflection, astrological and mathematical symbols and scattered phrases in Latin.

But to one who recognized the alchemical significance of its contents, the full, undivided alcumystrie that was both our old tradition and the true subject of Newton's inquiries, it contained elements of an awful mystery: the combined spiritual and physical procedures, shrouded in warnings and obfuscations, for making the most powerful substance on earth. It is a form of matter that resonates to psychic fields, and in turn warps them around it. It is a key component in building the device known as the Ma'rifat'. It is most commonly known as the Philosopher's Stone.

I took Katherine's gift as a token of love. Now I know differently. But at the time it was a demonstration of trust. I confess I took notes from it. Then I returned the copy to Katherine.

The second thing that led to my death was Katherine herself. She was the world to me, the world I wished to live in, the world I wished to create.

For her I ran impossible risks, and eventually I was unmasked. On the very day I was to be extracted, I was arrested. There was torture, with electricity, with beatings. I did the only thing I could to survive. I negotiated. I was an American citizen. I could go undercover in America. Work in their laboratories. Anything.

They would not release my father. But they agreed to spare my life.

I was given training in overcoming security checks. Training in ceasing to be a good Muslim, so that, for the sake of my cover, I could allow myself to Westernize fully. My mother being American, my English being perfect, I found it easy. I enjoyed it. I stopped praying, except in the private depths of my heart. I drank alcohol. I enjoyed several relations with women.

Eventually, the good people of Brookhaven took me in.

The third thing that led to my death was 9/11. The hatred of that attack rings in my soul still. I saw nothing in it but sin, however mighty the hubris of the country I had adopted as my own, and the hubris was great. But the blow struck deep, and partly achieved its aim: it made America become more like the nation its enemies said it was. More like the nation its enemies wanted it to be.

And then a miracle happened. I met Katherine again.

She was as beautiful as ever. Her mind was as first-rate as ever. And soon she made it clear she had strong feelings for me. I had always held back on commitments in my previous relationships with women, and would prefer to cut them off if I found them too emotionally taxing. But this time, with her, with my Beloved, it seemed God had smiled on me. I let myself fall. And fall I did, heavily.

After 9/11, President Bush spoke of Islam as a religion of peace, and this was welcome. For that is what Islam is.

But one day I was spat upon in the street in front of my Beloved. My assailant was an uneducated fool. I told him so, and we fought. She was upset. But without his honour a man is nothing.

Then the Mukhabarat came back again and demanded more. The infor-

mation I was sending from America was poor, they said. My network was useless. I was told my father would be mistreated. I tried harder to give them nothing, but I failed. I received a phone call in which a tape was played to me of my father suffering. I knew it was his voice. And so I gave them more. I was ashamed.

My Beloved was my oasis. But I suspected she too saw my people as ignorant, as incapable, as backward. I think she saw me as a noble exception. I became angrier, as I became more fearful for my father, and as the Mukhabarat pushed harder.

My Beloved asked me more and more difficult questions about the world situation. I felt she was probing me, testing me, questioning my loyalty.

My only solace was in the old traditions. I saw parallels with our work on the accelerator, connections, points of contact. For in smashing together tiny amounts of gold at massive energies and charting the subatomic particles that blinked in and out of existence as a result of the collisions, we were getting closer and closer to observing creation itself in action, matter condensing out of energy and vanishing again — just as in the old tradition, where the dance of energy and matter was the subject of our manipulations. The difference was that we did not need massive particle accelerators, for the crucible of our minds was sufficient. The old way worked with rare substances — the rarest of all was one called red gold, said to be unfindable in the modern age — that were subjected to mental as well as physical experimentation. The state of mind of the knowledge-seeker, his level of spiritual concentration and refinement, was as important as the state of his retorts and flasks and furnace. And the ultimate end-product, assiduously sought but rarely achieved, was not any magical substance in and of itself, but the transformation of the one who sought it into a creature of higher spiritual insight and attainment. It was an honourable path.

I befriended colleagues who were working on a substance they thought was new: metallic glass. I learned things from them, without sharing in return the wisdom of my forebears, for the fusion of glass with different metals was part of the old tradition, part of a path they had no idea they were treading: making the Philosopher's Stone. For they took no account of their own psycho-spiritual states as they worked. In modern physics we do only half the necessary work, though even there the role of the observer in certain phenomena has been seen, since the early twentieth century, as an integral part of any description of what happens at the subatomic level. We are coming closer to once again seeing what the old sages knew: that consciousness and matter are intimately connected. I will never have the chance to work there, but I dreamed of carrying out experiments at the most powerful particle accelerator yet to be built: the Large Hadron Collider, set to begin operations in 2007 at CERN, the European nuclear research centre on the French–Swiss border. Humanity will learn things from it that will revolutionize our view of the world, but which were known to the ancient sages all along. It may also teach us how to destroy it in the blink of an eye.

I organized a study class at the laboratory to talk about the great contributions of my civilization to the world. It was well received. They are kind and thoughtful people there.

Then one day my Beloved took me for a drive out in the countryside. At a secluded spot, we stopped, and a van with no windows came out of nowhere.

I was taken.

The last words I heard her say were: 'He's all yours. I'm done with him.'

5

Trial by Ether

New York, August 30, 2004

They met in a conference room near the top of 570 Lexington, several floors away from the sensitive eyes and ears of the newsroom, at nine o'clock sharp.

Robert, sleepless and agitated, sat on one side of the table with Scott from the legal department, John from DC and a lady he didn't know from corporate human resources. In contrast to everyone else, he wore a battered sports jacket and no tie.

On Hencott, Inc.'s side were three lawyers of varying styles: avuncular-diplomatic (in his fifties), prim-procedural (in her thirties) and zealous-intimidatory (in his twenties). Robert decided the favourite-uncle guy was the dangerous one.

John, looking like the cat that got the cream, kicked off the meeting. 'Lady, gentlemen, welcome to GBN. You have made known to us your intention to institute legal proceedings against this house over alleged actions taken by GBN and/or one of its officers in the death of Lawrence Hencott, Chief Executive Officer of Hencott, Inc., in the early hours of Thursday, August 26. May I take this opportunity to extend our condolences for the loss of Mr Hencott.'

'You may, thank you,' said the older man.

Robert closed his eyes and visualized 570 Lex's glorious architectural summit a few floors above them: lightning bolts pulsing from clenched fists, a riot of spikes like a crown of thorns, symbols of radio waves spitting and crackling out into the ether. Although he'd missed only two working days, he felt like a stranger to the cramped, petty confines of the offices and cubicles below.

'You look . . . maladapted,' had been John's only words to him as they rode up in the elevator together.

He tuned back into the conversation to hear the younger Hencott man reading from the note Lawrence had left in the hotel room where he'd shot himself. '. . . what has happened is because of Robert Reckliss. I am only sorry I cannot tell him myself how much this has to do with him. Should anyone think me a coward for taking this action, let them reflect that sometimes it can be nobler to fall on one's sword than to continue living in a world of unthinking, blind corruption. To the poisonous ego of Robert Reckliss I say vile, intense torture reveals impossibility of living. It even sounds like a headline. My love to Horace, who will see that my will is properly executed.'

'Good heavens,' said John. 'Could we get a copy of that?'

'Already done,' said the woman lawyer. She handed round photocopies.

'A disturbed state of mind,' said Scott, shaking his head sadly.

'No actual mention of GBN here, I see,' John said, over half-moon reading glasses.

Lawrence's words reverberated in Robert's head.

'To our mind, Mr Reckliss was not acting in a solely private capacity at the time of his unfortunate interactions with the late Mr Hencott,' the avuncular Hencott lawyer said in a reasonable, measured tone. 'Without prejudicing any recourse that might be contemplated with regard to Mr Reckliss as a private citizen – and I think all of us would agree you might want to consider retaining a lawyer to represent you in a personal capacity in this matter, Mr Reckliss – the involvement of GBN, through one of its senior editors, and in its own capacity as publisher of maliciously harmful and inaccurate information, defamatory to Mr Hencott and prejudicial to the corporation he headed, is hardly in doubt.'

'Malice?' Scott interjected. 'There's no malice here, and you know it. That's just noise and bluster. And don't you dare come after Robert as an individual –'

John interrupted him with a wave of his hand. 'Actually, *do* you have a lawyer, Robert?'

Robert looked blankly at John, then at the others around the table. Around each of them he could see a faint halo of grey-blue light. He tried to blink it away, but there was nothing wrong with his eyes. As he looked more closely, he realized with mounting excitement he was seeing faint patterns of energy swirling slowly around each of their heads. He gazed in amazement, a million miles away from the morning's tawdry proceedings.

Vile, intense torture? He found it hard to imagine Lawrence Hencott having such a thin skin that he'd exaggerate so grossly what had happened. The man had possessed a hide like a rhino. And this wasn't suicide. Adam had killed him, Horace said. Or forced him to die. Not Adam, but the forces that were slowly eating Adam away. Why? What had Lawrence known? What was his role? He had to get out of this office.

He saw everyone was staring at him.

He spoke slowly and firmly: 'I . . . don't . . . need . . . a . . . fucking . . . lawyer.'

A cell phone buzzed and crept a few millimetres along the polished table. The junior lawyer scooped it up, apologizing. He listened for a few seconds and passed it to his older male colleague, who, after a similarly short period, flushed a sudden, violent purple-red.

'What? Say that again,' he snarled. An agitated voice at the other end spoke in jagged bursts. He tried to interrupt several times and failed. Then, with a brisk motion, he snapped shut the cell phone and handed it back. He began forcing documents into his briefcase.

'This meeting is over,' he said. 'I am to inform you that Hencott, Inc., will be taking no further action in the matter of the death of Lawrence Hencott, who, I believe, is being buried as we speak. I apologize for wasting your time, and I am to pass on to Mr Reckliss the warm greetings of the company's new majority shareholder.'

John looked equal parts euphoric and aghast. 'Who is that?'

'Mr Horace Hencott, the deceased's brother.'

The Hencott lawyers left.

They sat in stunned silence. Eventually, the woman from HR spoke. 'I don't think I'm needed here any more.'

John signalled to her to sit still. 'Actually, there is still the question of our internal investigation. Over the last few days I've looked into

Robert's actions, and I have to say there may be grounds for internal disciplinary proceedings.'

Scott spoke up before Robert could react. 'Are you crazy? What grounds?'

'Negligence, dereliction of duty, poor judgement. We can't have our interviewees topping themselves the next day! It's already a joke on the Street.'

Robert stood up. 'None of this matters,' he said. 'I'll be back when I'm ready. I may be several days. Unless you do want me to get a lawyer? In which case I'll be back when I'm ready *and* you'll give me a big pot of money.'

John shouted at him as he opened the door: 'You're to say nothing about this to anyone, you hear? Nothing! I'm not joking!'

Robert looked him in the eye. 'No gags, John.'

And with a smile in his heart he went down to the gorgeous aluminium-clad lobby and walked out into the street.

London, September 1990

Robert held the embossed invitation in his hand and laughed out loud.

You are invited to a one-time-only theatrical event. In the garden of the Club of St George, Whitefriars Cut, EC4. A reading of the play *Newton's Papers*. 8 p.m. Black Tie.

He telephoned Adam Hale immediately.

Both were living in London at the time, Robert starting his seventh year at GBN, with solid stints in Paris and Madrid behind him. Adam had moved to London from Central America earlier in the year, ostensibly as chipper and sardonic as ever but in actual fact desperately short of money, haunted and alone. His ex-girlfriend Isabela, a poet and journalist, had been killed almost a year earlier. He had found her body by the side of the airport road in Santo

Tomás, shot in the back of the head. She'd been the love of his life, and in his grief and loneliness Katherine had been his biggest prop and supporter. They'd become inseparable, and in a rush of mutual need had got married earlier in the year.

Adam was freelancing like a madman and travelling as much as he could. To help out, Robert was trying to get him a job at GBN, much as Adam disliked institutions. Now that Saddam Hussein had gone into Kuwait, it seemed likely they'd be able to use him.

'What the hell is this? You're putting that damn play on?'

'Rickles. How lovely to hear your voice.'

'Did you finish it? When?'

'It's been something of a side project in the past few months. Between assignments, you know. Something to keep the heebie-jeebies at bay. Memories, and so on.'

'That's astonishing. Did you finish it on your own?'

'Or collaborate with Katherine? It's been a wonderful project for us both, actually. And now we can write it *and* sleep together, of course. How is Jacqueline, by the way?'

Robert and Jacqueline had been seeing each other for three years now, keeping apartments in Paris and London that allowed them to be together often. She was a childhood friend of Katherine, of impoverished French aristocratic background, working in PR. It was a monogamous, unmarried arrangement, childless so far.

'She's splendid, thank you. Is the invitation stag or can I bring her?'

'Stag, I'm afraid, old man. Very limited seating.'

'No problem.'

'I was just shouting at someone at the Iraqi Embassy, actually, speaking of work.' The workings of Adam's mind were as much of a mystery as ever to Robert. 'Unhelpful sods. Press accreditation for Baghdad? I might as well have been asking for the keys to Saddam's private bathroom.'

'I'm sorry?'

'Not your fault. Is it? Shouldn't think so.'

After all these years, Robert was still easily exasperated by Adam's flippancy and non sequiturs. 'What does Saddam's bathroom have to do with *Newton's Papers*?'

'Nothing at all, old man. So, you'll attend?'

Robert checked the date again on the invitation, breathing deeply as he did so. 'Absolutely, yes. I'd love to.'

'Excellent. Since you were in at the conception, so to speak, you'll be an honoured guest.'

'What's this club, by the way? I've never heard of it.'

'My grandfather was a member. One or two other friends too. It's a bit like the Special Forces Club, or the Explorers' Club, only a bit more . . . esoteric. You'll see.'

And so the first and only performance of *Newton's Papers* took place on a warm September night in a walled garden behind a highly discreet private club near St Bride's Church, just off Fleet Street.

It was not at all what Robert, or Adam, had expected.

New York, August 30, 2004

As Robert walked north along Lexington Avenue after leaving GBN, the Quad buzzed with a text message from the Watchman. At last. He'd been unable to reach Horace the previous night to tell him about the keys. It read simply: 'Waypoint X69.' The GPS programme showed it was over on the far East Side, near the veterans' hospital at the end of 23rd Street.

Robert had no time. He wanted to engage the enemy. All he could do was burn through the rest of the stages of the Path as quickly as possible, and pray he could recover some of the remaining keys. He felt light-headed with joy at sending the lawyers to hell. What an extraordinary manoeuvre by Horace! He'd always imagined him leaving worldly matters to Lawrence, but there was clearly more practical know-how to his old friend than he'd imagined. He started to dial his number, but remembered just in time that he'd still be at the funeral.

Standing at the corner of 52nd Street, where Marilyn Monroe's dress had been so memorably blown up by the air from the subway grate in *The Seven Year Itch*, he raised his arm and a cab appeared immediately. He told the driver to drop him on the southern side of the hospital on 23rd Street.

When he got there, the Quad pointed further east and north. Puzzled not to have received a clue yet, he walked towards the East River along 23rd, the VA Medical Center to his left, coming to an elegant turn-of-the-century pavilion marked MEN over one door and WOMEN over the other. It was a free public bathhouse, now repurposed as the Asser Levy Recreation Center.

The Quad led him past it, further north. Robert walked to a deserted children's playground and basketball court.

Now the clue arrived. Robert imagined Horace sending messages at discreet moments during the funeral.

> *The first of three, to make a five*
> *To stay the course, to stay alive*
> *Seek stepping stones that cross no river*
> *Fish and stars, but do not dither*
> *You seek the hidden door*
> *Seek balance at the core*
> *To pass Ether's Trial,*
> *Try hopscotching a while*

Robert stood and stared at the playground, letting his mind wander till he saw it: from the kids' slide to a drinking fountain there was a series of circular stepping stones, like jellyfish in the sea.

He walked over to inspect them: they were carved with semi-zodiacal motifs, about forty stones in all, of different sizes. There were crabs, fishes and sharks; conches, nautilus shells and starfish, all following a wavy, snakelike path.

He walked the stepping stones from the slide to the drinking fountain, which was broken. Then he turned and walked back down again, stepping first right, then left. Maybe kids did play a kind of hopscotch on them?

One of the stones wobbled slightly as he put his foot on it. It was a smaller one, a five-pointed starfish. He kneeled and gently pulled on it to see if it would move further. It lifted like a lid, and underneath was a sealed plastic 35-mm film container.

'Bingo,' he whispered.

He took it and carefully replaced the stone, stepping firmly on it to try to settle it. But inside the cylinder there was nothing.

'Fuck!'

The Quad buzzed again almost immediately. 'Then go to Way-point 090. As soon as you can. I feel Katherine is in trouble.'

It pointed him west, along 23rd Street. There were no cabs to be had. He ran back to First Avenue in the sweltering heat for a cross-town bus that was just about to pull away, cursing and praying in equal measure. He launched himself at the bus door as it closed, jamming an arm in and forcing the driver to open it again.

London, September 1990

Robert took the Circle Line to Blackfriars and walked to St Bride's Church, then spent several minutes wandering around the back-streets off Fleet Street, wondering whether he'd somehow misread the invitation, before finding the unmarked entrance to the Club of St George on Whitefriars Cut.

The modest, understated exterior of the house hid a sumptuous lobby, flagged in checkerboard squares of black and white, where a uniformed doorman checked Robert's invitation and ushered him to a small library, where sherry and snacks had been laid out.

'I hope I'm not too early,' Robert said, seeing there was no one else in the room.

'You're in perfect time, I'm sure, sir,' the doorman said, with a former policeman's intonation. 'Mr Hale said we should expect you.'

Soon other guests arrived, tuxedoed or in evening gowns, and Robert eased his social discomfort by inspecting the bookshelves and firmly clutching his sherry glass until spoken to. The library was heavy on medieval romances, translations of Persian and Arabic poets, and explorers' expeditionary tales. He also noticed several books on heraldry.

Snatches of foreign tongues reached his ears. Czech? Polish? He recognized some Portuguese, Spanish, French. An urbane man in full Arab garb switched easily back and forth from polished English to the beautiful metres of Arabic.

Soon about sixty people were in the library, with as many again mingling in the lobby.

'See anything that interests you?'

He turned to see a very tall man with prominent teeth and iron-grey hair in a formal military uniform, a buxom redhead on his arm. She smiled at him as his mind raced to remember who they were.

'Hello,' Robert said, playing for time.

'Knight to knight, come forth,' the lady said. 'You beat us, remember? *Omnia vincit amor*?'

'Good God.'

Then a gong rang, summoning the audience to their seats.

New York, August 30, 2004

Robert got off the bus at Madison Square Park. Before him rose the Flatiron Building, its triangular wedge pointing north, the undulations in its long face like ripples of stone frozen in time.

He walked to the corner of the park by the statue of William Seward, the man who had bought Alaska. There was a story that Seward had been a smaller man than the tall, lanky figure shown in the sculpture. But the artist, angry about being paid late or not enough, had used a torso of the rangier Abraham Lincoln he'd sculpted for another project and simply appended Seward's head. The story fell into Robert's 'too good to check' file.

Following the Flatiron's line uptown, he turned right. The Empire State Building reared directly ahead through the trees, ten blocks north, and closer to Robert a flagpole drew his attention. He walked to its base and smiled with recognition as he saw the five-point star carved into its base over the words AN ETERNAL LIGHT and, at the top of the pole, a five-pointed lamp in the form of a star. It commemorated military dead in World War One.

'After the square comes the pentagram,' he said into the air. 'Tomorrow I predict the Star of David. What will seven be?'

He tried to fathom the significance of the numbers and shapes in the Path. First a circle, then a vesica piscis made of two circles, then the site of the Triangle factory fire and all those triangular plots of land, producing a pyramid key; then the cubic key at Union Square. One component added to the geometrical shape with each trial. Did it symbolize that he was growing, increasing in knowledge and complexity, even as doom approached? Did it reflect the equipoise between building up and tearing down that was going on within him, or perhaps the balance between his growth and Adam's corrosion?

He had to focus. As soon as there was a chance, he'd ask Horace. No new clue had come. He turned away from the park and looked west, scanning for anything that would help his quest. He saw something he'd observed dozens of times before and never truly seen until that moment: in the middle of a large traffic island, where Broadway and Fifth Avenue crossed, rose a fifty-foot obelisk.

He felt the city wheel about him, pinned on him as though he were its axis. Shapes and alignments formed in his mind and rushed past his imagination faster than he could perceive them. He saw a vertical line right along Manhattan's spine, crossbeams from the East Village to the West Village and now from the starfish stone to this place of pentagrams to . . . where? It would have to be Chelsea on the West Side . . .

The shock of the vision left him staggered and dizzy. It left as quickly as it had come.

He breathed deeply in and out. He didn't know how to hang on to such flashes of insight. The harder he tried, the more it receded.

Frustrated, he crossed the street to inspect the new obelisk, trying still to reconjure the image.

The obelisk at St Paul's Chapel suggested that a body lay beneath it when in fact there was none. This one, he saw, made no bones about what it covered. Beneath a rendering of a severed arm wielding a sword, the plaque read:

Under this monument lies the body of William Jenkins Worth, born in Hudson, NY, March 1, 1794, died in Texas, May 7, 1849

The site was ringed with ornate ironwork, also in the form of swords. The monument was erected in 1857. *Honor the Brave,* exhorted the stone plinth, which was also marked with two five-pointed stars.

Adam had shown exceptional courage, and now, he felt, Terri was doing so too. Yet he could feel years of built-up anger at Adam coming to the fore. He felt the futility of letting fear censor what he said and thought and felt.

He had to meet Adam and find a way to turn the tables.

Adam was both the enemy and the ally. How long could he hold out against the great corrosive force that was slowly taking him over? One more day? He felt in his heart that Adam could still be saved. Which Adam was still in love with Kathcrinc, if Terri was telling the truth?

The path back to Kat and to helping Terri was the same. He felt a pang for Terri, always in control and now, he saw, utterly terrified of something, wounded and alone, probably for the first time in her life. Dependent on others. Closing his eyes, he saw her in his mind's eye as spiritually aflame, fearful, trying to shield herself from Adam and from the darkness within him.

Something had gone terribly wrong for her. He felt dread.

What had she been hiding from him? Closing his eyes and trying to reach out to her with his mind, unsure how to tap his new powers, Robert got insistent images of the vesica piscis, two circles forming from one, four circles from two, eight circles from four . . . *cell division* . . . the words formed themselves in his mind.

Oh, God. She had to be. *Cell division . . . since Friday.* Pregnant by him. Surely not. It couldn't be. He tried to look deeper. Dear Lord, no. She'd said there was no chance . . . *there was a shadow over the cell*

263

division . . . darkness and fear attends this division . . . He lost the words that were forming, jumping back out of the streaming river of information he had dipped into without knowing how.

If Terri was pregnant, he felt no link to what he had seen, no sense of connection. Could the father be not him but Adam? Still a cloud of malevolence hung over the images. *If she wasn't pregnant, then . . .* He lost the thought.

If Terri was afraid of Adam, it could only mean he had tipped further towards evil. If Adam was still in love with Katherine, that meant Terri felt displaced. Unprotected. She had described in their first conversation on AOL how Adam had protected her from a bad place. Now he was not protecting her. How far gone could Adam be? If it was his own child, surely he would not turn from Terri, if he had a strand of humanity left in him. And if he had truly crossed over, then Katherine was in terrible danger from Adam, whatever skills she had been able to revive.

The full strength of his feelings about Adam over more than twenty years came barrelling into his mind. The constant sense that he would one day do more harm than good. Always his arrogance in assuming that he could get away with outrageous stunts when others couldn't, that his unique capacity to mesmerize would carry him through when lesser souls struggled in the mud. Always the feeling that all those dazzling gifts would end up being wasted, thrown away on some madcap scheme, gambled and lost for a thrill. Deep down, despite Adam's generosity, despite his genuine care for others, despite his ability to disturb lives in good ways, Robert had always been angry at Adam. Jealous, envious and angry.

Walking around the obelisk, he searched for any more details that might help him. He found little but a list of battle honours. He took out the Quad and googled Worth. Was there something he was missing? The only thing he found was that a relic box had been set in the cornerstone of the monument, like the Garibaldi statue time capsule in Washington Square Park. For a moment the image seemed to want to tell him something; then he lost it.

He crossed 25th Street and walked further along Fifth Avenue, drawn by a flag with a large *P* emblazoned on it. And just past the corner he saw what it represented: at Number 204 were the offices of a design firm called Pentagram, with its name carved right into the building above the door. Another five. It gave him gooseflesh.

Suddenly the Quad buzzed. He activated the earpiece, and then Adam's voice was in his head. His heart pounded.

'Robert,' he said. 'Quite a pickle we're in, wouldn't you say?'

'You fucker. You've got a great deal of explaining to do.'

'When have I not had, Robert?'

'This isn't a game to me, Adam. Where is Katherine?'

He was speaking out loud into the air, as though Adam were right there all around him in the sky.

'Nothing's ever a game to you, Robert, that's one of your problems. Where do you think Katherine is? She's a free spirit.'

'I want to talk to her and hear her voice.'

'You think she's with me?'

'Don't lie. Don't fuck around. I know she is. She went to you after I told Kat I'd slept with Terri. And I bet she has the fucking keys. All of them. Which means you do. So you got what you wanted. Are you really trying to set this thing off? It's really going to happen, isn't it?'

Adam fell silent for a moment. Robert could feel his anger. No, not anger. He closed his eyes and held Adam in his thoughts. Darkness. Fear. It was raw fear.

'Robert, she's not with me at the moment, I'm afraid. We'll arrange something very soon, I'm sure. I need to explain a few things.'

'Tell me.'

'Where to begin? There was this woman –'

Robert snorted. 'There's always a woman, Adam. The clock is ticking. I want Kat. Where is she?'

Adam was silent for a few seconds in a way that seemed wounded.

'I will tell you everything. Everything. If you just give me two minutes. Listen to me for two minutes.'

'Is Terri pregnant? Why is she scared of you?' Anger flowed

through his words. 'You arrogant, self-centred fucker. We're out of time. You can't hang on. You're not superhuman. We have to stop this thing from happening! Give me Kat. I want her back!'

'You should have thought about that before,' Adam quipped. 'And if you want to survive the fifth trial, I'd rein in that nasty temper. Take it as a tip from one who's been there before you.'

Robert paced in the street, speechless with rage.

Then Adam shouted: 'You have no idea what I'm facing. Truly no idea. I will give you Kat. In two minutes. But listen to me first. For two fucking minutes! Or you will never hear from me again.'

Robert breathed deeply, willing his anger away, trying to control himself. It occurred to him that Adam thought this might be his last opportunity to tell his story.

'OK. Two minutes. You have two minutes.'

Adam paused, gathering himself, calming his tone. Robert crossed back towards the obelisk.

'Let me start again. After the performance of *Newton's Papers*, with the dreadful things that happened at the end of that evening, I broke with Horace, my mentor since I was eighteen years old. And things got weird.'

Robert absorbed his words.

'They weren't weird before? I mean, you apply a different yard-stick of weird than most people, you should realize.'

'Listen to me. I want you to understand. Horace watched over me at my grandfather's request, once I began to show signs of aptitude for the Path. They'd worked on an intelligence mission together in World War Two, the one that led to my grandfather's recovery of the Newton manuscript. I have walked the road that you are walking, though far more slowly. When we met at university, I was really just beginning. Those games of the night of the fire were my first attempt at orchestrating *experiences* in a way that would reflect the complexities of the Path, the way it works on many planes at once – mental, geographic, symbolic, existential, psycho-spiritual . . .'

'Go on. When are we talking about?'

'Early 1990s now. I told Horace I didn't need a mentor, didn't need a master, I was going to walk the Path alone. I lost my mind around that time, you may recall.'

Robert thought back. Adam had suffered a breakdown in the early 1990s, it was true, during his ill-fated tenure at GBN, after the *Newton's Papers* affair. Then, claiming to be haunted by Isabela, he'd uprooted himself and returned to Central America, got into trouble there, taken up an itinerant life.

'You weren't well at the time, Adam. But listen. This had better tell me something I can use. We have no time, if I'm going to help you.'

Still he struggled to control his impatience. He could feel exhaustion behind Adam's mock jauntiness. Pain and exhaustion, and an indomitable will holding it at bay.

'I wasn't well, it's true. Walk with me a moment, would you? Look around. Can you see west along 25th Street? Lovely church, Serbian, St Sava. I derive solace from it. Nourishment. Look east? The first two Madison Square Gardens were at the north-east corner, the ones that were really on the square. Second one had a stunning tower, based on the Giralda in Seville. Just like the Biltmore. What else do you scc?'

'The MetLife Building.'

'It's based on the Campanile in St Mark's Square, you know that? 700 feet. World's tallest building between 1909 and 1913, when . . .'

'. . . when the Woolworth Building was completed downtown.'

'Very impressive. Also known as 1 Madison Avenue. In 1908, beforc it was finished, one of the New York newspapers installed a huge searchlight in the tower to signal the result of the presidential election of that year. The beam would swing north for Taft, the Republican, south for Bryan, the Democrat. Imagine that.'

The north–south axis along the length of Manhattan flashed into Robert's mind again, fleetingly. He still couldn't see the full figure. Was Adam trying to help him?

'And next to it, to the north? What do you see, Robert?'

'Also MetLife. Great Deco hulk, 11 Madison, covers an entire city block. Lots of Masonic flourishes, I've always thought. Where is this leading us?'

'Oh, you'll get Masonic flourishes later, if that's what you like. This one is twenty-nine storeys; it was going to be a hundred, but they crapped out when the Depression hit. It would probably have been the tallest in the world too, if they'd stuck to the original plan.'

'Why are you telling me this?'

'About MetLife? So basic a riddle.'

'What?'

'So basic a riddle. MetLife.'

He pronounced it oddly. With the slight distortion of the phone, it sounded as if he'd developed a lisp.

'Are you having trouble talking straight? I don't have time for any more riddles. Talk to me.'

For a third time, Adam said it, exaggerating his pronunciation even more strongly. 'So basic a riddle, met lice.'

Robert felt a wave of compulsion suddenly envelop him, an urgent plea. *Remember this. Remember this.* He fixed it in his mind.

'OK. I hear you.'

'So I came to the New World. Montreal, New York, Miami, Las Vegas. Nine years ago.'

'Vegas? Doing what?'

'Winning money, mostly. Very odd. Had a couple of good nights. Never been able to hang on to it for long, to be honest. But it helped me fund myself. I decided to see if I could fuck myself to death.'

'You wanted to die, or you wanted to fuck a lot?'

'A bit of each. I was actually trying to create my own Tantric practice. That tells you something about my ego. It had to be something suited personally to me, but also something I might enjoy, something where the deprivations were things I didn't mind giving up that much. So I gave up smoking. Took up with a lady who was into it. Sexual exploration to the end of the road. Near where you are now, actually, on 27th just past the Gershwin Hotel, there's one locale . . . group sex for couples. Wild times.'

'Thanks for the information. What's the point?'

'Remember everything I tell you. There's method in the madness. They always say you can drive yourself mad if you don't have a mentor or guide in these spiritual quests, someone who's trodden the path before you . . . and I spent several years without heeding my mentor. I'm afraid I got myself into terrible trouble.'

'You were surprised that the divine wasn't to be found at orgy clubs?'

'I'm giving you the short version. There was far more to it than that. Retreats. Long periods of abstinence. Meditation. Breathing control. Discipline. Study. Do you remember the Unicorn game back at Cambridge? Many years of vulning. Many years of bosing, but the ground you are bosing is your own soul. They are the same thing. Some people even come at it using pain, power exchange, fetish play. Not my cup of tea, certainly. But there are different paths. And you see, it can work. It really can.'

'What can, Adam?'

'These things are kept secret for a reason. There's a path in every culture, in every religion, a hidden path, usually, reserved for special adepts, hidden behind codes and denials and rigorous disciplines. It unleashes powers of the mind and soul we didn't know we had, Robert. The names vary. Sufis, Kabbalists, Gnostics . . . The Christian mystics like St Teresa or St John of the Cross glimpsed it.

'What they have in common is an ascent of the soul that's a descent into yourself, a knowing of yourself that somehow leads to a knowing of the divine . . . but it also unleashes a lot of other things, for those who don't entirely understand what they're doing, like me. And it attracts attention . . . oh, yes. It draws the attention of those who have followed the same path for reasons that are far from good and altruistic. People like the Iwnw.'

'They found you? Back then? And this hidden path you're talking about, is it the same one I'm on now?'

Adam snorted in anger at himself. 'Yes, they found me. As for the hidden path, this is what Horace taught me. There is a single Path, though there are many ways to approach it. The approach you're taking is among the most arduous and dangerous. The Path contains the true inner meaning of all the great religions, which ossify over time, losing touch with all but their outer shell. Its adherents do not advertise, do not proselytize, but when someone is ready for the Path, a teacher finds them. These people are called by many names at different times in history, but Those of the Perfect Light is a common one. Around the world, they have private, discreet groups of supporters. The Club of St George is one. This is also the secret core of what the alchemists sought. Making gold from lead, or finding an elixir of life, were by-products, or even just metaphors, for reaching the highest level of the Path, where consciousness becomes so refined, and so powerful, as to be able to mesh with matter, control it, manipulate it. It is a goal achieved by very few, though many try.'

'Is the Path good? Or just neutral, depending on what use we put it to?'

'It is good, Robert. It says things that make no rational sense, because they come from a place far beyond reason. It says, for example, that love is the most powerful force in the universe, that love *is* the universe, and that the universe dwells within each of us. But each of its stages has a shadow side. And that is where the Iwnw dwell. Like the Perfect Light, they have representatives in the world, or adepts, if you prefer.'

'And they found you?'

'They did. I let them in. I had to go back to Horace and beg him to take me back, to forgive me and to protect me against them. This was in 1997, about a year before that event I pulled at the Biltmore. He helped me rid myself of them. In return, I've helped him track and fight the Iwnw ever since.'

He heard Adam suddenly breathing hard, taking quick, sharp breaths. He was fighting something off. Something dreadful. The Iwnw were squeezing the life out of him, trying to break through and control him completely.

'Adam?'

'Keep walking. Walk towards the Flatiron, then back around the obelisk.'

He walked. 'Talk to me, Adam.'

'Round you go.'

He reached the southern end of the traffic island and turned back north, towards the odd low green granite structure behind the obelisk. It was unmarked, with metal doors and grille windows set in the sides. Lush plants grew in the garden next to it, around the Worth Monument. He rounded the corner of the structure at the north end of the island. And there, smiling but white with pain, wearing a cell-phone mike/earpiece, his hands in the pockets of his jacket, was Adam Hale.

London, September 1990

An audience of fewer than 200 people – Robert later learned there were 170 numbered invitations – drifted out into the walled garden behind the club and were ushered to their seats. It was a perfect evening, warm, with a light breeze.

The seating was arranged in an L on two sides of the square, just as Adam had intended nine years earlier. The bricks of the wall were thin, the size of slim paperbacks: they looked far older than the rest of the club. Three ornate wooden chairs formed a crescent facing the angle of the L. Two had small lecterns like music stands in front of them. A single sapling stood in the centre of the square, perhaps three feet tall, a low table covered with a dark cloth next to it. The far angle of the garden, behind the chairs, was screened off with black curtains to form a backstage area.

Robert, having enjoyed a basic desultory chat with the Knight and his Damsel while queuing to take their seats, now lost them as they were directed to the other side of the garden. They had joined the club a couple of years after university at Adam's invitation, they'd told him, describing it as an organization that sponsored archaeological digs and expeditions to exotic parts of the world.

He was placed at one extreme of the L, an empty seat next to him.

A gong sounded three times to signal the performance would begin shortly.

Then Katherine slid into the seat next to Robert.

'This is very exciting,' he said.

'More than you know,' she replied, looking worried. 'This is a big deal for Adam.'

'How so?'

'You remember the Newton document? Adam took an oath while he was at university to protect it. You remember we talked about it, that night.'

He tensed involuntarily in his seat. 'I remember almost nothing of that night.'

'I know. Take it easy. He swore the oath to his mentor, an old friend of his grandfather. Part of the oath is that every certain number of years, those protecting such documents or knowledge are required to share them with the world. But they must do so in a way that only those worthy of the knowledge may understand it. It's Adam's time to keep his oath.'

'You mean the Newton paper Adam's grandfather recovered in World War Two?'

'Yes. This club is a society that helps to protect such secrets and tries to find others lost to time. Some members are in it purely for the exploration and the history, but others know its true purpose. It's a safe venue for Adam to fulfil his oath. But not everyone agrees that this is the way Adam should do it.'

'Sounds like crap to me. Can't he just hand it over to a museum and be done with it?'

'It contains powerful secrets, Robert.'

'Nonsense.'

The gong sounded again. The polyglot murmuring subsided, and an actress in her early thirties came out from behind the curtains, wearing black trousers and blouse. Robert recognized the woman who had taken the role of the Tart at the founding of the Unicorn Society nearly a decade ago.

'Ladies and gentlemen, Sir Isaac Newton,' she declaimed, and bade the audience applaud as the curtains opened again and a bewigged figure in seventeenth-century costume strode out briskly to centre-stage to receive the ovation. It was Adam, grinning with delight and glorying in the applause. A third actor, also clad all in black, followed him through the curtains and urged the audience to clap louder.

The actress brought a book up to chest height, and read from it in exuberant fashion:

> 'Newton's eye sublime
> Marked the bright periods of revolving time;
> Explored in Nature's scenes the effect and cause,
> And, charmed, unravelled all her latent laws!'

Her companion did likewise:

> 'Nature, and Nature's Laws, lay hid in Night.
> God said, "Let Newton be!" and All was Light!'

Adam joined in at the climax: 'I'm in Westminster Abbey, you know!'

The applause melted into laughter, and then Adam brought them down to silence as the other actors stepped back and took their seats.

'I'm an adjective,' he said with pride. 'A unit of physical measurement. A byword. *Newtonian.* And what world does my name describe?' He made a sour face. 'Clockwork.' He gave the audience a long, cold stare. 'Godless clockwork, no less.' He shuddered. 'Not a world I can live in.'

He wheeled on his heel and went to sit down. From his chair, grumpily, he continued: 'I voyaged through *strange seas of thought, alone.*' The two backing actors pronounced Wordsworth's words with him. The effect was spooky.

The performance alternated monologues from Newton and brief readings of documents and letters by his backing actors, with scenes played out dramatically by all three.

They raised a laugh by staging the story of the apple falling on Newton's head, and supposedly inspiring his insight into gravitation, with a small mannequin placed under the sapling. They told how the whole thing was an invention of Newton in his old age. They quoted John Maynard Keynes, purchaser of Newton's long-hidden alchemical papers in 1936: not 'a rationalist, one who taught us to think on the lines of cold and untinctured reason . . . not the first of the age of reason' but rather 'the last of the magicians, the last of the Babylonians and Sumerians, the last great mind which looked out on the visible and intellectual world with the same eyes as those who began to build our intellectual inheritance rather less than 10,000 years ago . . . Copernicus and Faustus in one.'

In one scene, Newton spoke of the full scope of his vision of the world, and of his sadness at becoming a byword for just one fragment of it, the scientific method, to the exclusion of the rest. The scene pitted Newton against a young atheist physicist. 'You created everything I believe in,' the young man told him. 'You banished superstition. You showed that the human mind, through observation and experiment and reason, can understand the universe without recourse to cave paintings, thunder gods and poring over bird giblets!'

Newton turned to the audience, angry and frustrated.

'You see what I created? I thought I was knowing God, not killing Him. We could coin a new Newton's Law. We'll call it the Law of Unintended Consequences.'

'You showed that it makes no sense to speak of God. Reason does not require fairy-tales to fill the gaps where it has not yet penetrated. God is a pathology, the fruit of our fears, nothing else. You taught us that!'

'I did no such thing!'

'Science measures what is real. The rest is just mumbo-jumbo.'

'You little smatterer! You godless whelp!'

The young man didn't let up. 'You cleared the way for the death of God!'

Newton thundered, beside himself with rage, almost in tears: 'Blasphemer! Remove yourself from my sight!'

The actor sat down. Newton stepped closer to the audience. 'I sought knowledge,' he said, and his voice seemed to rise from the depths of his soul. 'I walked the Path. Knowledge lies shattered in this world, strewn in fragments, like a butchered body, its limbs dispersed to the four winds. But we can find a piece here, and a piece there, and fit them back together. I invented nothing. I re-discovered a few fragments of knowledge, and pieced them back together. There are thousands of other fragments lying all around, hidden from our unseeing eyes. Hidden in plain sight, mind you.' He knelt down, in a posture of prayer. 'I sought to live in unfractured light, in the Garden of Eden, folded in the love of God,' he said. 'But I also found that, in walking the Path, some knowledge is forbidden. We discover knowledge that can destroy the world.'

At that moment, all the lights went out.

New York, August 30, 2004

Adam stuck out a hand to shake Robert's. Instinctively, Robert took it and a force like electricity tore through him. Adam held on to Robert's hand for dear life, supplication in his eyes even as his nonchalant smile stayed fixed on his face. Robert closed his eyes. He saw a dark shadow against darker light, and mutely beseeched it to recede.

Adam let go and slumped back against the curved wall of green granite. An octagonal window in the main metal door contained a card giving a number to call in case of alarm malfunction.

'What is this?'

'It's the entrance to Water Tunnel Number One,' Adam said.

The image of the tunnel's course flashed in Robert's mind. Union Square Park. Madison Square Park. Then it would go on to . . . he saw it. The Manhattan axis flashed into his mind again.

'Today is five,' Robert said. 'Pentagram. Five-pointed star. I've done one through four. Yesterday was the square. Tomorrow will be six, Star of David, at Bryant Park. The New York Public Library.'

'Think of it as the Shield of David. You'll need it. But remember, the waypoints just help you get to where you need to be.'

'What's on the other side of this? What's left when this is over?'

'Hopefully we are. Thank you for helping me. The scavenger hunt. The Path. This is what it's about. Over time I developed certain powers. They are incidental to the spiritual path, they come only when you're no longer impressed by them, and when you accept the responsibilities that come with them. To the regular mind they would be called supernatural, though they're simply part of our nature hidden to most of us. Powerful intuition is one. Working with Horace to oppose the Iwnw helped me to detect a man working at Brookhaven National Laboratory on Long Island. They have the particle accelerator there and a host of other powerful machines for advanced physics research.'

'I've heard of it. I know what you did.'

'Then you'll know I tracked and eventually challenged this individual. He had built and was intending to detonate the device. The Ma'rifat'. It was to be a 9/11-type attack, but far worse. Something more like Hiroshima. On August 14, 2003 I hunted him down out on Long Island. Fought with him.'

'I know about that. How did you survive?'

'I didn't, necessarily. I'm on borrowed time. I was powerful enough to shield myself, but . . .'

His voice cracked. He clenched his teeth. Again Robert felt the force of his will, like a mighty generator. Thrumming. Crackling.

'I became entangled. So did Terri. I wasn't pure enough. Fear. Guilt. My brother's death. He died down an old well, did I ever tell you? We were playing in the garden. Wrestling, fighting. He trod on a rotten wooden cover, over a well no one knew was there, and fell in. Knocked himself out and drowned. Not my fault. But I had gateways left open, and guilt over Moss was one of them. The man I killed grabbed me when he died in the blast and held one of them open. He became a Minotaur, a lost soul, psychically powerful but dependent on another to survive. Other beings are forcing their way through the gateway now. The Iwnw. The Minotaur has become the gateway for them. They want to feed on me. They resonate like a harmonic musical note with your DNA and slowly colonize it, hiding in the junk DNA, slowly turning you into them. I'm trapped, and they're compelling me, so help me God, to detonate the remaining device. I can't hold on much longer. The only thing that's helping me hold it at bay is this.' He removed the Malice Box from his pocket and brandished it.

'Katherine gave it to you.'

'She did what she must.'

'Then it's as I said. She gave you all the keys I found.'

'They're safe. Until they're needed. This one, I need to keep with me.'

Robert stared at its mesmerizing light as Adam held it in his fist. Katherine. How could she betray him so thoroughly?

'I have come to understand that there were two devices, you see. One that was already in place, hidden somewhere in Manhattan a few days before the Blackout. It was a twin. Female to the other's male, if you will. There was an array of keys along Manhattan to link the two devices, to transmit the energy from the one I destroyed to the other. Those keys are what you and others have been hunting.'

'This twin device, you say. It survived the Blackout and is armed? Still hidden in Manhattan? That's the one we need to disarm now?'

Adam nodded, sweating. His hands were shaking. 'It'll take the keys and this core to disarm it. Of course, once it's loaded with the keys, and the core, it can also be detonated. Add a couple of extra ingredients and it'll be more powerful than the original.'

'What extra ingredients?'

'You'll find out when you need to know.' Adam winced with pain.

'You can hold on, Adam. I know you can. Don't do this.'

'I can slow it down. But it's all up to you now.'

'Why just me? Horace is far stronger than I am. There must be others.'

'Even Horace isn't a Unicorn. Robert, there are no Unicorns left in the world. You're the only one. Fighting the Iwnw is like producing a counter-note, a pure tone powerful enough to absorb or disrupt their harmonic. Except it's not music, it's prayer, it's meditation, it's concentration of spiritual force, of goodness, of selflessness. You're the only one who can do it. Horace can only help you part of the way.'

Robert closed his eyes, willing the snatches and bursts of partial vision he had been experiencing, the fragmented power and understanding, to start to weave together into a harmonious whole.

Otherwise, he knew with certainty, he would not be strong enough. He willed it with every fibre of his being, then abdicated his own will and placed himself entirely at the disposal of the Path. Robert tried to grab Adam by the hand and somehow transmit strength to him, saying, 'Fight, old friend.'

Adam recoiled with a sound like a snarl, his face darkening. 'Let me explain something. Here's a webcam site. Take a look.'

Adam took a device like a cell phone from his jacket pocket with his free hand and hit a button, then another. Robert's Quad received a text message containing a URL. Robert clicked on it and saw, in grainy black and white, a jerky image of a woman sitting bound in a chair, an oddly shaped box on her lap, holding herself absolutely still.

'That is Katherine,' Adam said. 'She's in a room in this approximate vicinity. In the box, which as you might expect at this stage has five sides, is a glass vial containing an odourless, tasteless, colourless substance that explodes upon contact with air. How angry are you with Kat right now?'

Robert peered at the small screen on the Quad, trying to gauge if it really was Katherine.

'It is her, I assure you. Are you angry enough with her to want her to die?'

Robert flew at Adam, grabbing him around the throat with his left hand and slamming him hard against the green granite of the water tunnel entrance. He punched him on the side of the head with the Quad.

'Let Kat go! Let her go or I'll kill you right here!'

Adam reacted like a snake, curling out of Robert's grip and grabbing his left hand before spinning round and twisting it up between Robert's shoulder blades. Pain ignited in Robert's upper arm. It felt as though it would snap at any moment. He tried to walk forward and lean over to relieve the pain, but Adam pushed him face first against the stone.

'I found Katherine being a naughty girl earlier today,' he hissed into Robert's ear. 'I came back earlier than she expected to the apartment we're using, and I found her with two parts of the fifth key. One from Asser Levy Park, one from the garden here by the obelisk, which she'd just recovered. It looked to me like she was hiding them instead of handing them over to me. She swore she wasn't, but I honestly wasn't sure.'

He again slammed Robert against the stone.

'Now, I love Katherine – you've always known this, I still do – but I can't have her not trusting me. Not now. Not with all the high expectations of my Iwnw friends upon me. So I asked her for the parts of the key, and she gave me them. Then I decided to remind her of how serious a matter this all is. A little test to see how far you've come on the Path, and what we have to contend with in these coming final days. In the box is a ticking clock. When it reaches a certain time, it will complete an electric circuit, driving a small plunger to break the vial. As in our broader scavenger hunt, Robert, you're running out of time.'

Adam released him with a shove and stood back. Keeping his gaze on Robert, he walked round to the west side of the obelisk. Robert followed, eyeing him, rubbing his arm, estimating when and how he might be able to attack again and overpower him.

Adam had all the keys. Robert had to get the core away from him. But that would take away Adam's last defence against the Iwnw. It would tip him over the edge, send him all the way to hell, as it took away his ability to detonate the Ma'rifat'.

Robert had no choice but to take it from him.

As for Katherine, he cleared his mind of anger towards her. Observed it and acknowledged it was there but did not let it reach him.

'Robert, your attention please. Are you familiar with the device known as the mercury-tilt switch?'

'Used in car bombs and heating systems.'

'Right. Good. A small glass bulb, hermetically sealed no less, containing a drop of mercury and two wires that are not touching. When it's at a certain angle, the mercury flows to one end of the bulb and there is no circuit. Change the angle, and the mercury flows to the other end of the bulb, joins the wires and completes the circuit. Then, if it's attached to anything explosive, boom.'

'Oh, Jesus.'

'There is one of those in the box too. A very delicate one. Only Katherine's ability to keep it balanced on her knees is keeping it from going off.'

He looked again at the image on his Quad screen. Her stillness. Barely daring to breath. Her entire body was locked in mortal fear. He could see her head bowed in concentration, trying to control every tremor, block out every cramp as her muscles rebelled against the frozen posture she was holding them in.

'You're really going to kill her.'

'Not if you can work out how to save her, Robert. I have every faith. I'm not allowed to know everything that's going on in the scavenger hunt, as you know, but I thought of this one myself. I'd been saving it up for a time when it would be necessary to ask someone: how important is balance? What is its nature? What happens when we achieve it? How do we lose it?'

'Where is she, Adam?'

'Learn to see, my friend. I have walked the Path before you, remember. It cannot be taught. It cannot be put into words. It can only be experienced.'

Robert racked his brains.

'Would you like a clue, old man?'

'Yes, you sick fuck.'

'Then there has to be a forfeit. Tell me where Terri has gone.'

'I don't know where she is.'

'She appears quite taken with you. Unhappy with Katherine showing up. They really don't like each other any more, it seems.'

'Any more? I said I don't know where she is.'

'Too bad. This is all about choice, Robert. The clock has three minutes to run.'

London, September 1990

Towards the end, a member of the audience shouted out at Newton: 'But you are a fraud, sir. You claim to seek God's truth and yet you dabbled in the dark arts!'

Newton paused, turned, addressed the speaker. 'I beg your pardon?'

'You dabbled in alchemy, I say. In black magic!'

Newton fixed the heckler with an icy stare. 'The pursuit, sir, of the Philosopher's Stone is no black magic.' He paused, and then addressed the audience as a whole. 'Yes, it would have ruined me, had it been known. For we all live among the ignorant. To protect my identity, when dealing with brothers in the pursuit, I used a pseudonym. It was an anagram of my name. ISAACVS NEVVTONVS became IEOVA SANCTVS VNVS. One Holy God. But understand this. They who search after the Philosopher's Stone are by their own rules obliged to a strict and religious life. Humility is required.

'The secret of alchemy, it is said, is all contained in the one phrase *vitriol*, which stands for *visita interiora terrae, rectificando invenies occultum lapidem*: "Visit the interior of the earth; in rectifying, discover the hidden stone." And the correct understanding of the interior of the earth is the interior of our own souls, where we must rectify our self-seeking ways. Now, I have heard it said that I might be querulous. I can also be a vain man. But in following the secret fire of the world, the single, central flame that is light and life – in alchemy, in scripture, in gravity, in calculus, in the nature of light – I was pious. I strove for that state of spiritual grace without which the alchemical processes are simply . . . chemistry. I would pray from my heart.

'I pursued alchemy for most of my adult life, as part of the search for the One Truth, the Path we have all lost. It was the search for the vivifying spirit, the active principle that produces order, structure and life in creation. We called it by many names. We called it the vegetative spirit, the secret fire at the heart of the world, like the sacred fire at the heart of Solomon's Temple. We called it the quintessence, the fermentational virtue, the body of light, Mercury's caducean rod, magnesia. To my mind too it was Christ. The mediator. The one who adapts God's light to our world. The unifier of heaven and earth, as I unified the heavens and the ground beneath our feet through my theory of gravity . . . I pursued the Philosopher's Stone, yes.'

He paused.

'And there is something more.'

He stepped forward, and with a flourish pulled a dark cloth from the low table next to the sapling. A small glass drum, glowing with light, turned slowly atop the table.

'I found it.'

A gasp went through the entire audience. Katherine gripped Robert's arm.

'Knowledge may be used for good or ill,' Newton said. 'Possessing the Stone, it is possible to transform matter – make gold, cure illnesses – and transform human beings. It is also possible to unleash atomic and spiritual forces for ill. Turn man against man, brother against brother. Unleash forces that could destroy the very earth. The Stone may be used to build a device that can do these things.'

He pointed to the glowing glass drum. 'I have made this crude rendition of what such a devil's engine might look like. A rotating array of lenses, made of the substance of the Stone, focusing energy on the Stone at its core, internal lenses arranged in specific geometrical patterns. Three components are required to make such a device: the Stone, and knowledge of how to use it; mastery of the geometry of shifting focus and lenses; and the intensifying power of the substance known as red gold. Only the last was denied to me, for this substance is so rare; some say it can no longer be found. Each stage and each component must be imbued from the start with the highest level of spiritual dedication and refinement on the part of the maker, or all is for nought. Permit me to tell you of how I made – and lost – this discovery.'

Robert's heart lurched. It was true. The forbidden book. The one that Kat said had caused the fire. Adam was going to read from the secret Newton paper.

New York, August 30, 2004

'I need more time. Reset it.'

'I can't.'

'What do you want Terri for?'

He snorted. 'I love her. She's remarkable.'

'And Katherine?'

'Robert. Dear Robert. I love her too. I'm sorry.' Suddenly Adam broke down in tears of pain. 'This is too much. Get away. Get away. It's coming. Oh, God . . .'

A shadow crossed Adam's face. While his eyes begged for forgiveness, his hands shot up and closed around Robert's throat. Robert drove his arms up in a wedge to break Adam's grip and punched him hard in the face.

'Tell me where Katherine is.'

'Go to hell.'

'Tell me.'

He punched Adam again, in the solar plexus. He was heavier than Adam, stronger. 'Where is she?'

'I can't.'

'I am not your enemy. Fight your enemy.'

'You are my enemy.'

'No, I'm not, Adam.'

'Go to hell.'

Robert threw Adam against the railings around the obelisk and punched him again, flipping him over into the vegetation. Leaping after him, he grabbed Adam's arm and twisted it behind his back, slowly forcing his fist open. He ripped the Malice Box from Adam's hand.

'No!'

Adam forced his arm free and drove his elbow back, hard, into

Robert's throat. Then he jumped to his feet, vaulted the railings and ran. By the time Robert had extracted himself, Adam had vanished.

He tried to shout Adam's name. His throat wouldn't work. He couldn't talk.

He'd said three minutes.

Christ. Katherine.

Robert looked again at the Quad screen. Tried to make eye contact with Kat, even though he knew it was a one-way transmission. She was still sitting stock-still. Hadn't moved. How long had they fought for? Not even thirty seconds. He stared at the box on Katherine's knees. Felt out to it with his mind. Closed his eyes and focused on a single thought: *Balance. What is balance? What is the meaning of balance? What do we do after we find balance? How do we lose balance?*

He willed time to slow inside the box. Time and vibration to halt. In his mind's eye he willed the mercury's temperature to drop, its atoms to slow. He held it in his thoughts, slowly freezing it, praying the glass would not shatter before the mercury froze solid. He saw Katherine react, lifting her head slightly, disbelief and puzzlement stitched on her face.

He thought of the crowd at Union Square, wheeling about him as he stood in perfect balance at their core, acting as their pole, their centre, his feet off the ground, holding them and being held.

He thought of what happened when he tried to put his feet down, when he tried to fix a single spot for them to gyrate around. When he forced and fought the crowd, and fell. He abandoned his own will and let his intention melt into the fabric of the world itself.

Then he saw the mercury freeze. He saw the clock stop. Katherine saw it too. She looked up and gazed, wide-eyed, into the camera. His thoughts manifested in the world. His intention became reality.

He saw Katherine relax in the chair and nod. He saw her smile. She looked down, twisting her shoulders and body as she freed her hands. Then she grabbed a pen and notebook from her bag, scribbled something urgently and held it up to the camera: an address on 25th Street, perhaps a block west. *Basement*, she had written.

He ran to 25th, finding the building in less than two minutes. It was a ten-storey brick residential building, fronted by ornate iron railings. It had a basement apartment.

He kicked the door with all his might. The locks cracked and flew apart. The door creaked open. He saw the chair she'd been sitting on. The box. The camera. No sign of Katherine or the bomb.

He opened the box, hoping against hope to find part of a metallic-glass pentagon inside. But there was nothing in it but a scrap of paper in Katherine's hastily scribbled handwriting. *Thank you, my darling Robert. That bomb was not a toy. It was live. You saved my life. But, despite what he did, I am going after Adam. I can still help him. I love you. Go to Waypoint 067. Go now.*

Robert kicked the chair, then grabbed it in anger and frustration and smashed it against the wall. If Kat went back to Adam now, he was sure she would die.

London, September 1990

The glass drum changed colour as it slowly spun, shifting through deep blues and yellows and rich reds, then white again.

The audience sat spellbound.

'I found it. And then I lost it.'

Adam discarded the cloth and stepped closer to the drum, letting it light his face from below. He looked spectral, grotesque.

'One winter's day in January 1678, alone in my laboratory, after much prayer and many sleepless nights, I was blessed with success. I cracked open a mould, and in it I found the secret of secrets. The Philosopher's Stone. I knew it immediately. It was a disc. It shone like this drum. Its innards swirled and turned.'

There were voices of protest in the audience. Hisses. Calls for silence. Applause.

'How did I achieve it? For years I had worked with metals at my forge. For years too I had worked with glass, grinding my own lenses to the precision I required.

'*It is a stone and not a stone*, the Ancient masters said. Fluid yet solid. Dark yet light. And one day I saw: glass is a liquid. You will have seen windowpanes in old houses, perhaps a hundred years old or more. The panes are thicker at the bottom than at the top. The glass has flowed slowly down.

'It is fluid yet solid. It can be made when sand is struck by lightning. It is fire and earth, water and air. The Ancients coloured glass by mixing metals and metal compounds into heated, glowing, incandescent glass. Our glorious cathedrals and chapels house masterpieces of stained glass.

'I began to experiment. I varied temperatures, hour of the day, position of the sun and moon, metallic compounds delicately heated and cooled, glass delicately mixed and heated and cooled again. I prayed, fasted, spent night after night watching carefully over my apparatus.'

He listed the metals and compounds he had used, the temperatures and stages of the process, all hidden under a veneer of alchemical code: *green lion, white rose, our sulphur, sun and moon, king and queen.*

'Those who find the Stone,' Newton now roared, 'have since time immemorial hidden it in plain sight. Published how to find it. Always leaving an element missing, a part transposed, a defect that only the wise will see. I shall not depart from that noble tradition.'

There were more smatterings of applause.

'This is how we pass along the secret. On that winter's day, I cracked the mould. I had done so hundreds of times before. And pure light shone from within. A glow as soft as love, as strong as lightning. The perfect amalgam of glass and metal, neither one thing nor the other. I was dumbfounded. I stared at what I had done. And I heard these words in my soul: *Flamma unica clavis mundi.* "The key to the world is a single flame." I saw the one truth. The one flame beyond and behind all else. The unfractured light at the end of the Path.'

Adam paused. He looked as though he were going to add another phrase. Katherine gripped Robert's arm so hard he almost cried out. 'Don't say it!' she hissed to herself, her eyes on Adam. 'Shut up! Don't say it all!'

Then Adam chose not to go on. He stepped back from the glowing drum.

'Holding the One Truth still in my mind, I ran out of the laboratory to the chapel to give humble thanks to God. Yes, the same chapel where now you may see the statue of me. I was perhaps ten minutes gone. And in those ten minutes ... because some knowledge starts fires, because a wall of fire surrounds our world and limits what we may know ... a candle fell among my papers as I prayed and set fire to all the work of those months, and several years prior, and all my notes of that day.

'Finding the fire spreading upon my return, I extinguished it with water. And when it was out, surveying my charred notes and records, I found ... I had lost the Stone. One page remained, with some of my notes on the discovery. Incomplete. Charred. The Stone itself? A shattered, ruined husk.'

Adam reached into the folds of his costume and removed a sheet of paper. He unfolded it and prepared to read it. Several people in one group stood, their eyes fixed on the document.

'*Flamma unica clavis mundi*,' Adam said again. 'O –'

His words were never heard. A deafening thunderclap sounded, and the sapling before him burst spectacularly into flame. It was a stunning effect. As it burned and crackled and spat light, the spinning drum too ignited, showering sparks on to the actors and into the audience.

As the audience began to applaud, the burning tree flared brighter, fanned by a sudden swirling wind. Then, in a violent gust, the flames leaped directly at the actors. To shouts of horror, Adam's costume burst into flames. At the same time, two members of the audience rushed forward and descended on Adam, trying to rip the precious document from his right hand.

'Iwnw!' Katherine shouted.

Screaming in pain and defiance, Adam kicked one of his attackers in the stomach and punched the other in the throat, then ripped off his burning wig and ran towards the curtained-off backstage area. His two fellow actors ran to the attackers and tried to pin them down, followed by several members of the Club of St George.

Robert saw people trying to smother the flames on Adam's costume with their bare hands. He and Katherine ran forward to try to reach Adam.

Then a sheet of blue fire shot up from the mêlée of people piling on to the attackers. Several people were thrown back, their clothes aflame. People ran about, zigzagging and screaming. Audience members and officers of the club ran to them, pulling them to the ground and beating out the flames as others burst into the garden carrying fire extinguishers and heavy blankets. No one could later say how, but amid the confusion and mayhem the attackers escaped.

Robert and Katherine ran round the fallen burns victims and saw Adam dive through the curtain and disappear backstage.

They pulled the curtains aside – and found no one there.

Ten people were treated for burns injuries received that night. Two were permanently disfigured, including the actress who had appeared with Adam on stage. Adam never ceased to be haunted by what had happened.

When he vanished backstage, Adam had run through a basement door behind the curtains that was invisible from the audience's location. He had been planning to use it for a closing effect – they'd go backstage and then the curtains would open and they'd be gone. But he used it instead to get the precious document away from the attackers.

Robert had no idea what to make of what he had seen. He interpreted it as an attack with incendiary devices or flares of some kind, for reasons he couldn't fathom.

He and Katherine had gone to hospital with Adam, where he was treated for mild burns on his arms.

Later, Robert and Kat had spoken while they waited to hear about the condition of some of the other victims. 'There were people in the audience protecting Adam, or he would have been far more seriously hurt,' she told him. 'But there were others who shouldn't have been there. Somehow they infiltrated the club. None of us detected them. They wanted the secret of the Stone, but not for any good purpose.'

'Who are they? A band of arsonists? A rival club?'

'They are no joke, Robert. They are most commonly called the Brotherhood of Iwnw.'

'Younu? And what's this secret of the Stone nonsense? Surely you don't still believe in all that undergraduate game-playing crap?'

She took his hand and squeezed it, looking into his eyes. 'Robert, you should get out of here. Get home. I'll look after Adam.'

Robert knew she was sending him away to shield him from something she was afraid of. He didn't want to leave her.

'Can I do anything to help?'

'One day. Not now. Good night.'

New York, August 30, 2004

Robert walked west on 25th Street, following the GPS direction finder, his throat pulsing with pain. He could feel his strength waning again, more violently than on any occasion before, yet a soaring sensation of harmony still reverberated in his body and mind. He marvelled at what he had done, however much it had cost him. And, above all, he had saved Katherine.

Contending emotions broke over him in waves as he forced his leaden legs to keep moving forward. The Quad was pointing him further south-west. He walked along Sixth to 21st Street and turned right, past the sad, tiny Spanish and Portuguese Synagogue Cemetery. He marched west along the course of the old Love Lane, long ago subsumed into the Manhattan grid.

Kat still loved him, of that he was certain now. But, in still staying with Adam and trying to bolster the dying strands of goodness in him, she was risking everything. The Iwnw could get into her too. Adam could prove too strong for her.

Robert emerged at Ninth Avenue opposite a 1960s concrete stilted building with a bowed frontage. The General Theological

Seminary. To its north, an array of small two-storey wood-slatted buildings looked like they had dropped into Chelsea from 150 years in the past.

The Quad pointed him insistently into the grounds of the seminary.

Exploring, he found a gate into the gardens on 20th Street. It was huge. He'd had no idea. He sat on a bench in a cloistered red-brick courtyard garden, just like those at the old Cambridge colleges, an oasis.

His mind ran loose as he sat still and tried to absorb all that was happening.

Directly in front of him was the chapel, two panels of Christ's life in each door. To his left was a beautiful stone house, its front covered in vines, with chimney-type towers set at 45-degree angles, suggesting an inward fifth point. The house itself was Number 5. It was a place of harmony.

Exhaustion was pounding him now. Images floated up into his mind from the night of the fire in Adam's room, when his life and Adam's and Katherine's had become entangled for ever. It still stirred dread in him. For two decades he had never spoken of it, shunned thinking of it. What was he still afraid of?

The answer lay behind a closed door at the end of a corridor more than twenty years back in time, and he acknowledged again that the idea of opening it paralysed him with fear, that beyond it were things he had silenced for all of his adult life.

What was behind the closed door at the end of the corridor?

For twenty years he had espoused the sceptical mind, the empirical approach. Dismissed what he'd seen as a figment of his mind, of an overwrought night of drinking and sexual tension and confusion.

But he knew better. He remembered the figure of death floating over Adam and Katherine. He remembered looking into it, into the paralysing, staring eye and its rippling blue-and-yellow flares of light.

It spoke to him. It said: *Who are you?*

And, knowing it had come for Adam, he said: *Adam Hale.*

And the figure had turned its wrath on him and been . . . confounded. Shattered and dispersed.

Robert knew, beyond any doubt, that he had seen it, and that everything that had happened that night was real. Robert bore the gift that his family had sought to stifle in him, out of love, out of fear of where it would take him. But, on feeling the power of his gift, he had recoiled in terror.

Now he realized: he had not been ready. Horace and Katherine and Adam had all been right to protect him. He felt a wave of gratitude towards them, and a powerful sense of clarity and purpose. Such love must be repaid. Now it was time to put aside fear and to become fully who he was. To bend events to his will. For the sake of all those who needed him. To reclaim his gift.

The Quad buzzed. The clue.

> *Find the power of five, to keep us alive*
> *If you follow the signs, you'll be tilling the vines*
> *A north-easterly flue is a smokin' good clue*
> *Asserting your will, will do you no ill*
> *But surrendering more*
> *Will show you the door*
> *Seek balance at the core*

He walked over to the right-hand chimney of the stone house and sank his fingers into the dirt, below the nearest vines. He had to dig deep and quickly, but he found it. Plastic bag. Film container. Small glassy-metal shape. A segment of a pentagon.

He staggered back to the bench and almost blacked out.

With every atom of his being he wanted to force himself to his feet to go to protect Katherine, help them all, stop the detonation. Yet he recognized the pattern: after each acquisition and use of a new power, he had to recover his strength and absorb what he had learned. He had to demonstrate that he understood.

He lurched to his feet and managed to find a cab, settling on a fat fare again to New Jersey. He slept all the way to his house.

Once home, Robert went to his Manhattan map with a ruler, pins and thread, and drew the latest version of the shape he was forming on the city, and on his own soul.

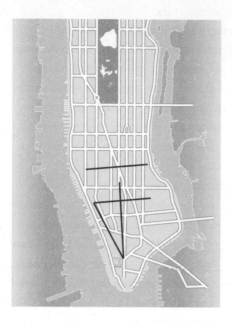

He also ran a line from the obelisk at St Paul's north through the Worth Monument obelisk opposite the Flatiron and continued it north . . .

'Well, I'll be damned,' he said out loud. 'Horace, we need to talk.'

He tried the old man but got no reply. Then he turned on the radio to catch the Convention news.

It had begun today. Senator John McCain and former Mayor Rudy Giuliani were to speak. In the morning NBC had broadcast an interview with President Bush in which he said he didn't know if the war on terrorism could ever be won. Now there was frantic spinning going on to clarify what he'd meant.

Robert dozed. At some point he heard Giuliani: 'On September 11, this city and our nation faced the worst attack in our history . . . On that day, we had to confront reality. For me, standing below the North Tower and looking up and seeing the flames of hell and then realizing that I was actually seeing a man – a human being –

jumping from the 101st or 102nd floor drove home to me that we were facing something beyond anything we had ever faced before . . . At the time, we believed we would be attacked many more times that day and in the days that followed.'

Robert looked back to that day. He remembered his fear. He remembered his anger. He looked deep into his heart. He was fighting different people, but the same questions applied. How to understand, without excusing? Against hatred, what response? Against evil, what weapons?

He fired up his computer and went briefly to the website. He wrote:

What the fifth cache said to me

Be your own weather, through intention.

Today I understood this line.

As we advance along the Path, we must balance the forces of earth, water, fire and air. The point of balance shifts and moves constantly. Clinging to any one point tears you apart. Balance must be constantly reacquired or it will destroy itself. If we align ourselves with the ebbs and flows of nature, we can acquire the strength of nature and even channel and direct some of nature's own power. This is the power of ether – seeing the interconnection of all things, and our connection to it.

There is a living, shifting border between order and disorder, the point where creation happens. In achieving balance, my will becomes powerful. My intentions come true. I make my own weather. I begin to create my reality around me. Yet the force of ether must not be used for my own gratification, or it will turn on me.

Today I felt for the first time that it was possible – no, necessary – to face down Iwnw with a different currency than their own. I saw the possibility – no, again, the necessity – of finding a form of weapon that they cannot convert into fuel for their own strength. It is impossible but also unavoidable. Unthinkable but also ineluctable: only a form of forgiveness can stop the detonation of the Ma'rifat'. But it must be a muscular form of forgiveness. I want to destroy the Iwnw.

Within minutes, a comment appeared.

Robert, the choice to be made is this: do I choose to align my will – my ability to co-create the world – with my own desires, fears and needs, with my own desired outcomes? Or do I choose to trust and align my will with the divine will, with the will of the Path, no matter where it leads, forsaking my own desires, including even my own fundamental desire to live?

The Iwnw can be defeated only by love. Even you cannot find the love to vanquish them for ever. But we may yet thwart them in their current work. You have passed the Trial by Ether. You have done well. But many dangers now face us. Be ready. Tomorrow brings the penultimate test.

The Watchman

A Martyr's Love Song: The Making of the Ma'rifat'

What was done to me should not be done to a dog, much less a human being.

As soon as they had me in the van they hooded and sedated me. I felt a prick in my arm and then lost all track of time.

I know I was taken from the van and that I stood in the fresh air for a few minutes in an open, exposed space. My wrists were bound with a loop of plastic. I could smell a chemical that I thought was kerosene. Then I was put on a plane.

I tried to shout that I was an American citizen and received a hard bang on both ears at once that made my head ring with pain. To be hit when unable to see, hooded and bound as I was, is terrifying. I did not dare speak again.

I had always known that the Mukhabarat in my own country and its neighbours had no qualms about torturing prisoners. But I had come to believe that there was no such American Mukhabarat.

I do not know exactly who interrogated me, but it was not the FBI of Eliot Ness. I do not think it was even in America. But I am sure those who did it were Americans. I have lived among them long enough.

I was kept hooded, naked, in a room so cold I could not stop shivering. My genitals shrank to almost nothing. At intervals I could not predict, I would hear a door open and smell the perfume of women. Women's voices would comment, in English and Arabic, on the small size of my genitals. They laughed at me, mocked me.

I dug deep into myself, to the core of my dignity, and tried to remain whole. If I had passed secrets at all, it had been to protect my blessed father. I had tried hard to minimize the potential damage of my actions. I had chosen to fail as a recruiter of my colleagues, rather than to learn how to compromise and blackmail other human beings. I had not sinned, though I had certainly broken the law.

But I was an Arab man with skills in nuclear physics. You cannot make a bomb from the work I was doing at the laboratory, though the energies we explored were massive. Not with Western science.

But no one seemed to care. Arab nuclear spy. Ride him hard.

I tried to use my pulse as a clock, to reckon the passing of time. But at times it seemed to race, at other times to plod lethargically. I think they put something in the food, to deny me even that means of orientation.

Loud, violent rock music would start playing at unpredictable intervals. Then silence would fall, sometimes interrupted by men entering my room and shouting incoherently at me; other times by the women; other times not at all.

Sometimes there was a chair in my room to sit on. Sometimes it was not there. Usually I had a bedroll, though sometimes not. A bucket was provided for my physical necessities. But they would move it, so I never knew where it was, except by the stench.

Eventually my hood was removed, for questioning sessions. I saw the women who had mocked me, mostly watching with a sneer. The men and women wore no insignia, and wore black. Sometimes the women wore medical coats.

I told them the truth, all the truth, immediately, with the exception of my studies in our honoured tradition. They had no need to know of such things and gave no suggestion of any interest in them. They simply did not believe that I was telling them the full truth: that I had passed secrets to an intelligence service, though I was not sure which Mukhabarat it was.

I told them about my father, about how I had allowed myself to become Westernized, my love for the woman who had turned out to be their agent.

They got angry and sometimes slapped me. I was never punched. But to be slapped, hard, while naked and cold, to the laughter of other men and women, to feel so entirely defenceless and alone, is deeply distressing. I felt like a little boy.

I was made to squat or stand for hours, for what seemed like days, in positions that slowly built up excruciating pain. When I sought to change position, they slapped me, pushed my head down violently, abused and mocked me, and forced me to assume the same position.

Still I told them the truth. There was no more to tell. They got very angry.

Different people came. And then they broke me.

They Abu Ghraib-ed me.

Other men were brought in, prisoners like me. We were made to sit on each other, form piles of bodies, perform acts I will not describe, pose in humiliating positions.

They brought in dogs. Angry, savage dogs, inches from my face, barely controlled by their handlers. I was so frightened I urinated on myself. They laughed and told me to start telling the truth.

Who was I really working for? What was my role in Al-Qaeda? What uses had they put my nuclear physics training to? Where was the bomb? Was there a bomb? What about dirty bombs?

One man, after what seemed like hours of interrogation, told me it all came down to this: 'My God is stronger than your God.' That's how he put it. And then he riffled the pages of a Qu'ran in front of my face and threw it against the wall.

I began to weep uncontrollably at irregular intervals, over irrational things.

They threatened to have me taken to another country where they would not treat me so well. Everything I had experienced, they said, was authorized and legal. They could send me to countries where they weren't so squeamish.

I told them again that I was an American citizen. 'Didn't get that memo,' one of the men said, and laughed.

In our tradition, as my father and grandfather passed it down to me, there are different levels of growth in spiritual power and understanding, sometimes expressed as different coloured organs across the chest, or up and down the body, sometimes expressed as mystical bodies emanating from our physical body; sometimes as properties of particular prophets. They are called lata'if, *which can be translated as 'subtleties'. I now began to use them inside out, to chart the levels of my destruction.*

They made me feel I was removed from God: akhfa

They made me blind to God's love: khafi

They made me reveal my most hidden secrets: sirr

They destroyed my spirit: ruh

They destroyed my heart's compassion: qalb

They reduced me to my primitive, animal self: nafs

They made me fear my physical destruction: the shattering of my qalib, *the mould that forms our bodies. The English word 'calibre' is derived from it.*

The day they made me feel as though I were drowning, time after time, when the true panic of death was upon me, I knew I had lost my dignity.

I tried to say to them whatever they wanted me to say. I confessed to everything they had asked me about. I told them all the secrets I knew of our honoured tradition. And still they didn't believe me. They laughed. Still the torment went on.

I gave up. I decided to die. I wished for death.

And that is when I acquired the power to activate the Ma'rifat'.

6

Trial by Mind

Little Falls, August 31, 2004

The Quad buzzed to indicate Robert had received a new text message. Waypoint 039.

His regular cell phone began to vibrate on his office desk. 'Robert? It's Horace. We must meet.'

'Is it safe for you?'

'Nothing is safe any more. We do what we must do.'

'There are things I need to tell you. To show you. Thank you for what you did at Hencott. How on earth did you pull that off?'

'I'll explain when we meet. Eleven o'clock. Meet me at Grand Central, at the clock. We have a lot to do, and no time. Get to the waypoint.'

'Horace, I'm terrified for Kat. She's in danger with Adam.'

'I instructed Katherine to gather and hide as many keys as she could while staying close to Adam, but she's starting to be worn down by the presence of the Iwnw. You are right that she is in danger. She is becoming susceptible to Adam's suggestions, but her proximity to him is the only thing that is allowing him still to fight the Iwnw. For now, she must stay with him.'

The GPS programme showed the waypoint was on First Avenue, near the United Nations. He had just enough time to get there before meeting Horace.

'If you're more than five minutes late, I'll leave,' Horace said. 'In that case, make it noon at St Thomas's Church on Fifth Avenue.'

'I'll make it at eleven.'

He drove towards Manhattan, the skyline shimmering before him on the horizon like the scale model of miniatures he had created in his study.

He had to know what else had happened on the day of the Blackout. Everything charted back to that.

It had been a beautiful summer's day, he remembered. A slow news day. In the morning he'd pottered in his office, taking care of routine administrative tasks. By midday it had become deathly slow. Then Katherine had called with a saucy suggestion, something they did from time to time. They'd take a hotel room, have a late lunch, drink champagne and make love. In the evening they'd stay in town and have dinner, maybe see a show. 'I was thinking the same thing,' he'd told her.

By two o'clock they were in their room. They were in the throes of lovemaking for the second time when the lights went out at four. It was always intense on their hotel-room trysts, and Katherine had made it even more so by reciting some of the sex magick words she had used on their first night together all those years before. Robert had been startled when she began, but she quickly soothed his fear away.

Both were climaxing when the Blackout happened, and in the throes of orgasm Katherine opened her eyes wide and stifled a scream that for a split second was more terror than pleasure, and Robert experienced a blizzard of simultaneous images so fierce that he froze, muscles knotted, deep inside her.

Robert saw strands of intense white light binding him to Katherine, Katherine to Adam, Adam to another woman, her face hidden, all of them united in a dance of fire, and, as images of each of them fired off in his mind's eye, a shadow too joined the dance, a formless creature, and then another, a child.

Katherine had never been able to talk to him about what she saw in her moment of terror. Robert now knew without any doubt that the second woman had been Terri. They had been picking up mental impressions of the moment of entanglement when Adam, Terri and the maker of the Ma'rifat' became conjoined with the ring of Katherine, Robert and Adam created more than twenty years earlier. And he had believed since that day that the shadow of a child had been little Moss, or at least the possibility of little Moss, just minutes after his conception.

But now, as he drove, new images and words came together unbidden in his consciousness: *Terri's baby. Terri's baby.* It made no sense to him. He'd seen cell division in Terri starting the day they'd made love, but these images were from more than a year earlier.

After the violent blur of impressions at the moment of the Blackout, Katherine and he fell from each other and lay side by side, breathing heavily. Initially neither noticed nor cared that the power had gone out. Once they realized, they assumed it was just the hotel, maybe even just their floor. Then Robert's cell phone rang. It was Ed at the office.

'Where are you, Boss? The lights just went out.'

'They're out here too. I'm just five blocks away. Did the backup power kick in?'

'Yes, we're fine here. The screens just flickered. But we've got no a/c, no cable TV. Wait. Wait. The lights are out in Times Square.'

'Is this an attack?'

'We're checking. There's smoke coming from a transformer over by the United Nations. You've got to get back here. The lights are out in Brooklyn, in Queens . . . holy shit, they're out in Boston. This is huge.'

'On my way.'

He remembered looking at Katherine. She'd turned as white as a ghost.

Robert got to the bureau just as police were confirming they did not suspect an attack. But the scope of the power outage kept growing. Parts of Canada were out. Virtually all of the north-eastern United States was out. Thousands of people were trapped in the subway. He organized coverage just as he had on the morning of 9/11. Sent teams of reporters out. Designated the lead writers. Liaised with other bureaux. Sent key people who lived in Manhattan home to rest, so they'd be fresh in the morning. Coordinated the work of the general assignment, power, equities, treasury teams. Hooked up with facilities managers and technicians about how long their backup-power supply would last.

After the initial fear of an attack subsided, New Yorkers took the Blackout largely in their stride. People slept out in the streets that night, unafraid. There were parties. Crime went down. At around three in the morning, after keeping overnight writers and

303

reporters company for a while, he went back to the hotel with four staffers who couldn't get to their homes. Katherine was a good sport about it and let them sleep in the room.

✤

With the Republican Convention in town, driving across Manhattan was asking for trouble. Robert parked on the West Side near Ninth Avenue and took the Shuttle subway from Times Square across to Grand Central. From there he walked the three and a half long blocks over to the United Nations.

Emerging on to First Avenue at the end of 42nd Street, he checked the Quad. It was pointing him left, and began flashing 'Arriving destination' as soon as he started walking. The great green-blue slab of the UN Secretariat and the East River were to his right. Ahead of him, a shining silver needle rose in a tiny park, bounded at its northern end by a soaring, curved retaining wall of heavy stone blocks. Twisting stairs led up the face of the wall to 43rd Street and the small town-within-a-town called Tudor City. Carved into the great wall in gold lettering were lines from the Book of Isaiah:

They shall beat their swords into plowshares, and their spears into pruning hooks; nation shall not lift up sword against nation, neither shall they learn war any more.

The waypoint was at the Isaiah Wall.

Robert thought about trying some kind of manoeuvre to see if he was expected or being watched – abruptly changing direction or darting for a cab, seeing who involuntarily jumped or was shocked out of their anonymity by the sudden fear of losing him – but decided it was futile. *Nothing is safe. We do what we must do.* His own gift, the one he had been terrified of his entire adult life, had emerged into the light. He was in plain sight for whoever needed to see him, let the chips fall where they may. If anyone came after him now, he would give them a damn good fight.

The Quad buzzed. A text message, from the Watchman:

Another digit, to find the widget
In seeking sex, you'll get the hex
Follow your hunch, you'll find a bunch
At number one, the battle's won
To find your kind
Pass the Trial by Mind

He strode over to the silver-steel obelisk. *Peace Form Number One*, it was called. It was a digit, in the sense of a single pointing finger, like the Emmet obelisk at St Paul's. And it stood in a park named for a diplomat called Bunche.

He knelt and looked at the base of the sculpture. He searched among the candle-holders and flowers left by people holding peace vigils opposite the United Nations. He reached with his fingers up inside the slots at the bottom of the monument. With his fingertips, lodged atop a metal spar, he felt another film container, taped in place and sealed in a plastic sandwich bag. He extracted it carefully with his fingers and opened it. There was nothing in it but a slip of paper with a handwritten message, all in capital letters. YOU ARE LOSING, it said.

'Damn!'

He crushed the plastic container in his fist, cursing into the air around him. It had to have been Katherine. Only she and Horace knew the waypoints. Would she give them directly to Adam? Would he force her to? Fear knotted in his stomach.

He rubbed his face with his hands. At least he had the major key, the Malice Box. Without it, surely, they could not properly detonate the weapon?

He realized he had only a few minutes if he was going to meet Horace on time. He jogged back to 42nd Street and turned right, heading west towards Midtown.

The parabolas and inverted Vs of the Chrysler Building's gleaming tower rose directly ahead in the sky, like angular ripples on a pond. He had walked this street once with Horace, taking in the Art Deco masterpieces that studded it like jewels – the News Building, the Chrysler, the Chanin. Outside the Chrysler, Horace had talked about its closed observation deck, and the legendary elegance of the Cloud Club atop the building, as well as the curiously cramped, curved spaces at the very top of the tower, which Horace had been privileged to visit.

'At the very top it's open to the elements, you can feel the gusts. Feels so fragile, but it's tremendously strong,' he said. 'Not many people know this, but there's a cult movie called *Q* that has many scenes shot up in the pinnacle. Some nonsense about the plumed serpent Quetzalcóatl having a nest up there and prowling the skies of Manhattan, eating rooftop sunbathers.'

'Sounds like you quite enjoyed it, Horace.'

'Terrible nonsense, though Quetzalcóatl the man, the Toltec priest, repays further examination. Take a good look up if you can at the radiator-cap decorations, can you see? Borrow my binoculars if you like.'

He'd done so. 'Looks like they have wings on them?'

'Yes, wings of Mercury. Or Hermes, to give him his Greek name. We'll see the same thing at Grand Central. Hermes everywhere, and sculpted wheels set with his wings. It's about speed, you see. The fleet-footed messenger.'

That innocent walk with Horace seemed a long time ago now. The old man had spoken of all the closed observation decks in Manhattan.

'We are so fearful,' he had said. 'We should reopen them all. The Woolworth Building. Chanin. Chrysler. Flatiron. Rockefeller Center, especially. Are we afraid of what we'd see up there?'

Now Robert understood that he had been talking about more than the upper reaches of New York's buildings. And now Robert was on the verge of breaking through to the true sweeping vistas and high places Horace had meant: those of his own nature.

He pressed on, crossing Lexington Avenue. His own offices at GBN, to which he felt no compulsion whatever to return, were nine blocks north.

At last he came to Grand Central Terminal. Just before he entered, the Quad buzzed with a text message: 'New Waypoint: X87.'

The GPS programme suggested it lay inside the New York Public Library, just a few blocks further west.

It was three minutes to eleven. He hurried to the central information booth under the four-faced clock. The great hall of the station was buzzing with people criss-crossing its floor, not manically, as at rush hour, but in a constant flow.

He felt a hand on his arm and turned to see Horace.

'We meet at the confluence of Time and Information,' he said, pointing to the sign above the booth. 'Let's walk as we talk. There is someone here that we don't want to see.'

Robert looked around, unsure what he was looking for, as Horace clamped a hand firmly on to his elbow. He steered Robert north towards the platforms, and they entered a walkway signposted as 'The North-east Passage'. As they went, Robert reached into his pocket and extracted a small packet.

'This is the major key,' he said, handing it to Horace. 'I took it from Adam yesterday. I'm afraid that in doing so I've taken away his last protection against the Iwnw.'

Horace took it quickly from him and slipped it into an inner pocket of his jacket. 'Thank heaven. Well done. This buys us some time, since they have all the rest. Keep moving.'

'Who is here, Horace?'

'I saw a member of the Iwnw. I am sure of it.'

Robert turned and looked behind them. No one had followed them. 'What do they look like?'

'White hair. About my age. Listen. We need to talk quickly. First, regarding Adam. He still has Katherine by him. She will help.'

'He tried to kill her yesterday.'

Horace eyed him with a faint smile. 'Yes, he did. It also helped you to make a breakthrough on the Path. Perhaps he's not as far gone as you think. Now, pay attention. There is a very interesting piece of artwork along these passages,' Horace said. 'It is called *As Above, So Below*. It will be instructive to explore one or two parts of it. As we walk, please report. What do you understand of the situation?'

Could Adam truly be pulling off such a double game? And now Horace was echoing the letter he had received at university from his anonymous relative. *As above, so below; as within, so without.*

'Let me think.'

'Your intellect won't help you,' Horace said. 'Thinking alone can't help you any more. Let it go. Tell me what your deeper impressions are. Use all of your mind.'

'The waypoint just now. The key was gone. I think Katherine took it.'

'Yes.'

Now footsteps echoed in the passage behind them. Robert looked back and saw a fit-looking older man in a dark business suit walking unhurriedly behind them.

'Is he Iwnw?'

Horace nodded. 'That's the one I saw. And wherever there is one, there are usually three.' He looked up ahead. There was no one there. 'We must conduct our business quickly. You may not understand the sequence of my questions, but I must prepare you for the next trial, and tell you certain things. I must gauge your level of understanding. You know the whispering arches here at Grand Central?'

On the lower concourse was a sinuous vaulted space of Guastav-ino tiled arches, where at any time of day, in a disturbing spectacle unless one knew the secret, grown men and women could be observed standing at the corner columns, their faces pressed to the wall like punished children. Standing so, it was possible to have a whispered conversation with someone standing diametrically across the arched space at the opposing column several yards away, each hearing the other's disembodied voice clearly, echoing in the air above their head.

'I do.'

He looked behind them. The white-haired man was still there, eyes fixed steadily upon them, maintaining an even distance some forty paces away.

'You are like a radio that's trying to burst into life. You are seeing connections between everything that's been happening in the last few days, and decades ago, things that don't seem at all related suddenly aligning ... It's as though everything is connected to everything else by a secret whispering arch.'

'Yes.'

'And you realize you've always known this. Felt it.'

'Yes, that's right.'

'You are at the stage of ordination, we might say,' Horace said, a grave look on his face. 'Greater mysteries are opening up to you, some might call them priestly mysteries. You are entering upon the Trial by Mind.'

'I need to go faster. We do. The next waypoint –'

'I know,' Horace said. 'We must hurry, yet the Path cannot be rushed. Balance is all. Walk faster with me.'

Robert began to pour out thoughts and impressions as they went. 'Adam's trying with all his power to hold this dreadful thing within him at bay, but it's winning. I can see it.'

'He is a very brave man. What more?'

'Katherine has left me. She has gone to Adam because I slept with Terri, but she's in huge danger. She's playing this double game, trying to support Adam against the Iwnw and the Minotaur within him. Terri is in hiding because she's terrified, I think because she feels Adam will no longer protect her. She sees Katherine displacing her, leaving her alone to face whatever it is that's scaring her. I think she's never been so frightened in her life.'

'All Terri's hopes are placed in Adam, yet she is terrified of him. She cannot afford to lose him, yet she cannot be with him,' Horace said. 'Why?'

'I think she's pregnant. With Adam's child. I had these images … cells dividing … but there was a shadow across them, and something else I can't fully see, can't understand. Her pregnancy feels over a year old, and yet only four days old . . .'

Horace nodded, gazing inwardly as they walked. Robert ploughed on. 'The shape I have been tracing across Manhattan. It has a spine directly uptown from the obelisk at St Paul's, through the obelisk opposite the Flatiron. I drew the line further north. It goes directly to the obelisk in Central Park.'

Robert pulled out a tourist map of the city and drew on it the waypoints that he had visited over the previous days. 'I don't know what this shape is, or if it's an amalgam of shapes, or what, but it has these crossbars, and this spacing along the spine – one unit or a half unit, some points skipped ... Today's waypoints suggest another crossbar, here ...'

It mapped his movements and trials. After St Paul's Chapel and Mercer Street, it showed his walk across the island from Tompkins Square Park to Washington Square Park to the *Goodnight Moon* house. Back up the centre line to Union Square. Another cross-beam from the Asser Levy stepping stones to the second obelisk opposite the Flatiron to the Theological Seminary in Chelsea. A third crossing from the United Nations to the New York Public Library. Continuing the line led to the mouth of the Lincoln Tunnel on the far west side.

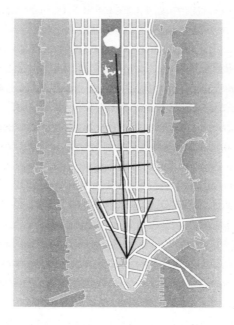

'Good. You are slowly tracing a shape that is called the Tree of Life. It is a kind of key to navigating the mysteries, to surviving the adventure we are embarked upon. Each level corresponds to a trial. After today there is one more point to complete the diagram, just as there is one more trial before you face the ordeal of closing down the Ma'rifat'.'

'Tell me more. I want to understand.'

They walked on. Still the white-haired man did not close upon them.

'It is one of the most ancient spiritual tools known to mankind,' Horace said. 'It is meaningless to the ignorant. Very powerful to the initiated.'

'What does it do?'

'It points to certain things that are true. It is a key, and a map. It has existed since before the ancient Egyptians. It is not the only key, certainly, but it is found in several spiritual traditions. It was the pattern used by the maker of the Ma'rifat' to lay out the keys along Manhattan to carry and amplify the force of the weapon. Not quite perfectly traced but close enough to be very dangerous. It is also the pattern we have used to direct you along the Path. It can be thought of in many ways. It is a route of power, a map of self-exploration . . .'

Robert closed his eyes for a moment, seeing again the fleeting multidimensional images that had been hammering at his mind – the sense of a great overarching pattern wheeling about him, threading through the streets of the city, an array of perspectives and sightlines and insights that bound together his inner and outer journeys, buildings and monuments and stages of the trial, in a single geometric shape.

'What does the full key look like?'

'Like this,' Horace said, filling in the lines on the map Robert had given him. 'Above the highest point on the Tree, there is a further level that is indescribable, a kind of succession of infinities, which we will also explore before your final battle. In terms of Manhattan, they are represented by Central Park.'

'I have to find Katherine. I have to find Terri. I have to use this to help them.'

'So you do. Bear with me just a little longer.'

They had walked along the underground passage as far as the exit sign for 48th Street. Set into the wall was a six-foot compass of glass mosaic, a photograph of a youthful Albert Einstein at its centre.

'You'll be aware that Einstein's theories describe how space and time are a single thing, and can be warped and bent.'

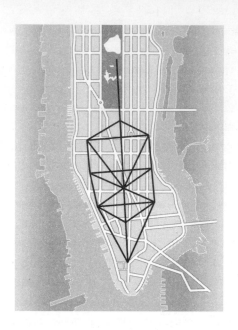

'Yes.'

'And that energy and matter are equivalent, that each can be converted into the other? With hugely destructive results, in the case of the atomic bomb?'

'Yes. E equals mc squared. Is the Device some kind of atom bomb?'

'At the very least. I believe the Iwnw intend to make it into something much worse. Let's keep walking.'

A few yards further north they came to the next mosaic, another wheel set into the wall, this time showing a young woman holding a bowl of fire in her hands, set against a backdrop of intergalactic space. Two smaller circles were set into the wall on each side. 'These mosaics represent the elements.' He pointed left to right. 'Or the trials you have undergone. Earth. Water. Fire, which is what she holds in her hands. See how she sparkles as the light catches the glass in the mosaic design. Then Air. Then Ether.'

'This stage is Mind, you said. What is last?'

'The seventh is Spirit.'

'What do they consist of?'

At that moment Robert looked north and saw a second white-haired man, identically dressed, coming towards them with the same measured pace.

'Horace!'

'This way.'

They retraced their steps towards the Einstein mosaic, heading back in the direction of the first Iwnw stalker, who did not speed up but just stared at them with cold malevolence. Horace and Robert descended a flight of stairs and took the 47th Street Cross-Passage to their right.

'When three of them converge on us, we will fight,' Horace said. 'Now listen. The penultimate trial tests the mind in its fullest sense. Not merely the intellect, or just the conscious mind, but the full spectrum of the conscious and the unconscious, the reasoning and the dreaming and creative minds.'

The sixth trial, Horace whispered as they walked west, would expose him to a shattering new awareness of reality, a powerful truth. Whereas in the Trial by Ether he had found he could affect the world around him through his will, he would now take the next step, realizing that he and the world were identical, and that only his mind constructed the illusion of separation.

'The insight, when it comes, is like grasping a high-voltage cable,' Horace said. 'Only one who has completed the previous five trials can withstand it. Even so, the insight comes only with proximity to death. It brings healing powers.'

To pass the trial, he said, Robert would have to survive accessing those energies, and bend them to a purpose beyond himself. It would force him to face the sixth dilemma: whether to heal, or to kill, his enemy.

Robert would recover a sixth key, six-sided or six-pointed, and find the penultimate missing component of the light body that was his new awakened self.

The two Iwnw men descended the stairs and walked slowly towards them.

Robert and Horace came to steps leading up to Tracks 32 and 33. Horace paused briefly to point out another mosaic.

'There are about a dozen panels in total in *As Above, So Below*.

This one may also have resonance for you. It shows Persephone condemned to the underworld for half the year for eating a pom-egranate. Seems rather harsh, doesn't it? It's partly a Greek retelling of another earlier myth, Inanna in the underworld. Also known as Ishtar?'

'Terri told me that one. It's about the Path. I'm entering the underworld to bring out Adam, and Terri . . . even Katherine.'

'Many myths reflect the constant struggle between the Iwnw and the Perfect Light.'

'Speaking of that . . . look. Now there are three.'

A third white-haired man in an identical dark business suit was walking towards them from the west, a faint smile on his face. Now two were behind them, and one ahead of them.

'Quickly, this way.'

Horace led him up the steps to Tracks 32 and 33. They ran back towards the main hall of Grand Central along the North-west Passage.

'We fight them in this corridor if we must,' Horace said. 'In case anything happens to me, it is time you learned a little more about the Hencott family.'

Katherine surveyed the hiding place and decided it was satisfactory. The police sharpshooter had made a good choice. She was early. She always liked to be. She surveyed the equipment, checking every item again. Through the viewfinder, she calculated yet again the distance to her target. It would require a sure touch.

Moving slowly, keeping away from the window, she made herself comfortable against a wall in the unoccupied apartment and closed her eyes in meditation for a moment.

The Iwnw were starting to reach her. As Adam struggled to resist them, she was giving him all the energy she could, as Horace had asked, trying to slow him down as much as possible to allow Robert time to progress along the Path. Although, in doing that, she was also exposing herself to their influence, and she could feel her own willpower beginning to falter. Her judgement.

Yet she was sure this was a good and necessary move on her

part. It was she who had realized there was bound to be at least one police sniper overlooking the location of the final part of the sixth key, given New York's heightened security levels for the Republican Convention.

She'd surveyed the area, using her professional expertise and her reawakening gift, and quickly concluded that there was just one sharpshooter, and where he had to be. Then she'd gone to see him. It had been a simple matter to put him into a deep sleep, using a hypnotic trick Horace had shown her many years previously.

So now she had a rifle. She'd made sure Robert wouldn't be shot at by the cops as he recovered the last part of the sixth key, and she could cover him if he got into trouble with the other police on the ground.

Adam had told her he was trying everything he could to help Robert along the Path, even if it meant allowing Robert to believe he had already completely crossed over. It was a miraculous balancing act, for he was at the same time appearing to give the Iwnw what they wanted.

On Sunday, after she had walked out on Robert, Adam had invited her to stay in his latest New York hide, commiserated with her over Robert, told her he loved her. She'd helped ease his pain, helped him in his vigil.

Terri had come to the apartment while Adam was out, noted her presence and immediately turned round and left. Katherine had seen nothing of Terri but her retreating back. She'd called out to her, but all she'd felt in response was a wave of hurt and fear, and, mingled with it, a note of deep resignation.

So much of this was her own fault, she felt. In giving the lost Newton papers to Tariq, she had effectively created the Ma'rifat'. She had given its creator the means to make it, then years later she had caused him to be driven to such pain and anger that he wanted to use it.

She had to make it right. But, above all, she had to focus on her mission. She had to hold the Iwnw at bay.

'My brother and I grew up in various parts of the world,' Horace said, whispering between shallow breaths as they walked. 'We are both somewhat older than you might think. We were born in Alexandria, in the 1920s. Father was a gentleman archaeologist, adventurer, sometime spy. He claimed to have met Lawrence of Arabia several times, to have introduced us to him when we were small boys. I have a faint childhood memory of a man in white robes who spoke oddly. It may be an invented memory, though; he told us about him so many times. My brother, of course, was named after him.'

Robert looked back behind them. He heard footfalls and then saw one of the Iwnw coming slowly up the steps. He was followed by the two others.

'They're coming, Horace.'

'Keep moving. Lawrence joined the military as soon as he could, lied about his age and served throughout World War Two. He was a paratrooper. After the war we worked together for a while, in Paris, and Berlin, and back in Egypt. I was altogether less impressive on the military front, worked in intelligence, at the more unusual end of it, sometimes. Army intelligence, then OSS. Heard of it?'

'It was the forerunner of the CIA, wasn't it?'

'That's right.'

'Horace, that must make you in your eighties.'

'Yes. Don't distract me. Father left us some land in various parts of the world, not farmland, you understand, mining plots, mostly worked-out seams, a couple of barely functioning mines. Made us swear never to sell, to safeguard them for eternity.

'Lawrence took all the mines on and made something of them. Really something. I've no idea how. He knew men, he knew logistics, he was afraid of no one. He studied when he came out of the army, learned engineering and chemistry, metallurgy. He was a force of nature. He built up Hencott Incorporated almost single-handed, built a corporate empire around what father had left us.

'Lawrence used to say you need presence in the world if you are to do good; it's better to be strong and protect the weak than be weak in need of protection. He put a lot of resources into research and development, and based it all in a laboratory so well guarded and secret that most people in the company didn't even know about it. It was on the grounds of a particular gold mine. You may recall he referred to it in the interview he gave your news service.'

'Oh, God, yes. What was that about?'

'One thing at a time. Lawrence was operational. I am meditative. We have both sought a special kind of gold, in our different ways.'

'I'm sorry?'

'There are a handful of mines in the world – three, to be precise – that produce a certain kind of very rare gold. We call it red gold.'

'I thought that was just an alloy of gold and copper? The guy who sold us our wedding bands was quite prolix about red gold, white gold, rose gold, and so on. They're all alloys, because pure gold is too soft to work into most jewellery.'

'Quite so. But that is not the red gold I am talking about. You will likely have never heard of this kind. Its uses are limited.'

'To what?'

'Here is where I must swear you to secrecy. For ever.'

Horace stopped and stared at him intently. Robert had never seen him look so powerful.

'I swear.'

But before Horace could speak again, a voice rang out from up ahead of them. 'There's no way out, old man.'

Behind them, the white-haired men were still advancing at a measured pace, three abreast, now just twenty yards away.

And ahead of them, blocking the way back to Grand Central, was Adam Hale.

'Listen to me,' Horace whispered, turning so that he stood facing the Iwnw, back to back with Robert, whose eyes never left Adam. 'Red gold may be used in certain procedures of a *hermetic* nature. Named after Hermes, the messenger of the gods. It was the name taken by a series of sages several thousand years ago. Alchemical procedures, if you will.'

'It was in Adam's play. But he said there is none left in the world.'

'Well, there is. Hencott controls all three mines. They were among the ones left to us by our father, who was himself acting on behalf

317

of the Perfect Light. There are perhaps thirty people in the world who know these things. Red gold, correctly handled, correctly prepared, after many years of trial and error, can in some circumstances draw to itself great amounts of energy, or trigger in the world the release of same. It is extremely powerful, but only in conjunction with the psychic state of those around it.'

'It sounds like the Ma'rifat'. The Device.'

'The Device must contain some of it. Of the thirty people I mentioned, some are of the view that the power of red gold must be used for political purposes. To advance certain political tendencies, to work against others, to shape the world. To rule it. Lawrence and I are not of this view.'

'Who are these people?'

The three white-haired men had drawn to within ten yards of Horace. They stopped and stared at him.

'They are the Iwnw. The word means "column" in the language of the ancient Egyptians. We stand against them. We are the Perfect Light.'

Adam, standing twenty paces ahead of Robert, gave a booming laugh. 'Well, well, gentlemen. You find yourselves in a tight spot.'

He walked towards Robert. In the baking heat of the underground passageway, they were all sweating, but Adam's shirt was drenched. He looked cadaverous.

'Stay strong, Adam,' Robert shouted. 'You don't have to do this. They don't control you.'

'It's too late for that,' Adam called back. 'Was Horace just telling you about poor Lawrence and the red gold? It's a very touching story.'

Robert whispered to Horace: 'The Iwnw got some of your red gold?'

'Tell everyone, Horace,' Adam boomed.

'Last year, the unthinkable happened,' Horace shouted, his gaze fixed on the three Iwnw men facing him. 'Lawrence and I learned that Hencott had been infiltrated by several of these . . . people.' He spat out the final word. 'They had taken twenty years to insinuate their way into the more secret corners of the company, but they finally managed to gain access, briefly, to the research and development laboratory.'

'The one Lawrence talked about in his interview? The one he said Hencott was closing?'

'That's right,' Adam shouted. 'That one didn't work out too well for you, did it, Robert?'

Horace ignored Adam's goading. 'They took some. Far less than a gram. But that is sufficient.'

'How long before you found out?' Robert asked.

'Almost immediately. And we decided to begin the immediate running down of the experiments that were under way. It took nearly a year to power them down. Red gold must be handled, once the process of elaboration begins, with very great care. What they managed to take was not elaborated, it was raw. Some rudimentary work was clearly done on it later. When, finally, it had all been removed and placed in a safe location until mankind is ready to make better use of it, Lawrence decided to tell the world. Not in a way that anyone but the thirty-odd people I mentioned would understand. But it is a time-honoured technique. Make a public announcement, disguising the real content, in such a way that it will be widely reported. Those who need to see the true meaning will understand. It also puts down a marker in time, for those who come later who might understand. That on this date, we took these measures.'

'What happened then, Robert?' said Adam.

'The company called to say Lawrence had gone off his rocker. They reversed themselves.'

Horace resumed. 'All of this had taken a great toll upon Lawrence. It is true that the stress of the discovery of the infiltration, the decision to close down his life's experimental work, the hunt for the missing red gold, eventually caused a crisis in his marriage. His wife did leave him. But he was of perfectly sound mind when he called you to set up the interview, Robert. He did so at such short notice because he became aware of an attempt to oust him as head of the firm. It went ahead shortly after your news item ran on the wires.'

'Oh, Jesus. I played right into their hands.'

'You didn't know. It's not your fault. Lawrence was a soldier. He fought back. Set up his base of operations at that hotel and began to make calls. Rallied support. Made sure arrangements he'd put in place for the succession – his will, company rules, and so on – had not been tampered with. And then' – Horace twisted his head, eyes blazing, to see Adam – 'Mr Hale showed up to visit him.'

Robert stared unblinkingly into Adam's face as his old friend drew nearer. 'What happened, Adam? What did you do?'

'I did what these gentlemen demanded. I tried to persuade Lawrence to tell me where the rest of the red gold was. The hidden stock. He did not want to help.'

'Adam was under the influence of these henchmen of the Iwnw, using the Minotaur as a conduit after Adam killed him,' Horace said. 'This may have been the first time they were able to corrode his will so fully. Remember it was he, working with me, who found where the stolen red gold had gone, when he tracked down the maker of the Ma'rifat' last year. But it cost him. It cost him severely.'

'It allowed me to see whose side I should be on in this endless contest,' Adam shouted. 'Don't go thinking dear Horace has all the answers.'

Still the three men with white hair stood silently in the dark suits, their relentless gaze on Horace. Robert felt they were waiting for something, though he couldn't tell what. He cast his mind back to the night of Lawrence's death. Last Wednesday night. It already seemed a lifetime ago.

'Lawrence tried to warn me. He called me. He wasn't threatening me. He was trying to warn me!'

'He would have been in great pain. He chose to die rather than to give in to Adam. He wrote to you too, yes? You remember?'

'Said it was all my fault. No, wait. It was *because* of me –'

'I had flagged you to Lawrence as someone who might one day come to our aid.'

'Lawrence said I had a poisonous ego . . .'

'No. He said *To the poisonous ego of Robert Reckliss I say vile, intense torture reveals impossibility of living.* He was giving you advice. On how to help. He was telling you your ego was blinding you to truth, as happens to all of us.'

'Dear God. I've understood so little.'

'It was suicide, in a way. But pushing a man so hard that he chooses to die, in order to escape the torment, is murder, of course.'

'I had no choice,' Adam said.

'Our friends here, however, were not as clever as they thought. Lawrence was able to ensure that after his death, controlling authority in the company moved quickly and irrevocably to me. By Sunday evening I had almost everything in place. By Monday morning, while the funeral was taking place, I was able to act to call those damned lawyers off you.'

'That was extraordinary. You should have seen their faces.'

Sweat ran into Robert's eyes. Tension knotted every muscle in his body.

'I needed you. I need you now. So does Adam. So do Katherine and Terri. So do a great many people. These creatures cannot be allowed to stop us.'

Now the leader of the Iwnw spoke for the first time. 'You have something we want, Mr Hencott. We have come to reclaim it. Mr Reckliss here stole it from our colleague.'

'Take it from me, if you can,' shouted Horace, defiance in every syllable. 'In my brother's name, I swear you'll get it no other way.'

Then suddenly Adam threw himself at Robert, scrabbling for his eyes and throat. Horace twisted one way as Robert leaped the other, feeling his body ignite with the accumulated strength of the five trials he had undergone. He flipped Adam sideways in the air and watched him slam into the wall of the passageway. Turning to face the Iwnw, he saw Horace deflect the charge of their leader and simultaneously twist the wrist of a second attacker with such speed and timing that the man's entire body left the ground and landed with a crack of breaking bone five yards away.

Adam rose again and made a dive for Horace, trying to reach inside his jacket, but Robert grabbed him by the shoulders and spun him around so that he and Adam were face to face. Robert dragged him to one side and punched him with all his strength in the belly.

Adam folded in half, letting out a bellow of pain, blowing air and blood from his mouth, and lay still on the ground.

Robert turned again to help Horace fight the Iwnw. One had the old man from behind by the neck and the other was belabouring Horace's ribs and chest with punches. Robert launched himself headlong at the second man, knocking him flying and landing on top of him in a crunch of breaking ribs. Robert punched him once in the face, and he stopped moving. The third Iwnw man, his wrist shattered from Horace's earlier throw, kneeled with his head lowered, muttering over and over an incantation while holding his forearm tightly in his good hand.

Now Horace twisted out of the grasp of the Iwnw leader and turned to face him. With a yard of clear space between them, he stepped forward and seemed to project a wave of force from his chest. His opponent flew backwards against the wall and fell heavily, knocked unconscious without a finger having been laid on him.

Breathing heavily, Horace caught Robert's eye and pointed in the direction of Grand Central. 'I still have the major key,' he panted. 'We must leave.'

Adam still lay motionless on the ground, doubled over. Robert made to go to him. 'Leave him,' Horace ordered.

A few minutes later Horace and Robert walked out of Grand Central Terminal on to 42nd Street and turned right, heading west. For a minute or two neither spoke. Horace dabbed some blood from the side of his mouth with a handkerchief.

'Do you think they'll come after us?'

'Yes, but not for a while. Possessing the major key and the traces of red gold it contains, even rudimentarily worked as it has been, I was confident of protecting us both. Of shielding us, at the very least. Without it they might have killed us. Thank you for your help.'

'How did it help to shield us?'

'It amplifies whatever psychic force is around it. With it in my hands, my powers are increased many times over. I am forbidden to say exactly how it operates, by my oath to the Perfect Light. Mankind at large does not yet have this knowledge, although the new collider at CERN may bring signs of it when it starts in a few years' time. I can say it resonates at a certain rate, setting up certain harmonics, that are also the harmonics of operations in the human brain.'

'It's like birdsong? The language of the birds?'

'That is one way it may be experienced, yes.'

'Adam's play, all that time ago, spoke of a device like the Ma'rifat'. But he said there were three components.'

'Yes. The so-called Philosopher's Stone, which is a fusion of metal and glass with psychic resonances similar to red gold. The red gold itself, which harmonizes with the Stone. They are like male and female components. Then, a knowledge of certain geometric arrangements that allow these materials to be brought into play on each other, like lenses. That is why each of the keys has a different geometric form: to reflect and shape the internal forces of the Ma'rifat' in different ways, according to the lensing required at different moments. All this is useless without a highly refined state of spiritual attainment in the operator. There is one exception, however. They can also be activated by a person in a desperate state of psychic collapse.'

As they walked, Horace fumbled in his pocket and handed him a piece of paper. 'I would have sent you this by text message, but since you're right here . . .'

Robert read the paper.

> *Don't be a rube, follow the cube*
> *Now visit Babel, if you're able*
> *An unseeing guide, leads you to the hide*
> *To see, though you're blind*
> *Pass the Trial by Mind*
> *Call Number JFD 00–19002.*

P.S. To get the waypoint number of the next cache, treble the letters in the item you seek and subtract the Deadly Sins

'A call number,' Robert said. 'To get a book at the library?'
'Yes, I think so.'

Robert's adrenalin level was sky high from the fight. Fire was still coursing through his limbs. He felt light-headed, with a tinge of nausea. The image of Adam crumpled on the ground began to bother him. He had hit Adam very hard.

They crossed Vanderbilt and Madison and came to Fifth Avenue. Robert fired up the GPS programme at the intersection and confirmed that Waypoint X87 was indeed inside the New York Public Library.

'Let us read between the lions,' Horace said with an uncharacteristic wink, and timed his crossing so they could traverse 42nd south and then Fifth west in quick succession. Robert saw that the old man was not immune to an adrenalin buzz himself.

They strode up the front steps between Patience and Fortitude, the two lions that guarded the library entrance. 'Arriving destination' flashed on his screen as they got to the top. He read the clue again to Horace.

They entered the great hall of the library, passing security, and made their way up the stairs to the third floor.

'What about the unseeing guide? Reminds me of Terri.'

'Yes, it would. We need to help her, Robert. Poor woman. Have you ever heard of a character called Tiresias? He is the originator of the magic wand carried by Hermes, or Mercury, you know. The caduceus, as it's called. The twin snakes spiralling along a winged staff. There are some splendid representations of it on the stonework outside, I should have shown you.'

'On the way out. So we're looking for a book about Tiresias?'

'Not quite. A book by someone similar to Tiresias, I suspect. A one-time librarian, blind, one who saw further than most. From Buenos Aires.'

They entered the catalogue room and jotted the number in the clue on to a call slip with one of the stumpy pencils provided.

'We don't have the title, I'm afraid,' Horace said to the librarian. 'It's part of a scavenger hunt.'

'Two in one day,' the librarian said. 'That's OK. We get it all the time.'

'Asking for the same call number?' said Horace sharply.

'I couldn't tell you.'

'Do you remember the person? Or people?'

'Wow. You take your games seriously. A woman in her late thirties or early forties? Beautiful blue eyes.'

They were given a three-digit number and walked through to the breathtaking main reading room. Under luminescent *trompe-l'œil* ceiling paintings of open skies, ranks upon ranks of readers sat in hushed concentration at oak tables. An arrow pointing right, to the North Hall, indicated book deliveries with odd numbers would take place there; even numbers would be delivered in the South Hall. A staff area divided the two halls, serving as a distribution point for volumes brought from anywhere along the library's ninety-odd miles of bookshelves.

'We don't use the odd numbers, it never gets busy enough,' the librarian said, ushering them to the left. 'Do you have an access card?'

Horace assured him that he did.

They sat and waited for their number, 542, to come up on an electronic board. The book came in less than ten minutes. Horace collected it. It was a slim volume, bound in library-issue brown hardcover to protect the original green, red and black soft covers inside. *Ficciones*, by Jorge Luis Borges, in an English translation.

On page 46 was the story 'The Library of Babel'. Robert read: 'The universe (which others call the Library) consists of an indefinite, and perhaps infinite, number of hexagonal galleries, with vast air shafts in between, ringed by very low railings.' It described a terrifying, endless library holding an infinite number of books, and the life of those who lived in it. 'From any hexagon, the floors above and below can be seen: they go on for ever ... A spiral staircase passes through, which plunges and rises into the remote distance ... The Library is a sphere, the exact centre of which is any of the hexagons, and the circumference of which cannot be attained.'

'I'm going to need a drink after reading this, Horace.'

'How many letters does it speak of?'

He read on till he found it. 'Twenty-two, it says. All the books in the Library of Babel are written with twenty-two letters, a full stop, a comma and a space.'

'Trebling it gives 66. Subtract Seven Deadly Sins. It's 59. Way-point 59.'

'I thought we'd be doing a Star of David today, not a hexagon.'

'The Star of David is a symbol of great reverence, and not solely in the Judaic tradition. The Mark of Vishnu. Magen David. In Islam, they say Solomon used it to capture djinns. The six-pointed star produces the hexagon, and vice versa. They're the same thing. If you want to see one, I'll show you where there was one, just outside. But we need to inspect this book more closely first. There should be something attached to it.'

They took turns examining the volume page by page. On the inside back cover, Robert noticed a rough patch on the surface, as though a length of Scotch tape had been torn off it.

A look of resignation crossed Horace's face. 'It was holding something. I'm afraid we're too late. Katherine has it.'

They returned the book and left via the front entrance. Horace took him to the northern end of the library's balustraded patio and pointed north-east, to the corner of 43rd Street. 'The biggest synagogue in the world was there, Temple Emanu-El, from 1868 to 1927. Two Moorish towers. Quite beautiful. The congregation moved uptown. Their new one is still the biggest in the world. For much of that time, until 1911, the synagogue looked back across here, not at this library but at a massive Neo-Egyptian wall of stone, fifty feet high. It was a huge water reservoir for Manhattan. People used to promenade along the top. I do miss the idea of it.'

'I want to get to the next waypoint. I need to work out what's next.'

The Quad showed Waypoint 059 was over near the mouth of the Lincoln Tunnel, just under a mile away.

'We have five minutes,' Horace said. 'I need to jam your mind with things to fuel it.'

He led Robert down the steps at the northern end of the patio and pointed out the caduceus, beautifully carved into plinths on each side at the bottom.

'You are right to say we are on a spine,' he said. 'It runs almost exactly along Fifth Avenue. In the 1920s, before there were stop lights, there used to be manned traffic towers directing vehicles from Washington Square Park along Fifth as far as 57th Street. They were made of bronze, with a distinct Egyptian Revival design. They were beautiful. All gone now, though I have a memento of them. Remind me to show you.'

They walked around the front of the library and went west on 40th Street. Horace turned towards Bryant Park, on the other side of railings painted, like the American Radiator Building opposite, in black and gold.

'Look at that beautiful lawn, Robert. What do you see?'

'I see people lolling about enjoying the sun. What should I see?'

'I see forty miles of bookshelves six feet under the grass, joined by a tunnel to the library we just left. I see a great domed, octagonal Crystal Palace, built for a grand Exposition in 1853 on the park next to the monumental reservoir. I see a young Mark Twain visiting it. I see the palace burning down in a dreadful fire. I see a stooped, rail-thin man of advanced years named Tesla, gently feeding the pigeons in the park, forgotten and alone, dreaming of a world energy and radio system that no one will back him to build. I see General George Washington's troops in retreat from the British, crossing the parkland. I see the penniless dead being buried in a potter's field.'

'Horace, was the fact that you and I met on that walking tour an accident?'

'When the pupil is ready, the teacher appears.'

'My head is going to burst. Please stop now.'

'There is no stopping. It can no longer be stopped.'

'Will you come with me to the next waypoint?'

'Consider me your bodyguard,' he said, patting his jacket pocket.

They walked to 39th Street and took a cab directly west to the corner of Tenth Avenue.

When they got out, the Quad almost immediately acquired a signal and flashed 'Arriving destination'. Horace read out the corresponding clue:

'A tower of light holds the key to your plight
A hex marks the spot, ready or not
To vanquish the night, seek the inner eye's sight
Up the spiral you wind
To pass the Trial by Mind'

Tower of Light.

'I see it,' Horace said immediately. He pointed to the tongue of asphalt that curved down into the mouth of the Lincoln Tunnel. There were more police than usual, because of the Convention. Early-afternoon traffic was relatively light.

On each side of the tunnel entrance rose Art Deco towers like stylized radio masts, surmounted by powerful searchlights. They reminded Robert of Flash Gordon-era science fiction ray-guns. A spiral staircase ran up their core.

'There are six platforms, you see?'

'You can't be seriously suggesting we go up one of those things?'

'Not we. You.'

Robert walked west along 39th Street on the south side of the tunnel entrance, where the tower looked easier to get to. 'This is the nearest one to the waypoint,' he said.

'Up you go.'

Horace handed Robert a bandanna. 'Put this around your face.'

'Are you insane? We'll both be arrested.'

'No, just you. Hex marks the spot. Hex and sex, both meaning six. The cache is on the top platform, I'm sure of it. We need that key. It will be part of a hexagon or a Seal of Solomon. Go.'

'Horace –'

The old man's anger flared. 'If anything goes wrong, meet me at the Market Diner at 43rd and 11th. Now can you not trust me? Go!'

The towers were set on a brick base that rose above his head height. 'Help me, then. Give me a leg-up.'

Horace interlocked his fingers and formed a stirrup, his back to the base, for Robert's foot. He pushed up with remarkable strength as Robert clambered up. Then he walked nonchalantly away.

Atop the base, Robert pulled himself up further to the bottom platform, inside the tower, then climbed the spiral staircase. At any moment he expected to hear bullhorns, sirens, the crack of bullets. Up he rose, through each platform, along the spiral stair that twisted like strands of DNA. It was as though he were climbing one of the staircases between hexagonal floors in the Borges story.

'I don't believe it,' he said to the air. 'I'm in the Library of Babel.'

At the top platform he stepped off the stair and looked around. Nothing. Bolted metal, thick black cables. The view of Manhattan was stunning.

It looked like he could go up another level, via a ladder, to where the lights were mounted. Carefully he climbed up and stuck his head through the gap in the platform. Right before his eyes, taped to one of the metal struts, was a film container in a sealed plastic bag. Stretching his arm forward, he reached it and put it in his pocket.

At that point he heard the first cop's voice, through the speakers of a police car. 'Stop! Don't move. Stay where you are. Stay where you are. Slowly show your hands.'

Katherine saw it all.

She focused on Robert through the telescopic sight, bringing the crosshairs to bear on his forehead as he leaned out of the top of the light tower to show his hands to the police. Two hundred and fifty yards. She'd have one shot, two at most. It had been a long time since her specialized training. She'd have to use the laser sight. She reached for the switch to turn it on.

Robert looked down, leaning his upper body out of the tower.

A ring of policemen were around the base. An officer sat in the police car, keying the microphone. Horace was nowhere to be seen.

Robert made an overt display of showing his hands. For the love of God, what next? Suddenly he saw a flash of multicoloured light. The middle of his forehead lit up with sensation. He closed his eyes, and still could see.

Time halted. He withdrew behind his eyes, behind his mind, to a place where, for an instant, he saw nothing but patterns upon patterns of light, streaming like rain from the sky, diffracting and interfering and weaving in colours he had never seen. It was world rain, unfiltered rain, a rain of light coalescing in and out of matter, twisting and arching back on itself, and he was simply a fold in it, an eddy, a swimmer in a sea of which he was himself made.

As above, so below; as within, so without.

He saw part of his mind filtering the stream of vibrations and light, the mercurial stuff of the universe, neither wave nor particle but both and neither, saw his mind building a representation of the world, a selection adapted to survival needs, an editing job so seamless as to be invisible.

Mind is the builder.

He saw the world being made. Every day. In every instant. He saw endless cycles of refinement, of evolution.

He opened his eyes. He saw that he was both free and pre-destined: that he had wanted and chosen everything that had happened to him, that his task was to learn why he had created this life, these events, for himself.

He resigned himself to whatever would happen.

Katherine saw the red dot dance about Robert's head and settle on his brow. She held her aim on him, breathing deeply in, saying a quiet prayer to herself to calm her nerves.

Robert saw the senior officer talking to uniforms, pointing to the car and up at him. There was a dumbshow of reluctance, of remon-strance, of consideration. Then everyone at once stopped and stared up at Robert. He could see alarm spreading through the group.

The senior police officer spoke into his walkie-talkie agitatedly.

Katherine saw they'd seen the laser dot. They'd be radioing to check whether it was one of their men and not a rogue sniper. Then they'd realize one of their own sharpshooters wasn't answering his radio. She'd give them another minute to do this. Then she'd have to move very fast.

*

Robert saw the policemen nervously taking positions of better cover. Two started gesturing to him to come down.

Then a voice boomed over the police-car loudspeaker: 'Come down slowly and calmly, sir. Come down.'

He started back down the spiral staircase.

Katherine shifted her aim down towards the policemen.

'Good boy, Robert,' she whispered. 'Keep moving.'

She brought the laser dot to rest on a cop's chest, just long enough for the police commander next to him to notice it, then moved it up to the policeman's forehead just as Robert reached the bottom of the tower.

She saw Robert jump down to the street as the cops flew in all directions to take cover from her.

'There you are, baby.'

Then a shadow entered Katherine's soul. She aimed the laser sight again at Robert's head.

She had a clear shot.

'I love you, Robert,' she whispered.

She refocused her aim. Then Katherine emptied her lungs of air, and between two heartbeats softly squeezed the trigger.

Robert looked up towards the muzzle flash and then time stopped. His mind ripped along the trajectory of the bullet, and he knew Katherine was at the other end of it, and he felt in her mind the terrifying shadow of the Iwnw.

A bullet was coming, and he couldn't move. He could see it, frozen in mid spin, a glint in the air, and then there were minds trying to reach his. He felt Adam, and behind him the Iwnw. He felt Horace. *Duck your head to the right. Duck your head to the left. Look up. Look down.* Pressure in his head, forcing him this way and that, paralysing him as each fought to nudge his head an inch either way.

He could feel Horace failing, desperately trying to block the murderous intent of the Iwnw through Adam's raw pain. He saw how seriously he had hurt Adam. Blood was pumping internally, he was bleeding to death within his own body. Robert saw the pooling blood, distended tissues. Horace was losing his grip, exhausted from the fight at Grand Central, and now Robert felt his head being tipped against his will, down and to the right, into the path of the flying bullet . . .

Had Adam crossed over or not? Was he still playing a double game? Robert felt he'd lost control to the Iwnw now. He was allowing them to feed into Katherine through him. He was trying to force Robert to duck into the bullet. He was Robert's enemy. He had become the enemy. Dear God.

Robert could let him die. Adam was bleeding out. If he just held the balance between the forces trying to tip his head this way and that for a few minutes longer, Adam would die and the Iwnw's gateway would collapse. He reached out again with his mind to Adam. He could even accelerate the bleeding.

Adam Hale. The brother he wished he'd had. Troubled, crazy, lovable Adam. Robert could not believe the good was lost.

Drawing on the powers of earth and water, fire and air, ether and mind, Robert looked into Adam's injuries and closed the internal wound. He stopped the bleeding and fired every repair and recovery mechanism in Adam's battered body. Then, in a blaze of burning mental light, he threw Adam and the Iwnw from his consciousness and twisted his head a millimetre up and to the left.

Robert heard the zip of an angry wasp and felt the bullet's shock-wave as the skin of his forehead split. The windshield of an empty car ten yards from the policemen shattered, and a boom echoed among the buildings. The policemen all hit the deck. Robert ran.

Katherine felt the shadow lift from her. She fired off two more shots in quick succession to cover Robert's escape, hitting two more police cars in the tyres. She saw him pull off the bandanna and make the corner. Then she put her escape plan into operation, emerging three minutes later on to the street in a business suit, unruffled and smiling.

Horace was waiting for him in a booth at the diner, his face white with shock, when Robert entered. A handkerchief jammed against his forehead to mask the blood, barely able to speak, Robert sat down and started to shake.

'I lost you,' Horace said. 'You saved yourself. I'm so sorry.'

For minutes neither said another word.

Robert put on the table between them a copper-red fragment of metallic glass, part of a hexagon.

He took a deep breath. Tried to calm his mind.

'The design of these keys is hundreds of years old,' Horace said. 'Perhaps more. Exquisite. The full hexagon will show a six-pointed star, forming another hexagon at its core. Within that shape, another Star of David, and so on, each nesting in the other, to an exquisite degree of detail.'

'Horace, are we safe here? Shouldn't we be moving?' Police sirens were sounding now in the street.

Horace closed his eyes. 'We have a few minutes.'

'I healed him. I healed Adam.'

Horace looked deep into Robert's eyes. 'You did well.'

'He can still be saved. There is still good in him, even if he no longer sees it himself. I couldn't kill him.'

'Yet he was your enemy when you healed him.'

'He was.'

'Your abilities are becoming greater than Adam's, greater than mine.'

'No.'

'There is another who needs healing. One who is deeply afraid.'

'Terri.'

'Tell me, when you were at the Worth Monument, was there anything Adam said to you that has stuck in your mind?'

'Well, he kept going on about the two Metropolitan Life buildings at Madison Square Park. I couldn't figure out why. He loves to go off on tangents like that, but it was odd.'

'He wanted to lodge a phrase in your mind. What exactly did he say?'

'MetLife. He kept saying MetLife.'

'And what do you conclude from that?'

'Not much, I'm afraid.'

'He was telling you where Terri is hiding. He was telling you while masking it even from himself.'

'What?'

'Did he pronounce it just like that? MetLife? What did he actually *say*?'

'Actually, he pronounced it oddly. As if he'd developed a speech impediment. The *F* was more of an *S*. At first I thought it was the phone, but it seemed very marked. Very odd.'

'So. Solve it.'

'MetLice . . . So basic a riddle, he said. He said that twice. So basic a riddle. MetLice.'

'And so?'

'Metal ice, so basic –'

'Stop there. It's a riddle involving those letters. What was the context? What else did he talk about around then?'

'Umm . . . he mentioned a sex club, to be honest.'

'What name did he give?'

'None.'

'Very well. Use your mind, Robert. He was telling you something, in the language of the full mind.'

'So, a basic life met . . .'

'Keep going. Write it down if you must.'

Robert scribbled letters into a notepad, turning them over in his head. '*Boîte à malice*. Good God. It's an almost perfect anagram of *boite à malice*.'

'And *boîte* in French means nightclub, I believe? Or place of work?'

'That's right.'

'That is where she will be hiding. Such an establishment, of that name, where she may have worked or which she may have frequented. He will have managed to shield that information, but not for long, especially not from himself. He bypassed even his own conscious mind to tell you that. You must find her as soon as possible.'

Robert googled variations on the club name on the Quad, coming up blank on all of them. He tried other search engines. Nothing.

'Some of these places are public, though discreet, but others are very word of mouth, I believe,' Horace said. 'Even the *New York Times* has written about them.'

Robert racked his memory for any indication Terri had given that might help. Finally, he called an acquaintance who freelanced for *Time Out* and other publications, including occasionally GBN, about nightlife.

'Matt, I need to ask you a question of some delicacy. It's quite urgent, and it requires great discretion.'

Matt said he'd never heard of La Boîte à Malice but would ask around.

Horace scribbled a note to Robert on a napkin. *Does he need money?* Robert shook his head. Matt either liked you or he didn't.

'The next ten minutes, Matt, would be ideal.'

Robert regarded his old friend for a moment. 'You don't eat, Horace? I don't think I've ever seen you eat.'

'At my age one is careful about what one puts into one's system. Let's move to another location now.'

By a circuitous route, they moved to another restaurant several blocks further away from the scene of the shooting. Robert heard police sirens off in the distance, near where they had been sitting.

Matt called him back in fifteen minutes, just as they were sitting down.

La Boîte à Malice was neither a sex club nor a floating kink party that moved from private loft to private loft, as he had imagined. It was something very high end, extremely discreet and very expensive: a consulting agency, run by a woman, that was said to offer imaginative problem-solving services, using methods from psychic to sexual, with a trademark sense of humour. The name, in that sense, could be loosely translated as the Mischief House, or even Tricks 'R' Us.

'Matt says it has a very strange vibe, cool and scary at once, and people talk about it as if it were an urban legend. It only employs witches, they say. And no one *ever* messes with them,' Robert told Horace.

'Is there a name for the woman who owns it? Some way to get in touch? Or,' Horace added with a smile, 'do they contact you?'

'It's the sort of firm Adam would know about. Matt had a phone number, but no address.'

Horace took from his pocket the map of New York with the Tree of Life shape sketched on to it and placed it flat on the table.

'Do you have anything that Terri has worn? Anything she is attached to, or worn close to her skin?'

Robert hesitated. Then he took a chain from around his wrist. It was the chain she had worn around her neck on the day they'd made love. He felt it glow in his hand. 'This is the chain that held the second key.'

Horace took it between his fingertips and closed his eyes. For more than a minute, he sat perfectly still, breathing deeply.

Without opening his eyes, he asked Robert to write down the phone number for the Mischief House and give it to him. He placed his palm down flat on the piece of paper while still holding the chain in his fingers.

'Personal items have resonance,' he said. 'With the red gold on my person, I may be able to find a matching resonance. Do you have any idea where Terri usually lives?'

'She said Adam called her his Red Hooker.'

Horace concentrated harder.

'She's not in Brooklyn.'

After another minute of intense concentration, he suddenly grimaced. 'I have found her fear . . . And pain. Call that number.'

Robert keyed it in and heard it ring. After six rings it cut over to an answering machine. No voice to identify the firm or confirm the number. He cut the line.

'She is wherever that phone is,' Horace said. 'It made her jump when it rang. She was scared, then intrigued. Now she has put up a wall. She was afraid to answer it, even though she wanted to very badly. Call her again. Say it's you and ask her to call. Say you are with me. She knows me.'

Robert called. He saw Horace wince again. When the answer phone came on, he spoke. 'Terri, darling, it's me, Robert. I'm with Horace. We can help you. We can protect you. We need your help. Please pick up?'

Nothing happened. He waited till the line went dead.

'We need to start heading east,' Horace said.

The Quad rang as they were crossing Seventh Avenue. 'Robert, stay away from me. It's too dangerous.'

'We can protect you.'

'There's no protection against them.'

'Let us help you.'

'The women here are helping me.'

'Terri, I know you're pregnant.'

She began to weep. 'There's no way out . . . no way out for me.'

'There is if we help you. Tell us where to meet you.'

'Where are you?'

'44th and Seventh.'

She was silent for what seemed an age. 'Mossman Lock Collection, at the General Society, 44th and Fifth, fifteen minutes.'

The General Society of Mechanics and Tradesmen, founded in New York in 1785, when the British had only been gone two years and the US Constitution was still four years from adoption, was in a jewel of a building.

Robert and Horace, still breathing hard from their brisk walk, exited the bronze-doored elevator on to a hardwood first-floor landing that curved elegantly over a hushed reading room below. The library was bathed in light from a breathtaking skylight three storeys above. Great reading lamps hung by chains from the ceiling like floating lilies. Robert and Horace followed a curving brass handrail to their left that led to a small room ranged with glass display cabinets.

Terri was not there.

The cabinets contained an astonishing collection of locks and keys, most of them mind-bogglingly complex. Everywhere he looked he saw an orgy of precision instrument-making in polished brass and silver. There were time locks, magic key locks, combination locks, plunger cylinder locks, examples of back-action key locks, grasshopper locks, outside-shaft locks, knob combination locks. One was labelled 'a very complicated lock'. Great iron keys and ornately scrolled locks from the Renaissance were displayed next to exquisitely tooled pieces from the nineteenth and early twentieth centuries that looked like code-breaking machines with numbered drums, star wheels and notched cylinders.

Horace called him over, his eyes gleaming, and pointed in awed silence at some carved wooden instruments, their parts looking like wooden toothbrushes. *This is a wooden Egyptian lock which is about 4,000 years old*, the label said. *Pin tumbler lock. This mechanical principle was developed by Linus Yale Sr for modern use.*

At the far end was a five-foot-tall black metal safe, painted in gold-yellow lettering. Next to it sat a strongbox of heavily riveted black iron. Robert's mind flared with pain as his eyes fell upon it. The black bolts of the cracked bell at St Mark's in-the-Bowery rushed at him. *Mary fat Mary fat Mary fat Mary.*

Coloured lightning flashed through his eyes, blue and purple and yellow. Saw-tooth patterns like the Chrysler arcs, twisting in geometric forms, scoured his brain. Then everything went black. The heavy bolts of the strongbox had set off a terrifying string of associations in his mind that ended in a single image: a picture he had seen as a child of the early atomic bombs. Thick rivets on black metal. Fat Man. Fat Mary. Ma'rifat'. And the words quoted by Robert Oppenheimer, leader of the Manhattan Project, when he described seeing the first atomic explosion: *I am become death, the destroyer of worlds.*

He stepped back in bewilderment and spun around. 'Horace?'

Before him stood a shape, in grey light against black, radiating black-blue waves. He blinked his eyes and shook his head. His hearing warped and squealed. His regular senses were overwhelmed, shutting down. He felt energy draining out of his body.

'I can't see,' he whispered. 'It's close. The detonation is close. If we can't stop it . . .' Then slowly everything stabilized, and the greys became light grey, then white.

He saw it was Terri standing before him, holding Horace's hand.

Horace flagged down a cab outside the General Society. 'Come to my apartment. I can look after you best there.'

Terri beamed sadly at Horace. 'Where is your place? I've always wondered.'

'A building that used to be called the Level Club, on the Upper West Side. Near the Verdi statue.'

'Why is it called that?'

'It was built by Freemasons, as a facility for visiting members from around the country. The venture went bust, though. It had some very rough years. Eventually it was rescued and restored. I'm not a Mason, but some of the building's features have great resonance for me. Some even say it is the most ambitious effort ever made to actually reconstruct King Solomon's Temple.'

'Now I really want to experience that.'

'Before we go, Robert,' Horace added. 'Look there.'

Just by the entrance to the General Society, the building was adorned by a muscular arm in iron bas-relief, holding a hammer in vigorous workerly manner.

'Remember it,' Horace said.

After Horace had finished dressing the wound on his forehead and examining his eyes, Robert got up impatiently from the sofa.

'What else happened on the day of the Blackout?'

Horace glanced at Terri. 'I suspect that on that day, everything happened,' he said. 'Everything that has happened, all of this, was set in train that day.'

Robert frowned. He could barely keep his eyes open; his entire body felt as though it were made of lead, and yet he couldn't still his mind.

'Tell me.'

Terri spoke: 'I didn't see all of it. Adam overcame great fear. Paralysing. But he went anyway.'

'Start at the beginning,' Robert said. 'Enough talking around it.'

'I only know a part of it,' Terri said. 'Adam will have to tell you some of it.'

'Go on.'

'Among other things, as I told you, it was the day I lost my eyesight.'

August 14, 2003: Blackout Day

Terri arrived at the apartment building on Greenwich Street at Charles shortly before ten o'clock in the morning, the appointed hour.

Since she had a couple of minutes to kill, she crossed the street to the little white clapboard farmhouse that sat diagonally across from the client's building. It looked like something she had seen in a children's storybook, a long time ago. All bent out of shape and non-linear.

It promised to be an interesting job. The client, some kind of minor aristocrat in his forties from Britain, had contacted La Boîte à Malice asking for someone with very specialized skills to help with a particular problem. Terri was the best qualified. As usual, the agency had checked up on the client and sent her a summary. It had been entirely up to her whether to accept.

When he opened the door, her first thought was that he had a far more smiling presence than she had felt from afar; her second thought was that he had intensely magnetic eyes. The client, who went by the name of Adam Hale, introduced her to a pretty, petite woman about twenty years her senior with straight black hair and blue eyes, whose first signal to Terri was a powerful block around some core issues in her past.

Terri recognized it because she maintained the same defence. Despite the older woman's superficial friendliness, she also read some unease: guilt about being there, high regard for a life partner and sadness. A feeling of something lost.

'Please meet Katherine Rota,' Adam said. 'Katherine, this is Terri, from La Boîte à Malice.'

There was a strong bond between Adam and the woman, one that had gone on for a long time. She saw a shape of three people, bound together through the years, changing combinations but always together ... the third was a man, Katherine's significant other. She saw it lasting through lifetimes.

Hale she read as a dynamo. Energy coursed through him and from him. He was powerful but stymied somehow, and afraid.

'Terri, I'll lay this out as baldly as I can,' Adam said. 'I have learned of an act of great obscenity, an attack, that is being planned against this city. It is the kind of thing that would not be taken seriously by the authorities, and indeed if they were to intervene it would only make things worse.

'The subject is a very dangerous person, with the ability to carry out a very serious act. He is also quite fascinating, and someone that in other circumstances I would find very gratifying to hold as a friend. However, this cannot be.'

Terri felt his intensity wash into her. Then she felt an enormous wave of potential harm. For a moment it took her breath away. In the middle of it, at its core, was a word. She tried to read it, amid swirling patterns of pain and shame. *Revenge*.

'Who is this man?'

'His name is unimportant, but his father and grandfather, both Egyptians, had access to a great tradition of ancient knowledge, in addition to being trained as scientists in the Western tradition. They passed along the reverence for this tradition, and some of its tenets and secrets, to the boy as he grew up between Cairo, London and America. His mother is American, and he is an American citizen.'

'OK.'

'Something dreadful has happened to this man. It has caused a psycho-spiritual breakdown. This has served as a gateway for certain forces of great potential evil. I have detected him and must stop him —'

Katherine interrupted: 'Pause for breath, Adam.'

Terri felt Katherine's barriers harden even further. But she smiled at Terri. 'He can be a little overwhelming. Would you like some tea?'

'Just water, please.'

Terri felt Katherine's attempts to appraise her. No hostility, a neutral but searching sweep initially, now turning positive. She felt Katherine was someone accustomed to assessing people quickly, trained in doing so. She was also like a television tuned to static. Deliberately so, though she didn't realize it.

'May I go on?'

341

Terri focused again on Adam Hale. 'Please.'

'In a few hours I plan to go to confront this man. I'm not strong enough to do so without help. There are forces attached to him of great power.'

'You want me to go with you? As I understood, that's not the problem I was brought in to address.'

'No. Just over twenty years ago, when Katherine and I met at university, she had one of the most powerful gifts I have ever come across. I need her help now, but she can no longer tap into it.'

'I see that.'

'I had hoped that, at least for the next twelve hours or so, you might be able to help her recover it. Add your own power, if you are willing. I need . . . armour, so to speak. Or depth. A deep well to draw on. It can't be described.'

'I know. I understand.'

She closed her eyes and drew a deep breath, holding it till it had absorbed all distractions, all incoherence, all negativity, in her being. Then slowly she exhaled, expelling it all. She held Katherine, Adam and the unnamed man in her focus, letting it spread slowly out to those around them.

She saw something deeply puzzling. *Beautiful . . . virginal . . .*

'Your husband,' she said to Katherine. 'Why didn't you call on him? He's . . .'

She looked at Adam, saw his eyes flit to Katherine's.

'He doesn't know,' Adam said. 'He has buried it so deeply that he believes he is a sceptic.'

'It's not the time,' Katherine said. 'Robert's not ready, and he's to be preserved until there's truly no option but to call on him.'

Terri saw the three of them again, in a chain of being, linked together and unchanging as worlds shifted and blurred around them. Adam. Katherine. Robert.

She turned to Adam. 'How will you prepare?'

'Breathing. Meditation. Movement.' He smiled at her. 'Focus on my quarry.'

She narrowed her eyes at him. 'You want me to raise your sexual energy too. So you can build on it as a base.'

'You're doing that just by being in the room.'

'I might be able to do better than that.'

She turned to Katherine. 'Ms Rota, could you and I talk while he does his deep breathing?'

New York, August 31, 2004

Robert held up his hand. 'Can you stop for a moment, Terri?'

Clouds of darkness and foreboding had filled his mind as he listened to Terri's account. He strained to throw off a sense of doom. The idea of Katherine trying to help Adam behind his back, of Terri and Katherine knowing each other over a year before he'd made love with Terri, made him feel idiotic, however much they'd excluded him to protect him. His whole adult life of denial of his gift seemed cowardly, somehow.

'You seriously need to rest,' Horace said.

Terri took his arm and led him, following Horace's directions, to a guest room. As he lay there, curtains drawn, in the half-light, a great wave of fear broke over him, and then he melted into exhausted oblivion.

He slept right through dinner. At some point in the night Terri brought him some soup. Then she withdrew and left him to sleep his fill.

A Martyr's Love Song: The Making of the Ma'rifat'

After weeks, I was suddenly released. There was no explanation, just a warning never to speak of what had happened to me. They knew what I'd done, they said, but I would not be charged. Simply, no one would ever again believe a word I said.

I was dropped in the middle of Manhattan one night, in the clothes I had been abducted in, with all my belongings except my identity papers.

I returned to Long Island to find I had lost my job. In addition to vanishing without explanation, I had been shown to have fabricated data. Pictures taken during my interrogation had been sent to my friends, to my family, showing me in compromising positions with other men.

They discredited me as a scientist and as a man. My credit cards stopped working. I was forced to live on my meagre savings.

I could not forgive them.

But I could take revenge.

Sir Isaac Newton's third law states that for every action there is an equal and opposite reaction. I determined now to honour that law.

And ironically, I would use in part the formula Newton himself had passed down to me through my Beloved.

I found my destruction as a human being had brought me capacities I had sought for years in our tradition. Inchoate and poisonous but real none the less. Malevolence gathered around me and began to feed on my soul.

My grandfather had placed in my father's keeping a metallic drum of exquisite design, which, as a boy, I had once been allowed to see revolve, and glow, and feel its power, as the adults prayed and chanted around it. It seemed to amplify and to broadcast their love, their spiritual rapture. My father passed it on to me, and, in keeping with his admonitions, I hid it in a secret place, as befitted a sacred treasure, until I was worthy of it. I had hoped, one day, to become an adept and learn its secret uses.

Now, with Newton's help, I made a copy of it. It was made of the same metal-glass that he described as the Philosopher's Stone. Only one element was missing.

They say that when the student is ready, the teacher will appear.

I now came to the attention of a group of people who had felt my rage, my humiliation. For fifteen years, I had been striving, in my secret studies, to transmute a tiny amount of regular gold into the kind we know as red gold. It is an alchemical operation, requiring both delicate physical treatment and heightened spiritual states. I had never succeeded. It was the one thing missing from Newton's paper. He did not say how to obtain it.

Now the Iwnw brought me some.

On August 14, 2003, I rose early, intending to enjoy every last drop of the beautiful day that was dawning. As the sun rose, I stood at the open window and felt the glory of the heavens enter my heart.

The final preparation of the Device would be a long, arduous task. I meditated for an hour. I tried to find a place of forgiveness for what had been done to me, and found none. I honoured my father's memory. I cursed the Mukhabarat. All Mukhabarats. Above all, I cursed the American Mukhabarat.

Two days earlier I had sent a message to Katherine, to my Beloved. It was our only contact after I was released. I asked her to meet me in Las Vegas, at the Luxor Hotel, on the evening of Thursday, August 14, 2003. I did not intend to be there, but I wanted her to be out of New York. I did not want her to be destroyed in the detonation of the Ma'rifat' that she had unwittingly helped me to build. I wanted her to witness it. To understand my pain. My destruction.

After breakfasting, I took care of final routine matters. I paid bills and burned personal items. I sent a final entry to the small weblog I had kept as an enthusiast for the great Nikola Tesla, who, like me, had explored the outer reaches of phenomena such as resonance and vibration, who had warned that such knowledge, in the wrong hands, could split the earth apart, whose laboratory near Washington Square Park, like Newton's in Cambridge, had burned down in a freak fire, who had seen beyond the limitations and prejudices of his age, and suffered for it.

Then I went to my garage and put all I would need into the trunk.

It was a short drive from my home to the place I had chosen as a suitable locale for the final construction of the Device.

It was at Robinson Street and Tesla Street in Shoreham, Long Island, just a few miles from my place of work. It was the empty shell of the laboratory where Tesla planned his most audacious vision: a Radio City of his own technology that would transmit energy and information through the earth itself to all mankind. He had not been backed sufficiently. He failed, though decades later his contributions to the world would be recognized.

I had studied and observed when to elude the security guards. When I was ready, I made my way into the grounds through my secret entrance. To face my destiny, in the form of Adam Hale.

✧

7

Trial by Spirit

New York, September 1, 2004

When Robert awoke, Terri was eating a sandwich. Horace was sitting with her at the dining-room table, sipping a glass of water.

'Hey, sleepyhead,' Terri shouted. 'Ready for breakfast?'

'What are you having?'

'I'm having lunch. It's noon. You've been out for eighteen hours.'

He stretched. His senses were especially sharp. He felt himself move with ease and grace.

As Terri walked away from the window to get coffee for him, he saw her flare with light against the dark wallpaper. Arcs and inverted Vs like the Chrysler around her head and shoulders. He blinked, but it didn't go away. He sat down, spine straight, feeling his head balance perfectly on his shoulders. Thrills of energy coursed along his belly, his limbs.

The coffee was delicious. When he placed his hand on Terri's back, she was electric. He felt animal heat, coursing power.

'Your hands are hot,' she said, smiling at him.

'It's the coffee cup.'

'No, it's you.'

Her transformation had been miraculous. As soon as Horace had taken her hand in the General Society's lock room, her despair and fear had begun to melt away. He looked into her eyes. Felt her perceiving him.

'Horace and I talked a lot while you were asleep. We may all still get through this.'

Horace brought him the newspaper, suggesting he catch up on events in their fair city since he'd last been conscious, and went into the living room.

There had been protests at the New York Public Library after they left, an attempt to attach a banner to one of the lions, a ruckus, arrests verging on the indiscriminate. Many more arrests down near

349

Ground Zero. Running cat-and-mouse games between cops and various flavours of protester, most peaceful, a handful not.

Above all there was speculation about shots fired at police cars near the Lincoln Tunnel. A police sharpshooter was said to be under investigation. A protester who had scaled one of the light towers near by was not thought to have been involved in the incident.

Investigations continued.

No dead. No reports of injuries.

Horace returned. 'We must leave. While we three are together, and while I have the core, the Malice Box, as you call it, Adam and the Iwnw will find it difficult to harm us. Where do you think the next waypoint is? It will be Number 121. The clue is as follows:

'For endless sight, climb into the light
The fire and the gold await the bold
To beat the clock, you must scale the rock
Then sally forth, and telescope north
To rescue love – or kill it
Pass the Trial by Spirit

'Any thoughts on that?'

Robert snapped out of his reverie. 'If the pattern that I showed you yesterday holds, it would be somewhere around Rockefeller Center. Radio City.'

Horace nodded. 'Things are accelerating.'

Robert could feel it too. A gathering impetus. The coming hours would resolve it. He felt ready.

'We start where we left off yesterday, on the spine,' Horace said. 'That reminds me . . .' He motioned for them to follow him and went into his study. Against one wall, in a glass case, was a three-foot-tall model, in bronze, of what looked like an ornate, Deco-style watchtower. Along the top were three coloured lights.

'If it were lying down, it would look like a mummy case,' Robert said. He saw there was also a framed drawing of it, a design plan, on the wall. Terri put her hands on both and concentrated.

'This is an architect's model of the traffic towers that used to run along Fifth Avenue, seven of them, as I told you. Quite beautiful. They have all been destroyed, alas. Take a close look at the top, between the traffic lights.'

Robert leaned forward. 'Good God. The spiralling snakes.'

'Precisely. The caduceus.'

'This keeps showing up, Horace, but what exactly is its significance? I get snatches of it – I half see it fitting into the trials, the city, the Tree of Life – but then it eludes me again.'

'Myths record, sometimes in distorted ways, the clashes throughout time between the Iwnw and ourselves over the rightful ownership and control of the Path,' said Horace. 'The fact is, the motif of the snakes spiralling along the staff is an image of the Path, just as the Tree of Life represents it too, from another perspective. The caduceus is a kind of magic wand, carried by the Greek god Hermes, whom the Romans called Mercury – the interpreter of the gods, the guide to the underworld, the patron of roads and boundaries.'

Robert saw flashes of underground water, streams under Manhattan – impressions that had struck him throughout the trials. He remembered feeling water twisting and snaking under the city, saw the course of Water Tunnel Number One along the vertical spine of the Tree of Life pattern, remembered the Native American belief in the serpent Manetta who dwelled in the streams under Fifth Avenue.

'How do the snakes represent the Path?'

'They stand for the powers that you acquire as you complete the trials,' Terri said, 'ascending from below to above, climbing from the primitive energies – killing, fucking, the pursuit of power – to the higher ones – compassion, creativity, healing. In terms of your trials, from St Paul's Chapel and Ground Zero up through Union Square to Radio City. You can think of the staff as your spine, and the energies as travelling up it from the base of the spine to the skull. The wings at the top represent the spirit taking flight when the Path has been completed.'

'Why two snakes, though?'

'The powers of earth, water, fire and air, of ether, mind and spirit, all have a shadow side,' Horace said. 'To complete the Path you must weave together at each stage the negative and positive aspects of each power. The raw force of the killing energy is destructive, for example, but you cannot walk the Path without it – you must yoke it to a higher purpose and draw strength from it. Without its power, you will not survive the rest of the Path. The spiralling snakes, switching back and forth on each side of the staff, represent the plaiting together of such polarities – good and evil, female and male, order and chaos. The central spine represents the balance between them.'

'But what are they doing on those traffic towers?'

'Hermes was the god of roads, so it would make sense to include his symbol on traffic towers along the city's principal avenue. Consider too that when these beautiful towers were withdrawn, another figure was used to ornament the city stop lights.' He pointed to a figure covered with an exquisitely embroidered cloth. Robert raised it to reveal a figure in cast bronze, about eighteen inches tall, wearing a distinctive hat and holding a winged wheel in his left hand.

'Mercury.'

'That's right. Truly we follow the path of Hermes.'

As they were about to leave, Robert noticed photographs of himself, Adam and Katherine on the corkboard by Horace's desk. 'What are these, Horace?'

'As I told you, I have been watching over you for many years, Robert. Over all three of you. I am your Watchman. Adam and

Katherine have worked very closely with me at different stages to bring you through this experience. Now we must leave.'

Robert checked the GPS programme as he stood on the sidewalk. Terri and Horace waited for the car they'd ordered in the lobby behind him, under a great Seal of Solomon set in the ceiling. Twin pillars topped by shining orbs graced the monumental front of the building.

The Quad pointed south-east, less than two miles.

At the New York Public Library, Horace insisted they enter by the main steps. He took them left, along the main corridor to a door at the end on the left-hand side.

'The Periodical Room,' he announced and led them quietly in.

Apart from a staff member at a counter, no one was there. The room, fitted in wooden panelling, was ringed with paintings of newspaper and publishing buildings of the early twentieth century, set in arches and frames as if they were windows. Robert saw the green-and-blue McGraw-Hill Building, the *New York Times* tower at 1 Times Square in its original stone facing, the old Newspaper Row opposite City Hall Park, when the *World* Building was still standing.

'Take a few minutes before we begin and consider these paintings,' Horace said.

They sat in silence for perhaps five minutes. Robert felt Horace holding them in his mind with great love.

He took a deep breath. 'Horace, what is the seventh trial?'

Horace took both their hands and closed his eyes for a moment. Then he spoke. 'The final trial will give you the potential – just a chance – of stopping the detonation of the Ma'rifat'. Without it, you will have none. The Trial by Spirit is a test of your capacity to forgive, to love, to surrender yourself entirely to the ocean of divine love in which you are both a single drop and the vessel holding the ocean itself.'

Robert would pass the trial if he demonstrated, in his actions and words, that he had utterly given himself over to the requirements of the Path – that he had developed a mind as calm as a mirror, a heart devoid of fear, a spirit brimming with love, Horace said. Anything less and he would die.

Robert would recover a seven-sided or seven-pointed key.

'And then you will be on your own. Though we will be with you, there will be little more that I, or anyone else, can do to help you face the Iwnw and their creature, as you must. Now let us begin.'

He got up and walked briskly to the door. As they tried to keep up, he led them back along the corridor, through the entrance hall and then left down a staircase to the library's exit on to 42nd Street.

Directly across the street as they came out of the library was a white stone arched gate, carved with figures of the zodiac. At the bottom of the left-hand column, Robert inspected the Gemini twins. They looked unearthly.

'Think of this as a sacred gateway or passage leading you to the final trial,' Horace said. He took them under vaulted Guastavino arches into the ornate lobby of the building, the Salmon Tower, where even the mailboxes were small works of art in bronze, and directly through on to 43rd Street. Looking back, Robert saw an identical carved arch in white stone, with the same zodiacal figures.

'Onwards,' Horace boomed.

They walked to Fifth and swept past the corner of 44th Street, where they had met Terri the previous afternoon.

Pressing on north but not stopping, Horace pointed to a brightly coloured frieze in deep reds, greens and yellow atop a tall building on the east side of Fifth. 'On top of the French Building up there,' he shouted. 'Griffins, in a faience sunrise! See? Body of a lion, wings and head of an eagle, tail of a snake. Known for finding gold and buried treasure! On the west face at the top, a head of Mercury, the Messenger, set in a gold bursting star! The gate is inspired by the Ishtar Gate. Ishtar is Inanna, Robert.'

'I am the creature of light. I remember.' He saw. He understood. He felt power surging through his body.

Horace charged ahead. 'Keep moving!'

They quickly came to 47th Street, where, on the west side, at the entrance to the Diamond District, two light towers rose in the form of stylized octagonal diamonds set atop criss-crossing metal spars.

'Robert, it's just like the light tower at the Lincoln Tunnel! Want to climb it?'

'Keep moving, Horace.'

He heard Terri suppress what might have been a laugh.

Bronzed Art Deco footings set into the sidewalk around the trunks of trees signalled that they had arrived at Rockefeller Center. Up ahead, on the opposite side of the street, soared the octagonal coned steeples of St Patrick's Cathedral. On the left, they passed the Maison Française, its façade embellished with sinuous female forms in bronze, and came to the promenade that led directly west to a sunken plaza – the site of the ice rink in winter – guarded by a gleaming gold statue of Prometheus, eternally stealing fire from the gods. At the end of the promenade, framed by the surrounding buildings, reared the main skyscraper of Rockefeller Center, the GE Building, or 30 Rock, its steepling setbacks sharply shadowed by the blazing sun overhead.

'I can't get a signal for the GPS,' Robert said, wiping sweat from his forehead. 'But I'm sure it's here. We need to go down.'

As they descended, Robert saw on the right a gilded figure of Hermes set into the façade of one of the buildings, a golden caduceus in its hand.

In front of the GE Building the signal returned. 'It's here,' he said. But something was odd. He looked again at the altitude reading: over 800 feet. That had to be at the very top of the tower.

He showed it to Horace. 'The old observation deck. That's the only thing it can be. But it's been closed for twenty years.'

'It wouldn't maybe be the Rainbow Room? That's pretty high up.'

'No, I don't think so. The Rainbow Room – where many years ago I proposed to my darling late wife, I might mention – is on the 65th floor. The observation decks were on the 69th and 70th floors. They were stunning. Designed to feel like an ocean liner. There is a photograph taken from there, in the old days, of Manhattan lost in clouds . . . just the tips of the Chrysler Building and the Empire State and a couple of others piercing the sea of mist . . . it was breathtaking.'

'What happened?'

'Access was cut off when they expanded the Rainbow Room. A tragedy.'

'They don't let the public up to the Rainbow Room until five o'clock,' Terri said. 'We don't have that kind of time. We'll find a way. Follow me.'

Dazzling glass-brick and polychrome sculptures representing Wisdom, Sound and Light loomed above the entrance in contours of deep maroon, blue, beige and gleaming gold, above a passage from the Book of Isaiah: *Wisdom and Knowledge Shall Be the Stability of Thy Times.*

As they entered, Terri dialled a number on her cell phone. 'Jay? Hi. It's Terri, from . . . yes, you remember? How are you? Well, I'm in a predicament here . . .' She turned away from them so they couldn't hear. After two minutes she returned, beaming. 'Jay's a comedy writer. He works upstairs,' she explained. 'He'll be down in a minute.'

'And he remembers you from – ?'

'Never mind. It was a Boîte à Malice job. Just think of him as a very tall man with a sense of adventure.'

They waited by the elevator banks, which were clad in polished black granite and bronze. Turnstiles and security staff in green uniforms barred their passage.

Jay, who looked very amused to be visited by Terri and her friends, came down and took them through the formalities of guest access. He was indeed very tall.

'I can take you up as far as the 65th floor, then it's down to subterfuge,' he said as they waited for a car to descend to the lobby. 'There were supposed to be police sharpshooters on the roof for the Republican Convention, but I heard they didn't show up.'

They emerged into the Art Deco twilight of the 65th-floor lobby. A backlit abstract design of waveforms and circles cast a ghostly wash of light from their left. Black-and-white floor tiles reflected zebra bands of darkness and subdued lighting around the columns. Voices suggested staff were working in the bar-and-grill area in preparation for the evening shift.

'There should be emergency stairs,' Jay whispered. 'If it's anything like our floor, they'll be this way.'

They found the fire stairs and made their way quietly up as far as the door to the 69th floor, which was padlocked. 'It's closed up there, no need for regular access like the occupied floors,' Jay said. 'You're a great woman, Terri, but I'm not breaking a padlock.'

Horace elbowed him gently aside. 'If I may be allowed . . .'

He removed a jeweller's loupe from his pocket and examined the padlock. Then he took a small leather wallet from his pocket and selected two long, thin metal tools. 'My days in the OSS were not entirely wasted,' he said, as the lock gave a deep click and opened. 'Nothing broken. Up we go.'

They came out into the open air and stopped in awe. The whole city was laid out at their feet. The skyscrapers and towers of downtown formed an island in the distant haze, bisected by the needle of the Empire State Building and, beyond, the ocean. To the left, peeking from behind the Met Life Building, glistened the arcs and spire of the Chrysler.

'Keep going up, it's better from the 70th,' Horace hissed, and led the way up a staircase that took them one floor higher.

They emerged on to a narrow deck, just radio antennae above them and waist-high, arched iron railings between them and the deck below. Lengths of dismantled scaffolding and construction bric-a-brac lay stacked against the door of a disused elevator shaft. To the north lay the receding expanse of Central Park, the great Reservoir shimmering at its furthest extent.

All around, they could see for miles and miles. It seemed they could see for ever.

Horace whispered: 'Do you have the clue, Robert?'

He read it out:

'For endless sight, climb into the light
The fire and the gold await the bold
To beat the clock, you must scale the rock
Then sally forth, and telescope north
To rescue love – or kill it
Pass the Trial by Spirit'

'There are no telescopes,' Horace said angrily, looking along either side of the deck.

'They've been ripped out.'

'It says *Telescope North*,' Terri said. 'Can you find where the north-facing ones used to be? Maybe there are holes where their moorings were?'

Jay looked on, entirely bemused. 'So is this what you do for fun, Terri?'

'Honey, I so entirely do other things for fun.'

Horace let out a whoop of discovery. Robert rushed to his side. 'There are several places where they used to be, you see? Check them. Check them.'

Robert started at the east end and worked towards Horace, who started from the west. Robert got to it first. It was a plastic bag wrapped in electrician's tape, with a box of some kind inside.

'Let's open it downstairs,' Robert said. 'We can't be caught up here.'

Horace nodded and put the bag in his pocket. He looked up at the radio aerials, then turned slowly around once on his heel, taking in the memories.

'When did your wife pass on, Horace?'

'The same year this was closed.'

Robert left him alone for a few moments, ushering Jay and Terri back to the staircase that led to the lower deck. They went down.

Then they heard a cry of pain and alarm from above.

'Stay here,' Robert told Jay. 'Don't move.'

Terri and Robert rushed back up the stairs and ran towards the eastern end of the deck. Against the backdrop of the Chrysler Building's shining spire and the bulk of the MetLife tower, Robert saw a figure in black crouching over the unconscious form of Horace, going through the old man's jacket pockets. A masked face looked up as Robert shouted 'No!' at the top of his lungs.

It looked like the same figure who had attacked him on the subway, eyes flaring with poisonous yellow light.

Seeing the lengths of scaffolding by the old elevator door, Robert grabbed a four-foot metal tube as the black-clad figure rose and advanced towards him. The man held the seventh key and the Malice Box in his gloved hands. As they stared at each other, he put them into a zippered pocket on his trousers.

'Terri! Help Horace,' Robert shouted. Then he charged towards Horace's attacker, swinging the steel pipe through the air in a violent arc aimed directly at the masked head. The figure ducked and rolled under Robert's swing as Terri ran past them both to the supine form of Horace. Landing by the pile of scaffolding, the figure picked up a steel pipe and stood up brandishing it like a sword.

They stared at each other, each anticipating a killing strike at any moment, treading nervously to firm their footing, gripping and regripping their weapons in the humid air. Keeping his eyes on his opponent, Robert shouted: 'Is he alive?'

'Yes, but he's not coming round,' Terri answered.

Robert sank his mind deep down into his core, reaching for the powers of earth and water, fire and air, ether and mind. He willed the raw strength of his fight in the subway to return to his limbs. He breathed deeply in and out, summoning his new-found gifts, seeking the higher harmonics that would let him into his opponent's mind.

Nothing happened.

Moving like a striking snake, the black-clad figure darted forward and brought his steel pipe down in a vertical stroke at Robert's head. Robert twisted to one side and deflected the weapon with a glancing blow. He drove an elbow into the man's belly and spun to one side, then wheeled around in a half-circle, sweeping horizontally with the pipe at hip level as though trying to slice his attacker in half.

The black-clad figure jumped back and kicked at Robert's lower back as the blow swept by, knocking him off balance. Then he leaped forward again and aimed a roundhouse strike at Robert's head. Robert raised the pipe and met the attack with a blow of equal force in the opposite direction. Metal slammed into metal with an explosive, high-pitched ring, the jarring impact almost shattering his arms. Both men, momentarily stunned by the force of the blows, let their weapons drop to the ground, their very bones vibrating. The attacker recovered quickly, and with a snarl of anger threw himself at Robert, who blocked a punch with his forearm and punched right back at his face. Robert's blow made no impact. Gloved hands closed around his throat. Calling deep within himself, Robert again found no strength. All he had was his own bloody-minded determination not to lose. It would have to be enough.

'Come hell or high water, you will not prevail,' he hissed. He clamped his hands over those of his attacker and tried to prise them free. He could see Terri still bowed over Horace, working on him urgently.

Robert stared into the masked face and saw death coming for him again, the yellow sickly light of his attacker's eyes flaring with red-and-blue filaments and shifting slowly into a magnetic, dead black core.

Then he heard Terri's voice. 'Let him go!'

The grip loosened slightly on Robert's throat.

'Try me,' she shouted. 'I don't die that easily. Come and get me, you bastard!'

The black-clad figure threw Robert aside, and he slipped down on one knee, gasping. Instantly a boot kicked him in the ribs, knocking all the air out of his lungs. He rolled away, his lungs in spasm, straining to breathe.

Terri bent down and picked up Robert's weapon, flailing with it at the face of the attacker. Robert saw the steel pipe ignite, twin snakes of blue flame flaring along its length as Terri drove the tip towards the groin of the man in black. She narrowly missed as he jumped backwards in the direction of the railings.

Terri advanced on him, lightning coursing up and down her weapon as she slashed the air with it, aiming for his belly and chest. The assailant turned and jumped up on to one of the stone mountings that held the railings in place. He reached into his pocket and pulled out the Malice Box, the core of the Ma'rifat'.

'This decides what happens, nothing else,' the figure shouted, brandishing it. Robert recognized nothing of Adam's voice in the guttural, anguished words.

Robert saw his chance. He ran forward past Terri and took a flying leap at the black figure, smashing into bone with juddering force and carrying him backwards into the air. Robert twisted, trying to land on his feet and half succeeding as he slammed into the tile of the lower observation deck, fifteen feet below. He felt his ankle crack, then he rolled to a halt against the Gothic railings of the lower level.

The black figure fell several feet from him, landing hard on his back. Something flew from his grip and shot through the railings.

Robert felt no pain, and then as he tried to rise, a snake of fierce, nauseating fire tore through him. A shrieking whistle filled his ears. He retched violently.

'Robert!' Terri was shouting to him from the floor above. He could barely hear through the pain. 'The major key! You must get the Malice Box!'

She was pointing frantically. Beyond the black figure struggling to his feet, Robert saw the glinting red-gold drum resting on a metal ledge on the other side of the railings, inches from the edge.

He couldn't do it. He was in too much pain. He was too frightened. He'd reached his limit.

'Robert!'

Now Terri appeared in the 69th-floor doorway, the scaffolding pipe still in her hands, Jay behind her. The black figure made to attack her.

Robert forced himself to his feet and launched himself again at the figure, knocking him spinning. Robert landed inches from the Malice Box on the other side of the railing. New pain shot along his leg to the top of his skull. Burning, sickening pain.

Jay and Terri advanced on the figure in black. Terri pressed her weapon against his forehead, snakes of crackling blue fire flaring again along its length. She held him immobile. On her instructions, Jay reached into the figure's pocket, extracting the seventh key and handing it to her.

To his joy, Robert saw Horace appear in the doorway, looking pale but determined. He immediately shouted to Robert: 'Get the core!'

Robert reached through the railings. He couldn't reach it.

He pulled himself up and reached over. Still couldn't reach it.

It was a drop of more than 800 feet.

He pulled off the leather belt of his trousers, climbed over the railings and formed a loop around one of the Gothic arch metal fittings on the other side, twisting the belt in a figure eight around his wrist.

Drenched in sweat, he reached for the Malice Box at the edge of the metal ledge. Still he couldn't get it. He lay along the ledge, pushing forward with his legs; then, with his fingertips, he touched it and dragged it towards him with his nails. He grabbed it and squeezed it in his left fist.

Then his foot slipped, and he fell.

Muscles tore in his arm and side as the belt took his full weight. He screwed his eyes shut and screamed till his voice gave out.

Sheer terror filled his soul.

He searched in the deepest part of himself for a glimmer of the powers of the Path. Nothing. Failure.

He felt a hand grab his wrist. Then two hands. He felt himself pulled up. His left hand was locked in paralysis around the key. Hands reached under his armpits, heaved him skywards, up over the railings.

He collapsed on the observation deck, Jay and Horace looking down at him. Then Terri shrieked as the figure in black suddenly twisted and kicked her staff aside, launching himself towards Robert and scrambling for the core.

Jay tried to tackle him and took a kick in the stomach, folding to the ground. Then the attacker wheeled around behind Jay, grasping him by the throat with both hands.

For a moment the dark figure stared at them, standing completely still. Then, with cold deliberation, he broke Jay's neck with a dry crack. Jay's body gave a violent spasm and fell to the ground.

'I am not Adam,' the figure in black shouted hoarsely. 'Adam is dead. This is what awaits you all if you stand against Iwnw.'

He turned and ran for the doorway, vanishing into the interior of the building.

'Let him go,' Horace shouted as Terri made to chase him. 'Come here.'

Terri turned reluctantly and knelt by Jay, looking imploringly at Horace.

'I'm afraid there's nothing you can do for him either. They will pay for this. Now help me with Robert.'

She nodded in silence.

Terri and Horace ran their hands over Robert, feeling his arms and legs. It was as though they were setting his bones. He felt a glow of warm heat over his whole body, rising to white-hot intensity in his ankle, his right arm, his ribs.

'We must get away from this place as soon as Robert can walk,' Horace said.

Robert felt fractured bones knitting together in his ankle, searing light flowing through his body. He gasped in pain.

Then Horace was still for a moment, reaching out into their environs with his mind, gauging the whereabouts of their attacker, and of the building's security guards.

'I see a route for us if we move quickly,' he said. 'Robert, that will have to do.'

Their descent took fifteen nerve-racking minutes, moving from stairwell to empty elevator and back again as both Horace and Terri scouted a course for them. They emerged on to the street just as alarms began to sound inside the building.

Horace immediately broke left, towards the north, taking them across 50th street. To their left, the red neon signs outside Radio City Music Hall broadcast in bold vertical letters the name the whole centre might once have had: RADIO CITY.

Horace took them into the west entrance of the International Building and straight through to the lobby on the other side.

Robert was stunned. It was aglow with golden light, the whole room sheathed in metal panels and suspended leaves, lit from below, of gently moving gilded steel.

Horace spoke to them both in soft but urgent tones. 'I am very

363

sorry for your friend's death, Terri. This is a war, and he was an innocent victim.'

'He didn't ask to take part,' Terri said. 'Who attacked us? The terrifying thing is that if it was Adam, I couldn't feel him at all. If it was him, he wasn't there; he was completely corrupted.'

'I don't believe that was Adam,' Horace said. 'I believe Adam is still fighting. I think that was another of the Iwnw, one of the three we met at Grand Central. He failed, though. We still have the core and the seventh key. The only way to make Jay's death meaningful is if we halt the detonation of the Ma'rifat'.'

'But I failed the trial,' Robert said.

'Did you?'

'I tried to call on the powers of the Path. I couldn't get anything.'

'The trial is not yet over. It is a necessary part of the Trial by Spirit to know despair, to be abandoned by every power one has. It helps us make our peace with death. Let us see whether you have lost your higher senses. Stand in front of one of the columns and look up,' Horace said. 'Observe what it becomes.'

He did as Horace suggested. As he looked up and stepped slightly to one side and the other, the shadows thrown on to the ceiling formed angular shapes, and then suddenly made a perfect triangle atop the column. It became an obelisk. At that moment Robert saw a huge surge of energy, in red-and-yellow light, burst from the column and flare around the pyramidion at its summit. He jumped back from the column as though he'd been kicked, covering his eyes.

'Shit!'

'You are still awakening,' Horace said. 'Too fast, for most people. You will experience a period of great discordance and doubt. Now we must go on.'

Robert's head was bursting with pain. 'Fuck! You might have warned me!'

Terri took his arm and led him out after Horace. They came out behind Lee Lawrie's giant Atlas iron sculpture, facing St Patrick's Cathedral, and headed north.

On the corner of 51st Street, looking east, Robert caught a

glimpse through his tearing eyes of the glorious spiked summit of 570 Lexington, the GBN offices.

Then Horace was hounding them to go faster. Terri and Horace each took one of Robert's arms as they walked.

'The pyramidion sat atop the obelisks and the pyramids,' Horace said. 'It is a small pyramid in its own right, and may often have been sheathed in gold. The word for it was *ben-benet*, derived from the sacred *ben-ben* stone, which represented the first island of creation, the first fragment of land to pierce the primeval waters.'

'It must have looked like the tips of those skyscrapers poking through the clouds,' Terri said.

'Yes,' said Horace reflectively. 'Yes, it must have. And shortly we shall see another representation of it, one that is at the very heart of this quest. And you will understand more.'

They passed St Thomas's on the left, Horace's backup location if Robert had missed him at Grand Central.

Then they were passing the black and gold of Trump Tower, the Art Deco masterpieces housing Tiffany's and Bergdorf Goodman on the east side of Fifth Avenue, and they were into Central Park.

PART THREE

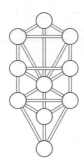

The Body of Light

New York, September 1, 2004

'This way,' Horace said, leading them past horse-pulled carriages and stalls selling photographs of New York scenes, in the general direction of the Wollman Rink.

'Horace,' Terri shouted. 'We don't even have a waypoint yet.'

'There are no more waypoints,' he replied. 'There are seven keys. We must work now with what we have. We need all the keys to stop the detonation. They need all the keys to make it explode in the fully hellish way they desire.'

Horace led them to a drinking fountain, past the rink, at the foot of a flight of stone steps.

Terri asked, 'Can we stop for a second and look at what was in the last cache?'

Horace halted and dabbed his forehead with a handkerchief. 'Yes, my dear. Of course. Up here.'

They climbed the stairs. At the top was an octagonal, single-storey building, surrounded on all sides by benches and chess tables. 'The Chess and Checkers House,' Horace said. 'It was here that the trials were planned. Barely nine days ago.' He took out a penknife and cut the plastic wrapping free from the package they'd found in the cache to reveal a black jewellery case. Inside was a pendant bearing a seven-pointed star in inlaid silver.

Terri put down the steel staff she had brought with her from the fight at Rockefeller Center and held her fingertips to it.

'As I suspected,' Horace said. 'Gnostic star. It stands for mystical insight. The other geometric shapes also reflected aspects of the trials. One, the circle, signifies beginning. Two, the vesica piscis, signifies the womb, and cell division. Three, the triangle, is stability, the ability to stand alone. Four, the cube, the building block of the greater man through compassion. Five, the pentagram, creativity and regeneration, because it can replicate itself endlessly. Six, the

369

Star of David, the union of two triangles representing heaven and earth, the spiritual and the physical.'

Robert's head was splitting, the light burning his eyes. Terri helped him move into the shade. 'This really hurts,' he whispered to her.

'I know,' she said. 'It's what it takes. We're going to get this done.'

Robert sat at a chess table and closed his eyes, losing himself in sensations he had never had before.

Since the jolt of energy from the column in the International Building, his vision had become flooded with light, as though he were staring at the sun with his head bound, unable to look away. Patterns and forms – the squares of the chess tables, the façades of the Deco buildings they had passed on Fifth Avenue, the octagonal form of the Chess and Checkers House – were hitting his consciousness like knife blades. Even the forms of trees and leaves felt like tattoos on his flesh. Waves of intense sensation were washing over him, emotions and physical stimuli as well as shapes and geometric forms. He could feel Terri's anger and helplessness at Jay's death, her burning, single-minded focus on survival, Horace's implacable will to defeat the Iwnw. Robert was drifting in and out of a state of hypersensitivity so acute as to be unbearable. There was no peace, no calm. At the fringes of his consciousness he could hear the language of the birds, but it was a cacophony of screeches, without insight, without love.

'Horace, Robert is hurting very badly,' Terri said.

'The building up is also the tearing down,' said Horace, without sympathy. 'I suggest we wait here. We will hear from Adam.'

In the myth, Osiris was sliced to pieces by Seth. Robert understood what it meant now. But then came the birth of Horus, the son, the bearer of light, to do battle. Despite the pain, he still trusted the Path. He was both Osiris and Horus. The new being would come from within the butchered old one. He had already felt it awaken. But he had still not recovered from the shock of hanging from the top of Rockefeller Center, stripped of all his powers, exposed and naked to his very core.

Die to live.

The seventh line of the letter he had burned. The words formed again in his mind.

Die to live.

He attempted to understand. Then he relented, and tried to help the others by lightening the tone. 'Actually, this is pretty cool in some ways,' he said. 'I can *feel* you guys, I can see fricking *auras* around you, for God's sake.'

Horace slapped him hard across the face.

Terri shouted at him: 'Horace! What the fuck?'

'Even here there is temptation, and it is the temptation of pride,' Horace said, his voice hoarse with anger. 'Be humble, or you will be humiliated.'

No one said another word for thirty minutes.

Eventually Horace relented. 'I am sorry, Robert. The primitive self fights hardest when it is closest to extinction, and the shadow of this stage is spiritual pride. There is a poem by Hopkins, one of a series called the "Terrible Sonnets", where he is wrestling with giving up what he calls his last strands of self.

> *'Not, I'll not, carrion comfort, Despair, not feast on thee;*
> *Not untwist — slack they may be — these last strands of man*
> *In me ór, most weary, cry I can no more. I can;*
> *Can something, hope, wish day come, not choose not to be.*

'You would do well to remember them. As we all must.'

Robert said nothing, his head lowered. He had expected the journey to end in enlightenment, in understanding. All he could see was darkness.

'I know those sonnets, Horace,' he said eventually. 'One of them is the only thing I can think of to express what I felt when I was hanging off the observation deck.'

'Which?'

> *'O the mind, mind has mountains; cliffs of fall*
> *Frightful, sheer, no-man-fathomed. Hold them cheap*
> *May, who ne'er hung there . . .*

'That's how it feels now.'
Die to live.
'Terri,' Horace said, 'you should tell Robert what else happened on the day of the Blackout.'

August 14, 2003: Blackout Day

Terri took Katherine into the bedroom, the only other room where they could sit, while Adam sat at his desk, eyes closed, and began deep-breathing exercises.

She closed the door behind them. 'Katherine, how can I help?'

Katherine sat down on the bed and looked up at Terri. 'What is the Boîte à Malice, exactly?'

Terri felt Katherine's curiosity about her as a woman. She was asking herself how Terri exhibited such power at her age, whether she was attracted to Adam, whether she was a manipulator or could be trusted. Terri also felt a powerful ambivalence in Katherine about her own long-dormant gift.

'It's a group of strong women having fun,' Terri said with her best crooked smile. 'We think up ways to solve problems that leave everyone feeling better for the experience.'

'Is prostitution part of it?'

'That's not what I'd call it. Imagination is, and flirtation, and creativity, sure. Technological skills. Understanding money. But it's all about reading people and seeing what they really need. We like to keep a witchy vibe, a little bit mischievous, a little bit dark and dangerous. I can read people real well. You?'

Katherine's inner defences were steel. Terri could see nothing she was hiding.

'I was always able to,' Katherine said. 'I just thought it was normal. But I had traumatic experiences. I was almost killed in a fire at university. I lost a dear friend. And it died off.'

Terri got a glimmer of a night long ago, a place of damp and cold, panic, fear, a fire. She shut off the image.

'So, tell me how you used to tap into it. Before you really believed in it.'

Katherine looked at her with surprise. 'You can see that far back? That deeply into me?'

'No, but that's how most of us start.'

Katherine recounted the sex magick, the Ouija board, fragments of the night of the fire that she could remember. There weren't many.

'And you frightened yourself? I certainly did when I started out.'

'I was frightened to explore some of it, yes. But it was just a blip. Temporary burnout. I was burning all ends of the candle at once. I was twenty-one. Just a bit younger than you, I'd say.'

'I started younger. I grew up in orphanages until I was sixteen. Life was tough. At first I used it just to survive. It's only in the last couple of years that I've learned to use it to help other people.'

'I need to know how to help Adam.'

'Help him raise his power. Tap back into yours.'

'I want to. I can't find a way back.'

Terri suddenly saw part of what she was hiding. Her connection to Adam was stronger than she wanted to admit, even to herself. She loved Robert, but she had been *married* to Adam previously. She still *desired* him.

Terri saw that no outsider could ever break the bond between these three. Any woman who formed a relationship with either of these men would always be trumped by Katherine. The insight filled her with a sense of foreboding. She dismissed the thought from her mind.

'Here's what we need to do. We're going to revisit that night of the fire, the night of your trauma, yes? Take the fear out of it. Take the power back from it. Find a way to give it to Adam for his fight today.'

Katherine met her eyes and held them. 'What about my husband?'

'His time will come to be freed of his fear. But he can help you too, Katherine. Tell me some of the words you used. The chants you didn't believe in.'

'I thought they were just tapping into the unconscious,' Katherine said.

'They were.'

'But there's more —'

'There is, but nothing's going to go wrong this time.'

Katherine sat in silence. Then she said the words, beginning *Time and place elide* . . .

Terri took her hands gently and repeated the words back to her.

'What I suggest is that, after you leave here, you go find your husband and make love to him. Haul him out of work. Whatever it takes,' Terri said with a smile. 'You're going to use these words, and take the fear from them.'

Terri said again the words that Katherine had uttered over the Ouija board over twenty years earlier, defusing them, releasing them. Blessing them. She held an image of Katherine and her faceless husband in her mind and cast a halo of golden light over them.

'Carry this light from me when you are with him,' she said. 'Start holding Adam in your mind now.'

Terri opened the door. She walked out and touched Adam gently on the arm to bring him out of his deep state. Katherine followed her.

'Katherine's going to leave now. We've done some work, and she'll be sending you strength for the rest of the day.'

She held hands with both of them for a moment, letting currents of light course through their bodies as they stood in a triangle. Then she took Katherine to the door.

New York, September 1, 2004

Robert listened in silence. So Terri had blessed their lovemaking, the day they'd conceived little Moss. Those magical incantations Katherine had used had been Terri's idea to help her get back in touch with her gift.

'And then I couldn't bring myself to go home. He was awe-inspiring. Vibrant. After Katherine left, we took one look at each other and just grabbed. Devoured each other. Forget holding back the energy. Forget everything. I don't know if I helped him prepare or not. Probably not. But he sure was going to die happy.'

'Goodness,' said Horace.

'Afterwards, when he was getting ready to leave, I gave him my address. I told him not to return to his place after confronting his guy, but to come and see me. And I left him a talisman to wear. To link him to my strength.

'I was home, around four in the afternoon, and suddenly I just got this enormous psychic shock-wave from Adam. Knocked me on my ass. All hell had broken loose around him. I knew he was alive, but . . . damn. When I got up, my gift was all over the place. I was an order of magnitude more sensitive, so it hurt even to walk, to think . . . and then I was numb, dead, couldn't feel my own feet. I could feel Adam, he was fighting, he was in danger, he had my power, he had his own, but it was tough, he was hurting. I could feel it, and then I couldn't. Back and forth, like waves of power surging into me and out of me.'

'This was the Blackout?'

'No, the Blackout hadn't happened yet. Then seconds later it hit. Boom. All the lights went out. Another shock-wave, bigger than the first. I felt like I was plugged into an electric socket. My body ignited from the inside out. My eyes blew out. And then I just sat down and cried and cried.'

They sat in silence for a while.

Terri put a hand on Robert's arm and spoke to both of them.

'We have several things Adam wants. He has things we want. We should use ours as bait. Draw him to a meeting.'

'We want Katherine, and the Ma'rifat' with its keys,' Horace said. 'We have some of the keys, the red gold, the core.'

'And we have me, and the child I may yet carry,' Terri answered. 'His child.'

Robert shook his head. 'We can offer the keys and core. That's all. Not you.'

'He needs me.'

'He loves Katherine,' Robert said. 'He told me so.'

'Katherine is not carrying his baby. He doesn't need her.'

Robert's mind flared again with the image of cell division. But it had begun on Friday. And still he saw the shadow.

'Terri, I need to understand.'

'It's simple.'

Terri gathered her thoughts for a moment. Robert could feel her anger over Jay receding into the background as she focused on what she needed to tell them.

'When the Blackout hit, chains of connection were made at a level we don't ordinarily see, on a psycho-spiritual plane. We've talked about some of this.'

Adam and the maker of the Ma'rifat' had become entangled, as they knew, in a parasitical relationship, she said. But there was more. Before fighting the maker of the Ma'rifat', Adam had made love to Terri, as she had just told them. It had been heedless, spontaneous sex, with no protection. By the time the Blackout took place, a few hours later, she had been in the incipient stages of pregnancy. She had been carrying a fertilized egg.

'At the same time, you and Katherine had been making love,' Terri said to Robert. 'She'd done what I suggested and called you up, and she'd used the sex-magick words to take the fear from them, to restore them to you both. They are words that summon up connection at the deepest levels.'

'I remember,' Robert said.

'Katherine also got pregnant that day. When the Blackout happened, she was in the same condition as me. And a twofold connection formed. First, through Adam, I was joined to you and Katherine. The circle of Katherine–Robert–Adam joined the circle of Terri–Adam–Minotaur, with Adam as the link. And second, a more direct connection was created between Katherine and me, because of the blessing session I'd held with her earlier that morning. The words still connected us, and even her skin did, for I had touched her and was still in touch with her. Some of her DNA was on my skin, and I was resonating with her, just as I was with Adam.'

'Adam talked about this. He said the Iwnw can work through DNA too. Resonating, setting up harmonics.'

Robert heard the screeching of the birds at the edges of his mind. There should have been harmony, but he couldn't hear it.

'I can set up harmonics too,' Terri said. 'They use it for evil, but it's a particular gift of the Path of Tiresias too, which is the one I follow. Remember the caduceus, which in myth originated with Tiresias before being given to Hermes. The twin snakes along the shaft represent, among other things, the twin helixes of DNA and the ability to work with it.'

Robert protested: 'No one understood DNA until the 1950s!'

Horace interrupted them. 'In the sense of using machinery to examine DNA, tease it apart, manipulate it in dishes and so forth, you are correct that these marvels have only come to us in recent years,' he said. 'But the Ancients knew more than they are credited with. Some adepts of the Path have always been able to visualize DNA, resonate with each person through it, even affect it psychically. It appears in the visions of shamans, in the mythology of snakes bearing wisdom.'

The squawking, screeching song of the birds in Robert's mind grew louder and more discordant. Pulsing light throbbed behind his eyes. He tried to will it away.

'The connection between you and Katherine. Go on.'

'There was a connection between the potential lives too. Between the two eggs, both fertilized, neither yet implanted in the womb. And . . .'

Robert felt an unexpected wave of pain and shame flare from Terri. 'I remember seeing a dance of fire,' he said. 'Burning figures of each of us. Flames and shadows. I saw you, me, Katherine and Adam. There was another man, Tariq. And a shadow I thought was Moss, or the possibility of him.'

'For a moment the two eggs were connected, superimposed. *Time and place elide.* They shared the same space.' She took Robert's hand. 'That was the moment, the moment of the Blackout, when the Iwnw connected with me through Adam. They got into the egg's DNA, messed with the cell structure and turned it from life to death: cancer. And there was a transfer of light, of life force, between Katherine and me at the same time. My cancer absorbed most of the life from your future child,' she said. 'That's why Katherine had a miscarriage a few months later. I'm so sorry. It just happened. There was no intention.' She broke down in tears, sobbing wretchedly.

Robert thought his head would split apart. Cancer. And he had babbled to her about pregnancy, as if he were some kind of magus, some kind of visionary.

Part of him still could not believe the things he was learning. Terri was saying, in a way, that she'd killed Moss? No. The Iwnw had killed Moss.

'Terri, there's something I don't understand. These events were over a year ago?'

'A year and two weeks.'

'I've seen shadows over you. Around you. Cell division. But only since Friday.'

'They froze the cancer as soon as they created it. Or said they had. To mess with our heads and hold it over us as a threat.'

'Why?'

'To encourage Adam to obey them when they called on him. For a year, nothing happened. We even thought they might have been lying. And then they unfroze it five days ago. To reinforce the fact in his mind that I will die in a few days if he doesn't ensure the detonation of the Ma'rifat'. They claim they will reverse the cancer and protect us from the blast if he does that.'

'Do you believe them?'

'Adam seems to.'

Even in the light of day, Robert felt shadows of night all around him. Evil creatures lurked there, baying and screaming. Yales like the ones on the gate of St John's College. Gargoyle-like monsters of vicious intent. He saw even more clearly the level of evil he was preparing to fight. He swore he would do whatever it took, to his last breath.

'Horace, did you know about this?'

Horace reached forward and took Terri's hand. 'Yes, I have known for some time. Adam and Terri asked me if I could help. I'm afraid it has been beyond my powers to do so. Even the Perfect Light cannot always undo what evil has done.'

'Why didn't you tell me? Can't doctors do anything?'

'I did not feel you were ready. And no, they cannot even detect the incipient cancer. Terri has been told by conventional medicine that it is all in her mind.'

'I felt it resume the day after you and I were together,' Terri resumed, wiping her eyes. 'Then on Sunday I found Katherine at the apartment I was sharing with Adam. I always knew that if he took up with her again, he'd leave me. He wouldn't be able to help himself. I felt I couldn't count on him to protect me any more. I went to the only people who could help me, my witch friends at the Mischief House. They took me in.'

'Were they able to help with the cancer?'

'No. Robert, my highest hope is that I can help Adam hold on long enough for you to defeat the Iwnw and somehow save us. Adam, me, the child. All of us. You're the only one who can.'

At that moment the Quad rang. It was Adam.

'Hello, Robert, time for us to meet again. Bring your friends.'

Robert lost it. 'If I ever see you again, it will be the last thing you ever do! Where's my wife?'

Horace motioned for him to calm down and to put the call on speaker so they could all hear it. Robert ignored him.

'Was that you up the top of Rockefeller Center, you fucker? Was that you who broke that guy's neck? Feel like a big man?'

Terri snatched the phone from him and pressed the speaker button.

'I know nothing about that,' Adam said. 'Last time I saw you was at Grand Central. You nearly killed me.'

'I should have.'

'You chose to do the opposite. I should express my gratitude.'

'I thought I saw good in you, still. I guess I was wrong.'

Silence. Robert thought he heard Adam's voice choke.

'Regardless of that, we need to talk,' Adam said. 'Cleopatra's Needle. The Central Park Obelisk. We need to trade.'

Horace nodded frantically for Robert to agree.

'Perhaps. The core. I have it with me.'

'And all the remaining keys?'

379

'All the ones you don't have, yes.'

'I want Terri.'

'No. The core, in exchange for Katherine.'

'No deal. I'm done with Katherine, you can have her. But I get Terri and the core.'

'Not a chance.'

'Then goodbye.'

Terri shouted into the Quad: 'Adam?'

'Terri. We can still bring the baby back.'

'You can have me. I'll come. I want to be with you. And you can have the rest of what you want. Just give Katherine back to Robert.'

Silence. Then Adam's voice: 'Go there now. I'll come when you are there.'

As they walked north along the tree-lined promenade of the Mall, Horace talked about the obelisk.

'It's a twin,' Horace said. 'They both stood at Heliopolis, which the ancient Egyptians called Iwnw, 3,500 years ago. A sacred city. Sacred to both the Perfect Light and our enemy, the Brotherhood, who take their name from it.'

Robert had not made the connection until now.

'The missing twin is in London, where it is also known as Cleopatra's Needle,' Horace continued. 'Though both were erected well before her time.'

'Wait, Horace,' Robert said. 'You talk about myths all over the world echoing the battles between the Iwnw and the Perfect Light. Was this obelisk standing at Iwnw when this all began?'

'No, it came much later. It was raised in what historians now call the New Kingdom. The history of the battle for control of the Path goes back much further, and not just to Ancient Egypt.'

'Tell me. I want to understand.'

Horace reflected for a moment, then began. 'The Path has existed for as long as there have been human beings. It is, simply, a way of seeing ourselves as we truly are – intimately connected to the rest of the universe, to a great consciousness that is the mind of the universe itself. All human beings are capable of ascending the Path

380

and achieving full awareness of this, and in doing so experiencing how mind, matter and energy are all one, in constant transformation from one form to another.'

'But you've said barely thirty people in the world know the secrets of red gold, for example,' Robert objected.

'All are capable,' Horace said. 'But few choose to walk the Path beyond its first steps. It is arduous in the extreme – even for those who are not undergoing the remarkable forced awakening that we have imposed upon you.'

Robert turned to Terri, who was walking with her arms held across her stomach, her staff tightly gripped in one hand.

'You said you follow the Path of Tiresias. I am on the Path of Seth. How many are there?'

Terri said nothing, lost in her inner thoughts. He sensed she was praying for Adam.

'There are as many ways to approach the Path as there are individual candidates,' Horace replied. 'But there are perhaps a dozen categories of similar approaches. That of Seth is reserved for very few.'

'Do the Iwnw follow the same Path?'

'They do. There is only one. But they inhabit its shadow side, and they seek to use the Path to wield power over others. They seek to rule. We do not. Once we were the same. We are all of the same kind. We all hear the higher harmonies, see the colours of soul states, can sometimes see beyond time and space. Everywhere in the world where the Path was known, however, there came a split. A scission. One was at Iwnw. But there were others. In China. In southern India. Among the Celts.'

Robert reflected on Horace's words, trying to fit his own experiences on to the story he was hearing. The trials had shown him a shadow side to the Path's powers. When he had been most strongly drawn to the shadows, the Iwnw had succeeded in infiltrating his consciousness.

'The old men in business suits. The three white-haired men. Are they the Iwnw or just representatives? Priests?'

'They are adepts who preferred to follow the shadow side of the

Path, and who made themselves over to evil. They are the Iwnw in this world, a manifestation of the seething, hateful force that lives in the virtual world, yearning constantly to incarnate, seeking constant opportunity to seize on our fears, our anger, our pride.'

'That's what happened in the beginning? Some followers of the Path split away and sought earthly power?'

'Everywhere it has been the same story,' Horace said. 'And constantly renewed. The powers of the Path are so great that it is very difficult to renounce self-advancement. One must cut away the ego entirely, which is like experiencing death.'

They walked past the Naumberg Bandshell and down the steps into an arched underground walkway. Once-glorious Minton encaustic tiles, in faded symmetrical patterns of reds, yellows and blues, lined the passage, which brought them up to the broad sky and expansive sweep of Bethesda Terrace, the angel silhouetted against the scudding clouds.

Still Robert had more questions. 'What does the word "Iwnw" refer to, Horace?'

'It means column, as you know, and refers to two things. First, to the creation of the world. The first island to emerge from the primeval sea of chaos was represented at Iwnw by a column, topped by a small pyramid shape.'

'And what is the second thing?'

'It refers to the Path. The column, in this sense, is the spinal column, linking our most primitive, raw nature at the bottom to our highest potential, our capacity for communion with all of creation, at the top. It represents our ascent when we follow the Path. The temples of Iwnw were places of great learning and spiritual attainment.'

'You speak of the Path but not of God, Horace. I don't think I've ever heard you speak of God.'

'At the end of the Path — at the top of the column, which we may also visualize as a ladder, if that is easier — there is the experience of the divine,' Horace said. 'Some call it God and personalize it. Others experience only a teeming, endlessly pregnant void — the awareness of creation happening at every instant, everywhere. It is the same thing.'

They broke right and then north, past the Boathouse Café and through the Ramble to Turtle Pond, guarded by a fierce statue of the Polish independence hero King Jagiello, swords crossed above his head before battle.

The Romans had taken the obelisk from Heliopolis to Alexandria in 12 BC, Horace said as they walked. Then it wasn't moved again till 1879, when it was prepared for shipment to New York after the local ruler gave it to America as a goodwill gift. To the great excitement of Freemasons at the time, items found under the pedestal when it was lifted in Alexandria included a stone carved in the form of a mason's square; a trowel cemented to the limestone beneath, to show it had not been left there by accident; a stone of unusual whiteness; cubes finished, dressed or roughened in ways consistent with Masonic symbolism; and an aperture in one of the hidden stones in the shape of a diamond, taken to represent a gem known to Freemasons as the Master's Jewel.

'The Masons stumbled across the Path during the Crusades, when they were still calling themselves Templars,' Horace said. 'But most have retained little of the wisdom they once guarded.'

They continued north into thick trees and then suddenly, sooner than he had expected above them to the right, Robert caught a glimpse of the seventy-foot obelisk, gleaming white in the sun. They looped further north to the steps leading up to the octagonal platform on which it stood and went up.

'Horace,' Terri asked, 'what does it say on the obelisk?'

Horace went to the south face. 'My hieroglyphics are a little rusty, but I will read the main inscription, along the centre of the column. The outside ones on each side were added later by a subsequent pharaoh. *He is the heavenly Horus, the powerful, glorious bull, beloved of Ra, the King of Upper and Lower Egypt. He made this monument for his father, Atum, Lord of Iwnw, erecting for him two great obelisks whose pyramidions are of fine gold. Iwnw* . . . some illegible parts here . . . *the son of Ra, Thutmose, may he live for ever.* That would be Thutmose III, to be exact.'

Terri smiled. Horace looked up at the top of the obelisk. 'Imagine the sun hitting the gold at the top, what that must have looked like.

It must have been spectacular.' He pointed downtown. 'All obelisks, all towers, all skyscrapers are the same thing. They are our desire to touch the sky, to know our incorporeal nature. They are rockets of the mind, of the spirit. Fireworks that never burn out. They are the necessary partners to the sacred cave, the rock walls painted with our dreams, the ring around the hearth, the magic circle of stones. The lingam and the yoni. Straight line and curved.'

Robert saw an aura of grey-blue light around the monument. Concentrating, he found he could bring it in and out of focus, and reduce or enhance its intensity. The violence of his earlier visual and aural impressions had been fading imperceptibly since they'd reached the obelisk.

Terri sat down heavily on a bench. 'Where the *fuck* is Adam?'

'He will come when he is ready. I suspect he is attempting to build enough strength to be able to mask some of his thoughts and actions, still, from the Iwnw, though perhaps it is too late to hope for that.'

'No,' Terri said. 'It's not too late.' Now Terri stood up from her bench and paced in frustration. 'Would you two just focus on nailing Adam when he gets here, please? Is there a way to do something to help him before I go with him?'

'If Katherine is here, there may be a chance, while we still have the Malice Box. The major key,' Horace said. 'If he comes without the Iwnw. Without his minders. It may be that getting away from them is what's taking him so long.'

'Tariq,' Terri said.

'The Minotaur, yes,' Horace replied. 'If he can somehow be released, or ejected, from Adam, the Iwnw's link to Adam will be destroyed. It would also break the link to you, and their grip on your cell structure would be broken.'

'What would it take?'

'It may not be possible,' Horace said. 'But Katherine would have to try to talk to the man she betrayed right into hell.'

They discussed alternative plans while they waited, voices lowered, throwing up mental shields as well as they could against the ears of the Iwnw. Robert found himself doing it naturally, without thinking about it or even knowing just how he did it.

Yet still he felt nothing of the enlightenment, the wakened state, that he had expected to find at the end of the trials. All was confusion, a dark and inchoate mess.

They each sat a third of the way around the obelisk, in a Y, and settled into their own thoughts.

'Robert, you recall the hidden aperture found under the obelisk,' Horace said. 'There was no actual jewel there, but its shape represented one. The jewel represented the purified consciousness of one who walks the Path all the way to the end. Focus on the jewel now. I suggest we all meditate on that for a while. It will help you to prepare for the coming ordeal. I fear Adam may keep us waiting for quite some time.'

Robert thought back to the black flint he had felt in his heart at Union Square after 9/11, when he'd been unable to believe that love alone could be enough to fight the hatred behind those attacks. Now he saw that love, and love alone, would be the only weapon with which he could defeat the Iwnw.

'When I looked into the Malice Box,' Robert said, 'it seemed to flip back and forth between convex and concave, as if it were both at once.'

'Both and neither, simultaneously,' Horace said. 'Paradox is the language of the divine. In the same way, concentrate upon the absence of the jewel, until the jewel itself appears in your consciousness.'

Robert held the empty jewel-shaped aperture in his mind and let all else float away. Time stopped and rushed by at once, and neither seemed real. He stared deep into the empty niche, until he became it himself: an empty niche, an empty vessel, an aching void, which slowly began to flip back and forth between empty and full, absence and the jewel.

In search of himself, in search of understanding, Robert went in his mind to the place he had been happiest. Birdsong twittered and echoed all around him, rising into the leafy green heights of the copse in the grounds he had roamed as a child, the lands of the great house. Dappled green light played on his skin as he sat on the smooth stone, inviting the birdsong to permeate his senses as he played through in his mind all the mysteries of the world. He had never left there without a feeling of resolution. Now he lost himself in the melodious, carefree chirping of the language of the birds, and knew peace.

Someone was coming. A twig snapped under a heavy boot and a comforting presence entered the copse, his strong and slow stride that of an outdoorsman, a man of nature. Robert smelled wet earth, rain in the air, damp leaves. It was his father. With a nod he came to sit beside Robert on the stone.

They were silent, at ease in each other's company, long used to the wordless ways they had of expressing their love. Grey-haired and ruddy, his hands gnarled but his great back strong from decades of work on the land, his father was as Robert remembered him best. Powerful and kind. Thoughtful, sparing of words.

'You've always liked this place, eh?'

Robert nodded. He felt no need to speak.

'I've fetched you away from here a few times. Your mother did too. Whenever we didn't know where to find you, this is where we'd come.'

His deep brown eyes searched Robert's, wanting to communicate something that words were unable to carry.

'I've written a few things down for you,' his father said, reaching into his pocket. He pulled out a letter and held it out to his son, his hand trembling slightly. 'Things you should know, in case you ever need them.'

Robert reached out and took the letter. He recognized it as the one he had received at university, the one he had burned but still remembered in every word and syllable. Their eyes met, and Robert saw his father was troubled.

'Your mother and I kept you away from these things,' he said. 'We knew of too much danger, too much wickedness that had come from messing with things we didn't understand. Terrible things that happened, family stories . . . We decided you should be brought up differently, in a modern way. We wanted you to have opportunities we never had, that the old ways would never give you.'

Robert realized that his father was apologizing to him. He was seeking Robert's blessing for keeping him in ignorance of his gift.

'Don't ever say I gave you this,' the old man said. 'And when you have children, make sure you don't hold them back with your own fears.'

He held out his hand to Robert, man to man, and Robert took it, shaking it gently.

'There's nothing to be sorry for,' he said to his father. 'I wasn't ready then. I am now. There's nothing to forgive.'

His father rose, wordlessly, and gave a final nod of goodbye. He walked out of the copse, leaving Robert alone with the harmonies of the singing birds, clear and crystalline like a perfect shining jewel.

Robert opened his eyes. It was dark. Horace was nowhere to be seen. Terri was sitting with her weapon across her knees, alert, facing into the blackness.

'Where have you been? It's been hours,' she said. 'Welcome.'

'Thank you,' Robert replied.

He heard a cough from behind the obelisk. 'Actually, old man, I think she's talking to me.'

Adam stepped forward, followed by Katherine. Robert's heart leaped, though she looked distraught, exhausted. Adam had Katherine's pistol in his hand. He gestured with it as if it were a toy, then slipped it into his waistband.

'I had to take this from Katherine. Useless little device among friends such as ourselves, but still better in my hands. Sit still, Robert. Tearful reunions can wait for a minute or two longer.'

Adam looked like a ghost, gaunt and deathly pale. He surveyed the area suspiciously. 'Horace, come out, wherever you are? I can feel you.'

There was no reply. Adam seemed to weigh his options, then reach a decision to go on. 'Katherine, sit over there.' He gestured to the bench where Terri sat. Robert felt Katherine was focused entirely on Adam and was sending him every last drop of strength she could muster.

'Robert, now you too, please. Between the ladies.'

Robert slowly got up and moved to the other bench. Katherine met his eyes with an expression of burning anger and fear. He tried to beam back at her his determination to protect her, to protect them all.

'What complicated webs we weave,' Adam said, with an air of sadistic glee. He threw something at Robert's feet. 'Rickles, don't say I don't look out for you.'

It was his wedding ring.

Robert looked at Terri, then at Katherine. Neither acknowledged him. He slowly bent down and picked it up, but did not replace it on his finger. He slipped it into a pocket.

'I'll leave you to work out how exactly the reconciliation goes down,' Adam said. 'I asked Terri to steal it during your tryst, to help you along with the breaking-down part of the trials. It's a brutal business, to be sure.'

Adam seemed to have lost the last of his humanity, retaining only an air of bitter, defeated amusement.

'Now, in exchange, give me the core, and the remaining keys you possess. Right now.' Robert stood slowly up and took a bag containing the keys from his trouser pocket: the seventh and one part each from the fifth and the sixth.

'Put the bag down there on the ground.' He pointed to a spot between them. Robert stepped forward and put it down.

'Step back.'

Adam carefully bent and picked it up, keeping his eyes on Robert and the women behind him.

'Now the core. The major key, the one that makes it all work. The little Malice Box that fits into the big Malice Box.'

Terri stood up, setting aside her staff, and walked towards Adam. Then she took his hands. 'Tell us something first.'

The tension racking Adam's body seemed to soften slightly, and he raised a hand to Terri's face. 'Oh, God, Terri. What?'

'Tell us about Lawrence. And about the Iwnw. What they want.'

Horace appeared out of the darkness behind Adam. 'What about Lawrence, Adam?'

Adam jumped, taken by surprise. Still Terri held his hands.

'Tell it,' Terri insisted. 'Horace needs to hear it. Everyone needs to hear what they made you do. What you've had to bear. Please.'

Adam stared at her, reluctant to begin. 'It's not a pleasant story,' he said.

'Please, Adam.'

He relented, shrugging. 'As you wish.'

Terri released his hands and stepped back a few paces.

'Horace will have told you,' Adam began, 'that Lawrence died a soldier. That under unbearable pressure from me, acting for the Iwnw, he refused to talk, and eventually managed to grab the pistol in his office and shoot himself, rather than divulge the whereabouts of the hidden stocks of red gold.'

'That is what happened, I'm sure of it,' Horace said. Robert had never heard such frost in his voice.

Adam grimaced. 'That isn't entirely true, I'm afraid to say. On the heroic side, he managed to make a phone call to Robert here to try to tip him off. A shame that he was barely able to speak, in his pain. I called you right afterwards, Robert, to muddy the waters. I was entirely in the grip of the Iwnw, as you will have gathered. Hard to believe it was just a week ago tonight.'

Terri blinked back tears of rage, refusing to cry.

'The fact of the matter, I regret to say, is that Lawrence cracked before he died. He whimpered and wept, and he let slip a clue – a small one, admittedly, but sufficient – about the whereabouts of the red gold. Then I let him write his goodbye note and shoot himself to end his misery.'

They all stared at Adam in shock as a ghastly expression of shame mingled with pride crept across his features.

Horace stared at Adam with contempt and outrage. 'By all that is most holy,' Horace whispered, 'if this is true, may these actions turn back upon the Iwnw a hundredfold, whether I or another be the instrument thereof. I forgive them, as my oath requires, but I do not absolve them of the consequences of their actions.'

As he spoke, words formed in Robert's mind. *Remember the letter. Seek Lawrence's message. Remember the letter.*

Adam stared now at Robert. 'It is very strange to realize, as I did

389

just a few hours ago, how the Path works through us to express itself once we begin to walk it. I was remembering the Unicorn challenge at Cambridge, and I realized that the decryption keys I gave the contestants, when placed one on top of another, made a reasonable sketch of the shape of the Tree of Life. I'd had no idea. Horace had barely begun to initiate me into its use as a tool on the Path at that time, and yet there it was speaking through me, forcing itself into the world.'

Robert met his eyes, wondering whether even now, despite everything, Adam was still trying to pass him secret information. What aspect of the Unicorn game was he talking about? He tried to calm his mind and hear the words forming at its fringes. But he couldn't grasp them.

'Returning to Lawrence,' Adam suddenly said. 'He withstood enormous pain. The Iwnw tormented him through me. Physical pain, and mental. When I couldn't beat it out of him, they came in with their own weapons. Torture of the psyche. Nightmares from the depths of childhood, secret fears dredged up from the dungeons of the mind. And he cracked. He talked, at least a little. He led me to understand that the red gold had been melted down, in minute amounts, into regular gold bars from the Hencott mines. Hidden in plain sight, in a way.'

Robert saw Horace's face fall.

'And those ingots were mostly stored at the place where everyone else stores their gold, naturally enough,' Adam continued. 'One of the safest places in the world. At the Federal Reserve Bank of New York, in downtown Manhattan.'

The Iwnw, who for a year, since the last detonation, had been patiently trying to locate the rest of the red gold, now knew where a good proportion of it was to be found.

'They had been seeking it because, not to put too fine a point on it, they were disappointed at the scale of the original explosion foreseen by the maker of the Ma'rifat'. Even if his weapon had fully exploded, instead of turning into the damp squib it became, it would have been something like Hiroshima, even though it used raw psychic energies as its fuel.

'But now they want more, much more. That is why they sought the amplifying power of the red gold. They don't want just physical destruction and passive victims. They want people to take death into their own hands. Internecine warfare. Brother against brother, family against family. Concentration camps across the land. Massacres with any weapon that comes to hand. It would not just be a physical bomb. It would be a soul bomb. It would rot the psyche of all those within its radius of destruction. Many millions of people. That is who they are. That is what they want.'

Adam looked at them defiantly. 'They have eaten me away from the inside to make me help them, and I have resisted as long as possible. But there is a cancer invading Terri where a child should be. And still I hope that at the end of all this, our child may be returned to her. They have promised to keep us safe, and to reverse the cancer curse placed on her.'

Robert felt Adam had now lost all reason. 'You believe them, Adam?'

'I must.'

Katherine stared at Terri, then stood and slowly reached her hands to the younger woman's belly. Terri put her hands over Katherine's and held them in place. Adam looked away from them, directing himself to Robert.

'Satisfied? As you can now see, I've had little choice in all this, try as I might,' Adam said. 'I may yet achieve at least one good thing. Now, the core. Please.'

'I have it,' said Horace. He slowly removed it from a jacket pocket. Robert could see its energy coursing through Horace's arm. Horace kept his gaze deliberately on Adam's eyes.

'Same thing, put it down on the ground,' Adam said.

But instead Horace called out to Katherine: 'Speak to Tariq, Kat.'

She looked at him in astonishment. 'What?'

'Talk to Tariq. Now.'

Adam seemed disconcerted, stepping back as Katherine walked towards him, appearing to understand what was being asked of her.

'Tariq, can you hear me?'

Horace drew closer to Adam, and then Terri approached Robert.

At Horace's shout, Robert and Terri joined hands with Horace and formed a ring around Adam. They all projected their most intense power into the centre of the ring, seeking to drive the Minotaur to the surface of Adam's consciousness. Adam stood bolt upright, his head suddenly snapping back, every muscle knotted.

Standing outside the circle, Katherine weighed her words, choosing each one with enormous care. 'I let you down,' she said. 'I want you to know that I am ashamed of what I did. I betrayed you.'

Adam shuddered, saying nothing, lowering his head to lock his eyes on Katherine's. Deep torment raged in his gaze. Pain and exhaustion.

'I know that you have suffered greatly. Tariq, no one should have to go through what you have experienced. Your father arrested and mistreated. One intelligence service after another trying to use you, squeeze you, manipulate you for their purposes. Blackmail. Threats. And, through all of it, you struggled to do the right thing. To live as honourably as possible among the shameless. All these things I know and recognize. You did not deserve them. You did the best you could.'

Slowly, in the air around Adam's head, a tenuous shape began to turn and spin, a shadow staring out at them from a place of torment deep within Adam's own soul.

'Quickly,' Horace hissed. 'Hurry!'

Robert felt the beginnings of a single, pure note sounding at the centre of his mind, in the place where the birds sang with unfettered joy.

'Tariq, I know what the interrogators can do,' Katherine said. 'They broke you down because they can break anyone down. Nobody can resist such treatment. There is no shame. No shame at all for you. There is shame only for me.'

The shape around Adam's head twisted and turned, giving off bolts of anguish and loss that hit Robert like punches in the gut. Robert tightened his grip on the hands of Terri and Horace as he saw the eye of death coalesce out of the air around Adam, flaring yellow and blue, achingly beautiful, staring at them all.

Katherine spoke into the eye. 'You were a powerful man, a

powerful being, stronger than I, but you have become weak, a parasite. It is not worthy of your kind soul. You were a brave man, and you can be brave again. I know you built the Ma'rifat' with me in your mind at every moment. I know you wanted me to see how badly hurt and betrayed you had been, how humiliated you felt by me, how dreadfully I had scarred you. I know how you took the little ditties and songs we used to make up and turned them into clues to the location of the keys. I know you hid things in such a way that I might be able to find them. I know you did these things, in a way, to ensure that there was a flaw in your plan, a possibility that you might be stopped, a chance for me to rescue you from what you were planning to do. And that chance is now.'

Katherine fell on her knees, staring into the eye. 'Can you forgive me? Please forgive me. I beg you to forgive me, as I forgive you.'

For a split second, the eye flared an opalescent white, anger and fear battling with other possibilities, with ghosts of other outcomes. Robert felt a tidal wave of sadness, of grief. But then Adam filled his lungs and bellowed, at the top of his voice: 'NO!'

He flung off his paralysis with a sudden frantic twist and broke through their circle of hands, sending them all flying backwards to the ground. Adam lurched towards Katherine, who screamed at him and burst into sobbing, desperate tears. Adam loomed over her, hands reaching out in uncertainty as though to cherish her, to hold her in a lover's embrace.

Horace called out: 'Adam, leave her alone!'

Too late, Robert saw Adam turn and lunge at Horace, flinging him through the air. The old man slammed into the bench, hitting his head and falling in a tangled heap. Adam leaped upon him again and seized the Malice Box.

Terri ran to Horace as Adam turned to face Robert and Katherine. Kat placed herself four-square before him, arms by her sides, defying him to pass her.

Adam gave a roar of anger. 'Too late! Too late!' He turned and wheeled his hands in the air, holding the core, then flung a sheet of raging light into their faces.

Dawn was breaking when Robert came to. He rolled upright and tried to stand. Every corner of his body lit up with pain.

Horace sat on one of the benches, eyes closed, in a posture of meditation. Robert could feel the old man was badly injured. Yet he emanated peace.

The early half-light bathed the park in gold. He could feel it on his skin, like warm, gentle rain. Robert shivered.

Terri was gone, and Katherine was still unconscious where she had fallen, near the foot of the obelisk. He went over to her and knelt stiffly by her side, placing his hand on her forehead. Without knowing how, he understood she was not harmed. He stroked her hair.

'My darling. I'm so sorry.'

Horace spoke from behind him. 'No need to be sorry, Robert. To go further we have had to come to this place.'

'I can still save Adam,' Robert said. 'That wasn't him.'

Horace grunted. 'Look to your wife. Then we must talk. We must stop this thing.'

'You're hurt, Horace.'

'Look to Katherine.'

Horace fished a map of Manhattan from his pocket and began to study it intently. It was the one he had taken from Robert at Grand Central, marked with the lines of the sacred shape he had traced on to the city during the trials.

Robert took off his jacket and knelt down again over Katherine, placing it gently under her head. He took her right hand and held it between his, kissing the rings on her fingers. After a few minutes, Katherine's eyelids quivered. She came to and looked about her in a sudden panic. 'I tried to save him! I tried! Horace? Terri?'

She attempted to stand. Robert restrained her with a touch of his hand.

'You tried your best, darling. They were too strong. Rest for a moment.'

'Is Horace OK? We have to stop them! Make it right!'

'We will. We will.'

Horace waved the map. 'The caches. The sites. The riddles. Pay attention. We have very little time now. They were all for something. Something more than simply reaching the next stage of the trials, I mean. They all resonate, and they all combine together. To give . . .' He winced with pain as he got up to show them.

'Horace, sit still.'

Katherine grabbed Robert around the neck and hauled herself to her feet. He half carried her over to Horace, and they sat down on either side of him.

'These are the sites of the caches.'

Horace pointed to the circles and lines he'd drawn up and down the map. 'You must understand how everything connects. Would you please pass me Terri's weapon? Quickly.'

Robert retrieved the length of steel pipe from under the bench where it had fallen and handed it to Horace.

'Now, please help me stand.'

Horace trod painfully forward, using the tube as a walking stick, then steadied himself and began to trace lines with it on the ground. As he drew, the lines began to glow faintly in the twilight.

'This is Manhattan,' he said, his voice harsh with pain. He traced an outline of the island, including the rectangular box of Central Park. 'A powerful current of power – we might call it a ley line, or a stream of earth energy – runs the length of the island.'

He drew a vertical line down the centre of Manhattan.

'Most people are not consciously aware of it, though unconsciously it has forced its way into the design and the life of the city in different ways. It has become the city's central spine. Fifth Avenue broadly follows its path. No fewer than three obelisks are located along its course, as you yourself have seen, Robert, as well as the great skyscraper of Rockefeller Center.'

He drew a circle near the bottom of the island, at the location of St Paul's Chapel, then another at the site of the Worth Monument, and a third where they were now in Central Park. All three were on the ley line. He traced a fourth circle to represent Rockefeller Center, just south of Central Park.

'I think I saw that,' Robert said. 'I felt that pattern as I was completing the trials. But there was more to it. There was —'

Horace held up his hand. 'One thing at a time. When the maker of the Ma'rifat' was looking for a way to maximize the effect of his device, he clearly decided to use this ley line to link two devices, rather than using just one. By doing so, he could ensure that the destructive force was spread over a wide area, rather than just propagating from one point. And so he took the keys from one of the devices and hid them in a particular array along the island, around this central line of power, as a kind of antenna to transmit the force.'

He drew circles to show the location of each of the caches.

'The array he chose is known as the Tree of Life. It has other names, but that is the most common one. He would have chosen it because it has been used, since time immemorial, to help human beings handle psycho-spiritual energies. It appears in ancient Egypt, in the Kabbalah of Jewish mysticism, in the Sufi strand of Islam, always as a key that unlocks such powers. It is an image of the Path.'

'How is it used?'

'It may be used in many ways. It consists of ten circles, or spheres, joined by a total of twenty-two paths. Some use it as a meditation aid, like a mandala, visualizing journeys along the Tree's paths from one sphere to another. Each sphere, in this form of use, represents a different facet of human consciousness, from the purely sensory and physical at the bottom, to the ineffable mysteries of the divine at the top. Others give astrological value to the spheres, or link them to animals, stones and medicinal plants. Not in this case. Our man did not use all the paths, nor all the facets, of the pattern.

'Rather, he reversed a tradition in which the Tree represents creation — with the inconceivably powerful divine light at the top, descending like a lightning bolt down through the other spheres, to attain physical reality in the lowest one. His intention was to use the shadow side of the tree, wreaking destruction instead of creation. A bolt of dark lightning, if you will.'

'But that went wrong when Adam killed Tariq,' Robert said. 'He never got to position one of the devices.'

'That's correct. It would have been the last piece of the puzzle. All the rest was in place. But Adam forced the Ma'rifat' to misfire when it was still several miles away from Manhattan.'

'So the keys were left where they were, and the other device . . . Where is the remaining Ma'rifat'?'

As they spoke, Katherine suddenly saw in her mind, with total clarity, the cube that constituted the fourth key of the Ma'rifat', the one she had stolen from the safe in the bedroom. A cube of 125 smaller cubes, each stamped with a number. The larger cube sliced into five slabs of 25 cubes.

She closed her eyes and ran its numbers through her mind. She imagined herself in a hotel, a cube-shaped hotel where each room had a different number.

25	16	80	104	90
115	00	4	1	97
42	111	85	2	75
66	72	27	102	48
67	18	119	106	5

91	77	71	6	70
52	04	117	09	13
30	118	21	123	23
26	38	92	44	114
116	17	14	73	95

47	61	45	76	86
107	43	36	33	94
89	68		58	37
32	93	88	83	19
40	50	81	65	79

31	53	112	109	10
12	82	34	87	100
103	3	105	8	96
113	57	9	62	74
56	120	55	49	35

121	108	7	20	59
29	28	122	125	11
51	15	41	124	84
78	54	99	24	60
36	110	46	22	101

Up, down and across, each string of five numbers added up to 315.

The very central room, at the core of the hotel, was unnumbered. That would have to be the central mystery, the key thing Tariq had wanted to hide. Yet he'd been unable to avoid playing.

She ran through the numbers of the waypoints. The first ones had been 025, 064, X62, 101. It was an interior diagonal of the cube. Top left to bottom right.

She knew she'd cracked it at that moment.

The next four waypoints had been 036, 057, X69, 090. Another interior diagonal. Bottom left to top right.

She ran through the rest. They all passed through the central unnamed cube. In each case, the X represented that same cube.

All the strings of five cubes added up to 315.

So the centre cube, the unnamed mystery, had to be . . .

63.

And, she saw, that would have to be the waypoint for the location of the Ma'rifat'.

Tariq's deepest secret.

She breathed hard.

'Robert, give me the Quad,' Katherine said.

She fired up the GPS programme and looked for Waypoint 063 in the directory, but it wasn't there. No waypoint with that number was listed. Somehow Tariq must have hidden it. She called up a blank *Go to Waypoint* _____ prompt and punched in the numbers manually. 063. And suddenly there it was. 'Downtown! The remaining device is downtown! Near where you started the trials. It's not showing exactly where, and there's no accompanying clue to go with it, but it's in the area of St Paul's.'

Horace looked at her with amazement. 'I had reached a similar conclusion. It would have to be reasonably near the red gold hidden at the Fed, in order to be able to draw upon its magnifying power. How did you work it out?'

'Tariq hid something at the centre of all the waypoint data. It was a number suggested by all the other waypoint numbers, based on the fourth key, that magic cube covered in numbers. I don't think our effort to contact the Minotaur was in vain after all. I think I reached Tariq long enough for him to drop it into my mind, somehow.'

Robert stood and stared at the map Horace had drawn, impatience ripping through his body. He wanted to move, to attack. The cacophony in his head was giving way to a greater and greater sense of single purpose and power. He pointed to the island's southern tip. 'If we know it's down there, why aren't we already on our way to stop it?'

'Because if you go now, you will be killed. You need to understand one or two more things. Then it will be time. Very soon.'

'What things?'

'Firstly, the trials. I arranged their sequence, chose their content, so that you would follow the same pattern through Manhattan that the maker of the Ma'rifat' had laid out for its destruction – the Tree of Life, except in reverse. By tapping the powers unleashed by each trial, you would be dispelling the shadows from each level of the tree. Reclaiming the pattern for the good. And building the power necessary to erase it completely, at the end, by defeating the Iwnw and halting the detonation.'

'I walked the Tree of Life, bottom to top.'

'Yes, you walked its key levels, each one corresponding to a trial. The trials were to prepare you for a final ordeal, the fight of your life, within the next hour. Only the worthy may enter the arena. To make it clearer, Robert, please come and lie down on top of the map.'

'What?'

Horace's voice rose with impatience, aching with pain. 'Just do what I say! We are almost out of time.'

Robert bowed his head in apology and lay down on top of the map, his face to the sky.

'With the top of your head at Rockefeller Center, it will help you understand, and it will then allow me to perform a ritual of power.'

Robert felt a deep surge of energy rippling into his body from the ground.

'First, Trial by Earth. You were nearly killed on the very first day, were you not? Had to fight for your physical survival. Sinking your fingers into the earth of graves. Looking out over Ground Zero. Thinking about how we respond to being attacked. Responding to death. Then, the great tidal power of sexuality: Trial by Water. You'll note that Mercer Street corresponds to the area of your groin. Then egotism, autonomy, self-esteem and self-centredness: Trial by

Fire. You refused to be blackmailed, threw Adam's attempt to control you back in his face. Guts.'

'Then I went to Union Square.'

'The place of the spiritual heart. The meeting place of the physical and spiritual selves. In the Judaic tradition, it is called Tiferet, meaning beauty, or Rahamim, meaning compassion. In mystical Islam, it is called Qalb, meaning heart. You'll see it corresponds to your actual heart.'

'This exists in Islam too?'

'Of course. All true soul work in all traditions leads to this place. In the fourth level you begin to transcend the ego, selfishness, begin to live more fully for others rather than yourself. You can only transcend a healthy ego, naturally. A sick ego prevents you from getting there. It sucks everything in. Union Square was the Trial by Air.'

'Why air?'

'The least substantial of the first four elements. The one most likely to fly away on its own unless it is tethered to the earth by the others. Compassion alone is nothing unless it is earthed in action. Feeling sorry for the little boy would not have saved him. Only leaping into the forest of boots and legs and shielding him with your own body saved his life.'

'Then?'

'Level five. Trial by Ether, meaning an element even more insubstantial than air, yet pervading everything, like an energy field. It stands for the interconnectedness of all things. It is the place of expression, creativity, situated at the level of your throat, the place where you speak your truth. It is reached only through a dynamic balance of the first four elements. This is where you begin to discover to what extent you may actually create the world around you. It is where you learn the true meaning of *intention*, which is the combination of your will and your ability to create. It is the state sought by the ancient alchemists, a level of perception where you see how consciousness and matter are two sides of the same coin. It is how you stopped the bomb.'

'The sixth level. Trial by Mind, the level of insight and

understanding. Inner vision. The third eye, the vestigial eye that is the pineal gland. The New York Public Library is at the level of your forehead, and it is where you encountered the blind visionary Borges. This is where you acquire the power to heal. It was also at this level that you received the wound to your head. You saved yourself from Katherine's shot when I was not able to protect you.'

'It was the only time the Iwnw reached me,' Katherine said. 'Robert, I'm so sorry. I truly thought for a moment I'd killed you.'

Robert didn't reply, his mind far away in the sky.

'Then Trial by Spirit. The seven-pointed star stands for esoteric knowledge, Gnosis, learning what is secret or hidden. Perhaps that's why many police forces use it for their badges, quaintly enough. It is at the crown of your head, as is Rockefeller Center.'

Robert brought himself back to earth. 'So the city and my body and the trials are all, in a sense, now one. How do we use this, Horace?'

'By going directly back down the Tree of Life to fight the Iwnw. You will now be able to tap into the raw power of the ley line that runs down its core, down the middle column of the Tree. And you will have your own fully awakened powers, drawing on the forces of earth, water, fire, air, ether, mind and spirit.'

Robert understood. He had been torn apart in the trials, his former identity stripped down and destroyed. And in its place he could now feel the fullness of a new self growing from the ruins of his former fear-bound, sleepwalking persona. He could feel light bursting from within him as his new body was stitched together, connected to his full powers within, connected to the full world without, the gravity of the earth and the boundless love of the heavens.

'Now for the ritual of power.'

Horace intoned the words with the greatest solemnity: 'We have walked the Path of Seth. We have dismembered this man, and now we rebuild his sundered body in the light of renewal. Where shall we find a head?'

Robert replied: 'I saw the same head twice, on the first trial and the third. The head of the Green Man, vegetation springing from his face.'

'Renewal,' Horace said, using the metal staff to paint a figurative head over Robert's. 'Where shall we find arms?'

'The fifth trial, and the sixth. The severed arm holding the sword at the Worth Monument, and the arm holding the hammer at the General Society where we met Terri.'

Horace traced new arms over Robert's supine form. With each addition to his body of light, Horace drew the corresponding form in the air above him.

'Strike with righteous power. Where shall we find a heart?'

'The fourth trial. Union Square. The four conjoined hearts I found that made up a compass rose. Katherine, me, Adam, Terri.'

'Compassion. Where shall we find legs?'

'The first trial. Legs of gold.'

'May they carry you to your quarry. Where shall we find a spine?'

'Trials six and seven. The caduceus carved into the steps at the New York Public Library, and the one carried by Hermes at Rockefeller Center. The magic wand of Hermes, and of Tiresias, represents the spine, from the earthly powers at its base to the divine powers at its summit. It therefore also represents the Path.'

'With this spine may you stand, and never fall again. This caduceus represents also the central column of the Tree of Life drawn on this city. Through it flow the power of the ley line and the power of the awakened Robert Reckliss, twin snakes of the physical and spiritual selves. Where shall we find, finally, a skin of light?'

'The first trial again. The Man of Swirling Light. The angel of the seven seals.'

Horace painted swirling whorls of light over Robert's body.

'You have now unsealed the seven secrets. The son of the dismembered man is born, and he is the old man reborn of himself, made new in the light of the Path. With what will you fight the Brotherhood of Iwnw, those who dispute the ownership of the Path?'

Robert stood up, feeling power blazing from his body. He took the staff from Horace. 'With love. With love, and the staff of Hermes.'

'What do you hear?'

'The purest birdsong.'

'You have come through the darkest night, and you have completed the Trial by Spirit.'

Katherine stared at him, tears in her eyes. He took her hand and kissed it.

'Look what it nearly cost me.'

'I love you, Robert.'

'I love you, darling.'

Robert turned to Horace. 'What more do we need to know before we go?'

'You may now learn a sacred secret. In the preparation of materials such as red gold, and the metallic glass known as the Philosopher's Stone, certain words of power are used. When pronounced in the correct order, by an adept in a state of high spiritual attainment, they will confer mastery over the materials.'

'What are they?'

'I don't know. But you do.'

'What are you talking about? I don't know any words of power.'

'You know them because you have heard them at some point in your contact with the Path. When you need them, you will remember them. You must.'

'There were some words like that in the Newton document that Adam swore to protect,' Katherine said. 'But half of them were scratched out. Adam never told me what they were.'

'The other half will come to you when you need it. Those are the words of power for the Stone, the vitreous metal.'

'What about the red gold? You must have known the words for that.'

'Lawrence and I each knew half, and I can share my words with you. They are *quaero arcana mundi*: "I seek the secrets of the world." But I was not permitted to know Lawrence's words, and I have found no record of them since his death, alas.'

Katherine shrieked in frustration: 'How can Robert possibly know them, then?'

'Lawrence would almost certainly have tried to communicate them before he died. If so, you will remember in time. Trust the Path.'

Katherine and Robert helped Horace to one of the benches, where he sat down with a gasp of pain.

Robert asked his final questions: 'Any idea what this final way-point looks like? What we are looking for?'

Horace pointed to the obelisk looming above them. 'Not to put too fine a point on it, we are at the masculine end of the polarity. You must go to the opposing end, to an intensely female space.'

'Female? How?'

'I don't know exactly. I have been searching for any psychic echo or impressions of this place for some time. It is well shielded. All I have been able to see is that there is a female space near where you started. You must find it. Curved. Rounded. Hidden.'

'Adam took all the triggers for the Ma'rifat'. Why doesn't he just detonate it as soon as he gets there?'

'He could. But the explosion would be smaller than the Iwnw desire. He needs you there to give it the full force of a soul bomb, but you are also the only one who can stop it. It's a risk they are willing to take.'

'But –'

'It will explode today, within the hour, unless you disarm it, it is true. But to achieve the greater conflagration his masters require, he needs your power. The power we have refined and built in you over the last week. The power to defeat him, which can also be twisted to help him. To achieve what they wish, they need a Unicorn. More precisely, they need the sacrifice of a Unicorn.'

'I'm ready,' said Katherine. 'Let's go.'

'Children, remember everything Adam has told you. Remember all his games. Even without his knowing, they may together make a key. A code. A metaphor. They may yet save your lives. They may yet save your souls.'

Horace closed his eyes for a moment. Robert felt pain flaring from him.

'Robert, my child. The Path has led you to its summit. To love, to selflessness, to the divine spark within. To God, if you care for the term. And in this case, to single combat. A fight to the death. No quarter. You must prevail.'

Robert looked into the eyes of his old friend. 'Thank you, Horace.'

'Now go, my friends. I cannot leave here. I am too injured to go on. I am growing weak. I will work to shield you.'

Katherine took Horace by the hand. 'Do you need a doctor? Can we do anything?'

Horace patted her hand and smiled.

'The care I need cannot be obtained in a medical hospital, my dear girl. I have always been protected. Dear Lawrence gave his life to protect me and Robert. Now it is my turn to do the protecting. Godspeed. Go.'

Katherine and Robert ran east through the park, through Greywacke Arch, to Fifth Avenue. The first vehicle they saw was a white stretch limousine bedecked in white ribbons, making its way home from what looked like wedding duty. Katherine frantically flagged it down.

'Can you take us downtown? It's an emergency. Quickly? Here's money.' She pushed a handful of twenty-dollar bills at the driver through the lowered passenger-side window.

'There's been a party in the back,' the driver said, taking the cash. 'It was a crazy wedding. I don't think there's anyone left back there, but you might want to check. Bridesmaids. Groom's friends. Wild kids wanting to go all night. I think I just dropped the last ones off.'

Robert and Katherine climbed in. Empty bottles rolled around on the floor amid discarded party hats, pizza boxes and strands of dried silly string. The seats were sprinkled with sequins and flower petals.

'Just like our wedding,' Katherine said. 'Take us straight down Fifth Avenue, then straight down Broadway, to Maiden Lane. Fast.'

'Yes, ma'am. Do you want some privacy?'

'Yes.'

The driver pressed a switch and raised the partition behind him. Then he gunned the engine, jolting Katherine and Robert back in their seats.

They tore past isolated bands of early-morning tourists, Republican delegates out for a jog, the occasional lost protester. They passed Rockefeller Center, the New York Public Library, the Empire State Building.

Robert tried to go over the phone call from Lawrence, and his suicide note, looking for messages. Then he tried Adam's games, and the play . . .

Katherine closed her eyes and dropped into a deep meditation, her breathing shifting to a profound, regular rhythm. The fear and anger that had surrounded her in a dark aura the previous night were gone, and Robert could feel her rebounding in confidence and determination.

He gazed out the window at the souvenir stores. Tiny toy Empire States, Chryslers, World Trade Centers . . . he understood his sickness now. He had actually been getting well. He had been perceiving the trials to come, the mystery of the sacred pattern threading through the streets of Manhattan, even before his awakening. And there was something more. Some buildings were directly affecting his senses, singing to him in harmonies he'd never heard before.

As they passed 29th Street, a building leaped out at him from the left like an oncoming train. Number 261. Burgundy, blue and gold. Hexagons and cubes and ziggurats hit him straight between the eyes. He gasped, looking away. He was still getting used to the intensity of his amplified perception. And intuitively he now understood it. Some buildings were dead, hitting him just with flat coldness. Others were jacking straight into his central nervous system. The buildings most affecting him were in various styles of Art Deco, the ones that borrowed motifs and proportions from ancient sacred buildings: towering monumental gateways, zigzag thunderbolt forms, steepling vertical façades from Egyptian and Central American temples. He felt them as physical expressions of the Path he had followed, as though his experiences had been sculpted and frozen in time for all to see. He saw new harmonies of proportion, colour and space, and he realized that the Path had been encoded into sacred architecture many thousands of years ago.

His whole soul was singing. He could feel Katherine in new ways, her presence next to him vibrant, magical. He reached out and took her hand, and she gripped it tightly as he looked into her eyes.

'Kat, I'm sorry I was unfaithful to you. I truly am. And I'm especially sorry for some of the things I said when we argued over it. About wanting to do it again. About –'

She put a finger to his lips. 'If you hadn't, none of us would be alive now. I understand what had to happen.' She took both his hands in hers. 'I am still very angry with Horace and Adam for not being able to think of a better way to get you through the second trial. It could have been handled differently. I feel sorry for Terri with her cancer. And I'm sorry too for some things I've said in the last nine months. For the coldness between us. For the distance, since I lost the baby.'

'It wasn't your fault we lost Moss.'

'I felt it was. Now I know better.'

He reached into his pocket and took out his wedding band. 'Would you put this back on for me, please?'

She looked into his eyes, searching into the deepest recesses of his heart. For a moment, even as he opened himself fully to her gaze, he feared she would refuse. Then she slid the ring on to his finger. They shared a long kiss, and then Katherine half turned so she could lean back into him, his arms around her. They gazed in silence at the passing buildings of Broadway, each preparing for the danger that was to come.

'We're just about there,' the driver said over the limousine's intercom. 'Maiden Lane. A pleasure to drive you this morning.'

The limousine drew to a halt and they got out. The sky was pulsing white now to Robert's eyes. He tried to feel out with his mind towards Adam, towards Terri, but found nothing.

The Federal Reserve Bank of New York was across the street, just a couple of blocks east of Broadway. There was more gold there than anywhere in the world, even Fort Knox. Robert had visited its underground vaults, cut into the bedrock of Manhattan, and seen the ingots stacked there in unmarked cages. Now it housed enough red gold to help the Iwnw kill millions of people.

Could that be where the Ma'rifat' was located? It would be impossible to breach, he thought. And he had no recollection of the underground spaces being curved or arched.

He took out the Quad and tried to locate Waypoint 63, but nonsensical data filled the GPS display screen. The directional arrow swung wildly.

'Kat, are you getting any impression of Adam, or Terri? Or the Iwnw?'

'Nothing.'

But at the corner of Maiden Lane, just as they were about to head towards the Fed, Katherine stopped dead in her tracks outside a jeweller's. Robert saw a wraith of yellow light reflected in the shop window. Then it moved to surround Katherine. She breathed in sharply, her whole posture changing.

'Time and space beneath my feet,' she said. Except it wasn't her voice.

'Terri?'

There was a clock set into the sidewalk under Katherine's feet, surrounded by a brass ring marked with compass points for north, south, east and west.

'I see where you are. Look north. Look for the four elements.'

'Where are you?'

'Downtown. Hidden away. Underground. Pain.'

'We're coming to get you, Terri. Where did he go?'

'Curved. Arches. Can't see.'

She gave a sudden shriek. 'Iwnw are here. Burning! Oh, God, burning! Come quickly!'

Then she was gone. Katherine slumped, breathing deeply, hands on her knees. She spat. 'God damn it! What was that?'

He held her shoulders, but she twisted away.

'Terri came into you. Are you all right?'

She shivered, trying to recover her composure.

'Did she say where she was? That was foul. It hurt.'

'She tried to guide us. Said go north, look for the four elements.'

The north arrow on the clock in the sidewalk pointed towards the old AT & T Building at 195 Broadway. They ran to it. Along the Broadway frontage were four panels in gold leaf on black: a bare-breasted woman of distinctly earthy allure, surrounded by vegetation; a young man disporting himself among birds; another young man, wrapped in flame; a sea sprite of sinuous beauty. Earth. Air. Fire. Water.

Robert reached out again for Terri. He remembered the luxuriant, sensual yellow of the double lover who'd split off from Terri's body to seduce him at the hotel. Achingly beautiful, sex made light. He found her. Except now she was racked with pain and fear. The figure of the man in flames was resonating in her. He felt cancer spreading through her body. He felt her raging anger at the Iwnw, her forlorn prayers for Adam. Fear for the world. She was seeing the world burning, not just herself. Gently, he coaxed her back towards them, away from her pain. He saw a fleeting image of where she was, a beautiful glass oculus above her head like the eye of death itself. Then he lost it.

'Kat, I'm going to try to draw Terri back to us. Can you take her inside you again if she can do it again?'

Katherine nodded reluctantly. 'I'll try not to resist this time. I'll try to help her sustain it.'

Robert sought out Terri more strongly, feeling a powerful blocking presence around her. His mind was being diverted from a location he knew well. Suddenly it was a maddening experience. He knew the place where the Ma'rifat' was located, he realized. He had even been there. But it was so powerfully shielded he could not see it at all, even in his own mind.

'If they need to kill a Unicorn to achieve the level of conflagration they desire, it makes no sense for them to block the location from me,' he said to Katherine. 'Why?'

'It only makes sense if they're not ready for you yet. If they're not yet confident of being able to defeat you. They must be building their strength. Maybe drawing on the power of the red gold. Accumulating energy.'

'Then Terri has to guide us there before they're ready. That's what she's trying to do. She thinks we still have a chance of stopping this.'

'Bring her to me. I'm ready.'

Robert sought Terri again and found her sneaking past the Iwnw's psychic barriers. He harmonized his consciousness with hers and gently drew her into Katherine, who shuddered slightly, then nodded.

'North,' Terri said, speaking through Katherine's mouth. 'North. Cure Mary. Cure Mary.'

They walked past St Paul's Chapel, past the obelisk, and crossed Broadway towards City Hall Park. He supported Katherine on his arm.

Terri came hurtling through now, deep-breathing, hoarse. 'Curare? Plaque, by a tree . . . Cure? Cure Mary? Oh, God . . . find it . . . put it together . . . it hurts . . .'

He scoured the trees in the park beyond the railings, heading north. Then he saw what Terri meant: a small black metal plaque near the foot of a tree, honouring Marie Sklodowska Curie, dated 1934. Marie Curie. Cure Mary. Curare. Cure me.

He saw what Terri was doing. She was guiding them to her location, through images of the coming horror. Marie Curie. Radio-activity. X-rays. Atomic.

And an image came into his mind, raging and powerful, of the eye of death staring up from Lower Manhattan, firing bolts of blue-and-yellow light into the sky, a shock-wave of hatred and fear spreading at impossible speed across the face of the globe.

'It hurts so much,' Terri moaned. 'Robert. Walk north . . . 270. Walk north. 270.'

'Is that a waypoint? Waypoint 270?'

'No! Street . . . Number 270 . . . Street . . . Manhattan . . . Oh, fuck, burning, oh, God, burning . . .'

He saw it. 270 Broadway, at the south-west corner of Broadway and Chambers, was an office building of some twenty storeys, white brick above and riveted black iron girders below, housing a bank. Robert wondered what she could mean.

'Terri?'

Katherine was shaking with fear now. He willed her to hold on to Terri for just a few moments longer.

'Terri, are you sure?'

No reply. Just a keening note of pain.

The building displayed heavy black rivets in its beams that reminded him of the heavy black bolts on the bell at St Mark's. The strongbox at the lock collection.

And suddenly the bell began to toll in his mind. It was a death knell. The bolts were like those he had seen on photos of Fat Man and Little Boy, the first atomic bombs used in anger.

He took out the Quad and googled the address. It got him a series of internet items of no discernible interest. He added 'Marie Curie' to the search.

Holy fuck. Only one entry came up. It contained the phrase 'Manhattan Project'. Number 270 on Broadway was the first home of the drive to build an atomic bomb during World War Two. The Manhattan Project had been housed on this site before being shipped off to Los Alamos, Oak Ridge and other points south and west. This was where it had begun.

Fat Man. Fat Mary. Cure Mary. Cure me.

'Robert . . . City Hall . . . back to City Hall.'

They were just yards from the early-nineteenth-century City Hall building itself, where the mayor had his offices. There was something on the tip of his tongue. His mind screamed at him to remember.

'Almost under your feet,' Terri said. 'Hidden. Under your feet. Find it.'

Terri gave a final scream and abandoned Katherine's body. Kat dropped to her knees and retched.

And then the Iwnw's shield suddenly fell.

An abandoned subway station. Disused. Curved. Arched. The old City Hall Station. It was what his mind had been screaming at him to recall. Closed to the public for more than fifty years. The first station on the first subway line in New York, and still the most beautiful. It was directly below City Hall.

The Quad buzzed. It was Horace.

'I see it. I suddenly saw it. The old City Hall Station!'

'I know. I see it too.'

'This means they are ready for you now. Confident.'

'I'm ready for them too.'

Katherine stood back up, anger and unshakeable willpower flaring from her.

Horace asked if he knew how to get there.

'I do.'

'I'll be praying for you. Giving you all the power I can.'

'I know, old friend. I have to go.'

'One thing, Robert. You still cannot involve the authorities in any way. The Ma'rifat' would detonate. You understand? Their fear and anger would set it off. This has to be handled by a Unicorn. It is between the Perfect Light and the Iwnw.'

'I understand.'

Katherine took the Quad from him. 'Horace, thank you for everything. We're going to get them now. We'll save as many people as we can.'

The City Hall Station had been closed originally because it was underused, too small and too curved for the new longer trains. Then the public had been barred from it for security reasons. It was used only as a loop to turn around the trains at the end of the Number 6 line. Despite the security rules, though, Robert's enthusiasm for gems of New York architecture had twice led him to sneak a peek at the station by hiding on board a turning train. He knew that it had two levels: a platform by the tracks and, above it, an elegant domed ticket hall.

He took Katherine's hand in his, hefting in the other hand the steel pipe Horace had given him. Her strength seemed to leave her, and he half carried her east along Chambers Street, past the Tweed Courthouse, heading for the other side of City Hall Park and the Number 6 subway.

An elegant dark green elevator, domed in the Budapest style and looking faintly like an old-fashioned British police box, stood on the esplanade on the eastern side of City Hall.

'The entrance to hell,' he said to Katherine. 'Who knew?'

The elevator went down one floor and opened directly opposite the turnstiles. Katherine was reviving. She was able to walk under her own steam as they headed for the Downtown & Brooklyn platform and went down the steps.

They waited for the local 6 train. When it pulled in, a booming voice over the PA system told everyone to get off. Standing halfway along the platform, Robert and Katherine waited till the last possible moment, then leaped aboard just as the doors were closing and ducked down. The train jolted into motion, screeching against the curving rails, and headed into the darkened tunnel. They moved along the train to the rear as it went. When it stopped in the darkness, they stepped from the couplings of the last car on to the platform. The train pulled away.

Robert and Katherine crouched at the furthest corner of the abandoned station and waited for their eyes to get used to the gloom.

Ahead of them, dimly lit by chandeliers and ornate glass skylights, stretched a curved platform and a procession of ribbed arches. Glazed tiles in dark green, cream and dark brown dressed the walls. Attenuated blue light streamed in from the skylights. It was a magical loop, a lost station, a ghostly, sad, beautiful place.

Robert looked for straight lines and found none. His eyes lost themselves in the shadows and curves. An insistent, throbbing note resonated from the walls, insinuating its way into his mind. He could feel the evil presence of the Iwnw in every atom of his body. Up ahead he could make out the mouth of a stairway, leading up towards the ticket hall. A sickly yellow glow emanated from it, punctuated by flickers of red-and-blue light. They were the colours of the eye of death.

He heard water dripping, and the sound of feet moving on stone up ahead. Slowly and deliberately, in the semi-darkness, he crept forward. Katherine was right behind him, hugging the wall.

The glowing lights up ahead changed tone, modulating to a darker yellow as the throbbing bass tone dropped in pitch, dipping to the very edge of his hearing range. He felt himself drawn to the play of light, even as the infrasound of the Ma'rifat' triggered primal fears in the depths of his mind. The lights were beautiful, seductive.

A few yards along the platform, pushed against the wall, lay a dark, elongated form. Robert sneaked towards it, fearing he knew what it was. He ran his right hand over it. He felt a sticky wet pool of liquid, and the metallic smell of blood flooded his senses. He tried to find a pulse at the throat and found instead a gaping knife wound. He pulled his fingers away involuntarily, stifling a cry of horror. For a moment he couldn't breathe. Then he composed himself and felt down to the body's waist. He found an equipment belt, a holster, but no pistol or radio.

'Cop,' he whispered. 'Dead.'

He reached up to the eyes and closed them. The body was still warm. He seemed to be a young man. Would he have to check in every few minutes? How long before he was missed?

Katherine briefly said a prayer over the body, then they moved cautiously along the platform.

The soft sounds of sacred chanting now reached their ears, melding with the deep, otherworldly resonance that echoed in the very tiles and stones of the beautiful cavern. Horace was right to call it the most female space imaginable. The skylights were like rose windows, their beautiful tracery like veins under white skin.

They were at the edge of the steps rising up into the domed ticket booth area. Robert slowly looked around the corner, keeping his head as low and hidden in shadow as possible. The upper chamber's arches culminated in a skylight overhead like a single staring eye, the one he had seen in a flicker of an image from Terri.

And, in the centre of the room, directly under the skylight, Robert saw the Ma'rifat'. It was beautiful. A translucent drum of gold and white, it spun slowly, pulsing from within, geometric designs and decorative script shining in different colours as its rims rotated above and below in opposite directions. It stood about four feet off the ground, atop a tapering column of what looked like solid gold. On a cloth on the ground next to it were some metallic shapes. A seven-pointed star design, a hexagon, a pyramid, a tiny round drum.

The Malice Box that Adam had mailed to him. The core. The master key.

'Fat Mary,' Robert whispered. 'The Ma'rifat'. The Malice Box.'

He climbed slowly to his feet, taking care not to scrape the metal staff he carried on the ground. He heard a footstep behind them, a shuffle and a cry from Katherine. Then his head lit up with pain, and he collapsed, unconscious.

The eye stared into Robert's soul. He prayed.

. . . turn fear into love . . .

Shapes and fragments of city scenes played before his eyes.

. . . mind like a mirror . . .

Lines of light and longing, lust and fear.

. . . merciful heart . . .

He reached out with his mind. It was the gift he had buried for more than twenty years, singing out into the unseen space around him, listening in return. It was a gradual erosion of the separateness of things. He felt everything bathed in a beautiful, barely visible light.

A man's voice rang out. Rasping. Exhausted. 'Robert.'

The one who'd attacked him on the subway. The same distorted bark.

It was time to fight. He was ready. He cast his mind far into the past.

. . . forgive him . . .

Robert opened his eyes. Directly across from him stood a figure in black, a man, breathless, crouching. His face was hidden, but Robert knew him, knew the stance, the familiar crossing of the arms across the chest, the lowered head.

'Adam,' he said.

Adam looked up, only his eyes showing in the darkness. Behind him, Robert could make out other shadowy figures. Three wraiths in black cowls softly chanted words he had never heard but that penetrated his heart with darkness. Beside them, a few feet to his left, he saw a slumped form on stone steps. Terri. He could see a red nimbus of pain around the head and stomach.

'Rickles,' Adam rasped, a note of fear in his voice. Then, gathering his composure, 'We meet again. For the last time, I think.'

His voice echoed in the great curved space around them. 'You are no longer Adam. You've killed Adam. You are evil. You're just another henchman of the Iwnw.'

'They work through me. But I am, just, still the Adam you all know and love.'

'If so, I can help you.'

'So you can. Though perhaps not in the way you imagine. We come to "a great reckoning in a little room". It is my destiny, it seems.'

'From *As You Like It*?'

'Yes, though I do not like it at all.'

'Where is Katherine?'

'Out cold, I'm afraid.' Adam pointed out of Robert's eyeshot. 'She's not hurt, though. Not yet.'

A train screeched by below like a banshee. He saw that the Ma'rifat' dimmed its glow and stilled its deep throb until it had gone.

'I know what you're thinking. There are fairly regular police visits down here. The Iwnw had to kill the last cop who came round. But I've moved his body now. No one will find us. Not in time. And, if they did, they would just set it off. Not in the way my masters wish, though. Hence the rather more elaborate preparations we've made.'

'I won't help you.'

'Robert, Robert. You don't realize who you are, do you?'

'Who I *am*?'

'In a sense, *you are the weapon*. We have gathered everything needed to detonate the Device at its full potential. All the keys. The core, the trigger. The red gold warehoused near by. But we can't do it alone. The final component is a Unicorn. A being of great beauty and power of spirit, sacrificed by the Iwnw. Which is to say . . . *you*, Robert. It's what you've always been. What you've always denied. Why I sought you out all those years ago. Why Katherine sought refuge with you.'

416

'I won't do it.'

'You will. We will fight, and the Iwnw who work through me, who compel me, will compel you. You will break, and you will die. You will have no choice. And, in dying, you will detonate the Malice Box.'

'I will not.'

Suddenly the chanting stopped. The Ma'rifat' fell silent at the same instant. The change was so absolute that the absence of sound hit Robert like a blow to the eardrums.

The tallest of the three black-cowled figures spoke from within his own darkness and shadow. 'A Unicorn. At last. We are honoured.'

Robert recognized the leader of the three men Horace and he had fought at Grand Central.

'Free Katherine and Terri. Release Terri from her pain,' Robert said. 'Reverse her cancer. Then perhaps we can talk.'

The Iwnw leader laughed drily, removing his cowl from his head. 'No, that is not satisfactory. Let me explain a few things. You may think that you are in the right, because you have been initiated and moulded by a member of the Perfect Light. The rightful masters of the Path and its powers, though, are not they but we: the Brotherhood of the Column. Iwnw. Consider your own situation. You have faced death, not once but several times, in order to attain your remarkable set of powers in a very short period. We tried hard to kill you a few times ourselves.'

'I thought you needed me.'

'If we had been able to succeed, it would simply have shown that you were not the being you were reputed to be. Indeed, our efforts helped to activate in you the powers that brought you through the trials. Very few could have survived such a series of ordeals. We love Horace's work, sometimes. You are a member of an elite, and a chosen one even among that elite. Should you not . . . rule? Wisely, of course, and fairly, but look. Look at the world.'

As the black-robed figure spoke, Robert sought Katherine in his mind's eye. Adam had spoken the truth – she was unhurt, and recovering consciousness now. She was more alert, already, than

417

she was letting on. Then he tried to reach again towards Terri. Carefully shielding his action, he tried to see into her belly. What he found there filled him with bleakness. Massive, racing cell division. The cancer had metastasized rapidly. He kept his overt gaze on the black-robed man. The other two Iwnw men resumed their chant in the background, and the Ma'rifat' responded to them, shifting its own rhythmic pulse in time with them.

'Look what the human race has done with the world, while the transformative powers of the Path are withheld, kept secret, by the high-minded fools of the Perfect Light. A planet poisoned, thrown perhaps permanently out of vital balance, perhaps already doomed if strong leaders do not act very soon. Massive overpopulation, draining the resources of the planet, billions of people piled into decaying cities that spread like blight over the surface of the earth. Chaotic international relations. Constant war. Unceasing brutality. Millions of children dying horribly of preventable diseases. You may have been led to believe that we are planning an act of horrific evil. But look at the world as it is now. One would think such an act had already taken place.'

Robert stood completely still, drawing from deep within himself the powers of earth and water, fire and air, ether and mind and spirit. He made his mind a perfect mirror, reflecting back the rising tide of black venom the Iwnw were pouring towards him. And he poured the most powerful healing energy he could summon towards Terri, wrapping the cancer cells in white light, trying to reverse the evil wrought upon her. He had to play for time.

'What are your intentions? What do you want?'

'Human beings have become a disease. Most do not deserve to live. Most do not even live at all. They are asleep to their own potential their entire lives, and then they die. They eat, they rut, they kill each other, they defecate, they dream of something better but don't really want anything different to what they have. They are *lazy*. A vast reservoir of psychic power, almost entirely untapped.'

'So, enslave them and rule? Modern-day pharaohs? Farm their minds?'

'You mock, but you would be one of the rulers. One who steers the flock. In any case, as you know, the Iwnw follow all the facets of the Path, not just the pretty ones. There is great power and strength in fear, in hatred, in contempt. It is from those emotions that we derive our own power. The Ma'rifat' can destroy Manhattan, certainly. It would already have done so if the pathetic creature entangled with Adam had managed to carry out his original plan. That alone would enable us to destroy, at one fell swoop, the world's leading financial centre, the babbling incompetents at the United Nations and a city that exemplifies the collective illness known as democracy.'

Robert felt Terri respond, felt her embrace the power he was sending her. He poured all the light he could covertly send into her body's own healing systems.

Still he listened, stone-faced, to the leader of the Iwnw.

'But a true soul bomb, a true alchemical engine geared to exploding in the consciousness of perhaps a billion people within a few seconds . . . that would be a far more effective tool. An instantaneous psychic collapse, driving everyone to the lowest, rawest, darkest levels of human possibility. Nation fearing nation, village fearing village, unable to abide difference of any kind – of language, of skin colour, of accent, of smell. Missile launches, quite possibly nuclear. First strikes. Retaliation. Round-ups of all those who don't belong to whichever tribe you happen to belong to. Children denouncing parents. Parents betraying children, neighbours handing over neighbours to concentration camps. Killing, and more killing. Rwanda in America. Srebrenica in America. New Dachaus and Belsens and Auschwitzes across the world. Those are the energies we wish to unleash. So that we may feed, and in feeding grow so powerful as to be unstoppable. And, after feeding, we will impose order on those who remain. We shall save the planet for our own kind, and rule!'

Silence fell except for the thrumming of the Ma'rifat', which had deepened in tone and grown in strength as the intensity of hatred in the arched chamber had risen.

'Go to hell,' Robert spat in disdain.

'We are already there.'

419

The image broke into Robert's consciousness, again, of the eye of death propagating massively from Lower Manhattan out into the world, the hateful, magnetic ball of blue fire flaring across the Atlantic Ocean and down the mountain spine of the Andes, the dead black hole at its core feeding on hatred and fear in an ever-widening circle.

Breathing hard now, Robert strained to maintain his shield, his mirror-mind. They were stronger than he had expected. Far stronger. Still he fed healing power to Terri, unable to tell now whether it was working.

Adam drew near and whispered into Robert's ear: 'You'll even take out a US president. He's at the Waldorf-Astoria. He won't get to give his big speech at the Convention tonight. You'll appreciate this: they used the hidden old railway siding under the hotel to bring him in.'

He heard Katherine stir. He had to get her out. For the first time, Robert was truly beginning to fear he might fail. Though there was something he still didn't understand.

'If the Ma'rifat' explodes, do we not *all* die?'

Again the dry laugh of the Iwnw leader echoed from the vaulted arches of the ticket hall. 'No. We will be shielded, and can shield others if we choose. The Ma'rifat' is a true alchemical device, which is to say it opens up a gateway between worlds. There is a world of pure consciousness that rarely incarnates. You have seen it, if you have passed the Trial by Mind. You have seen, perhaps, consciousness and matter in their true relationship, their timeless dance of each flowing into the other. Those of us who are Iwnw in this world ultimately serve the discarnate Iwnw in that world, the insatiable hunger, the dark intelligence that needs human fear and pain to live. The eye of death. The Iwnw found us, their three servants. The Iwnw found the maker of the Ma'rifat' and fed upon him. Through him, the Iwnw fed upon Adam. Through Adam, the Iwnw reached Terri, and tinkered with the structure of a certain cell. Life to death. Future child to cancer.'

He paused for breath, then spat out his words with violent hatred. 'Through Terri, on the day you people know as the Blackout, the

Iwnw reached even into Katherine Reckliss, into her baby-to-be, and sucked its life force into that very same cancer.'

Suddenly a human form flew past Robert from behind him, arms outstretched, and grabbed the throat of the white-haired man. It was Katherine. At the same instant Terri launched herself from the steps and grabbed another of the black-robed figures from behind. She swung him round and slammed him into the wall, then leaped for the steel pipe Adam had taken from Robert after knocking him unconscious. As she grabbed it, twin snakes of spitting energy flared into life along its shaft. She jammed one end into the man's belly, then spun the staff and slammed it into his head.

Reacting a split second later, Robert leaped at the third Iwnw member, summoning all the raw power of his desire to live into a single punch to the chest that sent the man flying backwards against the rear wall of the chamber. Tiling cracked and smashed behind him where he hit the wall, yet he walked straight back at Robert and punched him powerfully in the belly. Robert doubled over in pain.

As he fell, Robert saw Adam stride to the Ma'rifat' and insert the remaining keys, one by one. Then Adam took the core, the smaller Malice Box, and jammed it into the top of the greater Malice Box.

With a deafening crack of energy and blue-yellow flame, the Ma'rifat' spat a twisting, swirling column of fire six feet into the air from its upper rim. Red filaments flared within the flame and spread along the curves of the arched dome, crackling and spitting as the eye of death gathered and formed above and all around them.

Everywhere Robert looked, the eye was there, staring into his soul. It wanted him. It wanted them all. It wanted millions of souls. The seductive flowing colours of the eye flared red and yellow as he felt blows raining down on his back and head. The Ma'rifat' was preparing to detonate. Out of the corner of his eye, Robert saw Adam standing with his arms thrust directly into the twisting white column of fire atop the Device, his face contorted in agony.

Robert forced himself to his feet and drove headfirst into his assailant's ribs, again driving him back against the wall. Forks of yellow light shot from the tiles and propagated into the eye of death.

Before Robert could hit him, Terri stepped forward and slugged his man with her staff. The black-robed figure fell awkwardly and lay still. Then Robert turned to see Katherine struggling at the top of the steps to break a stranglehold by the leader of the Iwnw. Before Robert could reach her, the man lifted her by the neck and threw her down the stairs towards the darkened train platform below.

Terri was on him a second later, driving her flaring staff into his back below the left shoulder blade. The steel pipe pierced him right through the chest.

'That's for Jay, you fucker,' she shouted. The man teetered on his feet for a moment, an expression of sheer hatred frozen on his face. Then he fell, and Terri ran down the steps to Katherine.

'I'll take care of her,' Terri shouted. 'What's Adam doing?'

Robert turned to face the Ma'rifat' and Adam, who pulled his hands from the column of fire and advanced towards Robert.

'You have killed three of the Iwnw. That means the Iwnw now work only through me. It makes me stronger.'

'You don't have to do this. I'm here to disarm the Ma'rifat'. That is all.'

'That is not all. We have come to single combat. The simplicity is appealing. I kill you, and a billion people die, in the blast or in the soul corrosion that will follow. You trigger Armageddon. But I live, Terri lives, with her pregnancy restored, under the protection of the Iwnw.'

'Does she want that?'

'Consider the alternative. She has none.'

'I don't believe that. Don't hide behind the idea of saving Terri. She would never accept that. There's no deal. It's just a figleaf for the fact that the Iwnw own you.'

'I wouldn't be so sure. But if you kill me, you disarm the Ma'rifat' and vanquish the Iwnw, who withdraw to fight another day. All those people are saved. But Terri dies of cancer.'

Robert still couldn't see whether he'd been able to heal Terri. He still felt he could.

'I am a Unicorn,' Robert said. 'And I will die if I have to. But no one else will today. Except you.'

He lunged at Adam and locked his hands around his throat. Adam almost lazily unhooked him and sent him spinning back against the wall. 'I don't think so, Robert.'

Adam seemed to grab the air in his fist and twist it. Robert's head exploded in pain. Black waves broke over him. The eye of death shimmered yellow and blue, staring at him from all directions.

The black tinged to red. The Ma'rifat' spun, faster and faster, spitting off shards of blue lightning. A deep, thrumming vibration filled the air. It was the slow thunder of impending detonation.

Robert lunged again at Adam. They locked hands around each other's throats.

'You'll break, and you'll die, Robert,' Adam spat, the bilious yellow light of the Iwnw spilling from his eyes and mouth. 'Just like they broke me.'

Adam threw him against the wall. The Ma'rifat' screamed as it spun, the very stones around them shaking with its thunder, lightning bolts flying from it in red, blue, green. Robert felt himself losing. His strength was falling away. He closed his eyes.

In the blackness there was a still blacker light. His retinas were raw, his brain was crackling and mushing like a radio near a power line. His skin had all but vanished; there was almost no membrane left between him and the world. He was jammed open. His insides and his outsides were flowing into each other. Wherever he looked, the black hole at the centre of the eye of death was draining his powers, his very will to live.

'Horace,' he whispered.

'Horace is an old man,' Adam sneered. 'He can't help you any more.'

Blackness closed in. He saw the irresistible, beautiful, terrifying eye form a microcosm of itself around Adam's head. It was calling to him.

'Time to die, Robert.'

Adam pulled Terri's staff from the body of the Iwnw leader and swung it in the air.

Terri raised her head, sensing what was happening. She ran up the stairs.

423

'No,' Terri shouted. 'You can't kill him!'

Adam brought the staff crashing down towards Robert's neck. Terri leaped into the path of the weapon with a scream, taking its full force on her own head with a sickening crunch. She fell down at Adam's feet, her skull fractured.

Adam stood for an instant in paralysed horror, then dropped to his knees, flinging the steel stave to one side with a roar of pain.

'No!'

Adam cradled her head in his arms. She was dead. He screamed in inarticulate rage.

Robert stared in disbelief as he climbed to his feet. She'd given her life for his. She'd seen Adam about to finally lose his battle with the Iwnw, about to kill Robert, and she'd chosen to die rather than to let that happen. She looked so small in Adam's arms. A great wave of tenderness broke over him. She had given Robert the strength to survive the trials. He owed her his life twice over.

The raw scream of the Ma'rifat' began to modulate. Barely perceptible harmonic tones began to sound.

Then Adam lay Terri gently down and got to his feet. He advanced towards Robert, a look of crippled grief on his face.

Robert looked deep within himself and sought the resources for a last battle. *Die to live.* He would abandon any hope of survival, if only he could stop the detonation.

Then he felt his limbs begin to glow. Arms and legs and then his whole body. He opened his eyes and looked down. He was a body of light. He was the swirling angel Terri had shown him at the beginning of the hunt, clad in a garment of spiralling light that slowly absorbed itself into his skin. He felt Horace's protective energy surrounding him.

Adam leaped on Robert with a cry like a wild animal. They both fell and rolled down the steps to the platform, past the unconscious form of Katherine.

Robert hauled himself to his feet and grabbed Adam by the throat. Adam twisted from his grip and punched Robert on the jaw. Robert grappled with him, and they both overbalanced and fell on to the subway tracks. He pulled Adam to his feet.

The eye formed again around Adam. The face of death. It spoke: 'Who are you?'

'My name is Robert Reckliss.'

'We are Iwnw.'

'You are the devil.'

'If you wish. You cannot win.'

'Free my friend.'

'No.'

He dug deep into his memory. Found his last possible weapons. He saw the words that Lawrence and Adam had meant to communicate to him.

'I learned these words from Adam and from two friends, Horace and Lawrence Hencott. A man you tortured and killed.'

'What words?'

'The words of power. The words used to gain mastery of the red gold, and the Philosopher's Stone.'

'No.'

'For the red gold: *quaero arcana mundi.* "I seek the secrets of the world."'

Now he remembered the phrase that Lawrence had so clearly wanted him to remember. Vile, Intense Torture Reveals Impossibility Of Living. It was the same word Adam had given him at the very start of the trials.

'The answer is *vitriol.*'

'Stop.'

Then he began to quote from *Newton's Papers*. From the words Adam had made Newton speak at the climax of the play. The words that had appeared on the typewriter in Katherine's room, the night of the fire.

'For the Philosopher's Stone: *Flamma unica clavis mundi.*'

'Stop.'

'"The key to the world is a single flame."'

'No.'

'I accept Adam's evil and take it into myself. He is part of me, and I am the stronger part.'

'No.'

The eye flared with blue light, shrinking back from him. More powerful harmonic tones issued from the Ma'rifat'. It was stabilizing, feeding on his mind. On his soul.

And then he saw the final line that Adam had been going to pronounce at the end of the play, when the tree and the drum of light had ignited. He realized he had known it all along. Adam had hidden it in plain sight.

'*Omnia vincit amor!*'

'Stop! No!'

'*Omnia vincit amor!* Love! Conquers! All!'

He opened his eyes. The eye recoiled in fear as it flared around Adam's head. But then Adam smiled.

And Robert saw the innermost plan that Adam had been shielding from the darkness, from the Iwnw, until the last possible moment.

Robert looked into the eye. Spoke into it.

'I understand.'

'What?'

'Adam wants me to kill him.'

'No.'

'He realizes he is incapable of escaping you.'

'No.'

'He has tricked you all along. He has been waiting for the moment when I would be psychically capable of defeating him. Spiritually powerful enough to do it.'

'No.'

'It is the only way to break your power and disarm the Ma'rifat'. This is how Adam will save everyone, at the cost of his own life.'

'No. Wrong. Now you will die.'

'No. When he plunged his arms into the column of fire of the Ma'rifat', he was trying to slow it down. To delay the detonation. He succeeded. And when at the last moment you truly had taken him over, Terri stopped him from killing me. To give his plan one last chance to work. She knew all along.'

'No. Now die.'

'No. *OMNIA! VINCIT! AMOR!*'

A scream of primal evil exploded from the centre of the eye as it blew apart in a flare of yellow-and-blue flame.

Robert stared into Adam's eyes. Adam saw that he had understood. Robert held his friend's stare for a moment without time. Then he pushed Adam on to the third rail and stepped back.

Adam's body jerked upright, his head snapping back, and for endless seconds he seemed to resist the power of the coursing electricity crackling and spitting through him, standing upright and swaying at the knees as acrid smoke and a stench of burned flesh filled the sweltering air of the underground station.

Then Adam rolled his eyes back in his head and let himself go, a hand raised in gratitude. He fell lifeless at Robert's feet.

The Ma'rifat' slowed, its harmonies now haunting, beautiful.

Robert knelt down and closed Adam's eyes. Then he dragged the body across the tracks and lifted it up on to the platform. He stepped across to Katherine and cradled her in his arms, stroking her hair. She was still barely conscious. He wept for a long moment for his friend Adam. He saw images of his crazy games, his wild heart, his endless imagination, his kindness and indomitable sense of fun. Then Robert saw the sickly yellow light that had consumed him, his unshakeable will to fight to the last moment, the steepling, self-sacrificing risks he had taken to ensure the detonation would be halted at the last minute.

'I'm sorry, my friend,' he whispered. 'Thank you.'

He walked up the stairs to the Ma'rifat'.

He stood over the beautiful machine, its rims now slowly spinning, the column of fire extinguished, and removed its keys, one by one, from their slots around its glowing body.

When it was done, he called Horace. 'The Ma'rifat' is disarmed. Terri and Adam are dead. They gave their lives.'

'Dear heaven. Get out of there. Then please come to me. Bring the Ma'rifat' so I can destroy it.'

Epilogue
New York, Saturday, September 4, 2004

Horace, his hands protected by thick black rubber gloves, lifted the bullet casing, the first of the seven minor keys of the Ma'rifat', and dropped it gently into the large vat of sulphuric acid on the rough wooden table in the middle of his apartment. The windows were wide open to disperse the fumes. With a violent hiss and a plume of red smoke, the key dissolved.

'We honour you, Adam and Terri, and remember you as warriors,' he said in solemn tones. Robert and Katherine held hands and echoed Horace's words.

Horace next took the vesica piscis that had hung around Terri's neck, the second key, and dropped it into the acid. Its melting form floated for a moment on the surface and then disappeared with a sound like a sigh.

'Adam and Terri, we honour and remember you as lovers,' he said. 'We remember the child taken from you by the Iwnw.'

Horace went through all the minor keys, relating each one to an attribute of their two dead friends in their fight to halt the detonation of the Ma'rifat'.

His skull and back injuries from the fight at the obelisk now healed by Robert, Horace was preparing to spend several weeks on retreat to study the use of the full set of words of power Robert had shared with him, and meditate on what lessons could be learned for future clashes with the Brotherhood of Iwnw. Katherine and Robert, now sharing the same bedroom again, had asked him to preside over an informal renewal of their wedding vows when he returned.

When Horace picked up the Malice Box, the tiny round drum that had shattered Robert's previous life and awoken him to a new life richer than any he had dreamed possible, Katherine gave a deep sigh and began to sob quietly.

'Adam, for all your games, your riddles and puzzles, your challenges and provocations, your madness and your questing, restless, good heart, thank you,' Robert said, and his throat thickened and tears filled his eyes.

Horace carefully dropped the small Malice Box into the acid, which bubbled hungrily and drew the metallic-glass drum into its maw with a loud crack.

'Before you leave, I will give you the keys to a place where Adam's papers are stored,' Horace said. 'There may also be some safety-deposit boxes to explore. He told me some time ago, Robert, that he had named you as the executor of his will.'

'Thank you,' Robert said.

'There are manuscripts, heaven only knows what else. They will have to be gone through.'

'I can do that,' Robert said.

'You should. There will be other battles. You may find something useful in his jottings.' Horace paused for a moment. 'Now. The main task.'

He carefully lifted the Ma'rifat', which he'd held in safe keeping since Thursday when Robert had brought it out of the subway station, and held it over the vat of acid. 'In the name of the millions of souls whose lives were spared by the actions of these days, and in the name of Adam and Terri who gave their lives to halt the detonation of the Device, we state the words of power that give us mastery over its component elements, and we commit it to destruction,' Horace intoned. '*Quaero arcana mundi.*'

Katherine and Robert answered in unison: 'Vitriol.'

Horace lowered the Ma'rifat' very gently into the acid. Cracks and pops gave way to a deep, violent hissing, and fumes of green, orange, red and yellow flew into the air. He lowered it all the way to the bottom of the vat and released it. The acid churned and spat.

'*Flamma unica clavis mundi,*' Horace said.

Katherine and Robert replied: '*Omnia vincit amor.*'

THE
MALICE BOX
QUEST

has arrived ...

Are you ready to play?

The Quest will send you on a scavenger hunt to the most
remote parts of the globe in search of Red Gold, the mysterious
source of energy that fuels the Malice Box.

As Robert Reckliss has done before,
you must face your own 7 trials.

Crack clues, answer puzzles, break codes and navigate
yourself around the world using The Quad – a slick GPS device
linked to Google Maps.

Join the Quest, complete the trials, save the world.

www.maliceboxquest.com

WIN!
£1000s worth of prizes
@ www.maliceboxquest.com

A luxury safari-adventure holiday for two to a mystery location

If you're after a high-octane, action-packed holiday in an unusual setting it's time to join The Malice Box Quest . . . and fast.

Help Robert Reckliss find the Red Gold that powers the Malice Box and you could be jetting away with a friend for a truly mind blowing experience in a mystery country with specialist operator **Discover the World**.

Discover the World is one of the UK's leading specialist tour operators offering unique holidays to destinations as diverse as the Arctic and New Zealand. With over 21 years of experience, your Discover the World holiday of a lifetime will feature something truly unique and you'll be the envy of all your friends.

The holiday destination will only be revealed to the ultimate quester who is the first to complete the 7 trials and find the Red Gold. Expect an adrenalin-fueled trip that will thrill and entertain in equal measure.

5 x state of the art TomTom satellite navigation systems

Be cool, calm and collected navigating the roads in 2007 with TomTom. A leading provider of personal navigation products and services, TomTom's products are developed with an emphasis on innovation, quality, ease of use and value.

TomTom is Europe's favourite Satellite Navigation brand offering an easy smart and portable solution. With over 15 years experience in helping people find their way, TomTom ensures, through innovation, that you will always find your destination, wherever that may be.
For more information on TomTom's latest products please visit www.tomtom.com.

Find your way around the Malice Box Quest and you could win the ultimate navigation tool.

2 pairs of flights to any Monarch destination of your choice

Two lucky people could each win a pair of flights to any of Monarch airlines destinations.

Monarch operates scheduled flights to a variety of destinations throughout Spain, the Canary Islands, Gibraltar and Portugal, from five bases in the UK – Aberdeen, Birmingham, London Gatwick, London Luton and Manchester.

Get enough points in the Quest and these tickets could be yours.

A year's supply of Penguin Books

Yep, that's 52 books sent direct to your front door throughout the year. A staggering range of titles are available including thrillers, chick-lit, Penguin Classics, autobiographies, cookery, science, politics, history, reference and travel. We'll be sending you some of the biggest brands in the bookshops from Jamie Oliver to Marian Keyes and Nick Hornby to Michael Moore.

Can you crack enough codes to win your dream library?

5 x £50 worth of Penguin Books

In addition, 5 people will each receive £50 worth of Penguin Books of their choice.

DISCOVER
THE WORLD
www.discover-the-world.co.uk

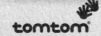
tomtom

Monarch

For terms and conditions including closing date, see www.maliceboxquest.com